Bailey Hannah's Wells Ranch Series

Alive and Wells

Seeing Red

Change of Hart

CHANGE OF HART

CHANGE OF HART

A Wells Ranch Novel

BAILEY HANNAH

DELL BOOKS
NEW YORK

Dell
An imprint of Random House
A division of Penguin Random House LLC
1745 Broadway, New York, NY 10019
randomhousebooks.com
penguinrandomhouse.com

A Dell Trade Paperback Original

Copyright © 2025 by Bailey Hannah

Published in the United States by Dell,
an imprint of Random House, a division of
Penguin Random House LLC, 1745 Broadway, New York, NY 10019.

DELL and the D colophon are registered trademarks
of Penguin Random House LLC.

ISBN 978-0-593-98401-7
Ebook ISBN 978-0-593-98402-4

Printed in the United States of America on acid-free paper

2   4   6   8   9   7   5   3   1

Title-page art: sharpner/Adobe Stock

The authorized representative in the EU for product safety and compliance is Penguin Random House Ireland, Morrison Chambers, 32 Nassau Street, Dublin D02 YH68, Ireland, https://eu-contact.penguin.ie.

For the fiercely independent.
I hope you find someone you can lean on.
Until then, you have Denver Wells.

Content/Trigger Warnings

- Alzheimer's disease (discussed in detail, on page)
- Abortion (discussed, not shown)
- Alcohol consumption, including underage (on page)
- Broken bone (on page)
- Cancer (on page)
- Depression (discussed in detail)
- Horse accident (animal unharmed, on page)
- Parental abandonment (discussed, not shown)
- Parental sickness/death (on page)
- Prescription depression and pain medication use (on page)
- Vomit (on page)
- Explicit sex scenes including cum play, sex toy use, rimming, breeding, praise, pleasure dom (mild), marking (hickeys/cum)

CHANGE OF HART

CHANGE OF HEART

Prologue—Blair

At 5:48 p.m. on Christmas Day, my life fell apart.

Rapidly blinking to clear the hazy film blurring the elaborate turkey dinner in front of me, I look toward the living room to avoid my mother's gaze. Not twenty minutes ago, I was curled up on the couch with my sister in our matching pajamas, teasing Mom for turning on the fireplace television channel. Now the loudly crackling faux-fire and accompanying sleighbell-filled music adds levity I don't appreciate.

Backdropped by the twinkling lights of the Christmas tree, my dad sits with a pained smile. "Sorry we didn't tell you sooner."

Alzheimer's disease: a neurodegenerative disease that causes memory and thinking ability to decline. The most common form of dementia; it is irreversible.

Outside the snow is falling in a swirling fury—the perfect representation of what's happening in my chest while I stare past my dad, cracking my knuckles to keep thoughts of hitting him at bay. Punching my loving father in the face won't solve anything. It won't change my mom's diagnosis, or the fact that they've kept it hidden from me for months. But it *will* upset my parents, my sister, and my ten-year-old nephew.

The muscles around my chest constrict my lungs, and I struggle to take a full inhale as panicked thoughts overwhelm my brain. Letting out a shaky breath, I do what I always do: smile.

"Okay, we'll handle it." I clasp my hands in my lap to keep them from trembling wildly. "People are living so much longer with the disease now. There are tons of treatment options. We can set up some safety equipment—locks, alarms, notes—and it'll be fine."

It'll be fine.

"It'll be fine," I repeat while fighting the waver in my smile. I give my younger sister a nod of encouragement, blinking back tears when I see marked fear in her eyes.

Of course, it won't be fine. Our mom is younger than the typical age for Alzheimer's. And while neuroscience wasn't something I focused a lot on during my six years of nursing and graduate school, I know early-onset Alzheimer's often progresses faster. Mom will forget everything she knows, piece by piece. Until her brain loses the ability to keep her body functioning. And nobody in this family will ever truly be fine again.

But for now—for the sake of protecting them—I'll say it's fine.

Fifteen minutes later, I excuse myself from Christmas dinner and pull out my laptop to spend the rest of the night in a deep dive on Alzheimer's disease. Except a distracting orange sticky note on top reminds me of a call I was supposed to have with the local doctor, Dr. Brickham, earlier in the week about a job. My dad set it up, suggesting I take the job because of how desperate Wells Canyon is for decent medical care. But from what I can tell, every conversation I've had with my parents over the past six months was a long string of lies. Now I realize this was his subtle way of getting me to move back home.

"Fuck," I mutter to myself, crumpling the paper and chucking it in the direction of the wastebasket.

Of course I forgot. My brain is essentially 2,875 sticky notes in a messy pile, so it comes as no surprise that adding one more to the chaos didn't make the information stick. Now Mom's diagnosis means I get to add a new batch of unhelpful notes to my muddled mind.

I flop back on the bed of my childhood room with a defeated exhale, staring at the spackled ceiling through tear-stained vision. I simply cannot be a thirty-one-year-old living in a room with fucking glow-in-the-dark stars across my ceiling. Sobbing, I stand on my bed and stretch until my ribs burn and I can barely lift my arms, peeling off every damn plastic star.

Like it or not, I'm moving back to Wells Canyon.

Denver

It's not that I'm trying to die—it's that I don't particularly care if I do. Not if I go out on the back of a horse, with the sun on my back and a smile on my face. Few people understand that, but my mom always did, which is why she's the only person I want to talk to in the moments leading up to every ride.

There's nothing but the gentle sound of stretching denim and leather when I squat down in the alley. A fiery course of electricity radiates up my thighs to crackle in my spine, and I take my time straightening back up. After a few slow neck rolls, I'm primed and ready to jump on the back of a bucking horse.

My hands skate up my worn chaps on their way to my mouth, and I press the pads of the index and middle fingers to my lips, then tap them gently against my mother's memorial plaque on the barn wall.

"Give 'em hell," I whisper on my way out the door. It's become somewhat of an incantation in the years since I last heard her say it. A message to wherever her spirit might be; a reminder that I'm not *trying* to die, if she wouldn't mind looking out for me.

After a long, harsh winter, the first rodeo of the spring is a sold-out show. The stands are packed, with spectators shoulder-to-shoulder along every square inch of fence rail lining the arena. But I'm not nervous about having a few hundred sets of eyes on me. It only ups the ante because, even if I don't win, I always come to impress. After all, putting on a show for the crowd is almost as important as winning—especially at these small-town rodeos with relatively lean payouts.

Swinging wide arm circles to warm up my shoulders, I track down Colt—one of the ranch hands at my family's 20,000-head cattle operation. Besides the local buckle bunnies, he might be my biggest fan around here. And since my best friend decided to start ditching me for dad duties, Colt's the only guy I can count on to rodeo with me.

Turning the corner, I spot him leaning against the rails of a bucking chute, talking to Peyton. Normally, Peyton would be a sight for sore eyes, with blond hair, blue eyes, great tits, and a penchant for cowboys. Plus, she's fun enough to hang out with short term, which is the most I can offer any of the women around here.

What more could I ask for?

A flash of brown hair in the background pulls my attention away. I'm shit at gambling, but I'd bet at least fifty percent of the women here have brown hair. There have to be a hundred brunettes in this place, so it couldn't be. Wouldn't be.

Right when I'm reminding myself that she wouldn't be caught dead at a rodeo in Wells Canyon, the sight of her profile as she dips into the crowd of barrel racers plucks at a too-tight guitar string in my chest.

I've just seen a ghost; okay, so *technically* she's not dead, but her presence here certainly feels paranormal. Even after all this time, I would recognize her anywhere. That face is one I spent hours memorizing, and years trying to forget.

Maybe I've been transported back in time.

I turn to follow the girl, desperate to find out if I'm seeing things, but a hand wraps around my bicep, and I'm tugged into the present.

"Hey, cowboy," Peyton coos in my ear, slinging her arms around my neck. In a place that otherwise smells overwhelmingly like sweat, livestock, and dirt, she's nothing but strawberries and honey. I inhale deeply, smiling at her like I can't feel each unsteady beat of my heart. Like my chest isn't slowly closing in on itself. Like I'm not tempted to toss her aside to chase after a memory.

"Thought I was gonna come find you after my ride," I say.

"Thought you might need a kiss for good luck." She smiles up at me, but I can't keep my thoughts from wandering to the empty space farther down the alley.

But what if it was . . . No, couldn't be.

Of all the rodeos, this isn't the one to be distracted at. It's been months without any real saddle bronc practice, and I can't safely sit my ass down on a thousand-pound animal when I'm not in the right headspace. So if I could quickly chase after her and confirm it was all in my head, I'd be fine. . . .

"Denny." Peyton interrupts my train of thought at the same time Colt grabs my shoulder to let me know it's time to ride.

"Sorry, gotta go. I'll see you after." I pull back, flashing her a smile before directing my attention to Colt. Pushing the apparition I saw into a faraway corner of my brain.

Colt's hand slaps down on the worn saddle, sending a cloud of shimmery dust into the air. "Saddled up and ready to rock."

Showtime.

I check over his work, tightening the cinch and taking a deep breath before climbing to straddle the chute's top rail. Thirteen hundred pounds of attitude sits below me, letting out loud snorting breaths, eager to get this show going. The thing a lot of people don't understand about bronc riding—all rodeo sports, really—is how much fun the animals find this, too. If a horse doesn't want to participate, they simply won't perform. It's a game to them, a moment of blissful free-dom to be wild, to play with humans the same way they play with other horses. Then they go back with the stock contrac-tor to live a pampered life in a lush, green field. If Wells Ranch's remuda could see these horses, they'd start bucking our cowboys off in hopes of finding a new job as rodeo rough-stock.

The haggard, braided bronc rein slides through my cal-lused hand, and I plop down into the saddle. Tuning out the cowboys slapping me on the back, repeating tips I've heard a million times. *Lift. Lean back. Chest up. Chin down.*

Eight seconds doesn't feel like a long time to most. Out-side of rodeo, I can't remember the last time I noticed exactly how long a second is. But when those may be your last eight seconds alive, it's a fucking lifetime. Yet despite the real pos-sibility of serious injury, I can't imagine ever giving up this sport. Life's short, and the adrenaline rush of saddle bronc is better than just about anything I've ever experienced.

I shift in the saddle, adjusting my seat and securing my boots deep in the stirrups. Readjusting the bronc rein in my hand exactly three times, in time with three deep breaths—the way my grandpa taught me.

Lift, chin down, mark out.

Licking my sweat- and dust-covered lips, I hold my free arm out. Strong and steady, not that it'll stay that way once this horse starts trying to throw me off. And before I have the time to overthink things, I give a nod.

The gate swings open with a bone-chilling creak. The only thing I have now is muscle memory. My heels hold tight to the horse's broad shoulders, and the front hooves stomp the earth. We're on fire—cemented in my seat, I'm spurring, lifting, riding out the wave with unwavering skill. We veer to the left and my focus snags on an apparition between the horse's ears.

The girl who used to be my everything.

It doesn't seem justified to call her the one that got away. Because that implies she slipped between my fingers; the truth is I dropped her and we both shattered.

The animal bucks and I tighten my core, gaze unbroken. When our eyes lock, I lose sense of everything around me. Forgetting where I am, what I'm supposed to be doing. Then I'm moving in the wrong direction and . . .

Blair

Bile rises in my throat as Denver climbs into the chute. It doesn't matter that I grew up here, that I've watched rodeos hundreds of times, or that I used to be sitting atop his bucking chute when he rode. The stress of watching anybody willingly put themselves in danger wears on my heart a little bit, but I can't deny that my anxiety's skyrocketing now. Seeping into every muscle, ligament, fiber of my being. It's different watching him.

Licking my lips, I wait with bated breath for the nod. For the release of the unruly bronc. The gate's flung open and Denver's feet are up, dulled spurs hitting above the shoulder blades, marking out his legal ride. For a qualified ride, he has to exit the chute in this position, and hold there until the front hooves hit the ground for the first time. Once he's marked out, the eight seconds are about showmanship just as much as staying in the saddle. And, *fuck*, Denver Wells has always been great at putting on a show.

One second. His form is perfect—heels firmly held high, arm unmoving, ass barely leaving the saddle. So much better than I remember him riding as a kid.

Two seconds. His heels drag down the horse's side with impeccable timing, before shooting back up to the shoulders.

Three seconds. The horse turns in my direction. The

quiet corner of the arena where I've been strategically hidden, avoiding locals. Avoiding him.

Four seconds. I swear his eyes meet mine, though I know there's no way he's paying attention to anything except staying on the bucking animal. Tell that to my skipped heartbeat, though.

Five seconds. The horse veers right midair, nearly tossing Denver out of the saddle with the unexpected, jarring turn. Suddenly, he's struggling to keep his seat, death grip on the bronc rein, free arm fighting for balance. His sand-colored cowboy hat flies in the opposite direction, floating through the air before settling on the ground.

Six seconds. Another sporadic turn, directly toward the fence. Denver is flung off the horse's side, his back and shoulders slamming into the metal rails, head ringing against a sponsorship sign from Al's Hardware. He hits the ground with a cloud of dust and emphatic silence from the crowd.

My stomach drops, breathing stops. Stillness hangs over the arena—both the event clock and the overall concept of time stopping as everyone waits for him to get up. Seconds pass, the pickup men get the bronc safely down the alley, and Denver's still motionless.

Slipping between the rails, I sprint through the thick arena sand, every muscle in my legs burning as I fight to get to him. I throw myself down to the sun-warmed earth, and my right hand clutches the identification around my neck.

"I'm the medic. Stop touching him," I yell at the cowboys attempting to jostle him back to life. "You want to be useful? Go grab the neck collar and spine board."

Two things I would've brought out myself, had I been in the right mindset at the time of the accident. Had I not been so caught off guard by something as stupid as my high school ex-boyfriend looking in my direction. I'm supposed to be a trained medical professional, not a silly, hormonal teenager.

This is why providing medical care to family or friends was against policy at my old job. Except now I'm a nurse practitioner in my tiny hometown, and a policy like that would mean being unable to help pretty much everybody.

"Denver." His name leaves my dry mouth in a whisper. Then a second time as a plea. "Denver. Denny."

His long dark eyelashes flutter slowly over his cheek, Adam's apple bobbing with a hard swallow. "Bear?" he whispers.

"Hey. Don't move, okay?" I place my hand on his tanned forearm to keep him still, catching a glimpse in my periphery of a cowboy running toward us with the equipment I asked for. "How are you feeling?"

"Never been better," he says with a wincing smile as I delicately slip the collar around his neck.

"Yeah, I'm sure." I stare at him, telling myself I'm only watching for abnormal pupil dilation. But I'm drowning in the molasses of his rich eyes—struggling to pull myself out of the hold they've always had over me. A brown hue so many overlook, assuming they're plain. Except his are flecked with amber and gold, an array of color only visible when you're close enough to kiss him. "All right, let's get you into the ambulance and head to Sheridan."

I motion at the cowboys to grab the spine board, and together we shift him onto it. He's not a lanky, thin teenage boy anymore, and it takes four of them to carry him out of the arena. Always the life of the party, Denver gives the crowd a small fist pump, which makes them wild. Raucous cheers ring out, and the announcer broadcasts well wishes for the hometown cowboy over the loudspeaker. A smile lights Denver's face, despite his glassy eyes giving away the intensity of his pain.

By the time we reach the rodeo ambulance, he's laughing with the guys about having a vendetta against Al from Al's Hardware now. They load him up while I check in with the other medical volunteer, then I slip onto the small bench seat next to Denver, fighting the urge to look into his eyes again.

It's a retired ambulance—significantly older than I am, and lacking most current medical equipment. But at least it provides a safe way to transport the many rodeo injuries to the nearest hospital an hour away. The heavy back doors shut with a thud and, less than a minute later, we're pulling out of the parking lot.

I didn't anticipate being alone with my ex-boyfriend when I signed up to provide medical assistance at the local rodeo. Thank God for the paperwork keeping me occupied. And for the potholed road which requires me to take my time, struggling to keep my printing legible as the rickety vehicle careens down the highway away from Wells Canyon. Without something to keep my hands and mind busy, I might make a stupid choice, like trying to talk to the man lying in front of me.

He looks older, but so many years have passed, it makes sense. *When was the last time I saw him?* A cursory glance at the café when I was home for Christmas a few years ago, I think. He didn't see me.

When was the last time he saw me? How much older do I look?

For a long while, the only sounds are rattling equipment and our driver, Johnny, singing along to a Creedence Clearwater Revival cassette tape. The way his voice cracks during "Fortunate Son" is very *unfortunate*, but I welcome the distraction.

Denver's eyes are boring into the top of my skull long before he speaks. "So, you're back in town."

"Seems so."

"Since when?"

I shrug one shoulder. "Few weeks."

"For how long?"

I sigh. "Don't know."

I didn't want to move back to my hometown in the first place. In fact, I've avoided Wells Canyon as much as humanly possible for the last decade. But now, thinking about leaving means thinking about my mom's Alzheimer's disease progressing beyond what my dad and I can handle ourselves. It means thinking about moving her into long-term care or hospice. So, as much as I don't want to be here, I can't stand the thought of what the end date of my stay means.

"Are you capable of answering with more than two-word sentences?"

I glance up to catch him smirking at me. I tap the pen against my clipboard and consider telling him I have *much* more than two words I could say to him. There are so many unorganized thoughts in my brain, I don't know where to begin.

"Yeah, *no*." I count the words on my fingers, shaking my head as I return to the incident report on my lap. Filling out the paperwork only serves as a reminder that I used to know every single detail about this boy. Now my knowledge is restricted to full name, birth date, and blood type.

"Is your girlfriend your emergency contact?"

"So you *are* capable of more than two words. I don't have a girlfriend."

"Does the blonde you were with behind the chutes know that?"

"Blair Hart, were you *spying* on me?" He flashes a lopsided grin, complete with his famous dimples. Dimples that stole my heart so many years ago. A smile I refuse to let envelop me again. "Nah, I ended things with her after my ride today."

"You . . . broke up? *After* your ride?" I squint at him, looking for any indication that he's suffering a brain hemorrhage. "You definitely need a CT scan when we get to the hospital, because I haven't left you alone since you hit the ground.

When did you have time to break up between then and now? I think you're confused."

"Not confused, and we didn't break up because we weren't actually together. Colt handed me my wallet and phone before you whisked me away in this dilapidated hunk of metal." He holds up the phone and wallet, trying to disguise the pain he's clearly feeling in his shoulder. "I sent her a text while you were busy ignoring me. *Terrible* bedside manner, by the way."

Some things, like the flirtatious teasing, seemingly never change. Other things, like the fuckboy attitude, are painfully new to me. Of course, I've heard snippets about his dating life since I moved away. It's a small town—everyone is dying to let me know what my ex-boyfriend has been up to whenever I come home to visit. As if I give a shit. It's been almost fourteen years, for God's sake.

"Wow, dumping her over text is a dick move."

His nose scrunches and his head rocks side-to-side as much as the neck brace allows, like he's weighing my words. "Desperate times call for desperate measures."

"Or you're concussed and making poor choices."

"Never thought this clearly in my whole life, Hart." He winks.

Jesus Christ, he is a total douche now.

"Anyway, is your *ex*-girlfriend your emergency contact?"

"Nah, Red is. Usually he's with me at rodeos, but he's a little preoccupied these days."

"At least one of you grew up," I mutter under my breath, pulling my phone out to text Red.

"Overrated . . . growing up, I mean. I'm happy for him and Cass—don't get me wrong. Hazel's adorable, and Red's the happiest I've ever seen him. But I don't want that."

An involuntary puff of air leaves my nostrils, and I do my best to play it off as a sniffle by running a knuckle across the tip of my nose. My phone buzzes and I glance down at the bright screen. "Well, Red's busy with the baby, but he says Austin will come pick you up when the hospital discharges you."

"You mean I don't get to ride all the way back to Wells Canyon on this uncomfortable-as-fuck gurney?"

"Fortunately, no." I tap my fingernails against the clipboard, checking my watch for the fortieth time. I swear this drive is taking significantly longer than usual.

"You could ride home with us, if you don't want to be trapped with Mr. CCR." He hooks his thumb in Johnny's direction, who's currently banging out a drum solo on the steering wheel. No, I don't want to spend another full hour listening to his singing, but I'll take that over another hour with Denver Wells. "Plus, you'd be saving me from a lecture. Austin's gonna want to skin me for this."

"You earned that lecture fair and square."

He groans. "I miss when you used to bat your eyelashes to get me out of trouble."

The corner of my lip ticks upward reflexively. *God,* I used to do that all the time. When I was a teenager hanging around the ranch, Grandpa Wells and Bennett both treated me so much like the daughter neither of them had. Which meant I got away with murder and, because Denver was always the one with me, he got away with everything, too.

"I can't, anyway. I need to get back right away," I say.

I promised Dad I would be home by dinner, because Mom's condition always worsens in the evenings. Early-onset Alzheimer's disease at just shy of fifty-nine years old. Something had been off for a long time before my dad insisted she see a doctor, and I kick myself daily for not being around more often to notice the signs. Not that it would help with a fatal disease. But I could have been here to help sooner. To spend more time with her. On the days when I really feel like wallowing in a pit of depression, I find myself wishing I'd never left town to begin with.

The clearing of a throat brings me out of my stupor. Denver raises an eyebrow, eyes locked on mine. "I *said*, what's the rush? The rodeo will be long over by the time you're back."

I stare back, narrowing my gaze. "I . . . uh, need to be around in case some intoxicated cowboys get hurt at the barn dance."

He seems to accept that answer, sucking his lips in for a moment of thought. The ambulance slows to a stop at a red light. *Finally,* we made it to Sheridan.

Rattling over a speed bump as we turn into the hospital emergency parking lot, Denver clears his throat. "Aren't you curious about why I ended shit with her?"

"Not in the slightest," I lie.

"Yeah? I guess you probably know why, anyway."

Because he's a fuckboy looking for his next conquest, is my best guess. Hit by a wave of claustrophobia, I frantically grasp the back door handles, needing out of this personal hell on wheels. I expected to grapple with mixed emotions about moving back to my hometown—*into my childhood bedroom, no less*—but not about him. I didn't anticipate his smug smile to send blood rushing up my chest and cheeks. I didn't anticipate Denver *fucking* Wells.

Denver

I slide my ass into Austin's passenger seat, avoiding the look he's giving me, and reach for the seat belt with a wince. Concussion and a broken collarbone. Could've been a lot worse, honestly. Maybe Aus should focus on the fact that I didn't die before he starts his parental-type speech.

"I don't want to hear it," I groan, leaning my head against the cool windowpane and shutting my eyes.

I held it together pretty well around Blair, still hopped up on adrenaline and probably a hint of shock—both from the fall and seeing her. Admittedly, I was unable to stop smiling because she finally came home like I prayed she would for years. Not that she noticed how happy I was to see her again, because she actively avoided interacting with me.

And the instant I watched her drive away, it all came crashing down.

"You good?" Austin asks as the truck lurches backward out of the parking stall.

The painkillers for my collarbone do nothing to ease the ice pick lobotomy going on in my skull—a seething halo of pain making it hard to focus. Even in the late afternoon, the cloudy skies are too bright and the truck engine is too loud. Plus, the carefully constructed wall around my heart's already threatening to crumble over the girl who was the reason for building it in the first place.

But aside from all that, yeah, *I'm good.*

"Yeah. You should see the other guy." Not opening my eyes, I hold my good arm up to shoot a finger gun in his direction.

I hear his hand scrub across his beard. "You're an idiot."

"You love me." This time I do open one eye, just enough so I can see to give him a little love tap on the upper arm.

"Know what I love more? Not wasting half my day to come pick your ass up from the hospital."

"Thanks, big bro. I love ya, too." I slouch down in the seat, tilting my head so the truck pillar blocks the sun. "It's like old times with you and Blair coming to my rescue. Didn't know she was back in town until she was suddenly doctoring me up right there in the arena."

She'd appeared like a fucking angel, cloaked in sunlight and staring at me wide-eyed when I came to. Of course, I saw her before that—it's why I fell off the horse in the first place. But having her so close, talking to me, face awash with concern, was unparalleled. She looked nothing like she used to, in fancy clothes that didn't suit a rodeo, hair neatly tied up, and more makeup than she even wore to prom. Nothing like the small-town girl I knew. Still, she's as stunning now as she was then.

"You didn't know? She's been at the ranch with Cassidy damn near every day."

Migraine be damned, I open my eyes and turn to look at Austin. *She has?* How am I the last to know about this?

"Huh. Must've missed the memo."

"Would you have cared anyway?" He raises a brow.

Maybe? Yes? I blink down at the floorboards. "Nah, you're the biosecurity guy. I don't give a shit who comes and goes on the ranch."

"*Right.*" He reaches for the dented travel mug in the cup holder and takes a long gulp. "So are you finally done rodeo-ing?"

Ah, time for the lecture.

I pull a face. "It's a concussion and broken collarbone. I'll be back out there in like a week . . . two, *tops*."

"Until you hurt yourself again. And we're down a cowboy *again*. Luckily this happened today, not a few weeks from now when we're really busy. You'd be paying out of your own pocket for a day worker to replace you."

"Pump me full of ibuprofen and whiskey, and I'm basically invincible. If anything, it'll make me stronger than I usually am. I can work perfectly fine."

He sucks his teeth. "Denver, quit being an idiot. You'll go home and sleep it off, like the doctor told you to."

It's been a full week since the rodeo, and either Blair has managed to completely avoid me at the ranch, or Austin was exaggerating about how often she's been coming here. Granted, for the first two days after the fall, I mostly stayed in bed. Then, against the judgment of the mother hens—also known as Beryl, Kate, and Cecily—I went back to work. So I suppose it's possible she's been here and I've missed it.

I'm not about to ask anybody and make it seem like I *care* that she was here. I can't let myself care that she's back, despite my concussed brain telling me to shoot my shot right there in the ambulance. My entire world collapsed when she left almost fourteen years ago. The thought of having her, and losing her all over again, scares the absolute shit out of me.

Did I break things off with Peyton on a whim because Blair's back in town? *Sure*. Was I thinking straight? *No*. But our casual situation was drawing to a close regardless. I never date women for more than a month or two—much longer and they start getting attached, and it becomes harder for me to break things off without seeming like a total piece of shit. Over text wasn't my finest work, admittedly. Especially be-

cause now she's mad, and real close to going full Carrie Un-
derwood on my ass.

"I'm in desperate need of a brewski." Colt claps his hands
together as we stroll across the parking lot of the local dive
bar, the Horseshoe.

"Fuckin' eh." With my good arm, I reach for the metal
door handle—shaped like a horseshoe, of course—and yank
it open. Turning the corner, I collide with something . . . or
rather, *someone*. "Shit, my bad."

On instinct I grab the arm of the person I crashed into.
And then it hits me like a fully loaded freight train.

"Shit, Blair. Sorry." I drop her arm, but make no move to
step back despite being practically on top of her. Just shy of
six-foot herself, she's face-to-face with me. Close enough to
kiss. And fuck me, do I consider going in for the kill. "We've
gotta stop meeting like this."

"Meeting like what? This is nothing like—" Her eyes flit
to my loose arm, and she lets out an irritated sigh. "Why
aren't you wearing your sling?"

"I'm totally fine now." I show off by lifting my arm to about
ninety degrees. Scorching heat radiates out from my injury,
but I grit my teeth, smiling as though there's no discomfort.

"Besides, he can't double-fist drinks with one arm," Colt
chides, brushing past us.

I raise an eyebrow at him. "Well, now . . . that sounds like
a challenge."

"Denver." Blair stresses the fact that my name has two
syllables. She tilts her head with a huff, giving me a look that
elicits a mocking chorus out of the ranch hands, who then
quickly shuffle away before getting swept up in her wrath.

With a smile, I say her name back in a horrific attempt at
a valley girl accent. "Blair."

If I thought she looked too preppy and polished for the
rodeo, she's *really* pushing the boundaries here. Her black
long-sleeve is so modest there's nary a sliver of wrist or neck

exposed, yet so tight it accentuates every gentle curve in her willowy, athletic build. High-waisted tan trousers. And *heels*. Blair Hart doesn't—*didn't*—wear heels. Not even to prom. She doesn't fit this town anymore, and there's a jogged memory flitting by of her teenage wardrobe: jeans, faded T-shirts, and a collection of Stetsons every cowboy in town was envious of. Then she grew up and moved away and changed. And, despite the passing of a decade, it turns out I'm still as affected by her as the day she left me for good.

"It's been a week. You should be wearing a sling. At the very least, try to keep your collarbone stable when you sit down—no double-fisting drinks. Got it?"

"Yes, ma'am." I give her a salute, hoping to induce a smile. Nothing.

"So, what are you doing here?" I ask.

A small crease forms between her eyebrows and she gestures to the small black server pouch tied around her waist. "What does it look like I'm doing? Helping Dave out because he hasn't found a replacement for Cass yet."

She starts sounding real similar to an adult in a *Peanuts* cartoon as my tunnel vision narrows at a dizzying rate.

A *fucking* ring.

She's wearing a ring. My Blair is wearing a fucking massive rock on her goddamn left fucking hand. It's too big for her slender fingers. Too showy for her personality. Too impractical for a nurse practitioner who probably wears latex gloves a lot of the time. But maybe the reason I feel every bruising beat of my heart is because at sixteen she promised that part of herself to me.

A *fucking* ring.

I scrunch my nose to calm the stinging sensation, and work to pull in a steadying breath.

None the wiser, she tucks her hands into the pockets of her fancy pants and turns to walk away. "Go sit down. I'll bring over beer in a minute."

I watch her go, telling myself I shouldn't. It was stupid to think she hadn't moved on after a decade away from this town. She's perfect in every way—naturally, she found a wealthy man in the city to make all her dreams come true. To be the man I could never be.

"Come dance with me." A rasping voice in my ear raises the hair on the back of my neck. Pointed fingernails drag up the goosebumped skin until Peyton's plucking the hat from my head and placing it on hers. Evidently, that text meant fuck all.

"Can't use my arm." My focus remains entirely unbroken from the sight of Blair's ass as she bends to clear a table.

She's taken.

Just because there's a goalie doesn't mean you can't score. . . .

No. *She's not that type.*

"You know what? Fuck it." I turn to Peyton, eyeing up her skimpy, shimmery halter top. Even her cleavage is glittery. "Let's dance."

I let her guide me to the dance floor, wrapping my good arm around her waist as Randy Travis croons over the speaker. And I probably should've worn the sling, because by the end of that first half-assed two-step, my entire upper body is throbbing.

Peyton suddenly grows by about two inches, raising up on the balls of her feet, presumably for a kiss. But as much as I'm willing to dance with her, I have no interest in bringing her home tonight, no matter what the cowboy hat on her head implies. So I take a large step back, dropping my touch from her waist.

"I need a drink," I mouth over the loud music, nodding my head toward the back wall where all the ranch hands are drinking around a large wood table. After so many years of spending every Friday night here, it's become our designated spot. No reservation placard required.

To my dismay, Peyton's hot on my heels. And she plunks

herself into my lap when I sit down, sending sharp jolts of pain from my armpit to my fingertips. A few weeks of casual dating and a breakup text later, here I am with a stage-five clinger.

And I could look past the fiery ache in my collarbone, or my annoyance at Peyton's bony ass on my thigh, if either thing ignited a single spark in Blair's eyes. But the full glass of beer clunks down in front of me, sloshing over the rim, and she carries on. No hint of jealousy or questioning, no eye contact filled with longing. It turns out seeing me with another girl has zero effect on her. Meanwhile, that ring on her finger—even without knowing anything about the guy—has me silently apologizing to my liver for the oblivion I'm about to drink it into.

"Hart." I catch a fleeting moment of her attention. "Bring over a tray of shots. Whiskey."

Denver
(thirteen years old)

My boots clapped together, sending dust and dried mud shrapnel into the air. Seated on the tailgate of Mom's pickup, I was watching her tack up a seven-year-old gelding. Somewhere, Dad and Austin were likely practicing their team roping. Jackson was in his own world—as always—slowly, thoughtfully brushing his mare. And I had nothing to do. Nowhere to be until it was my time to ride . . . in a little over three hours.

I loved rodeo. My entire family loved rodeo. So much, in fact, that my grandfather was the local rodeo association president for more than twenty years, and it was his dad before that. From April to October, each and every weekend was consumed by rodeo. Mom was one of the top barrel racers in British Columbia. Dad and Austin made a powerhouse team roping duo, with Aus heading and Dad heeling. Jackson was on track to be the top tie-down roper in the provincial high school rodeo circuit.

And then there was me. The only one not needing to groom or exercise my horse. No practice outside of jumping on unbroken horses and unruly cattle on our ranch. Despite my family's objections, I rode steers rather than roping or wrestling them.

Folding the ten-dollar bill my grandpa had given me at

breakfast that morning, I tucked it into the front pocket of my jeans and hopped off the tailgate.

"Gonna go buy a drink from the concession," I said, glancing over at Mom.

"Okay, baby. If you see Blair, buy her one, too."

"But Grandpa ga—"

"Denver Wells." Her tone was blunt, tightening around me at the same time as she pulled on the horse's cinch. "You be a decent boy and buy that girl a drink. She just had her best run of the season so far. She deserves it."

I rolled my eyes with a huff. I had mucked out extra stalls the day before for that money, and now I had to spend it on some girl. *Great.*

"And Denver," she called as I walked away. "Maybe it would be fun if you two hung out together. She doesn't really know anybody except us here."

Double great.

Now I had to spend my hard-earned money on her *and* hang out with her?

Should've slipped away when Mom wasn't looking.

Regretting my decision to open my mouth, I trudged across the rodeo grounds. Navigating between stock trailers, I kept my head down. The way I figured, I couldn't get in trouble for not buying Blair a pop if I genuinely didn't see her on my way to the concession.

Fat chance.

There she was. On a patch of grass directly in the middle of my route. Watching a steer wrestling slack event in dusty jeans and a hot pink rodeo shirt. Her dark brown hair was braided down her back, and the warm sun had it shining.

Blair Hart.

We'd known each other since preschool. Same age, same grade, and same class for our entire lives—not that it meant we were friends. Mostly, we passed each other in the hallways, and sometimes I'd be a middleman when she passed notes with her friends. We operated in separate circles until Blair decided she wanted to start barrel racing. The Hart family wasn't in the rodeo scene like mine, so Mom took her under her wing. She'd said something about wanting more estrogen in a house full of boys, on a ranch full of cowboys. Suddenly, Blair was tagging along for nearly every rodeo, and taking the school bus home with us three days per week to practice in our arena.

She was a nice enough girl. Smart, a bit quiet, and she could even be funny sometimes. Though I'd never admit that to the guys from school.

Still though, I wasn't interested in hanging out with her for the entire day. I *really* didn't want to buy her a stupid pop with my hard-earned cash. And yet, I'd rather do both than deal with Mom's rage.

"Hey, I'm headed to buy a cold drink." I stared down at her, waiting for her eyes to meet mine. "Whaddya want?"

"Oh, um." Blair popped up to her feet, brushing the dirt from her pants. "Let me see what they have."

She fidgeted with the sleeve of her pearl-snap shirt the entire fifty-foot walk to the concession. Keeping a gap wide enough for two more people between us, she clearly didn't want to be stuck hanging out with me any more than I wanted to be with her. Thankfully.

Two cans of pop and a measly amount of change back, I handed a can over to Blair beneath the thin shade of a pine tree. She grinned, wiggling a finger under the metal tab to open her Dr Pepper with an aggressive crack and carbonated hiss. "Thanks, Denny."

"No problem." I took a swig of my Mountain Dew while looking around for somebody to hang out with, stuffing my change into my pocket.

"Hey, I saw some train tracks down the hill when we drove in," she said with a mischievous grin. "We should go put those pennies in your pocket on the tracks."

I lifted a brow, talking into my open can. "For what?"

"'Cause it's cool. When the train runs them over, they get really big and flat. Although, it *is* a little dangerous." She gave me a look like she knew that last word was my kryptonite.

Not seeing anybody else around worth hanging out with, I shrugged. "Sure. Okay."

Blair was already turning on her heel and quickly walking away before I had the words out, and I had to jog to catch her. It turned out, the "hill" was a steep embankment filled with loose clay, and we were left with no choice but to slide down on our butts. No clue how we'd get back up, but Blair giggled the entire way down, and I couldn't help the smile teasing my lips.

"So, what do we do?" I eagerly awaited whatever risky thing Blair had planned for us, pulling the loose change from my pocket and presenting it to her.

"We lay the money flat on the tracks and wait for a train to come."

I squinted at the narrow steel. "Hardly sounds dangerous."

"Well . . . I guess it's probably not as scary as steer riding. But your foot could get caught in the tracks, or you might not hear a train coming in time. Also, it's illegal to play on train tracks. So if the conductor sees us . . . run."

Illegal—now we're talking.

"Okay." I grabbed the three copper pennies, jamming the rest of the money back into my pocket. Handing her two, I stepped toward the tracks and waited for Blair to show me what to do.

She diligently set the coins dead center on the steel, about a foot apart, then stepped back to admire her handiwork. I followed suit, putting my coin tails up before collapsing onto the soft grass a few feet from the railway.

We sat in silence for the next twenty or so minutes. Unable to ever sit still for more than a moment or two, I fidgeted to keep myself from walking away and hurting her feelings. Plucking grass and rolling it between my fingers, picking dried mud and horse crap from my boots, rationing sips of my pop.

"Sorry," she said softly. "I figured there'd be more trains coming by."

Her cheeks were a light shade of pink but, despite being painfully bored, I didn't want to make her feel worse about her silly idea of fun. "Let's sit here awhile longer. . . . A train has to come eventually, right?"

"It's okay if you don't want to. The flattened coins aren't *that* cool."

"I have nowhere else to be." I knotted a blade of grass carefully. "So, what made you decide to start running barrels?"

"My parents wanted me to take up a sport."

"And soccer wasn't an option, or . . . ?"

She laughed. "Have you seen our school's sports teams? Nobody takes it seriously. I'm too competitive to be on a team like that."

Explained why she had been practicing more than anybody I knew. Sure, she was at a disadvantage when she started a few months ago, having only been on horseback a handful of times in her life. But by mid-June, you'd never guess she was new to this.

"Fair. Rodeo's more fun than soccer, anyway."

"What about you?" She tucked a piece of hair behind her ear and leaned back on her elbows. "Why steer riding instead of roping like your brothers?"

"I can rope calves on the ranch. There's no fun in it for me." I stretched my legs out in front of me and relished the beating sun in my face, squinting up at the pale blue sky. "I need the rush."

"Fair," she murmured.

Another few minutes passed before either of us spoke again. Then we started talking, in small chunks of time at first. A quick mention of plans for the summer break, a comment about how few trains there seemed to be, talk about the next rodeo. By the time an hour had gone by, neither of us could shut up. Constantly talking over each other, laughing until our cheeks hurt, saying the same thing at the same time—I owed her at least six Cokes because she won every jinx. And doing the math about how many stalls I'd muck out to pay for those Cokes didn't bother me in the least.

The patch of sun we'd been sitting in was cast with late afternoon shadow when we finally got around to discussing favorite foods—having covered nearly every other possible conversation topic already.

"No way your favorite type of ice cream is maple walnut." I stared wide-eyed at her glowing face, freckled from the sun and rosy from laughter. "Nobody under the age of seventy eats that. I swear to God, if you say your second favorite is Neapolitan . . ."

"Neapolitan is pretty much the perfect ice cream." She giggled. "Seriously, if you add walnuts to it, you'd have my dream flavor. Call up Breyer right now."

I fake gagged. "They're going to think it's a prank call because nobody but you would be interested in that abomination."

Blair's fingertips grazed my upper arm in a halfhearted slap. "Shush, jerk. More ice cream for me then."

"Have at 'er. I'd rather go without ice cream for the rest of my life than eat that."

She dramatically rolled her eyes. "Oh, *as if*. It's just walnuts, drama queen. You're acting like I said to put sardines in your ice cream."

"Wouldn't put it past you. That's an old lady food, too."

A look I'd never seen darkened her eyes. Maniacal. Plotting. *Terrifying.*

"No . . . I wouldn't dream of such a thing." A small dimple formed in her right cheek as she spoke.

Crap.

"Well, great. I'm going to be terrified of eating ice cream anywhere near you from now on."

"You should be, Denny." She glanced down at the dainty silver watch around her wrist, and her shoulders fell with an exhale. "You should get back. They're probably going to be starting steer riding soon. Sorry for making you waste your time."

"I had more fun here than I would've with the stupid guys up there." My chin pointed up toward the rodeo grounds, and the small smile on her lips was contagious. I jumped to my feet and shook out each leg to wake the muscles back up. "Come on, we'll leave the coins and come back to check after."

I extended my hand, a little surprised by the soft warmth of her palm when she grabbed mine to pull herself up. "Come watch me ride?"

"Sure. I have nowhere else to be," she said, looking briefly over her shoulder at me as she started toward the hill. Blair began scrambling up the slippery, dusty bank on all fours. "Just gotta be back at the old folks home by five, or I miss out on a pudding cup."

My chest warmed, and not only from the intense cardio of climbing the hillside. "Well shoot, we can't have that."

"If you make me miss butterscotch pudding, you're *definitely* getting sardine ice cream next weekend, Wells." She stopped briefly on the hill to turn to me with a menacing glare and finger point, nearly losing her footing, which would've sent her toppling down to the bottom.

"*Of course* you like butterscotch. You're an odd duck, Hart."

Protective gear in place, I stood behind the bucking chute, eyeing up a steer by the name of Big Tom while my mom placed my number on my back. Despite not understanding my desire to climb on an untamed steer for eight seconds, she never missed a ride and she never tried to talk me out of competing.

"Give 'em hell, baby." She rubbed a firm hand across my shoulder, then moved to give me a final pat on the back when I stepped onto the metal rail. Poised to climb into the chute, I smiled down at her.

Adrenaline and excitement coursed through my veins. A rush of blood through my chest. A dull, steady drumming rhythm played deep in my ears, and radiated around my skull like a sturdy helmet—something to protect against natural fear. Arguably nobody *should* be comfortable climbing on the back of an animal that wants to see you die. And yet, knowing the steer could maim me was part of the thrill.

Sinking down, I tucked my hand under the steer rope, sliding the leather handle along my palm until I had a steady grip. Youth steer riders were permitted to hold on with two hands, but I wanted the real deal. I wanted to prove I had what it takes to compete with the men. I would've hopped on a bronc or bull, instead of a steer, if they'd have let me.

Swallowing the saliva pooling at the back of my throat, I heard Grandpa's voice in my ear. His baseball-glove-sized hand cupped my shoulder. "You got this, kiddo. Remember, three deep breaths—fix that hand—and let your body flow with the momentum. Don't overthink it."

I inhaled the dusty air, letting the animal odors settle in my lungs, and exhaled. Three times. Grandpa's hand left my shoulder, he nodded, I nodded.

The gate swung open and the steer flew out into the open air, jarring my body with every stomp. Swinging me in every direction. My grip tightened and I relaxed into the motion, letting my movements roll like an ocean swell. A train horn sounded in perfect harmony with the buzzer, and the pickup men couldn't get to me fast enough. The moment my boots hit the dusty earth, I was sprinting.

Over the fence rails, already tearing off my gear, I tossed my chaps in a heap next to where Mom had been watching, and breathlessly exclaimed, "Gotta go find Blair for a second. Be right back."

If she questioned me, I didn't hear it. Blood pounding behind my ears, I jogged down the alley to find Blair. She was sitting on a metal bench, watching the pickup men try to herd the steer out of the arena, when I plunked down next to her with a loud exhale.

"Oh," she said with a startled tone. "Hey. Wow, Denny. That was a great ride. Like . . . you were amazing."

She smiled at me, brown eyes taking on a gold hue in the sun, and I wasn't about to tell her it was merely an *okay* ride. Definitely not my best, and I didn't need to stick around for the score to be announced to know I wasn't winning.

"I heard the train. Let's go check our coins." I grabbed her hand to tug her to her feet.

"Denny, it's really not *that* exciting," she said as she followed me to the clay banks. "Like, they're just flattened coins. They aren't going anywhere. We could've stayed to hear your score."

"Meh, I'll find out what it is later." My feet sank into the fine, powdery clay and instantly slipped out from under me. I fell backward into Blair, who was smart enough to not even bother trying to get down the hill in any way but by sliding on her butt.

With a shriek, she threw a hand up to block me right before our skulls clunked together, and her laughter filled the air. "You can stay on a steer no problem, but can't manage to keep your own two feet underneath you?"

"I was just trying to beat you to the bottom."

Her tongue darted out to lick her lip, then she shoved my

shoulder hard as she stood. As she launched her body forward, her feet barely stayed under her as she ran. But, *shit*, she made it. With a triumphant fist pump, she turned to face me.

"Beat you," she taunted.

I ran down after her, skidding through the soft earth to stop before my chest crashed into hers. "Didn't know I was dealing with a cheater."

Ignoring me, she beelined for the tracks and held one of the flattened coins between her finger and thumb, letting the setting sun reflect off the smooth surface. Her doe eyes sparkled with a similar shade of worn copper, a kaleidoscope of browns and greens and golds.

She was right, the flattened penny wasn't *that* impressive. And I could tell she knew that.

"This is so cool," I lied with a smile, holding up my own to inspect it. "Dang, now I wish we'd done this with a toonie to see what the two colors all squished together would look like. Next weekend?"

She nodded thoughtfully. "Good idea. I'm going to see if I can figure out the train schedule this week so we can make sure we're down here to watch it go by."

God, she was weird. And I guess I was, too, because I enjoyed every second of hanging out with her. When we started back up toward the rodeo ground, I was already counting down the time until we'd be back here.

I smiled over at her, extending a hand to climb the embankment together. "I'll bring the butterscotch pudding."

Blair
(thirteen years old)

I spent nearly every summer weekend with the Wells family. Sometimes, it was only Denny, his mom, and me heading out on the road with her old ranch pickup and a bumper-pull horse trailer. We'd get a crappy motel room or camp out under the inky sky—giggling late at night about silly pictures we found in the stars or the motel ceiling stains. Living off nothing but processed sugar and laughter.

Other times, the entire Wells clan tagged along with massive gooseneck stock trailers, complete with live-in quarters. Then it was full meals, sleeping alone in the same trailer as the parents while Denny bunked with his brothers, and boisterous family hangouts around a fire every evening.

Regardless, it was Denny and I all summer long—attached at the hip, as Lucy loved to say. I learned Denny could say the words "chubby bunny" with six marshmallows in his mouth, his favorite color was blue, and he was deathly afraid of June beetles. We toilet-papered Austin's truck, ate our weight in ketchup chips, and stayed up way too late every night laughing. He was my best friend. I was also pretty sure I was in love with him—though anytime my bestie, Cassidy, asked me if I loved him, I'd lie.

The first day back at school was damp and dreary and daunting. Elbows linked with Cass, we walked into the eighth grade together. Wearing my favorite pair of jeans, a belt buckle I'd won a few weeks prior, and the pink, pearl-snap shirt Lucy Wells gifted me for my first rodeo, I was on top of the world.

"I wish we had more choices for electives. I don't even want to take cooking class." Cassidy stared down at her class schedule, checking once again that it hadn't magically changed on her. We both knew she'd had the schedule memorized since they sent it out weeks ago.

"At least it's better than taking shop class or band." I shrugged, clutching my binders to my chest as I scanned the crowded hallway.

"Barely." Cass huffed. "Why can't they give us something useful?"

I snorted. "Since when is cooking not useful?"

"I can just live off the French fries from the Horseshoe forever."

"I can't talk about fries right now. Denny and I ate so much poutine last weekend it made my stomach hurt."

Cass raised her eyebrow, a glimmering expression calling me out for mentioning Denny *again*. According to her, I found a way to work him into every conversation, which simply wasn't true. I only brought up Denver Wells when the story fit the conversation. Just so happened, I usually had a story involving him that fit.

Shaking my head with an irritated eye roll, I spotted him. Down the hall, past the band room, Denny was huddled with a group of boys by a bank of lockers. With his back to us, it was the perfect opportunity for payback. I raced up behind him and pinched his side—a move he'd done to me at least a million times over the summer. He jumped, twisting his torso midair to see who the culprit was.

I stupidly expected a laugh. Maybe a retaliation tickle.

Instead, he metaphorically slapped me across the face when his voice grew low and, in an annoyed tone, he said, "Oh, hi, Hart."

"Hi," I croaked, unsure why he was acting like we hadn't spent nearly every day together for the last two months.

Denny turned back to his friends, who stood with scrunched noses, staring at me like the biggest weirdo in school. And maybe I was. Any other girl in our grade would've swooned over Denny simply looking at them. But my eyes welled, my cheeks grew hot, and my intestines knotted with embarrassment.

Screw Denver Wells.

For the entire week, I made up excuses for why I couldn't go to the ranch after school—a stomachache, a headache, chores, tutoring. On Thursday evening, I was sprawled across my bed reading a *Seventeen* magazine, daydreaming about Chad Michael Murray, when the phone rang. The garbled sounds of my dad's low voice traveled down the hallway until he was knocking heavily on my door. I sprang to life, and cracked my bedroom door open, snatching the cordless house phone from his hand with a smile.

Expecting Cassidy, I didn't even say hello. Instead immediately jumping into conversation with, "Do you want to take this quiz with me to see which guy from *One Tree Hill* you should date?"

Lucy Wells's laugh filled my ear. "I think they're probably too young for me, but you do have me curious."

"Sorry, Lucy. I thought you were Cass. What's up?"

"Well, I haven't seen you all week. . . ." *Fudgesicles.* "Jackson said you were sick or had tutoring or something. Are things okay?"

The deceit came easily when I was simply lying to Jackson as we'd cross paths in the school halls each day. But I couldn't lie straight to Lucy like this. Not when there was clear concern in her voice, and I could so easily picture the worried maternal look that was definitely on her face.

"I just . . ." I picked at my fingernails, delaying the inevitable. "Things are weird with Denny and me right now."

"Are you sure this isn't a convenient excuse because you're afraid to tell me you don't want to compete anymore? If you want to quit, I promise my feelings won't be hurt."

"No! I *love* riding. I love barrel racing. I mean . . . I was serious when I told you I wanted to try breakaway roping next year. I definitely don't want to quit, but . . ."

"Okay, so I guess I'm not understanding the issue here. You two are best friends."

I let out a breathy exhale. I thought we were, too, before he went and acted like a moldy muffin at school. "We're not friends anymore, apparently. So I figured it would probably be weird if I was still at the ranch every day."

"Well, it's your choice. But if you still love riding, I don't think you should give up on your dreams because of a boy. If it's weird for him to have you here, he can learn to deal with it. This place is big enough—he can go somewhere else. *You* don't need to suffer for the sake of his comfort."

I couldn't help the small smile her words made crop up on my lips. "Yeah . . . okay, yeah. I'll come out. Maybe I'll see if my dad can drive me on Sunday."

"Perfect. You know where everything is, and you're welcome here anytime."

"Thanks, Lucy."

"So . . . who's my teenage heartthrob boyfriend? Maybe I'll see if their dad's available."

Megan Barlow's parties were the height of Wells Canyon's adolescent social scene—which wasn't saying much, considering our entire high school had about two hundred students spread across grades eight through twelve. I didn't particularly like Megan. . . . In fact, I don't think anybody did. But we collectively overlooked how much of a rude person she could be because her family was rich, and her parties were always incredible.

And with this about to be our first party as high schoolers, Cassidy and I spent our entire Saturday preparing. Manicures, pedicures, outfits . . . we even shaved our legs for the first time—only to the knee, because my grandma insisted anything further was reserved for when you were "entertaining company." Whether it was the phrase or the accompanying wink, I'm not sure, but it turned me off shaving past the knee for a *long* time.

"Do you think there will be older boys at this thing?" Cass mused as she thoughtfully twirled a piece of hair around her finger. She sat on the edge of my bed, waiting as I debated between outfits for the thirtieth time.

"I think there has to be. No way she invited the seventh graders, and I hope it's not *just* our class there." I wriggled into a pair of black skinny jeans and eyed my scrawny, tall body in the full-length mirror hanging from my closet door. "Why? Is there a certain redheaded boy you're hoping will be there?"

"Gross. No," she said, quickly dropping the hair from her clutches and pretending to be engrossed in the magazine on her lap.

With a snort, I shook my head and returned to layering my tank tops—tugging on the hems to stretch them enough for my long torso—then spritzed myself with body spray and gave a nod of self-approval in the mirror. "I think we're a good amount of fashionably late. Let's go."

We walked the two blocks to Megan's house with a spring in our step, and it wasn't until the front door closed behind us that I realized Denny would be there. Kicking my shoes off inside the foyer, I heard his laugh carrying up the stairs from the basement, and my stomach fell into my butt.

"Just ignore him." Cassidy squeezed my forearm, tucking her sneakers neatly against the wall.

Easier said than done. I'd survived the first week of the school year by keeping my distance, but that would be impossible at a party in Megan's basement unless I spent the entire night in the corner. Not that anybody would be surprised by Blair Hart tucked away somewhere petting the Barlow family dog instead of interacting with humans.

As we reached the bottom of the basement stairs, Megan immediately pulled Cass into an embrace. "Oh my God, I'm so happy you made it. There's a ton of food and drinks over there." She gestured toward the basement bar, which was covered in a spread of food. "Of course the usuals—pool table, arcade games . . . oh, and my dad hooked up *Dance Dance Revolution* and *Guitar Hero* in the theater room."

"Wow, sounds like fun." Cass smiled politely at her, taking in the chaotic scene before us.

"So much fun." Megan clapped her hands together before turning to me, her smile wavering. "Hey, Blair."

I awkwardly gave a wave, lips pressed together in a pained smile. In the movies, you can reinvent yourself when you start high school. But in a town as small as Wells Canyon, the reputation you earn as a little kid tends to follow you for life, unless you do something *really* gossip-worthy later on. Though I preferred being a generic "weird girl" over being Garrison the nose picker.

Cass grabbed my hand, tugging me through the sea of teenagers to the bar fridge. Cans of root beer acquired, we cracked open the tops and each took a long sip while surveying the land. For the next hour, she and I took up residence on a hot pink sofa close to the candy bar, making up pretend conversations for other party guests and consuming a concerning amount of gummy bears. Cassidy chatted with people as they perused the candy selection, and I became well acquainted with the Barlows' corgi, Gordon, through a shared love for Cheez-Its. I was doing a fantastic job of avoiding

Denny, maintaining my loser status, and giving myself a stomachache, when Megan popped up out of nowhere.

"A bunch of us are going to play a game in the next room, if you guys want to join." She slipped her straw between her lips and took a long swig of fruit punch.

"We should probably participate in *something* here." Cass grabbed my hand, yanking me to my feet.

With a groan and a longing glance back at Gordon snoozing on the couch, I followed my bestie across the room and through a wide archway. The Barlows' basement was likely bigger than my entire house, with doors and hallways heading off in every direction. Based on the yoga mats propped up against the wall, I assumed the room we'd been summoned to was their very own yoga studio.

Who has a yoga studio in their house?

The other participants were already seated in a perfect circle, which suddenly gained an awkward lump when Cassidy and I forced our way in.

"What are we playing?" Cassidy asked, shifting on the floor to get comfortable.

The circle shrugged in a wave, rocking into Megan.

"Well, my suggestion was charades, but some people think that's too boring." Megan rolled her eyes. "So, if you have any suggestions."

Cassidy's squinted gaze moved around the circle and she opened her mouth slowly. "Well, we could play . . ." Her tongue darted out to lick her bottom lip, leaving space for the last words to tumble out. "We could play Seven Minutes in Heaven."

I spun so hard to look at her, my neck cracked. Eyes wide, I mouthed, "What the hell are you thinking?"

Neither of us had kissed anybody yet. I'd thought about it a lot over the summer while hanging out alone with Denny, but it never happened. And I was absolutely *not* about to let the first time be in a musty closet at Megan Barlow's party, with some random boy I didn't like.

Apparently, that didn't matter anymore. I was outnumbered. The boys were all eager to participate. The girls were meeker about it, but they clearly wanted to play, too. An older girl—Jessica, I think—explained the rules while Megan left in search of paper to write our names on.

Sitting in uncomfortable silence, breathing in the noxious mingling of Victoria's Secret perfume and Axe body spray in the air, I waited as pairs of names were drawn from two metal mixing bowls. With the number of tiny, crumpled strips of printer paper dwindling, my heart rate was exponentially increasing. And in the midst of drying my clammy hands on the tops of my jeans, I heard Megan announce that Denny would be heading into the hallway closet.

I refused to look across the circle at him. If I watched him walk into a closet with a girl, I'd probably throw up gummy bears and Cheez-Its all over this nice hardwood. Simply thinking about it made it impossible to focus on anything beyond the rushing blood behind my eardrums, and the hazy vignette around my field of vision.

Was I about to pass out?

"Blair," Megan shrieked.

After a beat, Cass tapped my foot with hers. "It's your turn. You okay to go?"

I blinked away the blurry vision, swallowing the hard lump in my throat when I realized why everyone was staring in my direction. Denny was standing by the closet, eyes trained to the floor, white knuckles gripping the door frame.

The only thing worse than Denny being in a closet making out with a random girl was him being in that closet with me.

I shakily scrambled to my feet, my entire body on fire as I moved across the room. Although not a single cell in my body wanted to be in a closet with Denver Wells, it would be more embarrassing to be the one person who refused to participate.

So I stepped into the small space, which was humid with sweat and hardly large enough for two people, and Denny slid in after.

When the door shut, Megan's voice permeated the air. "Seven minutes starts now!"

I don't know how long we stood face-to-face, in perfect darkness, with only the sounds of our breathing. But finally, Denny lightly cleared his throat. "It smells really bad in here. Like fried egg and bologna sandwiches left in a hot car for two days."

"That's very specif—"

"Don't ask me how I know what that smells like," he interrupted.

Scrunching my nose, I held back the smile threatening to blow the lid off my sour mood. I missed him, and I hated how difficult that made it to hate him.

His hot, peppermint-laced breath hit my cheek with a long exhale. "Are you mad at me or something?"

"Yeah, I'm mad at you or something. You've been a real . . . piece of moldy cheese lately." I bit my lip to stop from tearing a strip off him.

"Moldy cheese? How have I been the moldy cheese when you're the one avoiding me every day? The only time I seem to exist is when you glare at me in math class."

He couldn't be serious.

"I'm avoiding you because you were rude to me on the first day. I thought we were friends, Denny."

"We are friends."

"Except when you're with your other friends," I mumbled, swiping a leaky tear just before it slid down my cheek.

"Blair," he breathed out my name, and his warm hands grabbed hold of my upper arms. "I didn't mean to. They're just . . . well, you know how those guys are."

"Yeah." I sniffled. Realizing I was crying, I wiped the back of my hand across my eyes. "I know how they are."

"I-I'm sorry."

"It's okay," I said to convince both of us. "I'm fine."

"I can tell you're crying. You wouldn't be crying if you were fine." He exhaled hard. "Okay . . . there's something my mom always says when we're too scared to fess up to something bad. It's like a Get Out of Jail Free card. She lets us have five seconds of honesty."

"What do you mean?"

"I mean that . . . Pretend I broke a vase. I get five seconds where I can tell her the truth, and there won't be any consequences or questions. Even if I was doing something I shouldn't have, like practicing trick roping in the living room, she can't get mad at me if I fess up during those five seconds. *But* there's no passing the blame, so I can't say 'I broke it, but that's only because Jackson told me to swing a rope inside.'" Denny's hands glided down my bare arms, leaving a wake of goosebumps he thankfully couldn't see, before falling away from me completely. "So, Blair, give me your five seconds of honesty."

I swallowed hard, weaving together a believable half-truth in my mind. Shoving away the sentences that would be too damning. The truth was, his actions hurt me not only because we were friends, but because Denver Wells was my first real crush. Because he made my brain float, my chest ache, and my insides somersault when he was near. Because he was the first person, aside from Cassidy, who seemed to *get* me.

"You were my best friend all summer. I thought you wouldn't treat me differently 'cause your popular friends were around. I know how they are. . . . I didn't think you were like that. So it hurt."

I wrapped my arms around myself in a hug, hoping to ease the shakiness in every fiber of my body, and ease the nausea bubbling in my stomach. Maybe it wasn't the entire truth, but it was a shard of honesty. And despite Denny's promise not to question me on it, I couldn't help but fear how he'd react.

"Five seconds of honesty—I'm sorry." He cleared his throat. "Okay, well . . . the truth is, those guys made fun of me, saying I liked you because we hung out all summer. It bugged me because . . . I don't know. I guess because I thought it was obvious we're just friends. You're more like a sister than anything. I was a jerk to you so they'd lay off. But that was very blue cheese of me, and I'm sorry."

Just friends. A pseudo-sister. *Obviously.* All those thoughts about kissing him were entirely delusional. I shook my head slowly, wiping the tears collecting on my lower lashes. "*Very* blue cheese of you."

"Can we be friends again?" he asked in a whisper.

"I don't know. Can we? Are you *allowed* to be friends with me?"

I heard the smack of his lips as he opened them in the dark, maybe preparing to give another five seconds of honesty. But before the words found their way off his tongue, the closet door opened and Megan stood with a devilish grin, hoping to catch us making out.

I blinked rapidly to let my eyes adjust before meeting Denny's own bewildered stare. And when he looked into my eyes—which were likely red and watery—his shoulders sank. I quickly reached to clean up any stray tears or dried salt with my fingertips before turning to face the crowd of partygoers. A catchy pop song played somewhere in the distance and, for a second, everyone stared at us in silence.

"You turned her down so bad you made her cry?" an older jock guy shouted from the other side of the room, clear pride and excitement in his voice.

There's that nausea again. My mouth was wet and dry all at the same time. I could've run away crying, but my brain couldn't convince my legs to move no matter how hard I tried.

Cass stood, stepping over and around people to get across the room, her eyes never leaving mine.

Then Denny cleared his throat beside me. "No. She turned me down, actually."

Liar. Though the slack-jawed expression on Megan's face made both me crying in front of everybody, and Denny lying, totally worth it.

"She turned me down, then got upset because I said something really rude in response—which I *didn't* mean to do, by the way," he said. Catching him staring in my periphery, I turned to meet his apologetic half-smile. "And I'm hoping she forgives me for being a jerk."

"I accept the apology, blue cheese."

Blair

Strolling into the kitchen, I spot Mom in the family room watching *Wheel of Fortune*, as always. Sitting on the old leather sofa, her silvery-brown hair atop her head in a messy bun. When she first got her Alzheimer's diagnosis, she kept a brave face. Now she's firmly in stage four out of seven for the disease, with no way of knowing how long before she forgets everything and needs 24/7 care. Whether it was the door alarms, the medic-alert bracelet, her eldest daughter moving home to care for her, or a combination of factors that made her depressed, we can't be sure. But the hopeful smile is gone.

"Morning, sweetie," Dad says, pouring himself a cup of coffee on his way out the door.

"Morning." I grab Mom's pill sorter and the mug of tea Dad has set out on the counter as I stroll past. The mug clunks onto a marble coaster, and I pop open the lid labeled Tuesday a.m., dumping the pills into Mom's open palm.

"Hey, I was thinking maybe we could go get a manicure after your doctor's appointment in Sheridan next week? I desperately need one."

Refusing to break her gaze from Vanna White's demonstration of a white hybrid sedan, she shrugs one shoulder as she swallows the colored assortment of pills. "Sure."

"Perfect. Let me do your hair for you before I head out to Cassidy's house to babysit, okay?"

She nods once and I head for the bathroom to grab supplies. Then spend a solid ten minutes teasing away every knot, dampening the strands with a light mist of water, and pulling her hair into a secure bun. It's not that she isn't physically capable of brushing her own hair—she simply doesn't care. And her depression is making things harder on Dad, who's been busting his ass to keep her safe and happy since the diagnosis. He installed the door alarms and cameras, spent hours googling medication options to ask the doctor about, and insisted I didn't need to move back in with them. And, for a brief second, I considered staying in the city; I loved my gorgeous apartment, my wonderful roommate, and my well-paid career at the Women's Hospital. But the relief in Dad's eyes when I pulled into the driveway with all my belongings made it clear this was the right choice. The *only* choice.

Seeing me grab my purse and sunglasses from the dining table, Mom asks with a warm smile, "Where are you going?"

"I'm going to help Cass out, remember?"

Crap. I knew as soon as the word slipped out that asking her if she remembered was stupid. The first bit of expression I've seen in her today disappears, eyes falling to my feet. "Right. Right, yes, of course."

"Dad's going to be home around lunchtime. Love you."

I double-check the oven lock, straighten the large sheet of neon yellow paper with my phone number on the fridge, and lock the front door behind me. The alarm alerts my phone on the walk to the car, and I send Dad a text to let him know I'm heading out. So many little steps which often feel entirely unnecessary when Mom's having a good day. But sometimes she leaves the house without knowing where she's going. Or she turns the stove on and forgets about it. Or she asks me questions about things that happened a decade ago. Those days—where she doesn't quite feel like my mom anymore—are the hardest.

.   .   .

I squint up at the worn WELLS RANCH sign hanging over the driveway. Once flanked by overgrown lilac bushes, the entrance is more clean-cut now, with manicured grass and tidy flowerbeds waiting to be planted.

Pulling into the ranch, I release a small sigh of relief when there are no cowboys in sight. It's not that I want to avoid Denver, but . . . I want to avoid Denver. Cassidy's on the front porch of the big house—the sprawling white farmhouse the Wells brothers grew up in, which is now where Jackson, his wife Kate, and their kids live.

Just my luck, my best friend had to fall in love and have a baby with an honorary Wells brother, then move to this ranch. A place filled with memories far beyond my high school boyfriend. His parents and siblings were a second family to me, and this ranch was home. My family's never been the tight-knit kind you see on sitcoms, but the Wells family was. And I adored them.

Denver and I traipsed over every inch of their land, explored every nook in every outbuilding, kissed on the same stupid porch Cassidy and the other girls are sitting on. Now for the two months since moving back, I've been sneaking on and off the property to visit my baby niece almost daily. Unable to take a full breath from the moment my car rumbles across the cattle guard at the end of the driveway.

I step out into the warm spring air. It's lightly perfumed by early floral buds, and my best friend has Hazel tucked against her chest, swaying gently in an old wooden rocking chair. Denver's two sisters-in-law, Cecily and Kate, sit stretched out on the front steps with steaming mugs in their hands. I don't know Cecily well yet, but I know if it were any later than eleven o'clock, Kate would be drinking something a lot stronger than coffee.

"Morning!" Kate's daughter, Odessa, calls from where

she's sitting in a pile of topsoil with her little brother, Rhett. They're playing with toy excavators and bulldozers, covered in dirt from head to toe.

"Hey, kiddos." I steal glances in their direction for the entire walk up the footpath. Wondering how so much time has passed that Kate and Jackson—who were in full denial about being a couple back when I left Wells Canyon—have *two* children now. It's an uncanny reminder of how much time has passed.

Kate waves as I approach the house. "Perfect timing—a fresh pot just finished brewing."

"Thanks. I need the caffeine to function," I say, climbing the front porch stairs. "I have to head to the clinic pretty soon, and I'm getting a migraine from thinking about Dr. Brickham's outdated filing system. I've been meaning to catalog it for weeks, but organizing is *not* my thing."

"I keep telling you to let me come help." Cass shakes her head in annoyance.

"With all the free time you have?"

"I can make the time."

"Babe, don't worry about it. I'm just complaining for the sake of complaining." I softly shut the screen door behind me, careful not to wake the baby.

It's surreal to be back in this house, and the strange tightening in my stomach isn't helped by the fact that the kitchen is the only thing that's changed over the past decade. What used to be firmly nineties style is now updated with modern wood cabinetry and quartz countertops. Otherwise, the same photos hang on the wall—with a few additions, of course. The same stair banister we'd grip to round the corner and fly up the stairs to the boys' rooms when Denver and I were running away from his brothers—typically after pranking them. I can't help but wonder how similar upstairs is. Obviously, the bedrooms have changed somewhat. Did they sand and stain the floors, or are there still scuffs from when Denny and I danced for hours?

My chest seizes, breathing choked with wistful nostalgia. If things had played out differently years ago, Denver and I could be the ones living in this house. It could be our kids playing outside. Our ranch, home, family.

"You okay, honey?" Beryl, the head of the ranch's kitchen, pokes her head out from the pantry with a lilting smile.

"Oh, yeah." My voice comes out thick with emotion, but I smile back and continue beyond the kitchen entryway to pour a cup of coffee. She watches me, not saying anything aloud because her expression does the job just fine.

I clear my throat. "Sometimes it's weird being back here. It's all so different and yet very much the same."

"Mmmm, yes. I imagine so. We always expect time will change things, but sometimes that's not the case."

I slowly stir the two sugar cubes, allowing them time to dissolve before adding creamer.

God, does this woman always stare into your soul like this?

"So, uh . . . need any help in here?" I ask.

"Oh, no, honey. Go sit with the girls."

I nod and turn to head back outside. Though there's a small bit of reprieve when I step out of the house filled with equal parts happiness and pain, the porch isn't a whole lot better. I doubt there's anywhere on this property that doesn't hold memories.

I sink into the chair next to Cass with a short sigh. "How's our little Hazelnut doing today?"

"She just ate, and I think she's saving up a big poop for Auntie B." Cass stands and delicately lowers the sleeping newborn into my arms. I tuck the thick blanket around her tiny body—though it's a warm day for late April, this elevation still has a good nip in the air, and her pink sleeper isn't quite warm enough. The fresh, cool air helps Hazel sleep like a rock, though.

"Perfect. I can't wait to get back at her one day for saving every bowel movement for when I babysit." Shifting in the chair to get comfortable, I motion my head toward the cabins in the distance. "Go. Take your shower and do your leather-working. I got her."

After one last glance at her sleeping daughter, she heads off to have coveted alone time. This is our routine, and I cherish every second of it, even if some days I feel like I'm the exhausted new mother with everything I have going on. The clinic, my parents, Cassidy and Hazel, and toss in overwhelming anxiety around seeing Denver—I'm run ragged and always feeling behind the eight ball.

"Aside from Brickham's old-school methods of filing, how's the clinic going?" Cecily asks, leaning back on her elbows to look over at me.

"It's pretty slow—which isn't the worst thing because it gives me more time to be here and with my mom." I shrug. "The old-school ranchers want Brickham because I refuse to perform medical procedures in the middle of a dirty barn or field. But I'm hoping more of the women will start wanting to come to me, at least."

Kate gives me a knowing look. I'm sure most of the cowboys at Wells Ranch would also rather see Brickham, the seventy-year-old doctor with techniques that are equally as old. But she says, "Count me in. I'm excited to not have to drive to Sheridan every time the kids get hurt or sick. Jackson can have Brickham bandage up whatever injuries he gets, but I refuse to let him work on the kids."

"As much as I don't want to talk shit about my boss, I can't say I blame you." I press the balls of my feet against the floorboards and push, sending the chair rocking backward. "I fell off a horse and dislocated my shoulder when I was a teenager. Brickham tied my arm up in a makeshift sling with baling twine. *In his office*. It's not like we were out in the middle of nowhere and he was forced to make do. And I know at least once he stitched Denver up right on this porch with questionably sterile tools."

"Jesus." Cecily widens her eyes at me, as Beryl's singsong voice floats through the fine mesh of the screen door, beckoning the two women to help knead bread dough for the hundreds of sandwiches they make for their cowboys each week.

I glance down at Hazel's fine red hair blowing in the slight breeze and pull the blanket up to keep her perfectly round head warm. Honestly, this tiny human might be the main reason why I haven't spiraled into a deep depression over moving back into my childhood bedroom. Sure, the prescription medication helps, but one hit of oxytocin from snuggling this little Hazelnut is enough to get me through a lot of bad moments.

Mid-sip of my coffee, the clomping of hooves on compact dirt deflates my chest. Typically the one thing I can count on here is that the ranch hands will be gone from sunup to sundown—my saving grace to avoid seeing Denver because the way he smiles at me makes my brain foggy, and seeing another woman all over him at the bar left me feeling like my heart had collapsed in on itself.

"Oh, it's lucky you're cute." I pull a face at the infant nestled into the crook of my arm when I feel her stomach rumble on my hand. "You literally save it for me, don't you?"

Her giant blue eyes blink up at me, and she starts to work up a cry when she realizes I'm not her mom. Her mom . . . who didn't think to leave a diaper bag with me. *Fuck, Cass.* She's supposed to be the organized one out of the two of us.

"Let's go for an adventure, Hazelnut." Up until now, I've spent my time with Hazel over at Cassidy and Red's cabin on the property. But I'm sure Cass isn't walking back there to change a diaper every time, so I head inside to find Kate wiping loose flour from the countertop.

"Hey, does Cass have diapers around here?"

"Upstairs in the first bedroom on the left. Her diapers are in the second drawer below the change table."

Upstairs.

I take the stairs at a painstaking pace, my free hand on the banister with a rigid grip. Thankfully, Hazel doesn't seem too bothered by what's happening in her pants, because I'm incapable of moving faster. I don't look to the right—to the bedroom I spent countless hours in. Instead, I slip carefully through the door of Austin's—*um, Rhett's*—room. Making quick work of changing Hazel so I can get back outside, away from the nostalgic smell of old wood and antique furniture.

But I lose every ounce of self-control when I step out and notice Denver's old bedroom door cracked open. I tread softly, wary of creaky floorboards, like I'll get in trouble for stealing a peek. With a gentle nudge, the hinges groan and the door swings all the way open. Everything in the room is pink now, so I don't know why I feel the urge to lie down in a bed that definitely won't smell like him. Or why I expect to open the closet and find a hoodie of his to steal. Despite the changes to the paint and furniture, the floor remains dented and marked up from the summer we taught ourselves country swing dancing, and it guts me. I blink away the burning in my eyes and take calculated breaths as I descend to the main floor, clutching Hazel to my chest like a security blanket.

"Wow. Feels weird seeing you walk down those stairs again." Denver's voice rings out from the doorway.

I should've handed the baby off to one of the women in the kitchen and left the moment I heard those horses outside.

"Since you're already here, mind doing a house call to save me the drive into town?"

Of course he's the appointment Brickham told me I have today. I would've known it was Denver, had I been able to navigate the office's stupid appointment system. But at this point, it feels like his method of booking is partially done via Post-it notes scattered across his desk, and partially kept nowhere but in Brickham's head. Which is an organizational method I can appreciate, except when *my* appointments are in *his* head instead of mine.

"I don't do house calls."

He tilts his head, giving puppy dog eyes. "Not even for an old friend?"

Old friend? That's what we boil down to?

"Call Brickham and get him to come out here."

"But I need *you* to sign off that my collarbone is fine so I can ride this weekend."

"The collarbone you broke a little over three weeks ago and haven't been letting heal properly? Not a chance." I shake my head and move to brush past him. Though I'm not sure where I'll go, considering I have an infant in my arms. Can't exactly hop in the car and flee.

Unsurprisingly, he follows me out the front door and leans against the porch rail when I sit back down in the rocking chair.

"Please, Blair. It's totally healed up, I swear. No pain." He makes a crossing-his-heart motion, and I can't help but notice it's done using the uninjured side of his body.

"You know I don't have X-ray vision, right? I'm not signing anything based only on your word. I know how cowboys are—you could be dying and you'd lie straight to my face, telling me you're fine so I'd let you ride."

"Come on. Brickham would do it."

"Go see him, then. The most I can offer you is a requisition form to get an X-ray in Sheridan. Then we can talk about it."

"The powers that be want your signature since you were the one at the rodeo."

I squint at him, rocking the chair more aggressively to keep Hazel calm. Would love for Cass or Red to come collect their child now, so I could get out of here. "Then it sounds like you won't be able to show off on a bronc for any women this weekend. Though I bet if you wore your sling around the rodeo grounds they'd feel real sorry for you. Might work out better in your favor than being flung off again."

"Would you feel sorry for me?" The dimple in his right cheek hollows until it's so deep I worry I'll be pulled into his charm like a black hole.

I sharpen my gaze, ensuring my lips don't transform into a smile. Regardless of how warm I feel right now, I refuse to fall victim to his shameless flirting. "Yeah, I typically feel a lot of sympathy for grown men who can't be bothered to take proper care of themselves. Nothing hotter."

The indent in his cheek flattens out as he becomes serious. "Okay. You win. Give me the form, and I'll go get X-rays."

"I'll send them to the clinic when I get to my computer."

"Great. Thanks."

I press my lips together with a small nod. Manifesting my best friend walking around the corner to grab her baby, so I can leave this ranch in my rearview mirror for a little while. Because the more time I spend with Denver, the more likely it is one of us will say something about what happened nearly fourteen years ago. The more likely it is he'll make me laugh and I'll be right back to who I was at eighteen. The more likely it is I'll regret ever leaving this place.

He turns to head back down the porch steps—all six-foot-whatever of him with tanned, muscular arms, dusty Levi's, and shaggy brown hair. With him unable to see my face, I let my eyes drift up and down his body. Slowing in a few places that make the hair on the back of my neck stand.

"Oh, and Blair?" He spins, undoubtedly catching me ogling. "Thanks for the house call today. Super helpful. Aus will be happy I can get right back to work."

My tongue tucks into my cheek. "You got me. Consider this your one free house call."

"So next time I have to pay? Got it." He winks. "Do you accept payment in the form of dinner? Or maybe ice cream—Neapolitan with walnuts still your dream combo?"

I'm already paying for this conversation with the knowledge that I'll be up all night replaying it, self-aware about how pathetic I am.

"I'll forever stand by the belief that somebody needs to make that."

He snorts. "Good to see all those years in the city didn't make you less weird."

Shoving his hands into his jean pockets, he mulls over a thought as the dimple in his right cheek bobs in and out. I stare at the boy I never stood a chance at moving on from. You would think a decade away, thousands of dollars' worth of therapy, and the knowledge that he's moved on with plenty of other girls would keep my heart in check.

Time is a fickle bitch; days are long, years are short, and it seems to stand still altogether when Denver and I are involved.

Denver

This X-ray better be enough to get Blair's approval to ride, since I dug myself a hole by saying I specifically needed her signature. I didn't. Any doctor's signature would've worked and, truthfully, I've seen Dr. Brickham's signature so many times, I'm confident I could forge it. But Blair's inhabited every waking thought since I found out she was back in town. I knew she wouldn't be able to turn me away if I was a patient, so I stupidly booked an appointment with her. Recklessly desperate for the opportunity to talk to her again.

Of course, she couldn't make it easy, insisting I get an X-ray to prove my collarbone healed before I can ride again. Turns out, Blair Hart still has the ability to make me do anything she asks, which is why I drove an hour and a half to Sheridan and sat in the dingy waiting room for an hour on a random Wednesday. Not even Austin's questioning stare-down from across the kitchen table this morning was enough to keep me from coming here.

I step out into the unseasonably warm May afternoon, adjusting the brim of my ball cap to block the sun, and pulling my phone from my pocket. A lively laugh carries across the strip mall parking lot, and my ears instinctively perk at the familiar sound.

It can't be. . . .

Christ, I need to get laid or something to get Blair out of

my brain. I haven't slept with anybody since she turned up here. Whenever I think about it, my stomach knots up. So I haven't . . . despite Peyton blowing up my phone to the point where I'm debating changing my number. I couldn't have been clearer with her from the start that our situation was casual—I don't do relationships. But I guess my words bounced in one ear and right out the other, because even after I officially ended it, she didn't back down. Ignoring her calls, leaving messages unread, and turning down advances at the bar hasn't been enough of a hint, either.

But maybe I can get drunk enough for a one-night stand.

Whatever it'll take to stop me from thinking about my high school girlfriend anytime I hear a woman's laugh or see a flash of brown hair. So hung up on her presence in town, I'm booking doctor's appointments for the first time in my adult life solely so I can see her, and I'm hearing her voice everywhere I go. It's pathetic.

She's engaged to somebody else. My soul can't take another crushing blow from her. And yet my nights are filled with sweet dreams for the first time in ages, and there's no stopping myself from adding "what ifs" to my days.

What if she became single again? What if there was a life someday in the future where we worked out? What if, in the meantime, I settled for being her friend?

Stepping out from under the shaded canopy outside the clinic, I hear that haunting laughter again. This time, I allow myself a hopeful glance, squinting to make out the people standing on the opposite end of the parking lot. Losing any control over my body, as if being pulled by the invisible string that's always tethered me to her, I weave between vehicles.

"Morning, ladies."

Blair spins on her heel at the sound of my voice, a crease forming between her brows. While she's not giving me the warmest reception, her mom, Faye, immediately envelops me in a hug. Arms wrapped tight around my waist, her small frame presses into me and I smile over at Blair, who rolls her eyes. I have a way with moms—they fucking love me.

"My boy," Faye says excitedly, letting go of her grip to stand back and beam at me. "Oh, I was just telling Blair to invite you over for dinner."

"Oh yeah?" I look over Faye's shoulder at Blair, who's animatedly mouthing the word *no*. She makes it *too easy* to rile her up. "Sounds great—I'll bring the wine. I seem to remember you drink white. At least, that's what Blair used to steal from your liquor cabinet back in the day."

Blair scoffs, but Faye blows her off with a grin, smacking me across the arm. "Oh, you cheeky little monkey. Yes, bring plenty of wine. Maybe plan to stay the night."

"Ya know, that's a good idea." I tilt my head, stealing a glance toward Blair, trying to gauge whether she's remembering all the nights I snuck into her bed as vividly as I am.

While I probably wouldn't turn down a chance to sleep with her after all these years—even platonically—I don't think the man who put a huge rock on her left hand would appreciate it. On impulse, my eyes travel the length of her arm to find her hand stuffed deep in her jacket pocket. I need the sight of her ring to remind me she's not mine anymore and calm my rapid pulse.

"Okay, Mom," Blair interrupts, placing her right hand on Faye's shoulder. *Shit. Of course it's her right hand.* "Can I have a minute alone with Denver?"

Faye gives my fingers a squeeze goodbye before opening the car's passenger door and slipping in. And Blair's mouth flies open at the same time the door slams shut. "Ignore all that. She just got confused, so you're off the hook for dinner."

"Maybe I don't want to be off the hook. Your mom makes great lasagna."

"Regardless, she'll probably forget she invited you before the date even comes." She blinks rapidly a few times; she's fighting to keep her emotions in check. "Seriously, don't worry about it."

While I don't normally hang around with the gossiping crowd in town—I'm too busy to loiter at Anette's Bakery during the day, and I don't stick around long enough to make small talk with most women I sleep with—I've heard about Faye's diagnosis. I know that's why Blair's back in town.

Blair's arms cross against her chest, moving too fast for me to catch if there's a ring on her finger. Or maybe it's that I get caught up in the way the movement pulls her black ribbed tank tight across her boobs and pushes them together slightly. They may not be massive but, *fuck*, there's no way of stopping myself from taking a torturous glance. Whether she has a fiancé or not, I'm not sure I care. Anyway, I had her first—which should count for something, if you ask me.

I finally remember how to form words. "I'm sorry . . . about your mom."

"It's fine." She gives a thin-lipped smile. "Anyway, we gotta head home."

"Oh, I came over here to tell you I just had my X-rays done. This collarbone is feeling better than ever. Honestly, I think it healed stronger than it was before." I lean against the trunk of her car and take in her irritated posture. Arms crossed, a scowl painted in the grooves between her eyebrows, and a sporadic twitching in her left eyelid. "Think you can sign that paper for me now?"

"That's not how this works, and you know that." She shakes her head at me. "I need to *see* the results before I consider doing anything."

"Great, when should I come by your office?"

"Call the office and make an appointment. I think there's some availability next week."

"Perfect. Then we can make a plan for family dinner, too. I've missed your mom's lasagna."

"You can keep missing it. Get Red to cook for you." She turns, rich brown hair swishing over her shoulders—*God,* I hate to see her go, but I *love* watching her leave. Blair's leggings ride up her ass a bit, leaving me on the verge of panting like a fucking dog as she walks to her car door.

"Bye, Blair. See you soon!" I shout as she disappears from sight.

My gelding, Vegas, stamps through the muddy creek bed and grunts his way up the embankment alongside a couple thousand head of cattle. The scents of fresh pine and newly thawed earth flood my nostrils as we climb away from the creek. The mountain's bursting with early wildflowers and all the grass our herd could hope for. Spring couldn't have come soon enough, after a winter of dealing with a hay shortage. Even from at least a hundred feet away, I can feel Austin take his first relieved exhale in months. This ranch may technically be in all three of our names, but as the oldest brother and the one responsible for tracking finances, he's always bearing the brunt of hard times. And it shows in his gruff tone and sullen attitude—made slightly better now that he has his fiancée, Cecily.

I feel guilty sometimes, like maybe I need to take more weight off his shoulders. Occasionally, I hate that I've given up just as much of my life for this place as he has, and he's the only one allowed to be pissy about the hand he was dealt. Since Blair's been back in town, I've been feeling the latter more often than not.

When Blair and I were teenagers, she helped with a few cattle drives. And *fucking hell,* I can still picture her riding across this clearing with her cowboy hat pulled low over her eyes, long hair flying behind her. Fully in her element, Blair's smile shone brighter than the sun, and was more beautiful than the hillside blanketed in blue and white flowers. I try to imagine what she might do for fun now, with her city-slicker clothes, fancy nurse practitioner job, and city-boy fiancé. If there's anything in her life that makes her face light up the same way.

Clearly I'm in a daze, because I don't notice Red riding up beside me until he taps me on the arm. "Made it through another winter."

"We always do." I run a hand along the brim of my Stetson, adjusting it so I can look at him without squinting in the harsh midday sun. "Bet you're ready to get back to your family."

"Definitely." He spits chewing tobacco on the ground between us. "You know . . . this used to be my favorite part of this job—getting away from everything for a few days, drinking whiskey and playing cards with you guys at night. But, *fuck*, now I can't stop wondering what Cass and Little Spud are doing."

"Makes sense."

What doesn't make sense is why I keep wondering what Blair's doing. As if it's any of my business.

"Blair's staying with Cass to help with the baby while we're out here," he says like he can read my mind. "Bet they're doing nothing but binge-watching those ridiculous dating shows on Netflix and eating junk food."

I don't want to assume she's avoiding me, but she sure likes to be at the ranch anytime I'm not around. With the exception of the day I finished work early and caught her off guard—the day I nearly threw caution to the wind and kissed her on the stairs of my childhood home, just to see if it still feels the same as it used to.

Then a sentence slips free from between my lips, because my brain's too busy spiraling to think before I talk. "You'd think her fiancé wouldn't be too thrilled about her hanging around a cattle ranch with a bunch of cowboys all the time."

"Her fiancé?" Red snorts. "Unless something's changed over the two days we've been away, Blair's not engaged to anybody."

"But . . . she was wearing a ring at the Horseshoe. I could've sworn—a massive rock on her left hand. Impossible to miss."

"How much did you have to drink? Maybe you were seeing things."

"Yeah . . . maybe."

It could have been a hallucination. This isn't the first time I've questioned whether I've conjured things up when it comes to her. For years after she left, I'd have moments where I questioned if Blair Hart was only ever a figment of my imagination. If my brain had dreamt up this perfect girl—one who would ruin me for every other woman—as a nasty trick.

But now that I know she's real and fiancé-less?

I'm not sure if what we had as kids means anything to her anymore, but there's no way I can pass up the opportunity to attempt to make things right. If there's one thing I learned from losing so many of the people I loved in one fell swoop, it's to not take things for granted. For months after my life fell apart, time seemed to stand still. And then it dawned on me that I was the one not moving. I was ignoring the people who meant the most to me, I wasn't fighting to get Blair back, I wasn't even living.

Standing on the edge of a literal cliff, I tossed my portion of Mom's ashes into the wind and made a pact with myself. Tell the people I love that I love them. If someone asks for help, be there. And if the love of my life ever decides to give me a second chance, make sure she doesn't regret it.

It doesn't seem likely that Blair has any interest in giving me another shot. But even if she still hates me, I can't sit here wondering anymore. Not after years of dialing her number, then canceling the call before the first ring. Not after years of briefly stopping at the end of her parents' driveway, questioning whether it's worth asking them to pass along a message.

Red snaps a finger in front of my face and stares at me with furrowed brows. "You good?"

"Yeah, yeah. Just thinking about the rodeo in a couple weeks," I lie. "You coming? I miss having you behind the chutes, man."

If he doesn't buy my lie, he does a good job of not giving enough of a shit to call me out. "I have to talk to Cassidy first, but maybe. I'm sure she'll want to get out of the house, too."

"You and Cass being together—having a kid together—still feels crazy to me. Can't believe you went and grew up."

"Best thing that could've happened to me, man. This time last year, I would've never expected it." He rubs his palm across the stubble on his jaw. "Don't get me wrong, it was fun hitting up rodeos every weekend, drinking, being a stupid kid. But if I had known there was a chance I could end up with Cassidy, I would've given that all up a long time ago. Would've gotten my shit together sooner."

"Well, better late than never, right?"

He looks pointedly at me, then gives his mare a little kick, trotting to rejoin the rest of the guys back on the north side of the creek. I take another minute alone to watch the cattle slowly disperse before turning and following after the other cowboys.

Catching back up to Red, I say, "For the record, I have my shit together. I'm just not interested in anything long term. No kids and wife in the cards for this guy."

"I said the same thing at one point." He reaches into his saddlebag and pulls out a bottle of water. A far cry from previous cattle drives, when we guzzled beer the entire ride back to the ranch. "Now I have the girl I always wanted, and the world's cutest baby."

"And the dad bod to match." I slap him on the stomach

with a laugh and give Vegas a little kick, escaping right before Red's hand can hit me upside the head.

At eight p.m. I'm settled on top of my bed with a beer, holding my phone to my ear for my routine chat with Dad. Jackson doesn't necessarily have an issue with our father, but he also doesn't put in the effort to talk to him regularly. Austin hasn't spoken with him since he left, and the two of them are too alike to work it out.

He comes for dinner on the anniversary of Mom's death, and her birthday. But somewhere through the years—when Dad realized how much he was missing by not being here—he started calling me in the space between those dinners.

His gruff voice comes through the phone, "Hey, kid."

After a deep breath, I dive right into it. Word-vomiting all over the place. "Blair's back home to take care of her mom—remember I told you before that she's sick. Anyway, maybe it's a real bad choice . . . but *damn*, I want to get her back. I have no clue if she's still mad about everything, or if she'd even be interested in me anymore. . . ."

"Blair's back," he muses.

"Yeah, she is."

"Is it going to make anything worse if you try to fix things?"

I take a swig of my beer, unsure how anything could be worse than not speaking for over a decade. "Guess not."

"There's your answer. Now that'll be a hundred bucks for your therapy session."

"Yeah, put it on my tab." I roll my eyes—not that he can see. Probably a good thing, too, or I'd get smacked upside the head. "Speaking of which, Odessa's got this swear jar set up and some of us might as well toss our entire pay in there the moment we get it."

Dad laughs wistfully.

I know he misses it here. Misses us. Things were hard after

Mom died, and he needed to get away from the memories. Aus refuses to forgive him for it, but I'm too much like my dad in some ways to stay mad. I can't blame him for running away, because I did the same thing. Sure, after losing Blair I didn't physically leave Wells Canyon, but I still ran. To liquor, parties, misbehavior, women . . . I ran to anything I thought could help with the pain, just as he did.

For twenty minutes, I fill him in on the ranch, the lack of rain, and what his family's up to. He blows me off every time I hint at him coming home. And when we hang up, I lie back on the pillow and fall asleep dreaming up all the ways I might be able to get my Blair back.

Denver
(fourteen years old)

I stepped off the school bus behind Blair and started up the long, sloping driveway. With a running start, I expertly jumped clear over the cattle guard and turned to smile at her.

"One day you're going to screw that up and break your leg," she said, carefully stepping on each metal bar laid across the driveway. "And your mom is gonna be *mad*."

Sure, Mom had given me crap about jumping over cattle guards a few times. But I never missed. *Worrywarts*.

"Anyway"—Blair grabbed my forearm, holding me back so Jackson could get ahead—"look what I stole from my mom's craft kit."

With a shoulder shrug and shimmy, her backpack fell to the ground, and she crouched in the middle of the gravel driveway to dig through it.

"Ugh, where is it?" She huffed, tipping her backpack upside down and letting the contents spill across the rocks. A giant bag of gummy worms, a rubber duck, at least thirty pencils, and an apple so bruised it was almost unrecognizable were only a few of the random objects that caught my eye.

"Blair, what the heck are you doing?" I laughed and grabbed a stuffed bear keychain holding a heart with her name on it. "*Cute*. A little Blair bear."

"Look, I *never* find souvenirs with my name on them so how was I supposed to turn this little guy down when I saw him?" She snatched the bear from me. "Anyway, that's not what we're here for."

She continued rummaging through the pile of items for a moment, and I watched with a stupid grin on my face.

"Ta-da!" she exclaimed, holding up a bag of googly eyes. "Let's stick these on the most random things we can think of in your house."

The way her eyes were lit up, there's no way I could say I thought her prank was silly. Nothing like the ideas I came up with, which usually involved potentially dangerous situations and pissing at least one of my brothers off.

"You're going to give Grandpa a heart attack if he opens a cupboard at four a.m. and there's a bunch of googly eyes staring back at him."

She giggled, starting to cram everything else back into her backpack. "This isn't any worse than the time you snuck a whoopie cushion onto his chair at the dinner table."

"Good point," I said, kneeling beside her to clean up the mess—namely the concerning number of colorful rubber bands strewn everywhere. "Why do you have a thousand hair ties in here?"

"Because I have to put my hair into a ponytail anytime I need to focus. But I constantly lose them, so I keep a bunch in my backpack."

I dumped a handful of hair ties into her bag. "Huh. I've only ever seen you with your hair up at school. It's down when you barrel race."

"Because I don't really focus then. I don't know . . . it's different for some reason. Like . . . I just *do it.*" She shrugged, zipping the backpack shut and tossing it over one shoulder as she stood.

"I think that's called being a natural, Blair Bear."

"Oh, shut it." She tucked a strand of hair behind her ear, kicking rocks at me—clearly thinking I was teasing. "Come on, it's time for our great *eye*-scapade."

"Great, *I* can't wait," I said, drawing out the *I* while winking at her.

We walked the rest of the way to the house plotting our attack. Dad, Grandpa, and Austin would be out on the ranch working. Jackson was probably holed up in his bedroom already. But Mom could be anywhere, and she was always catching us in the middle of pranks, which meant being sent to muck out stalls.

As luck would have it, she was in the garden when we strolled up the porch steps. And the moment the screen door slammed shut behind us, Blair was kicking her sandals off and sprinting toward the kitchen. I followed down the hall, tossing my backpack on the counter and watching her crafty mind work. An impish smile tugging at the corners of her lips as she pulled her hair into a high pony.

"I'm eyeballing everything in the fridge," she announced, unzipping the bag of stick-on googly eyes.

"Okay, um . . ." I racked my brain for ideas.

She interrupted my thoughts by slapping a handful of eyes into my open palm. "Don't think. Just do."

We stuck googly eyes to just about every possible item in the kitchen before carrying out our mission through the rest of the house, until the bag of two hundred was empty, and we fell to my bedroom floor. The wood was warm underneath us, thanks to the afternoon sun streaming in through the open window, and Blair tapped her bare foot on the hardwood to the sounds of Dolly Parton coming from the garden.

"Denver! Blair!" My dad's voice boomed up the stairwell.

Blair looked at me with a grimace, mouthing *oh, crap.*

"Do we run?" I asked quietly.

"Nah, we take it like men." She pretended to wipe sweat from her brow as she sat up, her shoulder brushing mine. Then with a salute, she said, "If we die, it was nice knowing ya."

I snorted and reluctantly got to my feet, pulling her up with me. The two of us marched down the stairs, preparing for the wrath of my dad. Bennett Wells was the polar opposite of my mom—gruff and quiet, as opposed to her outgoing personality. But he also loved Blair like a daughter, and that regularly saved my ass from a whupping. Even when he was mad because I'd failed a test or forgotten to do one of my chores, she'd jump in and defuse the situation.

"What the hell is this?" Dad stood next to the open fridge, pointing to a jar of pickles with googly eyes. Both the eyes and the contents of the jar were wiggling slightly—likely from the force of his opening the door—and I clamped my mouth shut, doing my best to hide my reaction.

Blair, however, couldn't stop a giggle from escaping, even as she held a closed fist to her lips. It *was* funny. Every jar staring back at us. Even the milk jug had eyes . . . and a smile Blair must've drawn with a marker when I wasn't looking.

"I got a bunch of googly eyes from my mom," Blair said through her laughter.

"We thought it would be funny." I bit my bottom lip to stop from laughing. It wasn't only the prank that was funny—it was my dad's scowl as he presented a head of lettuce with lopsided eyes stuck to it, and maybe even more, it was the gasping bursts of laughter coming from behind Blair's hand.

"What's not funny is the way I almost crapped my pants when I opened the fridge."

Another muffled laugh from Blair.

"We'll take the eyes off the stuff in the fridge." She pulled herself together enough to smile sweetly at him.

His dark eyes flitted between us before he gave a single nod. Grabbing his can of Pepsi from the counter, Dad brushed past us and out the back door.

"You like how I specified the fridge?" she whispered. "We better peel those off and get out of here before he sees what I did in the bathroom."

· · ·

Since school let out for summer vacation the week prior, Blair had been running barrels for hours every morning. She caught a ride to the ranch with one of our day workers, which meant arriving at five o'clock in the morning. And she practiced from daybreak until the mid-morning sun was too hot.

Rays beat down on the open arena, and I wiped a bead of sweat from my forehead as I watched her. On the back of her chestnut gelding—a gift from my parents at the end of the previous year's rodeo season—Blair held tight around the last barrel, hair whipping out from under her cowboy hat as she gave a kick. Her own sounds of encouragement for her horse were drowned out by my mom clapping and shouting, "Bring him on home, girl!"

Mom treated every practice like it was the finals at the Calgary Stampede, hollering and clapping her hands together, screaming as if Blair was running for fifty grand. She didn't even bother timing most runs because she insisted the time didn't matter as much as the ride itself. I leaned against the fence next to her, jokingly using my hands as earmuffs, and watched Blair storm toward us with a Cheshire cat grin.

Slowing the horse, Blair yelled, "That run felt really good!"

"Damn, that was about as close to a perfect ride as you can get." Mom beamed. "Let's quit while we're ahead for today. You run like that on Saturday and you'll blow all those other girls out of the water. Incredible, kiddo."

"*Holy*, wish I got half as much praise when I have a good ride." I shook my head, eyes flitting between the girls. "How does it feel to be the favorite child?"

"Oh, shush." Mom slung an arm around my neck, pulling me into a tight hug. She planted a kiss on my head, and I replied with a hearty, embarrassed groan, doing my best to slip out of her grasp. But her fingers only dug deeper into my shoulder with a bruising grip. "You know I don't pick favorites, my sweet baby boy."

"Okay, okay, okay. Forget I said anything." I laughed, managing to pry her hands off me.

Blair sat on her horse a few feet away, watching the interaction with a raised eyebrow and a smile that I knew meant she'd be giving me hell for this later. Mom reached for me again, and I playfully shooed her hand away.

"Enough embarrassment out of you today, thanks, Mom."

"Okay, kids. I'm gonna head inside and make some lunch. Love you."

"Love you," I replied before turning to Blair. "Wanna go down to the river?"

She hopped from the saddle and took her hat off, shaking out her hair. Her fingers combed through the dark brown locks and she nodded eagerly. "Yes, please. I'm *sweating*. It's so hot out here. I need to go for a swim."

Grabbing her horse's reins, I turned toward the barn. "I bet Chief's sweating hard, too. You wanna turn on the spigot, and I'll untack him so we can hose him down?"

"My hero," she said with a melodious voice, hands clasped against her chest. "I'm too hot and tired to lug that saddle anywhere."

Rounding the corner of the barn, I said, "You're a weirdo. Go get the hose."

She stuck her tongue out at me before dramatically dragging her feet across the dusty earth toward the water spigot. I watched her, tongue in cheek, while slowly removing the bridle. *Such* a weirdo.

A few minutes later, I walked back out of the tack room into the blazing heat and found Blair spraying cold water over Chief's shoulder. My T-shirt clung to the sweat on my back, and I plucked the hat from my head to fan myself.

"Hit me with that, would ya?" I gestured toward the hose in her hand.

Without a second thought, Blair lifted the nozzle above Chief's withers, shooting me directly in the face with a jet stream of cold water. A chill ran through my veins as I instinctively turned away, feeling the spray move from between my eyes to the nape of my neck. Water cascaded down my back, rinsing away the sweat and soaking my jeans.

"Ayyyy, okay, okay, okay. That's enough."

I held a hand up for protection and turned to look at Blair. A mischievous, crooked grin swept across her face, and I narrowed my eyes. Then I launched toward her, ducking under Chief's neck and frantically grabbing for the hose. Blair bolted, shooting water in my general direction as she ran down the length of the barn.

"You're dead, Hart," I shouted.

Her giggles filled the air and, nearly tripping over my own boots, my fingers made contact with the hose. I ripped it from her hands with a laugh, instantly turning to spray her. A jet from her shoulder down to her knees, dousing her body like I was putting out a fire.

"Denny, stop!"

Backing away, Blair's foot hit a divot in the ground, and before she had an opportunity to save herself, she fell backward onto the damp soil. Immediately filled with regret, I dropped the nozzle and rushed toward where she was lying.

"You okay?" I asked tentatively.

She nodded as she sat up, but her face told a different story—scrunched nose, eyes squeezed tight, and lips pursed like she was holding back a scream.

Shit, she's hurt.

My gaze traveled her body, assessing her for injuries. Hands and wrists seemed okay, no blood or obvious breaks. Same for her feet and ankles. Reaching her chest, spit filled my mouth and I swallowed hard to get it down. My heart thundered like galloping horses, and my brain screamed at me to look away, but it felt as though my eyes were fixed in place. I homed in on Blair's chest in a soaking wet white

T-shirt. Light purple bra with a floral pattern on full display through the translucent fabric.

I hadn't thought . . . That wasn't the plan. I didn't. I would never.

Blair Hart?

The girl was more like my sister—I'd even made a comment about her being the favorite child to my mom no more than fifteen minutes earlier.

So why was a shiver creeping along my spine despite the sweltering heat?

Her arms came up to cover her chest, breaking my stare. "Yeah, I think I'm okay. Are you?"

I winced at her catching me gawking. "Good. Yeah, I've never been better."

Not like that. That did nothing but make me sound like *more* of a pervert—like I'd never been better because I'd never seen Blair's boobs before.

"I mean . . . yeah, let's go put Chief away." I gulped.

"Could you? I think I need to sit for a minute . . . my ankle." Her eyes were watery when they met mine, and she slowly interlaced her fingers around her left ankle to cradle it.

"Yeah, of course. Do you . . . uh, d-do you want me to carry you somewhere?"

She shook her head no. "I watched you struggle to pack a square bale across the barn last week. I think I'd rather be left here to rot than trust you wouldn't injure me more."

Normally, I'd make a snarky comment back, but my thoughts had turned to soup—brain matter was likely about to start oozing from my ears. Plus, it was taking every ounce of willpower I had not to steal another glance at her chest.

Gingerly rolling her ankle under her palms, she squinted up at me. "You gonna put Chief away or not?"

I nodded like an idiot, springing to my feet and leading the gelding to his paddock. Taking deep breaths of hay-scented summer air, I tried to scrub the thought of Blair in her see-through shirt from my brain. She was my friend. My partner-in-crime. A complete weirdo.

When I strolled back around the corner, I found her lying on the grass. Sun strewn across her, she had an arm draped over her eyes and one knee bent. Catching a sunbeam, her charm bracelet scattered a kaleidoscope of color across the ground. Blair Hart was the prettiest thing I'd ever seen. And, even though she had no interest in me, I could *never* comfortably say I thought of her like a sibling again.

Blair
(fourteen years old)

D enver and I peered out the thick, musty curtain of our motel room, struggling to see beyond a swarm of moths hovering around our yellow porch light. The rural motel parking lot was filled with trucks and stock trailers, and not a soul was loitering outside.

"Your turn," Denny whispered, careful not to wake his mom sleeping on the other side of the room.

After a long Saturday at the rodeo, we penned the horses, grabbed pizza, and settled into our outdated motel room for the night. It wasn't long before Lucy fell asleep, and now, at a little past nine o'clock, Denny and I were getting antsy. Unable to sit through another episode of *The Simpsons* airing on the small, grainy television, we decided it was an appropriate time for one of our favorite motel games: Nicky Nicky Nine Doors.

The game was simple. Immature. Stupid. But we loved it. Something about knocking on a door and running away—the thrill of potentially being caught by an irate adult—filled us with immense joy.

"Nuh-uh," I protested. "I did it last weekend. Remember that big guy wearing only tighty-whities answered the door and yelled at me? Your turn."

His lips pressed together, and he let the curtain fall to cover the window, leaving the television as our only light source. "Okay, I'm gonna try to get room twelve."

The door he was aiming for was at the very end of the row of rooms. If he didn't want to get caught, he'd have to sprint—a serious feat in clunky cowboy boots.

Stepping into his boots, Denny shook out his jitters and released the door's safety chain. With a shiver-inducing squeal, the motel door popped open, and I held tight to the knob, watching Denny creep down the concrete sidewalk in a fitted gray T-shirt and plaid pajama pants.

He shot a devilish grin over his shoulder at me and held a closed fist in the air.

One, two, three loud raps reverberated through the door.

And then he ran. Barreling toward me, his boots hit the ground with a thunderous sound. Just as he started to slow, expecting to leap through the open doorway to the safety of our motel room, I shut it and flipped the deadbolt.

"Oh, you're going to pay for that." Denny's voice was clear, but was quickly followed up by a muffled sentence in a deeper tone.

"Oh no, no, no. They got me, too," Denny replied to the stranger. I gently pulled the curtain aside to get a glimpse of Denny's back and the front of a tall, irritated man in his fifties. "I opened the door to see who was knocking and accidentally locked myself out. That's all."

After another few seconds of chat—the man clearly not believing any of Denny's weak attempts at a believable lie—the irritated room-twelve resident turned to walk away, and I let the curtain fall.

"Blair, I'm going to kill you if you don't open up."

I pressed my cheek against the door. "What do I get if I open it?"

"The satisfaction of knowing your best friend didn't wind up murdered outside a sketchy motel."

Something about the way he said *best friend* made my chest ache. I knew we were friends. I also knew I considered him my best friend. So there was no logical reason why hearing him say it made me want to curl up and cry. Except I was hopelessly in love with him, and he'd made it clear time and time again that I was only ever going to be a friend to him.

Flipping the lock, I turned back toward the beds with a heaving breath. Before he'd even had the chance to kick his boots off, I was in my bed, eyes shut tight to keep the tears at bay. Covers tight around my chin. Ears perked, waiting for him to settle onto his cot for the night so I could feel all my silly teenage emotions alone.

Blair

With Mom napping, the dishwasher running, and a sinking feeling I've forgotten to do something this morning, I say "fuck it" and head outside with my yoga mat tucked under my arm. I haven't had the time or energy for exercise since moving back home two months ago, and I can feel it in the creak of my bones and the anxious nattering in my head. In Vancouver, I went to the gym daily and, while it didn't magically fix my depression like all the online health gurus promised, it definitely helped. The endorphins clear my head and calm my nervous system in a way nothing has since the last time I barrel raced at eighteen.

With a flick of my wrist, I unroll the mat across the spongy grass and settle into Virasana, deeply inhaling the mountain air. Exhaling the exhaustion. Inhaling the sweet honeysuckle aroma. Exhaling my consternation.

As my breath moves my body into a table position, I close my eyes, reveling in the momentary peace. Just as I feel a soothing wave roll over me, the loud vibrations of my cell phone on the glass patio table disrupt it. I breathe intentionally, trying to tune out the noise. But it buzzes. And buzzes. And buzzes. Until I feel like I might flip the table if I have to hear it one more time.

I snatch the phone and hold it to my ear, not bothering to check the call display. *"Yeah?"*

"Whoa, somebody's in a mood," my sister, Whit, says in her obnoxiously calm voice. You'd think she's the one in the middle of yoga practice. The voice is fake—her way of masking the fact that she's about ten seconds from a nervous breakdown. She's always been better than I am at suppressing impending explosions.

"Sorry. What's up?" I sigh and roll the mat back up, chucking it on the ground before sinking down into a wooden Adirondack chair.

"I'm at my wit's end with your nephew. He got himself suspended today for graffiti. *Graffiti*. On the principal's office door, no less."

"Was it *good* graffiti, at least? People pay big money for that."

The other end of the line falls completely silent. Whit clearly isn't finding me as funny as I find myself.

"Sorry. That's stressful. Um . . . I can take him while you work. I'll have to move some things around. . . ." My brain's going a mile a minute trying to work out how I'll take care of my troublesome ten-year-old nephew, give Cass a hand with Hazel, go to work, and check in on my mom throughout the day. "Yeah . . . I'll tell Cass I can't go out to the ranch, I guess."

"Thank you, you're a lifesaver. Do you think you could take him to grab some new sneakers, too? Sorry . . . I know it's a lot to ask. I've just been run off my feet here, and I've asked Alex a thousand times, but you know how he is."

My sister became a mom at nineteen, and a single mom at twenty. Her baby daddy, Alex, is only ever helpful when he's single and trying desperately to get back in her pants. So if he's not willing to buy his own kid shoes, he must have a new girlfriend.

"Of course, Whit." I pull the elastic from my hair, set it on the table, and comb my fingers from my temple to the nape of my neck. "Has Alex tried talking to Jonas about his behavior at all?"

"What do you think? He doesn't give enough of a shit. 'Boys will be boys' is his go-to phrase, which is entirely unhelpful."

I gag directly into the phone. "If Alex wasn't partially responsible for creating my nephew, I would despise him for that statement alone. How long is Jonas suspended for?"

Whit groans. "Two days, this time. They said if there's another incident, he's out for the rest of the school year."

A breeze drifts around me, coaxing out an army of goosebumps on my bare thigh. "He won't. He's not stupid, he's just . . ."

"A boy."

I laugh. "Sure, I guess. Not that it gives him a pass." I rub at my leg like I'm trying to get a stain out, hoping the friction smooths the spackling on my skin.

"Speaking of boys . . . how has it been seeing Denny?"

"Awkward, to say the least. He's been acting like nothing ever happened between us, so I guess he's over everything. Which is . . . nice." Certainly eases some of the guilt I've carried over the years. I loved him and I never had a doubt that he loved me, but we were eighteen. We made stupid choices, and abandoned each other. I don't know—maybe your first love is meant to hurt.

"And you're not over it?"

"I was until I came back here. It's a mindfuck going to the ranch all the time and . . . Okay, I told you he injured himself at the rodeo when I was there, right? Now I have to see him as a patient." I groan and slump farther down into the patio chair, remembering how Mom mentioned inviting him for dinner *again* this morning. "Also, Mom won't shut up about him since we ran into him last week."

"She's always had a soft spot for him. . . ."

"Bet she'd be less than impressed with him these days. Out fucking everything with blond hair and tits." I roll my eyes.

"Well, he is a boy."

I scoff. "If you start sounding like Alex with the 'boys will be boys' crap, I swear I'll disown you. Anyway, he's hardly a boy. He's thirty-two, Whit."

I bet he has a couple of gray hairs. I bet he has a bad back and gets heartburn. Nobody with gray hair and heartburn has any business fucking around at rodeos every weekend.

"So then why don't you appease Mom? Invite him over so she can see how different he is, and maybe she'll quit talking about him."

"Oh, yeah, as if he won't come in and turn on the charm for her. I'm banking on her forgetting about this soon. Anyway, I'll see you tomorrow when I pick up Jonas. I'm gonna try to"—I pull my phone away from my ear to check the time—"*never mind*, no time to finish my yoga. I have to head to the clinic."

Dr. Brickham's office—which I suppose is also mine now—is a hole in the wall at the far end of Wells Canyon's Main Street. An unassuming brick building, likely one of the first things constructed in town, nestled beside the Anglican church. The glass front door swings open, tripping a trio of tinkling bells to alert Wanda, our receptionist, of my presence. Despite the dingy walls and worn parquet flooring, Wanda maintains a relatively warm and welcoming atmosphere in the small waiting room. It always smells clean, the room's lined with neatly arranged chairs, and magazines are perfectly fanned out across the coffee table—if Brickham could be bothered to put a little money into this place, I'm confident Wanda would make it shine.

She pops up from behind the oversized oak desk with a smile that nudges her thick glasses up her nose. "Good afternoon, Blair. Mr. Davidson canceled his appointment for today."

"Of course he did." I sigh. It's not surprising. I saw his wife a few weeks ago, and she was eager to have somebody other than Brickham to help manage his diabetes. But like nearly every other farmer and cattleman around here, I knew he wouldn't show from the moment his wife booked him in.

At least that gives me a minute to breathe.

I stride across the empty waiting room to my office door and slip inside. The candle warmer I evidently left on last night gives the room a moody, amber glow, and I don't bother with the overhead lighting. Instead, my body melts into the plush desk chair, and I take the first full exhale of my day.

Then I stare down at the stack of files Wanda color-coded for me. I'm still not entirely sure if it's hazing or him making the best use of an extra person in the office, but Brickham's managed to slam me with every bit of paperwork possible. Prescriptions, supply orders, exam requisitions, doctor's notes . . . you name it, I'm the one filling it out.

Homing in on a thick binder of workers' compensation paperwork, which I accidentally put off for so long Wanda felt the need to add hot pink Post-its indicating *urgent*, I pluck at my wrist blindly, searching for a hair elastic. *Nothing.*

Fuck. I must've left it on the outside table at home.

I groan and sort through the cluttered top drawer of my desk, until I finally come across a bright green rubber band. It'll probably rip out a bunch of my hair with it, but that's a price I'm willing to pay so I can focus on work without the distraction of hair in my face.

After securing the ponytail, I wrangle a pair of earbuds from their case and pray Taylor Swift can help me through this mind-numbing task. And she does. I'm so deep into data entry and the *folklore* album, I don't notice somebody entering the office until they're scaring the ever-loving shit out of me by yanking a stack of papers from under my nose.

"Denver." I breathe out his name, trying to calm my racing heart now that I know I'm not about to be murdered. My earbuds slip into the case, and a harsh exhale blows the wispy baby hairs fallen across my eyes.

"Blair," he says with that stupid singsong voice and that equally stupid smile. "Terrible bedside manner, as usual—keeping a patient waiting for fifteen whole minutes. Thanks to you, I now know all about Wanda's Yorkiepoo . . . though I still don't really know what that is. A dog, maybe?"

He drags an empty chair across the room with an obnoxious screech and plops into it on the other side of my desk.

"Yes, Winston is a dog." I gather the paperwork I'm in the middle of completing, pushing it to the side of my desk before sifting through the remaining stack to find Denver's X-ray results. "Well, it looks like your collarbone healed fine."

"Told ya so." He smiles, leaning forward and tapping the paper between us with his finger. "Now you can sign this, and come watch me kick ass at the rodeo this weekend."

"I'll sign the form because it's been six weeks, and I don't have a legitimate medical reason not to. But I'm not going to sit there and watch you hurt yourself again."

I can't. I lost all my senses last time. I don't know how I managed to watch him risk his life weekend after weekend when we were kids, but just thinking about it makes my palms clammy. And he's not even mine to lose now.

Mouth agape, he clutches his chest like he's been stabbed. "Damn, that's how little faith you have in my riding abilities? I'll have you know I almost never get hurt."

"Good. That means I don't have to worry about you being a frequent patient here." I bite my cheek and wince as his face falls.

Quickly recovering from my verbal slap, his tongue darts out briefly, leaving his lower lip glistening as his sullen expression turns into a small smirk. "On second thought, I might start throwing myself off the horses. Make a habit of getting injured."

"Of course you would."

"You know . . . I probably need a complete physical. Full body exam." He makes like he's about to undo his belt, and I throw a hand up to stop him.

"Great, I'll schedule you an appointment with Brickham. I'm sure he'd be happy to give you the full rundown. Maybe even a prostate exam." I nod, pretending to be looking at scheduling on my computer—as if Brickham would ever keep a digital schedule.

"Hard pass."

I sign the rodeo association's health form and slide it across the wooden desktop toward him. "There you go. Have fun this weekend."

"Still think you should come. Red and Cass are going to be there."

The only good reason I have for skipping the rodeo is knowing I'm playing with fire by being around Denver. But I can't say that. Knowing him, the admission would make him try harder to get me to engage in flirtatious banter. And for what? So he can have another fuckboy conquest?

"No, thanks. I should really stay home with Mom."

"Speaking of which . . . when are you going to quit denying me my lasagna?"

I roll my neck with an irritated exhale. "Forever, Denver. My mom's confused, and even though she won't shut up about you right now, it doesn't mean we need to do dinner. She'll forget about it—and you—eventually."

He leans forward, scooching his chair until he's practically on top of my desk. "Sounds like I need to come visit her while she still remembers who I am. And if she can't make her famous lasagna anymore, it's no big deal. I'll bring pizza. Friday night at seven?"

"No. I don't want you coming over to hang out at my house."

"Well, I'm not coming there for you, Hart. I want to hang

out with your mom in *her* house. I'd love to have you join us, but if it makes you too uncomfortable . . ."

My leg begins to bounce uncontrollably—my stiletto heel tapping against the floor is the only sound in the room for a moment.

"I know what you're doing," I finally say.

He raises a questioning brow. "Oh yeah?"

"You're acting like a sweet, charming guy so you can get another notch in your bedpost. You're a fuckboy who's trying to win me over by being kind to my sick mother. I'll save you the trouble—I'm not interested in sleeping with you."

He snorts, and those dangerous fucking dimples pull in slowly as a beaming grin spreads across his face. The corners of his eyes crinkle in the dim glow of my desk candle warmer, and he leans in close enough I catch a faint whiff of musky cologne.

Denver Wells wears cologne now?

"Blair, if I were the type to keep notches on my bedpost, we both know yours would've been the very first. That's not what I'm doing here." He folds his hands on the top of my desk. "Thanks for enlightening me about the kind of person you think I am, though. But you're wrong—I genuinely want to come visit and make your mom happy. You can be there. You can hide out in your bedroom. You can go out with your friends."

Side-eyeing him, I think about the genuine smile on Mom's face when we ran into Denver in the parking lot. She talked about him nonstop for the hour drive home, and even after a full week she's still bringing him up.

"Why are you so invested in this?"

"Because I've lost enough people to know you don't take shit like this for granted. If your sick mom wants me to come over for dinner, I'm not going to turn her down."

Fuck. I can't argue with that.

"Okay . . ." I sigh. "Okay, you can come over."

"I'll come over Friday with pizza. And Saturday you're coming to the rodeo." His dark eyes meet mine as he stands, and my stomach flip-flops. I open my mouth to protest it, but he taps his hand on the desk and turns to leave. Looking at me over his shoulder when he reaches the door. "It'll be fun. You'll see."

Jonas shifts in the car's backseat, and I steal a quick glance up at him in my rearview mirror.

"Sorry, kid. Just checking the cameras back at the house because Grandma tripped the door alarm."

He nods silently, and I continue scrolling through the camera views on my app. When I'm confident she hasn't left the house and wandered off, I toss my phone into my purse and throw open the car door.

"Okay, let's be super speedy in the shoe store, please. I have a patient coming at eleven, and we're already running behind."

His freckled nose scrunches, and he looks up at me while kicking a rock across the parking lot. "I thought you were hanging out with me all day."

"I am. But it's also a weekday, which means I have work I can't get out of. Unfortunately, drawing a penis on my boss's office door would earn me a lot more than a two-day suspension."

He smiles to himself, trying to hold back a laugh—no doubt about the word *penis*.

A rush of frigid air hits us when I open the door to the small, quiet shop. Spotting a kids' section, I gesture for Jonas to follow me, and we silently peruse the sneaker selection. I clock the employee staring at her phone behind the cash register, but otherwise it's only us and the haunting voice of Celine Dion in the room.

As I should've anticipated, a text message rattles among the metal shelving, and Jonas gives me a whale-eyed stare, as if he's prepared for us to get in trouble for making a noise.

Cassidy: quick Q: can you pick up
some diapers for me? <3

I can. Although we'll be even *more* behind, so I'll have to call the clinic and let Wanda know I'll be a few minutes late. And then I'll also have to ask Whit to check on Mom, since I don't have time to pop in before my afternoon is full of patients. *Shit*, and I don't know what I'll feed Jonas for lunch—a ten-year-old boy can't skip meals the same way I tend to do. Hopefully Wanda can help with that, too.

I glance over at Jonas and hold up a plain black pair of sneakers. "How about these ones?"

His face contorts. "Mid."

"*Okay.* So, like, is that a yes?"

"Dad said I could get some Nikes." He continues down the aisle, then holds up a gray Nike sneaker. "This one's good."

"Well, your dad isn't paying for them." I start scanning the tower of boxes to look for his size. "And if I'm spending over a hundred bucks on a pair of shoes, they're going to be for me. What size shoe are you?"

He shrugs. "Dunno. But I need these ones."

With an irritated exhale, I hold my empty palm out toward him. "Give me your shoe so I can check the size."

My phone beeps again in my back pocket while I wait for him to untie his sneaker.

Dad: Hey kiddo, I'm gonna be
late tonight, so you're in charge
of dinner.

Frozen pizza, it is.

"Jonas, can you *please* pick up the pace?" I snap my fingers at him, and finally he hands over a sweaty sneaker, which I have to bring disgustingly close to my face in order to read the worn number printed inside.

"All right. They don't have your size in these black ones. So, how about gray?" I point to the neighboring shoe on the shelf.

"How about Nikes?"

"*Jonas.*"

"*Blair.*"

I huff. "Okay. First of all, I was in the room when you were born, so you'll put some damn respect into the *auntie* title. Secondly, you don't deserve shit after getting suspended, so you should be thankful you're getting anything at all."

I toss his stinky old shoe, and it lands with a thump at his feet, but he makes no move to put it on.

"I'm not wearing them." He pops a shoulder with discontent, staring longingly at the stupid shoes that cost a ludicrous amount, given how quickly kids outgrow or ruin them.

"Well, that's a fight for your mom to have with you." My fingertip jumps between the boxes to find his size in a charcoal pair. "Please put your shoe on so we can leave. We're seriously running late."

The shoebox I need slips out of the pile like a Jenga block, and I stand back up triumphantly. He shuffles his old shoe around with his foot, but doesn't put any real effort into slipping it on.

Watching him is *excruciating.*

My blood pressure's a percussion playing behind my eardrums, and I anxiously lick my lips. "Jonas, *please.* I'm gonna leave here without you, at this rate."

"*Relax,*" he chides, finally sliding the stupid shoe over his stupid little foot. And by the time it's tied and he catches up with me, I'm almost done paying for the "mid" sneakers.

"My dad is just gonna buy the Nikes for me when I see him."

I roll my eyes discreetly, knowing damn well I'm only here buying shoes for a preteen boy because his dad is a deadbeat. And if he buys his kid some nice shoes, it'll only be because he's trying to win my sister over in their appalling on-again-off-again situationship.

"You know what, kid? I hope he does."

Denver

Five seconds of honesty?

I'm not standing on the Harts' doorstep simply because I want to make Mrs. Hart happy. Just like I didn't waste time with X-rays and doctor's appointments because I needed Blair's signature to register for the rodeo. And now that Kate and Cecily have reassured me that Blair was likely wearing a fake ring to fend off creeps at the bar, I am fully committed to having her back in my life.

Pizza boxes balanced precariously in one hand—bottle of white wine tucked into my side—I rap the knuckles of my free hand against the cream-colored door. I've been here a million times, but only through the front door a handful of them. Blair spent almost every waking hour at my family's ranch, but that still wasn't enough for us. When my mom started taking regular trips to the city for chemotherapy, I would sneak out and come here at night. Before getting my driver's license, I'd steal ranch trucks and drive illegally down backroads to get here. Park a few houses down and slip in through Blair's bedroom window. Then sneak back out before her parents woke up, getting back to the ranch in time for morning chores.

The front door opens and Blair's dad, Frank, appears with a warm smile. Stepping aside so I can walk into the foyer, he says, "Long time, no see. How's it going?"

"Never been better." I follow him to the kitchen as if I don't know the way, setting the pizza boxes on the counter and taking in my surroundings. Oak cabinets, nineties furnishings, and a large sliding glass patio door looking out at a vibrant green space. The only thing that appears to have changed in the Harts' home over the last decade is the addition of Blair's nephew among the dozens of family photos. I know I didn't spend a lot of time here growing up, but the nostalgia carries a tinge of pain.

Is this how Blair feels when she's at the ranch?

"We thought we'd eat out on the patio—it's such a nice evening, and Faye can use the fresh air." He pulls two bottles of beer from the fridge and hands one over to me. Whether it's my nerves or the slick condensation on the outside of the glass, I struggle to hold the bottle steady.

Each of us grabbing a pizza box, I follow him through the open sliding door onto the covered patio to find Faye sitting alone at the table. I know I told Blair she didn't need to have dinner with us. But a tiny, masochistic part of me was hoping she'd be here. Even if it was only to glare at me from across the table and shoot down my attempts at banter.

Maybe I made a big mistake in coming here.

"Pretty as always, Mrs. Hart." I plaster on a fake smile and relax into a chair opposite her with a sigh.

"Oh, *shush*, you." She flaps a hand in my direction, pink blush splashing across her cheeks. "How are you? Did you bring us the biggest bottle of wine you could find?"

"I don't know about *biggest*, but the cashier promised me it's a good one. It's just inside. . . ." I move to stand, but Frank beats me to the punch and lumbers his way back into the house. Faye smiles softly at me; she still looks like a stereotypical kindergarten teacher, with a bright-pink knit sweater with daisies all over it and faint lines around her eyes and mouth.

After a few seconds of staring at each other, I break the awkward silence. "So, no Blair tonight?"

"She's here. I think she's taking her time getting prettied up for you."

The last thing she would be doing is anything specifically for me. And even if Blair wanted my attention, she knows hair and makeup isn't the way. "She never needs to do anything special."

"Tell that to her. She's been in a tizzy all afternoon." She smiles to herself. "You two are just the cutest."

Before I can respond, the sliding glass door opens and—*fuck*—Blair steps out in a knee-length light-blue dress with thin white stripes on it. As she turns to softly close the door, the fabric swishes around her bare legs. Then she sits, prim and proper, in the chair next to mine, and the warm summer evening carries her spicy scent over to me. Perfume, makeup, dresses—nothing like the girl in dusty jeans I fell in love with all those years ago. Even still, I lose my breath in her presence.

Blair pulls open each box. "You brought meat lovers and supreme?"

I nod. "Your favorite."

Pride rushes through me as I prepare for Blair to be ecstatic about me remembering her favorite pizza after all these years.

"I'm a vegetarian," she deadpans.

"O-oh, well . . . um, I could go grab something else," I stammer, considering every alternate takeout option in my mind. In Wells Canyon, the options are basically pizza and cinnamon buns. "Want me to get a different pizza? Salad, maybe?"

"I'm kidding, Denver. Supreme is still my favorite. It looks delicious." She brings a steaming hot slice to her mouth and slowly nibbles, nodding politely toward her dad when he sets a half-full wineglass in front of her.

"So, Denny, how are things going at the ranch?" Frank asks, shifting side-to-side in his squeaky metal chair.

"Better now that we have the cattle out on the range for the summer. We just got done driving them out there."

Blair's watching me with keen interest as she chews.

"You should've come. We could've used your help," I say to her.

"I doubt I even remember how to ride." She shrugs nonchalantly. Blair—who used to *live* for horseback riding—suggesting that not only does she not remember how to ride, but she doesn't care? If my mother were in a grave, she'd be rolling in it.

"*Bull.* You're a natural, right? You don't just forget that sort of thing."

The corners of her lips pull into the closest thing to a smile I've gotten since the ambulance ride weeks ago. That's a win, in my book.

The four of us talk until the pizza is gone, the sun is low, and the air has a sudden crispness. Then Frank and Faye head inside, leaving Blair and me to clean the dinner mess in silence.

Stepping back outside from clearing the plates and pizza boxes, she picks up the nearly empty wine bottle. "We may as well finish this. It's a felony to waste good wine."

I slide my glass over to her and sit back down, watching her carefully divide the remaining liquid between our cups. Wine definitely isn't my drink of choice, but I'll take that over being kicked out of here the second we finished eating—which is what I expected to happen.

"Thanks for coming over. Mom definitely had a good time. She's been so reclusive. . . . It's good for her to socialize a bit." Blair swirls her glass before taking a hearty drink.

"I'm glad I came. It's been a fun night."

She looks at me over the rim of her glass. "I *know* you have better things to do on a Friday."

I laugh under my breath. "Like what? Go to the Horseshoe like I do every Friday? I think I can afford to skip a week."

Plus, you'd have to drag me in there kicking and screaming right now. My phone's been vibrating in my pocket all night—no doubt it's Peyton. I was sure to tell Colt I'd be at Blair's tonight, knowing damn well he'd relay that information to Peyton. With any luck, she might think Blair and I are *together*, and decide to finally leave me alone.

"Don't you have a rodeo to get ready for? Considering how committed you were to getting a clean bill of health, I would've guessed you'd be practicing or something tonight."

"Nah, when you're as good as I am, you don't need to practice."

Blair smiles. For a fleeting moment that makes my entire chest ache, until she catches herself and tucks it away with a roll of her lips. "I don't know . . . the only time I've seen you get on a bronc recently, you fell off."

"Has nothing to do with my riding skills. I'd have gone pro if I was shorter."

"*Right.*" She playfully rolls her eyes, that smile threatening to pop up again to spite her. "So what's the excuse for why you fell off?"

"I saw you."

Glancing away, her head nods softly. And I watch her watch the evening breeze swirl around the garden. She and I have always been comfortable in the silent moments, so this discomforting quiet makes me wonder if I should've lied to her. I could've made up something about the horse being absolutely rank, an old injury flaring up, maybe a beesting to my eyeball.

Wind chimes clink together, wind whistles through tall decorative grasses, and I don't know how long we sit in silence, but one by one various small, dim solar lights begin to light the backyard.

"So, you said your mom had a good time tonight. What

about you?" I finally get the nerve to say something, and she takes a long, thoughtful sip of wine, her free hand fiddling with the neckline of her dress.

"Yeah . . . yeah, I did."

Maybe she doesn't hate me. Maybe. Maybe there's a chance here.

"Blair, about what happened when we were—"

"Let's not talk about it." She cuts me off. "Please. Tonight has been really nice, and I don't think bringing up ancient history is really necessary."

"Okay, I just—"

"Denver, *please*. Can we talk about present-day stuff?"

I exhale long and hard into my wineglass. "Sure. Pulled any good pranks lately?"

She wraps her arms tight around herself. "It feels a lot more like the world is pranking me. Patiently waiting for Ashton Kutcher to jump out and tell me this is all a very elaborate episode of *Punk'd*."

"Sorry." *For now. For then.*

"It's fine. Plenty of people out there are going through a lot worse things, so . . ." She looks over at me with flattened lips, shrugging her shoulders and finishing off her wine.

Everything in my body aches to be her comfort, her safe space, her person. But she simply switches the subject with forced enthusiasm. "What about you? Any pranks? Piss Austin off lately?"

"You know I live to piss him off." I laugh halfheartedly. "How long are you going to be in town for?"

"I'm not helping you prank him, if that's why you're asking." Her tongue darts out to lick a drop of wine from the corner of her mouth, leaving her lower lip glistening in the dim patio lighting. "I'm here indefinitely, at this point."

"Come to the rodeo. It might not be the sort of thing you city slickers do, but if you're in town indefinitely you should have some fun, at least."

"I should head to bed," she says in a clear effort to end the conversation, reaching to collect the wine bottle and glasses from the table.

I steal a glance at her bedroom window. "Remember when I used to sneak into your room after your parents went to bed?"

She stands, cradling her empty glass against her chest. Her eyes meet mine and her voice is barely audible. "Yeah, I remember. 'Night, Denver."

I start toward the backyard gate, feet dragging because the last thing I want to do is go home. "See you tomorrow, Blair."

"Maybe."

"See you tomorrow," I say over my shoulder.

"We'll see. . . ."

I turn and walk backward, staring her down with a grin on my face. "See you tomorrow."

She rolls her eyes from the sliding patio door, corners of her lips slightly upturned, blue dress billowing around her legs. "See you tomorrow."

Blair
(fifteen years old)

Slipping the curry comb from my fingers, I turned to find Denny staring at me from the barn alley. Leaning on the stall door, he tossed a handful of something into his mouth and chewed. Even in dirty jeans and a ratty T-shirt, he looked good—definitely better than the shape I was probably in. And I frantically reached up to smooth a hand over my hair, stopping to fix the scrunchie holding up my ponytail.

"Thought your grandpa had you fixing fences?" I brushed past him, swinging a bucket of grooming supplies on my short walk to the tack room.

Denny was hot on my heels. "Finished already. Was gonna see if you wanted to go fishing?"

Fingers running along the hem of my T-shirt, I peeled the thin cotton from my damp lower back. With the weather unseasonably warm for late May, I had to stop running barrels before lunch. Which meant a full afternoon with nothing to do until Kevin, one of the ranch hands, could give me a ride home in the evening. Hanging out with Denny under the shady canopy lining the riverbank sounded perfect.

"Heck yes."

His dimpled grin filled my chest until I could float to the barn rafters, and he held a box of Nerds candy out to me. "Want some?"

I made a face. "That's what I imagine eating aquarium gravel is like."

He followed behind me, chomping as loud as possible, definitely aware that each crunch was sending shivers down my spine. "Maybe in texture, but not flavor. I don't think algae is this sugary."

"The texture is enough to turn me off, thanks."

"More for me."

We walked side by side down the gravel road toward the big house to grab Denny's fishing rod. Funnily enough—and I pointed it out to him—the rocks under our boots sounded an awful lot like the handful of Nerds jostling around inside his mouth. Without hesitation, he reached down and scooped a handful of pebbles and dirt, then shook it in his cupped hand, as if he was considering eating it.

"Denny. Gross," I warned him with a disgusted look. "That's probably full of horse poop and whatever else."

"Good for the immune system." He shrugged, lifting his hand, poised to pour the fistful of earth into his open mouth.

"Denny!" I grabbed his hand. "Stop. That's how you get worms. Don't be such a boy."

"You're one to talk, Hart." He gestured to my body and I looked down, suddenly filled with regret about my outfit. Jeans that were dustier than his, worn so thin in the knees you could catch a glimpse of skin when the lighting was right. And a Coors Light shirt I robbed from Cassidy's beer T-shirt collection after a sleepover séance went wrong. I clung to the frayed hem, keeping my lips compressed as I swallowed hard.

As we approached the big house, Grandpa Wells rose from the wicker chair on the front porch and cleared his throat. A strange sight to see in the middle of the day—he preferred to work with the cowboys rather than sit around twiddling his thumbs. "Denver, you, uh . . . best head inside. Your parents want to talk to you. Blair, hop in the truck and I'll take you home."

Confused, I shook my head and looked at Denny to see if he knew what was going on. His nose crinkled, and he squinted in the harsh midday sun. "I finished up the fences already—*swear*. Blair and I were gonna head out fishing for a bit."

"You can fish another day." His chin jutted toward the screen door. "Do as you're told and go inside."

While Grandpa Wells was the type of guy to give the shirt off his back, and he treated me and the other non-Wells kids around the ranch like his own grandchildren, we also knew better than to disobey him.

"Yes, sir," Denny said, turning to give me a goodbye half-smile. "Guess we'll go fishing tomorrow."

I nodded, spinning on my heel to climb into Grandpa Wells's rusty blue Ford.

I awoke with a start, my room cloaked in darkness save for the small, horse-shaped night light by the door. Wind whistled through the trees outside—a sound our house's old single-pane windows did little to mitigate.

The storm must've woken me up.

Yawning, I rolled to face away from the window, tugging the comforter to my chin and willing myself back to sleep.

Thunk.

Something hit the glass, and I jolted upward, clutching the bedding for comfort. Heart racing, blood rushing behind my eardrums, and a stutter to my breath. My eyes squeezed tight, pretending that not seeing the danger would be enough to keep me safe.

Another small object hit the windowpane, and I felt around the dark bedside table for my cell phone before quickly darting fully under the covers. I blinked at the painfully bright light, taking a moment for my eyes to adjust enough to see three missed calls and ten text messages, all from Denny.

All vague.

All desperate.

Blair: R u ok?

Denny: Let me in. It's raining

I stared at the message.

Let me in. What the . . .

Tiptoeing, I made my way to the window and peeked from behind the curtain. Sure enough, there was Denny, slumped down in a patio chair with the rain and wind howling around him.

"Denny," I whisper-yelled, sliding the window open with a grating squeal.

Within seconds, my best friend—also the boy I had the world's biggest crush on—was dripping wet and shivering in my bedroom in the middle of the night.

"What's going on?" I gawked at him, awkward and unsure of how to handle the situation. Whatever the situation was.

"It's . . . uh . . . ." He let out a ragged breath. "Sorry for waking you up. I-I wanted to talk to you."

"It couldn't wait until I see you tomorrow?" I asked through a loud yawn.

"No. Well, yes . . . I guess. But, no. I need to talk to you now. I couldn't sleep." Everything about him was off—unlike any version of Denver Wells I'd seen before. No self-assured confidence behind his words. No warm smile. No light. "I just . . . Blair, I don't know why I'm here."

A shiver racked his body and, without a word, I turned and opened my closet door. Then felt around in the dark for a pair of buffalo plaid pajama pants and a baggy old T-shirt.

"Here. Get out of the wet clothes," I said, thrusting the pants and shirt toward him. And when he stepped toward the door, I shuffled to block his path, my palm falling to his damp chest. "You can't go out there and get us caught. I'll go so you can change."

I gingerly stepped into the hallway and padded to the kitchen, pretending to get a glass of water for enough time I could be sure he was fully dressed. Fighting to stop myself from thinking about him half-naked in my room. I'd had a crush on him for so long, I forgot what it was like *not* to have a crush on him. But it was painfully obvious those feelings were never going to be reciprocated. He told me about girls who passed him notes in class, teased me relentlessly for being weird, and introduced me to people as his best friend—there had even been times where he referred to me as his *sister*.

I desperately needed to get over my crush. And picturing his bare chest, cold and damp from the rain, wasn't helpful. Picturing him slipping out of his wet jeans wasn't helpful. And picturing him naked in my bedroom *definitely* wasn't helpful. But there was no stopping it. My glass of water went down in slow, painful gulps as the tiny clock hand skipped forward.

He was sitting cross-legged on top of my bed when I slipped back through the door. Denver Wells was in my room. Wearing my clothes. On my bed.

Crying.

"What's going on?" The door shut behind me with a soft click, and I crawled across the floral bedspread to sit in front of him.

"It's Mom," he muttered. "She's sick."

"What?" I croaked, feeling as though my ribs were imploding.

"Cancer."

The world stopped, air falling still. I couldn't breathe or think or see. In the dark quiet of my room, I reached for his hand, looping my fingers around his. His grip held strong, clung to my touch like a life raft, squeezing around my knuckles with each slow, shaky breath. The bones in my hand pressing together hurt, but the pain was dulled by the excruciating ache in my chest.

"Is she . . ." Scared of the answer, I struggled to ask the question. "Is she going to be okay?"

"Mom and Dad say she will be."

"Okay. So then . . . it's okay. She'll be fine."

She had to be.

I didn't see how there could be any option other than her being fine. Aside from the junk food when we were on the road for rodeos, Lucy Wells was the healthiest person I'd ever met. She was young. She was amazing. Everyone loved her. People like that *need* to be okay, because the world is counting on them to stick around.

And if I was wrong, I had to pretend that things would be fine. That's what Denny needed from me. It wasn't my time to be emotional or scared.

I ran my thumb across the back of Denny's shaking hand. "Your mom is the toughest person I know. She's going to kick cancer's butt."

"Yeah."

And then it dawned on me. . . .

"Wait. How did you get here? It's like one o'clock in the morning."

"I stole Grandpa's truck," he said matter-of-factly. As if it wasn't a big deal for a fifteen-year-old to steal a truck and drive through a storm in the middle of the night.

"Denver Wells," I whisper-yelled. Regardless of the fact that he couldn't see a single detail of my face, I shot him a look. "That's seriously illegal. What if you got caught or crashed the truck?"

He shifted on the bed, releasing the death grip on my hand. "I've been driving around the ranch since I was six. I'm fine."

"Even still. It wasn't worth the risk to drive here. You could've texted or called or waited until I saw you tomorrow to talk to me."

"I couldn't." His rough exhalation was hot against my cheek, and I realized how close we were. "I tried to sleep. Forget about it. Everybody else in the house seemed to have no trouble sleeping. . . ."

"She's going to be okay."

"And if she isn't?" He sniffled, and something wet landed on my calf, quickly soaking through my thin pajama pants. "What then?"

My voice was thin. Wavering. "She will be."

"Thank you."

"For what?"

"I came here because you were the only person who I thought could make me feel better."

"Oh," I murmured. *Crap. Think of something to lighten the mood.* "Well . . . uh . . . I'm struggling to think of a joke or something under this kind of pressure."

He chuckled under his breath, the mattress dipping as he moved even closer. Prickling heat flooded my capillaries, no doubt turning my skin red, and I focused on the tenderness of his fingertips as they grazed my knees.

When his hands settled on my outer thighs, my stomach warmed and churned as if I'd just chugged a large mug of hot cocoa. I licked my lips, staring at the silhouette in front of me, wishing I could see his face well enough to gauge his emotions.

Was he going to kiss me?

No, I told myself. Having him in my bedroom in the middle of the night was messing with my head. Simple as that. He was upset over his mom's cancer diagnosis, and thinking he had anything else on his mind was disgustingly selfish.

"Bear," he whispered.

Normally, Blair Bear was a nickname he reserved for when he wanted under my skin. But this time, it felt special and filled with love. It was us.

"Sorry, I want to help cheer you up, but I don't know—"

His closed lips pressed to mine. Soft, yet firm, and salty from his tears. I held still, embarrassingly unsure of what to do. Sure, I'd fantasized about kissing him a million times, but the real thing was different. Of course it was. Denny's lips were perfect. He was perfect.

As quickly as it happened, it stopped.

When he pulled away, I was frozen in place, everything inside me aching to kiss him again. Only I didn't know how. I'd practiced kissing my hand a lot, learning the techniques descriptively outlined in *CosmoGirl* magazine. But in the moment, nothing was happening in my brain, and my entire body was hot, and—*oh god*—I screwed it up. My eyes shot open, desperate to find his face in the blackness, naively hopeful I'd get some indication about how he was feeling.

Before I had the chance, he flopped backward, head landing on the pillows with a huff. "Can I stay here tonight? I want to be with you."

With me.

We kissed.

He wants to spend the night.

With me.

Unable to form words, I simply lay down next to him, our shoulders and upper arms touching. I was painfully, zealously consumed by him. And when he rolled to his side—slinging an arm across my stomach and shuffling close enough I could feel his steady, sleepy breath throughout my hair—I stroked a finger across my bottom lip and prayed it wasn't the last time I'd get to kiss Denver Wells.

Denver
(fifteen years old)

I didn't expect to fall asleep at Blair's house. After all, I spent hours tossing and turning in my own bed before saying "fuck it" and grabbing Grandpa's truck keys from the bowl in the kitchen. I planned to just enjoy her company—even as she slept—because she had a way of making me feel better without trying, and the last thing I wanted was to be alone. But I inhaled the subtle scent of her shampoo, felt the rise and fall of her breath against my chest, and I was a goner. Arguably, the best sleep I'd ever had.

I also didn't go to her house intending to kiss her. Sure, it was something I had considered doing a number of times. I'd even been close: when she bumped into me coming out of the tack room and her hands fell against my chest, when she leaned her head on my shoulder as she helped me with math homework alone in my bedroom, or when she grabbed my hand as we ran away from Austin after pranking him with a bucket of water on top of a door.

Okay . . . Maybe subconsciously I went to her house with the intention of kissing her. Because I definitely didn't hold back the moment I had the opportunity. I dreamt about our kiss all night, then woke up with the worst problem a teenage boy sleeping next to a girl can possibly have, and got the hell out of her house before she woke up.

. . .

Blair sat on Chief, listening to Mom give critiques about her last run. It was a dreary day—fitting for the day after we learned of Mom's diagnosis—and a distant thunderstorm rumbled across the ranch. Chief's ears perked, and both women turned their heads toward the sound, which was conveniently in my direction. Blair's eyes met mine for a split second, and even from a considerable distance, there was no denying the ruby red hue on her freckled cheeks.

Mom waved before turning to walk back to the house, and Blair trotted toward me . . . then past me without a word.

Weird.

We kissed and now she was actively avoiding me, and I had no idea why. Granted, I'd only kissed one other girl before, but she didn't take off running, so I was pretty confident I wasn't a bad kisser or something.

"Hey, good job out there," I shouted as I walked around the side of the barn.

"Thanks," Blair mumbled, pulling Chief's saddle off.

"How's Mom doing?"

"Seems fine."

I reached to take the saddle from her, but she shrugged me off, moving quickly past me.

Oh my God.

It dawned on me that I didn't waste any time leaving this morning, and I might've left *evidence* behind in my panicked, embarrassed state. I pressed my back against the wall with a groan. Of course she was avoiding me. She was probably completely disgusted. Muttering curse words under my breath, I scrubbed a hand across my jaw, and turned to escape the barn before having to face her again.

As luck would have it, Blair stepped out of the tack room and crashed into me. Her chest pressed against mine, hands wrapping around my arms to stop herself from falling over.

When she released her grasp, I stumbled backward. Desperate to have as much distance between us as I could manage, despite every tendon in my body aching to be close to her again. She and I had been in close proximity a thousand times over the last two years of friendship. But suddenly it felt different.

"How are you feeling today?" she asked quietly, looking down at her feet and shuffling a few pieces of hay around on the concrete floor.

"Oh, um . . . okay. How about you?"

"Yeah, okay."

For a moment that felt a decade long, we stood on opposite sides of the barn alley. Shifting on our feet, refusing eye contact, but unable to walk away.

Blair broke the silence. "Five seconds of honesty?"

I nodded, though I was convinced this was about to be the most embarrassing moment of my life. If she was about to call me out for what happened this morning, I'd need a quick explanation. A list of lies ransacked my brain: I was eating ice cream and made a mess (stupid), the roof had a slow leak (she'll know it's a lie as soon as she gets home), I peed my pants (equally as embarrassing as the truth), *she* peed her pants (not believable whatsoever).

"I really like being your friend, and I don't know what I did last night to upset you, but—"

"Upset me?" I interrupted. "You didn't. Being with you made me feel better after the worst day I've ever had."

Her nose crinkled in the cutest way. Small freckles bunching together. A crease forming short ridges between her eyebrows. And I wanted to kiss her scrunched, confused face.

"Why did you leave before I woke up then?"

Shit.

"Um . . . Well. I had to go." I fiddled with the end of my leather belt, praying she wouldn't pry further.

"Five seconds. Please."

I stuffed my hands into the pockets of my jeans, crossing my fingers. Hopefully it wouldn't lead to a bunch of bad karma or something—I had no choice but to lie. "I had to get back here before my dad and grandpa woke up, or I'd be in a ton of trouble. And I didn't want to wake you up that early."

Okay, not a complete lie. But I definitely would've woken her up to say goodbye, if that was the only reason for my early morning escape.

"Oh, God, I'm an idiot. Of course. I thought . . . I thought you left because you realized you made a huge mistake. Let's forget about it. It never happened," she rambled, hands flailing. "I mean, you had just found out about your mom, so your emotions were probably all over the place. And, like, you definitely wouldn't kiss me otherwise."

"I wouldn't?"

She snorted like I'd made a stupid joke.

And something about that sparked a flame in my stomach. My boots scraped across the barn floor on my way to her, until we were mere inches apart, and staring at each other with heaving breaths. Her captivating brown eyes swallowed me whole, pulling me the final distance until they shuttered closed, and my mouth crashed into hers. Her lips parted with a sigh as she relaxed into me, arms draping around my neck. Exploring each other with soft strokes, her tongue was warm against mine, and she tasted like cinnamon gum. And when I pulled away, it took a few extra seconds for her eyelids to flutter open.

"Denny." Her tongue slowly swept along the ridges of her teeth. "You're my friend—my *best friend*. Sometimes you even tell strangers I'm your sister."

I grimaced. That was something I definitely wouldn't do again.

She continued, "I don't want to wreck our friendship."

Nervously reaching for her hand, my heart racing, I made a promise with myself to *never* let anything come between me and Blair. "We've argued about things before and always stayed friends. Remember the spit swear we did last year? Kissing is no different."

Well, it was a *little* different. Better, for sure.

"A kiss swear?" She looked up at me, freckled cheeks rosy and eyes smoldering.

"A kiss swear." I delicately pressed my lips to hers again. "I promise I won't let any amount of kisses ruin things, Bear."

That was an unintended five seconds of honesty, and a promise I had no intention of breaking. I wanted to kiss Blair Hart every single day for the rest of my life. And I wouldn't let *anything* get in the way.

Blair

I spin in circles on the old wooden bar stool, listening to Cassidy give her dad a list of instructions a million miles long. You'd think we were leaving the baby with him for a week, not a few hours . . . and we'll be less than five kilometers up the road. But Dave nods along, doing a great job of at least *acting* like he intends to listen to her rules. I've seen my parents with Jonas enough to know grandparents *never* follow the rules.

"We ready to go?" I ask Cass as Dave turns, diaper bag slung over his shoulder, to head for his attached apartment. Years ago, he learned to shut the bar down when Wells Canyon has a rodeo—it's not worth paying to keep the lights on when everyone in town is drinking in a makeshift space in a parking lot, built with livestock panels and a utility-shed-turned-bar.

"Just waiting for Shelb."

I check my phone for the text message to let us know she's on her way. "Hey, so . . . we've awkwardly skirted around the topic before, but I need to know. Is it going to be problematic for Shelby, Denver, and I to all be in the same place?"

Cass looks up at the shelves of liquor behind the bar with pursed lips. "Why would that be an issue?"

"Well . . . he and I dated. They hooked up at the rodeo last year . . . maybe even continuously after that?"

"Mmm. As far as I know, they didn't hook up continuously. And I thought you were okay with it?"

Of course she thinks that, because I insisted I was fine approximately two hundred times after I found out and asked her to confirm the rumor. Not her fault she couldn't tell there were tears in my eyes and my voice was squeaky through text messages.

"I am." My nails drum on the bar top. "I just . . . I guess I wanted to know what I'm walking into."

"You're walking into nothing. I wouldn't let you come if I thought there was even a chance you'd have to watch them flirt. Promise." She crosses her heart. "And anyway, I can only think of one reason why you suddenly care so much about this a year later. Are you two . . . ?" She gives me the *look*.

"We are not. Forget I asked."

"I get being mad at Shelby. I would be pissed if one of my best friends made out with my ex, too."

"It's not that. Her and I hardly even talk anymore, except when you're asking us both to hang out, so she can do whatever she wants."

It has nothing to do with Shelby, and everything to do with the way Denver kept looking at me last night.

"All I know for sure is that I saw them make out a full year ago. Shelby has since moved on with God knows how many people. And I can only assume the same is true for Denny. I've seen them in the same vicinity multiple times since then, and there was zero funny business. Not even a flirty comment or sideways glance." She grabs my hand on top of the wooden bar and looks into my eyes. "Happy with that?"

My phone buzzes, and I immediately stand to leave. "Yeah, I'm good with that."

Rum and Coke in hand, I settle onto the bench next to Cassidy and stare out at the dusty, sunbaked rodeo arena. As

Shelby leans forward to clink her plastic cup against mine, her rhinestone cowboy hat catches the evening's sunrays and cascades a scattered rainbow across our laps. "Blair, I'm *so* happy you moved back. We missed you."

"I missed you guys, too."

"The troublesome trio is back in action." Shelby grins, raising her cup to her lips.

I don't even remember exactly how Shelby ended up becoming friends with me and Cassidy. One day, shortly after she moved to town in high school, she sat down with us at lunch and the rest was history. Our duo became a trio without warning. While I'd still call her a friend, I'll admit I haven't put as much effort into staying close with Shelby like I have Cass over the years. In fact, aside from the occasional girls' night when I was in town visiting my family, and the rare trio FaceTime, we stopped talking almost entirely after I moved away almost fourteen years ago.

"Back in action for approximately . . . three hours." Cass flips her wrist to look at her watch. "Once the boobs start hurting, I'm out of here."

"I'm out of here right alongside you," I say before taking a long gulp, letting the strong drink burn its way down my throat.

"You guys suck." Shelby scrunches her nose in disappointment.

Cass shakes her head with a small laugh. "I give it an hour before you've ditched us for a guy, anyway."

"Fair point. Have you seen Wyatt lately? *Damn.* He moved back from college a whole-ass *man.*"

"He's like twenty-two. Basically a baby." Cass flashes me a look that says *can you believe this girl?* And I smack my palm against my forehead because, yes, I absolutely can believe Shelby is into a guy a full decade younger than her.

"Whatever. Man enough." Shelby takes a long swig as the rodeo announcer begins his introductions.

Considering the size of Wells Canyon, the rodeo crowds never cease to amaze me. Hosted semiregularly from April through October, you'd think people would get bored. But, with nothing else to do in town, everyone within an hour radius comes here.

I down the rest of my drink the moment women's barrel racing starts. Eyes fixated on the riders, nitpicking their movements with Lucy's voice filling my brain. I want so badly to look away before any tears fall, but I can't, and I fucking hate it. Thankful for my large, dark sunglasses, I reach up and pretend to itch the side of my nose, dabbing at the dampness with the pad of my finger.

I knew from the moment I submitted my application for nursing school in Vancouver that I'd be giving up horseback riding. And I told myself it would be fine, because I'd visit the ranch on holidays and during summer break. School was temporary. When I was done, Denver and I would buy a house with enough property for our horses. Maybe we'd even live on Wells Ranch—build a house and have a family of our own.

I'm still staring at the closed alley gate following the last run of the evening when Shelby's fingers rap against my thigh, stinging my skin even through the Wranglers.

"Told you he's man enough." She points toward the chutes where a kid is climbing on the back of a horse. It's hard to tell what she sees in him from this distance, but I give her an approving nod.

Cassidy starts talking about how much hotter her baby daddy is—comical considering mere months ago she was denying having any interest in him. With my gaze darting from cowboy hat to cowboy hat, the thought train running through my brain derails entirely.

Denver's sitting on the fence rail, laughing with the cowboy getting ready to ride. His hat's low over his forehead, and he pats the guy firmly on the back before turning to talk to Red.

I stare for so long, I start to worry he can feel my eyes boring into him, though he never looks in our direction. The gate opens, and Denver disappears. Ride after ride, I scan each chute with the eye of a sniper, keen for another glimpse. Refusing to spend any time dwelling on *why* I want to see him so desperately.

Just like last night, when I sat in my darkened living room—away from the window, so he couldn't see me—and watched him sit in his truck for far too long before driving away. For a moment, I thought he might get out and come back to the house. For a moment, I thought I might run out to the truck and ask him to stay.

Denver finally pops up at chute number four, adjusting his hat as he climbs inside. His gaze cuts to where we're sitting, as if he's known exactly where we were all along. Staring into my soul, he presses his hand to his lips, then swings like he's lobbing a softball toward the grandstands. The discreet motion hits me like a gut punch, and I swipe my clammy palms against my thighs.

I shouldn't have come here.

I moved back to town with the intention of staying well away from Denver Wells. When we broke up as kids, the only thing that kept me from hauling ass back to Wells Canyon, and throwing myself down on my knees in front of him, was the physical inability to leave my dorm. Then I got antidepressants, my emotions became callused, and I knew I couldn't love him the way he wanted anymore.

Now he's blowing me a kiss from the bucking chute before his ride, as if we're back to being sixteen and in love.

I won't survive losing my person again.

The gate opens, and Denver's on the back of a reckless, bucking horse doing everything in its power to toss him into the thick blanket of dirt below. Without taking my eyes off him, I set my empty cup down and rest my hand on my shaky knee. He's well seated, his movement fluid, and the seconds are ticking by. I move my tongue around inside my excruciatingly dry mouth, counting each second in my head. In backseat-driver fashion, my feet flex instinctively each time his legs kick up toward the horse's shoulders. Time's dragging, and I'm not breathing. Not even sure if my heart is beating.

When the buzzer loudly sounds, he's quick to release his grip, lunging to grab on to the pickup man next to him. And when his boots safely hit the ground, the pent-up breath I'd held for the full eight seconds comes out in the form of a whooping cheer.

Fresh drinks in hand, the three of us girls plop down at an empty table. With the rodeo about to end, a wave of people will be flooding into this space any moment, grabbing drinks from the bar and milling about until the sun sets and the local country band starts to play. But for now, it's quiet and the evening air around our shaded table is refreshing.

Cass checks her phone for approximately the three hundredth time since we dropped Hazel off with Dave, and a smile lights her face. "Wait, have you ever seen something cuter?"

She holds the phone toward us, and I lean closer to Shelby to see the screen. She's right—I don't think I've seen anything cuter than my niece, swaddled up in a buffalo plaid blanket, sleeping peacefully.

"What are we looking at?" A man's voice breaks our focus on the screen, and I blink up to see Red slowly rubbing Cassidy's shoulders.

"The most perfect baby in the world, that's all." Cass shows him the photo just as Denver approaches, setting an armload of red plastic cups down in the center of the table.

"Tequila shots for the ladies," he says with a grin, pushing one of the cups toward me.

Cassidy shakes her head. "None for me."

"Thanks, Denny." Shelby picks up a cup and swallows it before standing. "I have a cowboy I need to track down now. Bye, girlies!"

"Well, Hart." Denver sits down, the bench flexing under his weight, and places his cowboy hat upside down on the table. Running a hand through his hair, his knee knocks into mine, fanning the sparks ignited under my skin. "Looks like you and I are getting drunk tonight."

"No way. One shot. That's it." With a shiver, the fiery liquid burns through me, and I reach frantically for my rum and Coke to chase the foul taste.

"I don't think two would hurt."

"Blair's alcohol tolerance isn't any better now than it was in high school. Two shots will knock her on her ass." Cass laughs, cozying up to Red.

"Good thing I have a lot of practice carrying her drunk ass home," Denver says, cracking a beer can open. "Didn't even drop her the time she puked down my back when I tossed her over my shoulder."

I bury my face in my hands, a hot flush building in my cheeks. "Okay, let's not relive those times. I'm an adult now. I can handle my liquor."

The mostly empty plastic cup clunks against the wooden tabletop with a hollow sound. "Prove it, Hart."

A hypocrite at heart, I don't care that a mature, rational adult would turn down the challenge. And Denver's taking full advantage of my competitive nature, egging me on with a waggling eyebrow and a nudge of the cup. The tequila's gone in seconds and I hold my lips firmly together, not letting any disgusted reaction show on my face.

"Can take the girl out of the country, but can't take the country out of the girl, eh?" He smirks, and my entire body warms at the way his eyes rake over my body. "Country looks better on you, anyway."

For an indeterminate amount of time, I nurse my mixed drink and pretend my skull isn't filled with TV static. Letting them know that the Earth is rotating at an alarmingly fast pace isn't going to help my "I can handle my liquor" argument. So I rest my chin in my hand, pretending to be engaged in the boys' conversation about the ranch, and fight to keep my mind from wandering to the way Denver's leg is constantly bumping into mine, even though every graze makes my heart flutter.

In my periphery, he swallows his beer, the short stubble along his jaw catching my eye in the golden light of dusk. So much of him is the same—strong shoulders, slender body, dusty brown hair. But there's a few permanent creases on his rugged face. New scars on his deeply tanned, veiny forearms. Maybe even a gray hair or two, though it's hard to tell in this lighting. Stupid men and their ability to age like fine wine in spite of their crappy diets, too much sun, and lack of a skin care regime.

Cass turns to Red, crinkling her nose in the way she always does before she asks a question she's anxious about. She leans in closer, whispering something. He whispers back. At least . . . I think they're whispering. I certainly can't make out what they're talking about over the drum solo on stage behind us.

Denver's hand falls to my thigh, and I practically jump out of my skin—instantly sobered. When my startled stare meets his molasses-brown eyes, he silently mouths, "You good?"

I give a curt nod, turning back to where Cassidy and Red are simultaneously sliding off the picnic bench.

"We're heading out—you coming?" Cass asks me.

I should go home and sleep off both the alcohol and the weird feelings rattling around in my head. Continue avoiding

Denver as much as possible. I came back to Wells Canyon to take care of my dying mother and help my best friend with her baby, not to get wrapped up in local cowboys. *Especially* not the one creating pulsating heat between my legs just from touching his knee to mine.

"Nah, I'm gonna stay awhile longer. I think I want to dance." My traitorous mouth speaks without warning. Cass looks me up and down—without a doubt, she's going to give me hell for this later.

"Okay, don't get into too much trouble."

"Yes, Mom." I bat my eyes at her.

God, I really am drunk.

"Love you guys," Denver adds as Cass gives me one final side-eye before turning to leave, Red's arm wrapped snugly around her waist.

Denver hardly gives our friends time to get out of earshot before he turns to me. "You're hammered, aren't ya?"

I purse my lips at him, glaring, not appreciating being called out like this. "Am not."

With a cocky eyebrow raise, he snickers. "Still awful at hiding it, I see. I kept hitting your knee to check if you were okay. I know you tend to hurl after too many drinks."

Good to know I wasn't imagining the knee knocks. But my stomach drops unexpectedly at the realization that he was only doing it to slyly get my attention to check whether I'm about to vomit or not. Not because he wanted to touch me.

Fuck, Blair. Get it together.

"I'm actually super sober," I say. "I could go for poutine, though."

"I can't wait for you to ruin poutine for me when you throw that up everywhere later." He looks at me with a smile, dimples so prominent I would happily do another shot of tequila right out of them. "Maybe we dance first, eat poutine after. Slightly decreases the chance of spewage."

"Zero chance, because a couple shots of tequila is nothin'."

He snorts in disbelief. *For good reason, arguably.*

I'm pleasantly surprised to find that I'm capable of standing—albeit with a slight sway. Nothing some fries smothered in cheese and gravy won't fix. Denver's immediately beside me, fingers tightening around my elbow while we navigate through the crowd.

"If you must know, I actually can't remember the last time I threw up." Or drank tequila . . . but that's beside the point.

"Too grown up to drink to excess now? I guess in the city you probably sip on twelve-dollar cocktails and talk about the stock market instead."

"The cocktails taste better *and* get you drunk faster than the water you call beer."

"Damn, shots fired." He pretends to be taken aback for half a second, then holds out his hand to pull me onto the dance floor.

His fingers graze mine, stealing my breath. And when he pulls me into him, I almost throw up from the whiplash of memories—dancing together in his childhood bedroom, making love on a picnic blanket, holding him tight after losing his mom. He's broader in the shoulders than he once was, but familiar enough to make my heart ache.

Falling into sync like no time has passed, we traverse the dance space, two-stepping and twirling. We take it easy for the first song, sticking to the most basic moves, keeping space between our bodies. But by the third round, our hips fit together like puzzle pieces, and there's a fire when he looks into my eyes. His hand spreads across my lower back, letting me lean back so the ends of my hair kiss the concrete, before yanking me in tight. Close enough his cologne floods my senses, and his breath blows hot on my cheek.

With a flick, he has me unraveling across the dance floor until our arms are outstretched, and a laugh bubbles up from my chest at the boyish grin on his face. Connected only by our fingers, I'm dying to be back in his embrace. Skin stinging at the loss of his touch.

When I come back in, our mouths nearly collide out of habit. It feels right to kiss somebody when you're lost in each other on the dance floor, and the thought of kissing *him* in particular feels like kismet. But I roll my lips together and push on, refusing to let the way he cradles my body against his be enough to break down my resolve.

Denver dips me again. This time, while I'm entranced by the blurry street lamps outside the rodeo grounds, he grabs me by the belt buckle to whip my body upright. I'm so fucking close to him my breasts collide with his chest during every gasping breath. He keeps his hold on my buckle for longer than necessary, eyes locked on mine. Tucked under the waistband of my jeans, his fingertips are softly grazing my bare lower stomach. Inches from where I'm suddenly wet and throbbing with need. My hips roll instinctively toward his touch, forcing it a tiny bit lower, and I nearly forget all the reasons why I shouldn't kiss him right now.

Heartache on the dance floor is damn right.

My name leaves his lips and I stare at the smooth, pink skin, wondering for a split second if he's about to kiss me.

Breathlessly, I mutter, "We should go get our poutine before the food trucks close."

"Right . . . *right*. We should."

He lets go of my body, and it takes every ounce of my quickly fading self-control not to tangle my hands in his hair and kiss him with years' worth of pent-up longing. But instead I settle for letting him take my hand to lead me out of the crowd, toward the scent of French fries.

"It's been way too long since I danced like that," I say, catching my breath and dropping his hand, hit by a blast of cool night air outside the swath of people.

"No country bars in the big city?"

"Can't say I actually looked into whether there are or not." I shrug, as if the thought never crossed my mind. To tell the truth, I didn't go looking for country bars because the idea of country swing dancing or two-stepping with anyone else sounded like a surefire route to lying in bed in a depression coma for two days straight.

Stepping up to the food truck's window, Denver orders a large poutine. I try three times to pay for it, but he shuts me out—blocking me from getting to the window, gently pushing my hand away when I thrust a wad of cash at the food truck employee, and shushing me when I start to insist.

I give up with a dramatic sigh, and the moment Denver has our heaping order in his hands, I'm grabbing a too-hot fry and nibbling it carefully. "You know, I have money. If anything, it would just be paying you back for all the times you bought me food when we were kids."

"Then technically you owe my mom. She was the one slipping me a secret allowance for you every week."

"*Great.*" I lick a dollop of gravy off my fingertip and scrunch my nose. "Now I feel bad about the disgusting amount of sour key candies I consumed growing up—knowing Lucy was paying for it."

"I see how it is," he says with a smile that reaches his eyes, picking up a fry and tapping it against mine. "You were fine with bleeding my wallet dry all summer, but feel bad when you find out my mom was bankrolling your candy addiction?"

"Absolutely."

"Are you shitting me?" Denver buries his face in his hands.

Suddenly regretting my snarky response, I tilt my head to try and get a glimpse of his face. "Sorry, I didn't mean—"

"No, sorry, not you," he interrupts. "You're all good. Real quick—can you do me a favor?"

I raise an eyebrow, bringing a French fry to my lips. "Let's hear it."

"Well, there's this girl . . . fucking *obsessed* with me."

I cut him off, holding a finger up between us, stopping him from digging a deeper hole. "Immediately no. I've heard enough."

"Blair."

"Denver."

"The girl you saw me with at the rodeo—"

"And the bar."

"So you did notice Peyton refusing to leave me alone at the bar."

I chew on a cheese curd, pretending to be unfazed by the thought of him with another woman. "You seemed pretty content."

He definitely wasn't shoving her away. Not that he had to. He doesn't owe me anything after all these years, especially when my actions broke us up in the first place. It's a good thing he moved on, even if it kills me. Actually, the nagging pain of rejection I'm currently feeling deep in my chest is tolerable. Much better than what might happen if I let myself get attached and end up hurt again.

"I had an injury and was trapped, but I didn't want her there. I wasn't lying to you when I said I broke things off in the ambulance. Besides, we were never serious, and I made that *very* clear from the start. But she's having some trouble understanding that, and now she's a bit of a stage-five clinger."

"Sounds like you need to communicate better."

Shaking his head as he swallows a mouthful of beer, Denver sets his drink down and digs into the front pocket of his jeans. Then he holds his phone out to me, wiggling it slightly to encourage me to grab it. "I don't know how much more clear I can be."

His fingertips brush over my hand when I reach for the phone, and I'm *totally* unaffected by it. "I feel like this is a bad idea. I don't want to accidentally see or read anything that'll traumatize me forever."

Or that will make me completely unravel at the seams.

He laughs. "You won't."

"Nothing I won't be able to unsee? You're sure?" I look tentatively at the phone in my hand.

"Nothing you haven't seen before."

Thinking about him sending pictures of himself to somebody . . . My sinuses burn and an uneven breath rattles in my lungs.

"Denver. If this is an elaborate prank to get me to see a dick pic . . ." I thrust the phone in his direction, needing the pictures, and God knows what else, as far away from me as possible.

"It's a joke. I'm trying to get her to leave me alone, not have her begging for more. No pictures, I swear."

Sighing, I glance up at him through my lashes. "What's the password?"

"Zero, nine, sixteen."

My birthday. His lock code is my birthday.

There's simply no way that's a coincidence. Not with Denver, who used to sneak into my bedroom and decorate my room for my birthday every year. Even if he hated me— even if he moved on—he wouldn't have forgotten that date.

Clearing my throat, I quickly look away from him and tap the four digits.

Hit with a barrage of incoming texts from Peyton the moment I unlock the phone, my eyes widen. Invites to go on a date, asking what he's up to incessantly, and getting increasingly persistent because he hasn't answered her.

Looking up from the phone, I grimace in his direction. "Well, she's certainly . . . *passionate*."

"Hear me out. Can you just . . . pretend like you're here with me?" His eyes cut to where the girl is presumably standing, then back to me. "Nothing weird. You can be quiet if she comes over here but let me pretend we're *together* together."

A pawn. That's what I am now.

"Why should I help you get yourself out of this hole you

dug? You toy with people's feelings and you're bound to end up in messy situations like this."

Before he can answer, a cutesy voice breaks through the noisy rodeo after-party. "Denny! I was looking for you after your ride." Her eyes narrow upon seeing me, and I slowly pull my hand away from the paper plate loaded with poutine. I imagine this is what it feels like to be a prey animal. "Oh, you're the new waitress from the Horseshoe."

"Actually," Denver pipes up immediately, "she's a nurse practitioner."

I nod. "Blair. I'm helping Dave out at the bar from time to time."

"Peyton." She thrusts her hand toward me, and I look her up and down as I reach out to shake it. She seems nice enough. And I can't blame her for having a crush on Denver—Lord knows I haven't been able to shake mine since I first noticed how cute he was at thirteen. "How do you know my Denny?"

My Denny plays on repeat until the words don't sound real anymore and, genuinely, I think I might throw up. Not to be dramatic. Cheese curds, gravy, and tequila are coagulating in my stomach, churning and threatening to ruin this *lovely* conversation.

Would it be uncalled for to turn a little to the right so I puke all over her cute outfit?

I swallow, looking from Denver to Peyton and back again. "Oh, uh. We were childhood friends."

"We were a lot more than friends." Denver smiles, grabbing my hand on top of the table. To my surprise, I don't pull back. In fact, I let the warmth of his hand fill me with hopeful elation. Or maybe it's the hot gravy raising my internal body temperature. "Now she's moved back home, and we're picking things back up where we left off."

Is that what's happening?

No. No, he's only saying that to scare this poor girl off.

His callused fingertip languidly draws hearts on my palm,

and all the arguments about why I won't pretend to be with him melt away. Sign me the fuck up for future heartbreak, if it means having a few minutes of pretending to be his.

God, I'm pathetic.

"Absolutely." I squeeze gently around his fingers and smile over at him. "Making up for lost time."

Denver

P eyton's fake smile falters for a second. "Oh, that's super cute. . . . Well, I'll see you guys around."

"Really nice to meet you." Blair gives her an apologetic look, like she feels bad for stealing my heart as a kid and making me emotionally unavailable for everybody else.

We quietly watch Peyton disappear in the crowd gathered near the bar, neither of us racing to remove our hands from their clasped position on top of the table.

"She's out of your hair now." Blair slowly unfurls her fingers from mine and tucks her hands into her lap. "Consider it my repayment for the poutine."

"I think that's worth more than a shitty rodeo poutine. Getting her to leave me alone—especially without causing a scene—is easily worth at least two dinners. Next weekend maybe?"

"Denver," she breathes out my name, shoulders rolling forward slightly. "I can't."

"Okay, so the weekend after. Or . . . midweek? I can probably make that work."

I mean, *hell,* if Red could drive to town every night after work to win over his lady, so can I. I'll tell Austin to kiss my ass if he fights me on it.

"I can't go out with you. I came back here to help take care of Mom, not to partake in whatever it is you do to women. If that's what I wanted, I would've come home before now."

My heart plummets to my stomach. She's made it clear she thinks I'm nothing but a fuckboy now. That all I want is to get her into bed. And I can see why she gets that impression, if people have been filling her head with rumors.

What if it's all my fault she didn't come back sooner? She thought I'd moved on, or I was a manwhore, or whatever the fuck. When the truth is that I wouldn't have even looked at another woman, had I suspected Blair might be back one day.

I want to tell her that, but instead I blurt out, "What I'm doing *to* women? Damn, people caught on about my serial killer M.O., eh?"

"Yup, that's it."

I nudge the fries toward her, because suddenly she's pounding back the rest of her drink, and she's going to need something to soak it up.

"Anyway, it doesn't matter. You're free to do whatever—*whoever*—you want. But I r-really need to go." Her voice cracks and she stands up, white-knuckling the table edge.

"I'll take you."

"No, it's fine. I can get myself home." All the progress it felt like I was making with her is gone in the blink of an eye. A couple minutes ago, I held her soft, warm hand in mine and, even though it was only for show, the glimmer in her eyes was the first sign of hope I've seen from her.

"I can't let you wander off alone at night. I'll throw you over my shoulder, if I have to."

"You wouldn't dare." Her lips purse in defiance.

"I wouldn't?"

I step into her and my hands find their way to her waist in the same way they have hundreds of times. Only this time I'm shaking, and she jolts like I've electrocuted her, jumping back and bumping into a passing stranger. Wide-eyed, she runs her fingers across her bottom lip.

"Come with me to find Colt." My tone's more pleading than I intended. Although, it seems to convince her, because she nods silently.

With Colt secured, the three of us weave between vehicles until we find his truck. His blue heeler, Betty, barks aggressively as we approach.

"Betty, don't be a hag," Colt yells, shutting her up immediately. Then he turns to Blair and adds, "She's really a sweetie. Don't let the bark fool you."

He unties the dog from the flat deck of his truck, and she rushes to hop into the small single cab, settling onto the middle of the bench seat.

"So, uh, we'll have to get pretty friendly, if we're all going to fit. Betty doesn't share her spot."

Colt walks around the side of his truck and climbs into the driver's seat, and Blair's staring at me. The moon's reflected in her doe eyes, and she fidgets with the hem of her shirt. It's nice to see her like this—dressed in jeans and a simple T-shirt, looking a lot like the way I remember her.

"I guess I'll sit on your lap?"

"Guess so." I try my best to hide my excitement, slipping onto the seat and taking a deep breath of night air and diesel fumes, waiting for her to settle onto my lap and shut the truck door.

"Hi, baby," she coos, reaching out to give Betty a scratch behind the ear. And even though it wasn't directed at me, Blair saying that word makes me desperate to hear her call me "baby" again.

When the truck dips into a pothole, Blair's back presses firmly into my chest. Instinctively, I wrap my arm around her waist in a makeshift seat belt, holding her warm body to mine. And I can smell her—*fuck,* the same spicy perfume I caught whiffs of at her house, and a clean shampoo scent as her hair brushes my cheek.

"You good?" I mutter, my free hand clutching the edge of the seat for dear life. Fighting like hell to stop myself from rubbing her thigh.

"Great," she says under her breath.

We turn onto the main road, and she rolls her hips slightly, sending a rush of blood to my cock. *Not the time,* I remind myself. This isn't a flirty ride home before a one-night stand.

Colt careens the truck around a corner, a little faster than I would've taken it, and Blair's hand clutches mine against her stomach. Body heat permeates through her thin shirt fabric and I can feel her racing pulse. She relaxes into me, letting our fingers subtly interlace in the dark of the pickup truck barreling down the side streets toward Blair's home. I need to know if she feels the same spark between us.

There's nothing to lose.

My free hand slides across the upholstered seat and up my denim-clad thigh before resting on the side of her leg. Drawing slow circles, I take notice of how her breathing pattern changes when I touch her.

When I slip to the top of her leg, fingertips toying with the inner seam of her jeans, cautiously moving up the length of her inner thigh, I almost become completely feral. Because Blair's breath stops altogether, and her knees fall away from each other. Melting under my touch the way she always has. Her grip on my hand tightens, and there's no way she doesn't feel my chest thundering against her back.

Then we pull into her driveway, and she straightens up, swiftly pulling her hand away from mine. The harsh roof lights temporarily blind me when Blair opens the truck door and hops out. And I'm hot on her heels, walking up to the front steps.

"Thank you for coercing me into going out tonight." She

unlocks the door with the slow turn of a key, and it swings open. "It was fun."

"Does that mean I can do it again?"

"Denver." She exhales hard. "I told you already—I can't do this with you."

"Can't do what?" I step toward her and she doesn't move back, letting the air between us become electric.

I glance at her full lips, and can't help but wonder if she tastes the way she used to, if her naked body feels the same against mine, if she sounds the same when she's coming.

"Can't pick back up where we left off. Even if things hadn't ended the way they did, I didn't come back here for this." She gestures to the invisible tether between us. "For whatever happened in the truck tonight, or for whatever you think is happening now."

"Of course not. But would it be so bad to hang out with your 'childhood friend' again?"

A childhood friend who crawled across her bed to bury my face between her legs hundreds of times. A childhood friend who begged her to marry me. Having her reduce our relationship to that felt like a slug to the chest, but I'm clearly not above throwing it back in her face as a way of convincing her to spend time together.

"I missed my best friend." I let one small truth sneak out of my lips. I missed her more than she'll ever know. "We can be friends and nothing more. Can't we, Blair?"

"Yeah . . ." The corner of her mouth quirks. "I guess we can."

I chance another step toward her, until there's only the wooden door frame acting as an invisible barrier. The singular thing keeping up this charade about being friends. Then I lean against the frame with a smug smile, reveling in the way her eyes are so clearly tearing my clothes off. She's never been good at hiding her emotions—not from me.

She should've closed the door in my face by now, but instead she stands quietly, eyes locked on mine, chest rising and falling with slow breaths. And, because I know her cues intimately, I know she's thinking about kissing me. Her tongue darts across her bottom lip, and her body sways a little closer.

My name leaves her lips in a whispered plea. And I reach up to brush her hair behind her ear, ready to give everything up for the taste of her. I don't care that she doesn't want to live here. That she doesn't want me. That we didn't work out when we were younger.

I've never stopped loving Blair. Now I know for certain that I never will. I wish I didn't have to go the last fourteen years without her, left only with a toxic habit of constantly reliving every moment we shared. Begging the universe to turn back time so I could have her back.

Finally she's home, and I refuse to lose her again. So I rest my forehead against hers, combing my fingers through her wavy brown hair. Breathing her in. And she does the same—embracing the connection we've gone so long without.

"Blair? Is that you?" her dad calls out from the hallway. Heavy footsteps move toward us, and Blair frantically backs away.

"Hey, Dad. Sorry if I woke you up. I just got home from the rodeo."

She turns to me with a small smile and mouths, "Good night."

"'Night," I whisper as the door shuts on my big moment. My first—*definitely not last*—attempt at getting my girl back.

Blair
(sixteen years old)

To teens in the 2000s, the most meaningful gift anyone could give was a perfectly curated burned CD. And that's exactly what I found displayed on my nightstand the morning of my sixteenth birthday.

When Lucy had started chemotherapy a couple months prior, it meant trips to the city every couple weeks. And after Denny and I had become an official couple, he snuck into my room in the dead of night to share a bed anytime his mom and dad were gone for cancer appointments. He insisted it was lonely and weird in his house with them gone, and I wasn't about to argue that he still had his grandpa and brothers around. Having Denver Wells in my bed made my nights a lot less lonely, too.

I left the window open, waiting patiently in my cutest pajamas for him to slide it open and hop in. Then he'd strip down to boxers, crawl under the covers, and wrap his arms around me. Sometimes he wouldn't say anything, planting soft kisses on my shoulders until we fell asleep. Other times we'd talk in hushed voices until our words started slurring from exhaustion. In the morning, he'd kiss me goodbye and duck out long before daybreak. Driving his stolen truck back to the ranch with enough time to slip his grandpa's keys on the rack and sneak upstairs.

And on my birthday, I woke up to find he had gotten up

extra early to blow up sixteen balloons and hang streamers everywhere. Then there was the CD, which he'd drawn on with permanent marker—our names inside a red heart.

"Happy birthday, beautiful." He kissed me softly on the cheek the moment I sat up to take in my decorated room. "I need to head home before they realize I'm missing, but I had to see your face first."

"Denny, this is the nicest thing ever." I laid my head on his chest, wrapping my arms around his waist.

Squeezing me tight enough I groaned, he spoke into my hair. "Put the CD in your backpack, we can listen to it in my room after school."

Then he kissed me, pulling me onto his lap on top of my bed. My pajama shorts rode up my thighs, and his callused hands gripped my bare skin, rocketing electricity up to my groin. We hadn't done more than some kissing and over-the-clothes touching, but after months of that, I was hungry for more. So I rolled my hips, eliciting a strangled groan from deep in his chest.

"Bear," he mumbled into my mouth. "We can't. I need to go or I'll be grounded for life."

I glanced past him to the small wall clock above my desk. He was right—already cutting it real close to the time his grandpa typically woke up.

"Soon?" I kissed him desperately.

"As soon as the time is right, baby."

Within seconds he had slipped out of my window into the still-dark early morning. And I lay spread out on my bed, counting down the minutes until we were holding hands in the school hallway, kissing between classes, and snuggling up on the bus ride to Wells Ranch.

Stalls mucked and various chores done for the day, Denny and I sank to his bedroom floor, backs propped against his bed. I pulled the homemade CD from my backpack and watched as he crawled across the floor to the boombox a few feet away. The muscles in his arms flexed, and I was powerless against the way his butt looked in taut, faded denim. When he settled back in next to me as the first few chords of a familiar country song played, I breathed him in and took a million mental snapshots of the moment.

His thumb circled my knee, and if it weren't for his parents' open door rule, I would be jumping his bones.

"This is the perfect playlist." I let my eyes drift closed, smelling his body wash and feeling the warmth of his arm around me.

Nuzzled into my hair, he whispered, "Dance with me."

Then he was tugging me to my feet and pulling me tight to his chest. We stumbled for a moment, entirely unable to find the beat.

"You know what we should do?" I ran my hands down his solid arms. "Learn how to dance properly. Like we see people do when there's live music at the rodeos."

A smile lit his face, and it wasn't long before he was searching for how-to videos online. We pulled up a promising-looking tutorial and sat with our eyes glued to the screen for three full run-throughs. Then with a confident nod, Denny stood and held out a hand.

It was horrific. I stepped on his foot, he tripped and hip-checked the dresser. But we laughed. *Hysterically.* Until tears streamed down our cheeks, and Denver's face scrunched up with a mixture of frustration and determination. He repeated the words "we're going to get this" with each screwup. And, for some reason, I believed him. So we kept trying.

Finally figuring out the basic footwork of a two-step, we danced around the small room. Wearing a pattern into the old floorboards, grinning at each other, we didn't stop until Lucy yelled at us to head downstairs for dinner.

Denny didn't let me go, though. He pressed his hand to the small of my back, despite the way my shirt had become damp with sweat, and he kissed me deeply.

"Happy birthday, Bear," he said against my lips.

I held my hands on either side of his square jaw, feeling the sharp bristle of new-to-him facial hair on my palms. "Thank you for the best birthday ever."

His deep brown gaze met mine, and he relaxed into my touch. "I love you."

Some would've said it was too soon to say those words. Sixteen, dating for approximately four months, and had only told our parents a month prior—when I no longer had rodeo-related reasons to come to the ranch, so we needed to explain why I was still there every day.

But I'd loved Denny Wells since the day he sat with me by the railroad tracks, only cemented by his sweet words and caring gestures since then. So it honestly felt like a long time coming.

"I love you, too, Denver."

He kissed my nose, cocking a brow. "Denver? You *never* call me by my full name."

"One time I read in a *CosmoGirl* issue that calling a guy by his full name—not a nickname—means you're in love with him."

By that measure, I should've called him Denver since day one. But when I read the article, I made a mental note to stop calling him Denny once we'd exchanged "I love you's."

He chuckled. "I'm not sure that makes sense, but *you* can call me anything you like."

I tapped a finger against my chin, faking deep thoughts. "Even Capybara?"

"The hell is that?"

"The largest living rodent," I stated, and was met by his fingers pinching my sides. I shrieked. "What? They're cute!"

"Okay, anything *but* that. I'm not a rodent. How did you—never mind, I know how your mind works. I don't need to ask where Capybara came from."

"I just have a constant list—"

"Of random crap running through your mind."

"Exactly." I kissed him just as Lucy yelled for us once again, so our arms fell to our sides and he followed me out of the room. "My brain is a bizarre place. Random thoughts freewheeling through my synapses, leaving no room for practical information."

He kissed me at the top of the stairs. "But that's why I love you."

"Please never stop saying those words to me." I kissed him one step down. And then each one after that. Until we were kissing on the bottom step, pressed against the railing, and Austin walked in to ruin the moment. His shoulder smacked into Denver's, urging us to quit making out and continue on to have dinner with both of our families, complete with a birthday cake for me.

"I'll tell you every day for the rest of my life," Denver whispered, squeezing my hand as we practically floated into the kitchen.

"I'll hold you to that, *Denver*."

Denver
(sixteen years old)

I was waiting outside the barn, our horses already tacked up, when Blair hopped out of the truck at six a.m.

"What on Earth are you doing?" She laughed as she spoke, jogging down the driveway toward me. "The sun's hardly up."

"Exactly." I beamed, bending slightly to kiss her. A hint of spearmint toothpaste still lingered on her tongue, and she wrapped her arms around my neck, kissing me deeper.

Finally coming up for air, her lips curved into a smile against mine. "What do you have planned for us?"

"Well, it's the anniversary of our first kiss, in case you forgot." I could never forget the date.

May twenty-sixth. A blessing and a curse. I wished I had kissed her a single day sooner, so the kiss wouldn't be forever associated with finding out about Mom's cancer. A diagnosis which quickly changed from "she'll be fine after some treatment" to "we're going to sign her up for trials because her body isn't responding to conventional cancer treatment."

Blair pulled my mind from the dark place with a single hand on my jaw, thumb rubbing across my bottom lip. "Hey. Let's have a good day, okay?"

"That's the plan. Let's go, we have a long day ahead of us."

Giving Chief's neck a firm scratch, she laughed. "You better not be conning me into helping fix fences or something."

"Damn, you caught me." I smacked her ass, eliciting a shriek, and mounted my gelding, Rune, before she could get me back.

For the next hour, we rode side by side along dusty trails and across wildflower-blanketed fields. Talking about our plans for summer, our plans for college, our plans for the rest of our lives together. We raced across a field—naturally, Blair won. And I wasn't even mad about it, because the sight of her flying through the tall grasses with one hand on the reins and the other holding her hat down, hair flowing behind her, was worth losing miserably.

She hollered loving insults with a glowing smile when I caught up.

"Never met such a sore winner before," I yelled back, continuing past her.

"I just don't want to pass up an opportunity to humble you."

"Such a loving girlfriend. I'm so lucky," I teased.

She followed me through a stand of poplars, to the shady grove somewhere in the middle of nowhere. I'd stumbled across the spot while driving cattle the previous fall, when I ventured off to move a rogue cow back to the herd.

"We're here." Rune stopped and I hauled my ass out of the saddle.

"We're . . . where?" Blair looked around confused as she dismounted and tied Chief to a tree.

"Our special spot." I rummaged through my saddlebag. "Grab the snacks from your bag."

She did as she was told, pulling out the picnic snacks and bringing them over to the patch of grass where I was fighting with a blanket my mom had given me, struggling to get the silly charcoal fabric to lie flat in the clearing, filled with thick grass and tiny blue flowers.

"Den . . . I can't believe you planned this."

"Yup. I planned a whole romantic thing just to have my lovely girlfriend make fun of me on the ride here." I shook my head, gripping the cork from a stolen bottle of white wine. My mom had woken up before dawn to lovingly help pack apple cider alongside the snacks and blanket into the saddlebags. And I promptly switched the bottle out after she left the barn in an attempt at making this picnic a little fancier—more adult.

The cork flew off with a loud *pop*, and I handed the wine to Blair, who took a swig, wincing at the taste. Eyelashes fluttering closed, she leaned into me, gripping the neck of the bottle and snuggling in tight against my side.

"You know I tease you because I love you," she whispered. "I love you more than anything in this world."

"I love you, Bear."

She set the bottle on the ground beyond the blanket edge and took my face in her palms, kissing me with the taste of wine on her lips. Never breaking contact, she swung a leg over mine and kissed me hard.

"Please. I'm ready for this," she murmured against my mouth.

I gulped, chest heaving, and Blair worried her bottom lip as she waited for my reply. Likely expecting another rejection. It wasn't that I didn't *want* to do it. But spending so much time around my grandpa's rowdy ranch hands had me feeling nervous I'd get it all wrong.

"Are you sure?" I asked, already knowing the answer. Because Blair had been hinting at having sex for months, and it was me who was too scared to go for it.

Her hands tenderly held my jaw, and her rich brown eyes searched mine. "I'm sure, if you are."

I nodded. With more privacy than we'd ever had before, no rush to get back home, and an entire box of condoms—*another thing packed after Mom had gone back to the house*—I planned this trip with a goal. It was finally the perfect moment, and Blair deserved nothing but perfect for our first time.

I watched her peel off her jeans while I did the same. Then I kneeled on the blanket, unable to breathe, hands shaky as I fought to open the condom wrapper. "You're beautiful."

Blair sat up and raked her nails through my hair, pulling me into a kiss that erased every anxious thought. And when she lay back down, she brought me with her, never breaking contact with my lips.

Later, she packed away our belongings, and I pulled a folding knife from the pocket of my jeans to meticulously carve our names in the bark of a towering cottonwood.

"There," I said triumphantly, shoving the closed knife deep into my pocket. "Now you'll always be able to remember the exact spot where you had the best time of your life."

Laughing, Blair wrapped her arms around my torso, and kissed me. "As if I would ever forget."

Smoothing a hand over her mussed-up hair, I whispered, "You're okay, right? No regrets?"

"Denver, I love you." Her lips punctuated each word with gentle presses to my cheek and jaw, until she was brushing them against my ear. "That was better than I ever imagined."

Blair picked a bouquet of wildflowers, tucking them into her saddlebag while we exchanged glances. We didn't get back to the ranch until well after dark, and there was no doubt in my mind that I'd be marrying Blair Hart at that exact spot on the mountainside one day.

Denver

Strolling into the big house shortly after eleven a.m., I follow the scent of freshly brewed coffee to the kitchen. Beryl, our kitchen manager and pseudo-mom, is armpit deep in the oven, scrubbing every last speck of grime away.

"Morning," I say as I squeeze past her to get to the coffeepot.

"Morning, honey. There's fresh coffee and some scones." Her voice echoes from inside the oven. "What are you doing bumming around here in the middle of the day?"

My niece, Odessa, and nephew, Rhett, are playing at the kitchen table, Play-Doh and Play-Doh accessories scattered across nearly every square inch of the massive wooden tabletop. Odessa looks up when she hears my voice, sticking her tongue out at me. Naturally, I return the gesture.

"Gonna head to town shortly," I answer Beryl.

Her head pops up to look at me with confusion, and she drags her wrist across her forehead. "If you need something, Austin and Cecily just went to town for wedding stuff."

"Oh, no. I don't need anything."

A smile creases around her lips and eyes, glimmering as she stands and sinks her hip into the edge of the kitchen island. "Ah, I see. You're going there for some*one,* not some*thing.*"

Taking a long swig of black coffee, I mumble a *yeah* into the cup.

"Does someone happen to be a woman? About *this* tall"—her hand raises above her head—"with gorgeous brown hair and a very lovely personality?"

"It might be."

She slaps the countertop with a yip that makes me and the kids jump. "Your brother owes me five dollars."

I pull a face, clunking my cup down and staring at her. "What the hell?"

"Bad word. I get a quarter," Odessa pipes up, pointing to a mason jar sitting on the china cabinet, covered in bright flower stickers and a SWEAR JAR label with the E facing backward.

"Hell no. That's not a bad word." I shake my head at her, trying not to laugh as she places her tiny hands on her hips in defiance. "I'm not giving you any money."

"It *is* a bad word. Just like the S-word, and D-word, and *fuck*."

My hand shoots up to cover my mouth in a failed attempt to stop from laughing, and an even worse attempt at keeping the mouthful of coffee from spraying out between my fingertips. Brown liquid splatters across the white countertop, and I cough repeatedly into my elbow. Beryl's no better, doubling over until her forehead is firmly against the counter, shoulders shaking vigorously. And Odessa's watching it all with a shit-eating grin on her face. Even if she's not fully aware *why* her words were funny, she's always going to repeat anything I laugh at. She and I can be a bit of a hell-raising duo because of that.

Throwing my head back, I stare up at the white ceiling to compose myself. "Odessa . . . kiddo . . . I think we're even now. Unless you're gonna put some money in the jar, too." I risk another sip of coffee, turning back to Beryl. "Now, what in the H-E-double-hockey-sticks do you mean, you bet my brother?"

"The boys were all placing bets, and I decided to get in on

the action. It's been a long time since I've done any gambling and, well, I knew I'd win." She looks awfully pleased with herself, leaning against the counter and wringing her weathered hands together. "I bet Jackson that you'd be dating Blair before the end of the summer."

"Don't go buying anything with your big winnings just yet, then. We're not dating."

"It's only June, and you're driving to Wells Canyon midday to visit her. If you aren't dating yet, I'd wager you're well on your way."

I wish that were the case, but Beryl doesn't know our history. This isn't as simple as Blair moving away for college and us losing touch.

"Wouldn't count on it. I'm going to have to pull some miracles." My knuckles scrape across my jaw. "I really messed up back in the day."

She leans across the counter, grabbing my hand in hers. And after a comforting, motherly rub of her thumb across my knuckles, she raps them hard with her fingers. "Then quit wasting time. Go show the girl how much has changed since she left . . . how much *you* have changed. Nothing you did as an eighteen-year-old should carry so much weight when you're in your thirties."

"You should use that as your platform for justice reform. Get all the eighteen-year-old serial killers out of prison before they turn thirty."

"Making jokes isn't going to get the girl."

"Works pretty well for me most of the time, actually."

She tilts her head, silently calling me out.

"*Okay.* She needed me, and I wasn't there. And she implied that part of why she didn't come back to town before now was because she thought I'd moved on with other girls. So when I should've been here waiting for her, I wasn't. It's a bit deeper than the shit I did at eighteen."

She clears her throat, raising a brow, preparing to call me

on my shit. And, truthfully, that's why I come to Beryl when I need to talk things out. She knows when I need a quiet listener, and she knows when I need a whupping. Looks like today is a whupping.

"Hadn't you moved on? Lord knows you never bring these women around here, but the way I hear you boys talk? It's no wonder why she thought you'd gone on to greener pastures, if even a fraction of the gossip got back to her."

"It was never anything serious," I protest, but Beryl slaps my hand again.

"Then prove that to her." She grabs the coffee mug from in front of me, dumping the contents in the sink. "You said you have your work cut out for you, right? As much as I enjoy your company, you being here right now seems like killing time because you're scared. What you should be scared of is losing her all over again because you F-worded your second chance."

Who am I to argue with that?

I pull into a parking spot outside of Blair's office and straighten myself out before heading through the glass front door. It's been a little over a week since the rodeo, and when I saw her at the ranch a couple days ago, she straight-up ignored me when I asked her to go for dinner. Essentially ghosted me while face-to-face by pretending to be preoccupied with Hazel.

So when it looked like a relatively easy day on the ranch— the kind I could sneak away from without much interrogation from Austin—I figured it was now or never.

"Mornin'," I say to the receptionist pointing to Blair's closed office door. "Just here for Hart."

My entire arm trembles when I lift it to knock on the heavy wood door.

"Come in," Blair's voice fills the dark spaces inside me, and I take a deep breath before entering.

Instead of being prim and proper behind her large oak desk, she's sitting cross-legged on the floor. Heels tossed aside, hair up in a ponytail, and a sea of scattered paperwork around her. Despite the warm lighting, sugar cookie aroma, and instrumental music playing softly, the vibe of the room is tense.

She looks up at me and confusion washes over her face. "Hey, what are you doing here?"

With false confidence, I smile. "Taking you for lunch. Repayment for dealing with Peyton, remember?"

Narrowing her eyes, she gestures to the stacks of disheveled paper. "I'm too busy for lunch today. I'll eat something later."

"Good thing my plan A came with a built-in plan B." I wink and head back out the door, leaving her sitting on the floor with her eyebrows pinched, mouth agape.

I knew she'd blow me off, even if she had no reasonable excuse. Although it looks like she genuinely has a good excuse today, and that makes me even more thankful I'd planned a picnic-style lunch. Though I'd hoped for an impressive mountain view while we ate, I'll take whatever I can get.

I stroll out to my pickup and grab the brown paper bag from the passenger seat, then walk back past the bewildered receptionist and plop down facing Blair on the cold linoleum floor.

"I think your receptionist hates me because she can't see over the counter, so she has to stand up every time I go through the door."

"I heard about the face you made when she showed you pictures of her dog last time you stopped in. Bet *that's* why she hates you."

"That dog looks to be at least four years past its expiry date."

"Oh my God, she might hear you," Blair whispers in a threatening voice, eyes nearly bulging from their sockets.

"Enough talk about living taxidermy when we're about to eat. Thought we could have a nice picnic outside . . . enjoy the sunshine or whatever. But I guess this cave you call an office works just as well." I start unpacking the bag, handing her a can of Diet Coke. "Seriously, though. How can you work when it's this dark in here?"

She leans forward to look at the small cardboard boxes I'm pulling out of the bag, clearly interested in lunch despite saying she didn't want it. "The overhead lights are obnoxiously bright and make a revolting humming sound. It's too overstimulating."

"Right. Sorry, I should've guessed that was the reason."

A huff of air blows from her nose. "No need to apologize. You're not expected to know every single thing about me anymore."

I expect that of myself, though.

"What if I want to know everything?"

Wiggling a finger under the metal tab, Blair opens the can of pop with a fizzing hiss. "Then you can ask me questions. For now, though, you can know about my time-consuming project—organizing every single file in the office so Wanda can upload the info to the server."

"Organizing? Blair Hart? You're right, I don't know everything anymore."

She laughs. *Fuck me,* I want to hear more of it. Sweet and soft, but with a rasp to it. To somebody who didn't know her, they'd likely assume she was getting over a cold. But I know her voice has had a permanent rasp at certain pitches ever since the winter she came down with a bad viral infection in ninth grade. I love that it's still there after all this time.

"Only for as long as this hyperfocus lasts, which is why I can't risk taking a break for lunch."

"Fair enough. Get back to it, then."

I slide a box of chicken strips and fries toward her, watching with a smile as she grabs three fries and shoves them into her mouth without taking her eyes off the paper resting on her lap.

"Want me to feed you while you work?"

Her eyes briefly flit up to mine once she's finished chewing. "If you could blend this and give me a really long bendy straw, that would be wonderful."

"Don't tempt me, Hart."

We sit across from each other while we eat, and I watch her focus intently on sorting medical records—tapping a pen against her chin in thought, then simultaneously scribbling and reaching for food. I offer once to leave her to her work, but she doesn't respond, and I assume that's an invitation to stay. I don't mind at all; I've always loved watching her when she gets in the zone, with laser-focused eyes, a tiny crease between her brows, and a concentrated worrying of her bottom lip.

At one point, she mixes up her hands, bringing her pen to her mouth instead of the chicken tender and smudging blue ink on her top lip. When she realizes the mistake, she cracks up and looks over at me, a smile extending beyond her eyes.

"Tell me how stupid I just looked." The pen falls to the floor and she rubs at her lip, missing the ink stain entirely.

"I didn't even question you trying to chew on the pen because you seem like you totally know what you're doing. Thought it was part of your process." I laugh and rock forward onto my knees. "But I don't know if blue lipstick suits you."

She doesn't pull back when I reach for her, and the pad of my thumb swipes across her upper lip. I rub delicately at the mark, taking my time because the last thing I want to do is remove any part of my body from her smooth, plump lips.

"Tough stain?" she asks quietly.

"You must use some pretty fancy pens. It won't budge."

Without hesitation, her lips part and she slowly licks the pad of my thumb, sending shivers down my spine and arresting my breath. And now I'm fucked, because all I can think about is her doing the same motion to the tip of my cock. How badly I'd love the pen ink to leave streaks down my shaft. I swallow hard and resume scrubbing, unable to do anything else right now. Every thought in my head's gone, and the blood responsible for keeping my brain functioning is relocating to my hardening dick.

"Better?" she asks.

I reluctantly let my hand fall from her face.

"Better," I say about the fact that her lip is mostly back to its normal color. But absolutely nothing is better about the situation between us. It won't be until I feel those beautiful lips on mine, and I find out if her kisses are as honey sweet as they once were.

She takes a sip of her drink, muscles in her jaw tensing in the dim light.

Still leaning into her personal space, I ask, "Can I ask you a question?"

Those big brown eyes of hers are searching mine. "Sure."

"Do you ever think about me the way I think about you?"

She scrunches her nose with a small laugh. "I don't know. What way is that?"

And I guess the blood flow still hasn't returned to my brain, because the next words I say do nothing to help the case I made to her about being nothing more than friends. "Your body wrapped around mine, my cock buried inside you, moans muffled by our kissing, feeling so fucking good we'd both be happy to die right in that moment. *That way.*"

She shifts in her seat, staring at the patch of floor between us. I'm the world's biggest idiot. *Friends.* I asked her to be friends—and then we almost kissed mere seconds later, but that's beside the point. She'd been drinking the night of the rodeo, and it was late. Now she's sober and seemingly sitting in combined disgust and shock.

"Blair, forget I said—"

"All the time."

Her gaze cuts to meet mine, and I'm about half a second from launching myself at her, kissing her until she can't breathe, and fucking her on the office floor. That half a second is all it takes for my plans to be kiboshed by a loud knock, followed by Dr. Brickham barging in. Blair and I must look absolutely bizarre, sitting on the floor surrounded by paperwork and fast food, our faces flushed. And Brickham does a double take.

Smiling awkwardly down at me, clearly realizing he was interrupting something, he says, "Denny, how are ya?"

I clear the pooled saliva in the back of my throat with a rumbly cough. "Oh, uh, good. And you?"

"Good, good. Looks like we're in for another hay shortage this year."

Fucking hell, I was about to indulge in the girl of my dreams, and this man interrupts to talk about hay?

"Sorry, we were kind of in the middle of something," Blair speaks up. "Can we have a minute?"

A minute isn't long enough for what I want to do, but I'll take anything I can get.

"I need you right now. This stupid space-age system you insist on having is absolute junk."

"You mean the electronic record keeping?" She bites back a smile.

"All I know is I have a patient coming in ten minutes, and everything is gone. The damn computer won't even let me log in. I need you to come to my office."

Blair looks at me, and I open my mouth to protest, but she shakes her head. "Um, we'll . . . get back to what we were talking about later, yeah?"

"Bet your ass we will."

Blair
(sixteen years old)

In a crowd of other barrel racers waiting in the August heat, I leaned forward to drag my nails along Chief's neck, in that perfect spot about an inch below his mane where he loved to be scratched. I looked around at our competition and smiled at the only face I recognized—a girl from Sheridan who ran barrels faster than anyone I'd ever seen. And sure, their runs were rarely clean, but when it worked, it freaking worked.

Denver weaved through the throng of horses, stopping next to me and giving Chief a firm pat. "Hey, Bear. You two ready to kill it? You're gonna ruin all of these girls' days when you make their runs look like peewee barrels."

"Den." I pulled my foot from the stirrup to kick it at him. "Shush. You're going to make people hate me."

"Okay, okay. I'm just speaking the truth, but I guess we can rub it in later. I need to go find the best spot to watch you win from. Love you."

"Love you, dork." I leaned down to kiss him, feeling the heat of the other girls' stares on me.

Turning back to the arena, I adjusted the straw cowboy hat on my head and tucked a sweaty lock of hair behind my ear. Then walked ahead, gearing up to take the next crack at the barrels. A clover pattern around three barrels, then straight on home. After hundreds of runs, Chief could do the pattern in his sleep, and my job was primarily to hang on and let him do what he loved.

With a deep breath, my heels squeezed against his side, ushering him forward. When Chief saw it was a straight shot from the alley into the massive outdoor arena, he took off like a bullet out of a gun. Around the first big barrel on the right-hand side of the arena, sticking so close to the barrel I had to pull my foot up and back to keep from knocking it over. Then the second, where I heard Denver whistling over Kenny Chesney blasting from the loudspeakers. The third barrel wobbled as Chief rounded it—I doubted it was enough to tip, as long as the ground was relatively even, so I didn't hold back. Storming toward the finish, I egged him on to push faster, hooves kicking up dirt and mane whipping around in the breeze. Once we passed the timer, Chief slowed to a stop just before slamming into the fence panels. And I didn't need to see the time to know it was a damn good run.

If Lucy had been there, she'd be cheering so loud my entire face would turn crimson. She was never one to care that the other girls stared, or that her children found it mildly embarrassing to have her literally jumping for joy regardless of how well they competed. But with her illness, she hadn't been able to travel to rodeos since the spring.

Instead, Jackson, Denver, and I drove around the province by ourselves. The boys took turns hauling the stock trailer, and I made sure they followed the rules Lucy set for us. One of those rules being that we took videos of every single run to show her when we got home.

Sidling up next to Jackson's roping horse, I climbed off Chief and tossed my hat on the trailer fender. In the middle of combing my fingers through my hot, damp hair, somebody pinched my side, making me squeal.

"Baby, you're incredible." Denver wrapped his arms

around my waist and lifted my boots clear off the ground—no small feat, given he only had all of two inches and ten pounds on me.

"Denver Wells, if you drop me and I have to go collect my first-place buckle with a limp, I'll kill you." I laughed, leaning into him as my feet touched back down.

"Marry me." He held a palm to either side of my flushed face. "Marry me, and we'll travel to every rodeo in North America all year long."

"You just want to claim half of my cash prize." My fingers slapped across his bicep. "Hold your horses—we still have a whole year of high school left, then college. Plus, I don't think my dad's going to allow underage marriage."

"Okay, well . . . *agree* to marry me. Say you will one day. Promise me you'll be mine forever."

"Denver, what the hell has gotten into you?" I shook my head, and his eyes grew wide, waiting for an answer. A confirmation that . . . I would *marry him?!* "Okay, okay. I promise I'll marry you one day, and I'm yours whether there's a ring on my finger or not. Even though you're insane."

Then he stole every last bit of oxygen from my lungs with an all-consuming kiss.

Days later, I walked into the big house to find Lucy in the kitchen for the first time in weeks, sipping on chamomile tea. Noticing me enter the room, she looked up and smiled weakly. "Hey, kiddo."

"Hey, Mama." I wrapped my arms around her small body, inhaling the musky scent of her favorite body wash—it was technically "formulated for men," but she said it made her skin soft for half the price of women's body wash. And anyway, it wouldn't matter what she smelled like, because her husband, Bennett, would love her even covered in cow shit.

"You feeling good today?" I asked, pouring myself a cup of coffee.

"Great, actually. I was thinking I'd go sit on the back porch in the sun for a while. Boys probably won't be back until dusk."

I nodded, stirring the sugar cubes until they'd dissolved, then I led the way to the porch swing. "Maybe the meds are working, if you're feeling better."

Lucy didn't say anything, but she sipped her tea and looked out at the lush hayfield separating the big house from the main road. And I took in her frail, pale body in my periphery—so different even from the last time I saw her. Her house slippers dragged on the wooden floorboards with every slow swing.

"Thank you for being in our lives, Blair." Her voice wavered as she said it, and she stopped to clear her throat. "I know you're sixteen, with big plans for university, and a whole life ahead of you. It's a big ask, and I promise I'll love you all the same if you tell me I'm being a selfish jerk."

I turned to look at her, catching the glassiness in her eyes and the way her small smile faltered. "You know I'd do anything you asked me to do."

"Look out for my boys? When . . . when they don't have me here to make sure they're staying out of trouble, and not fighting with each other, and . . ." She stopped to aggressively wipe the tears running in rivulets down her cheeks. And I did the same, my jaw quivering as I struggled to find words.

"I will," I choked out. "You know I will."

"I really hoped I would be having this conversation with you before your wedding one day. You know the whole 'look after my baby for me' speech." She sniffled, blinking rapidly to clear the pooling in her eyes. Denver's seemingly random proposal suddenly made perfect sense to me; she'd likely had a very similar heartfelt conversation with him recently. "And we can hold out hope for a miracle, but I don't think it's coming. So I want you to know now how lucky we are to have you—how lucky he is. I couldn't ask for a better daughter."

I grabbed her hands in mine, smoothing my thumb over her soft skin. No longer caring enough to keep up with wiping away every tear hanging from my jaw, or the snot running from my stinging nose. I swallowed thick saliva, fighting to breathe as I stared into the eyes of the woman I considered my second mother. A woman who had given me so much, and who looked completely at peace with this conversation—as if she innately knew I would follow through with looking out for her boys and taking care of her baby. Lucy trusted me like I was her own daughter, and I fell into her. My head resting on her shoulder as I wept, letting her stroke my hair softly.

"I know, honey. It's going to be okay. You'll all have each other, and it'll all be okay."

Denver

July seventh is a weird day on the ranch. Has been since the last birthday we had with Mom, when Dad carried her out to a lawn chair set out on the grass and we pretended like she'd be around for a hundred more birthdays to come. We ate our weight in the delicious food Kate made, while filling the hot summer air with stories and laughter. Blair sat on my lap, drinking fruit punch and running her fingers through my hair. When Mom got tired, Dad brought her to bed, and the rest of us stayed up until two o'clock in the morning around a bonfire.

But it's been different without her. Dad shows up at the ranch twice a year—to commemorate her birthday and the day she died. We have an uncomfortable family dinner, always without Austin, and I try my damnedest to keep things lighthearted.

Hopping out of the shower, I send Aus one last text invite for dinner. I know he won't come, but I can't help shooting my shot at getting everyone together. For Mom. For Grandpa.

The walk to the big house is slow and torturous until I see Blair's vehicle parked out front. Then my pace quickens, until I'm practically at a jog. Taking the front porch stairs two at a time, and blowing through the screen door. With one long exhale as I stroll down the hallway, I play it *totally* cool walking into the kitchen. In a split second, the wind deflates from my sails when Blair is nowhere in sight.

But my dad is.

"Hey, Dad." I give him a nod hello, immediately heading for a cold beer out of the fridge.

He briefly looks up from where he's drawing with Odessa at the table. "Hey, kid."

I fish a key out of my pocket to crack open the beer, then take a swig and lean against the counter next to where Kate's chopping up vegetables. Mid-dice, Kate casually mutters, "She's over at Cassidy's. Maybe you should text her and ask if she wants to stay for dinner."

I nearly choke on my drink. Does *everyone* around here have bets placed on us getting together or what?

"I'm not subjecting her to this shit show," I say under my breath.

Just then, Blair walks into the room, instantly invigorating the overall energy with her sunshine smile. "Bennett Wells? No way!"

She rushes around the side of the table, wrapping him in a hug, and Dad smiles for what's probably the first time all day.

"I heard you were back in town," he says. "Didn't expect to find you out here causing trouble after all these years, though."

Probably also the most Dad has *spoken* all day.

Blair steps back, smiling at him. "Yeah, my best friend is Red's baby mama, so I've been here a lot lately. But what are you doing here?"

I wince and take a sip of beer, waiting for the hammer to drop and all the happiness in her tone to dissipate in an instant.

"Oh, uh . . . w-well . . ." Dad starts to stammer.

Jackson clears his throat. "It's Mom's birthday. Dad always comes to have dinner with us."

"Oh, shit." Blair turns to look at me, eyes awash with concern.

"Bad word," Odessa pipes up.

"I didn't . . . Somehow I didn't put two and two together when I looked at the date this morning." Blair crosses her arms over her chest. "I'll leave you all to your family time."

"Stay," Dad takes the word right out of my mouth. "Lucy would want you to stay."

"I don't want to intrude. . . ."

Clearly not in the mood to argue, Dad pulls out Austin's chair for her with a huff. And Blair cautiously takes a seat— fully aware that Austin sits in that exact spot at the table, and always has.

Looking at me from across the room, she mouths his name with a confused knitting in her brows.

I mouth back that I'll tell her later and head to the pantry to hunt for a bottle of wine. Finally finding a white that seems like it might be fancy enough for Blair, I step back into the kitchen to find her and Dad in a lively conversation about her time in Vancouver.

Kate and Jackson seem equally as confused by Dad's change in demeanor, but the three of us breathe a collective sigh of relief. Because this is infinitely better than any previous dinner with Dad, where conversation was stilted, and nobody mentioned Mom despite it being her birthday.

I slide a glass of wine to Blair and sink into a chair, watching her be the daughter my dad had always hoped for.

"You okay?" she quietly asks when Dad gets up to grab himself a fresh drink.

"So much better now." I study the summer freckles starting to pepper her cheeks, craving the soft feel of her skin under my hardened fingers. "You don't have to stay, if you don't want to."

"I want to stay." She raises her glass to her lips. "If you want me to . . ."

"I do."

"Where's Aus?"

"He . . . uh." I lower my voice so it's barely audible. "He doesn't speak to Dad, so he doesn't come to these."

The surprise on her face makes sense, given the fact that our dad was always closest with Austin growing up. I guess that's why his leaving seemed to have had the biggest impact on my eldest brother.

When Dad sits back down, Kate is right behind him with food. Setting plates in front of us, heaped with smoked chicken breast, salad, and green beans straight from the garden.

Thanks to Blair, there's dinner conversation for the first time in over a decade. There's laughter. There's reminiscing, and talk about rodeos, and even a very heated debate over the best current country artist.

Blair glances over at me with every break in conversation, filling my heart until I'm sure it'll burst. And when her foot taps mine under the table, I'm sure of one thing.

Beryl is winning five dollars.

Blair Hart is going to be my girl again before this summer ends.

Blair

Cecily saunters through the screen door holding two of the largest pitchers full of sangria I've ever seen, then points her chin toward the river trail, and our girl gang starts toward it. Odessa's running far ahead, insisting she get to the riverbank before we show up and "scare the frogs away." Kate—with Rhett on her shoulders—is loaded up with sand toys, sunscreen, and beach towels. Cass has Hazel in a baby carrier on her chest, and a cooler backpack on her back. Cecily's carrying drinks, with a sleeve of plastic cups precariously tucked under her chin. And I'm packing enough food to keep us fed for a full week, on the off chance we somehow can't find our way back to the big house. Though those pitchers of sangria might be the trick to accidentally getting lost.

A ragtag bunch, sweating and struggling to make it to the river in the sweltering July afternoon. When we finally drop our things on the rocky shore, I'm immediately stripping down to my bathing suit and gingerly stepping across hot rocks until the cold water rushes around my legs. Then I plunge into the glacier-fed river, letting it clear my mind and rejuvenate my body like it has so many times in my life.

I emerge with a body spackled in goosebumps, watching as the best group of girlfriends I've ever known sits together, laughing and drinking. I didn't get to know Kate as well as I would've liked to before I left Wells Canyon back in the day, and I only met Cecily a few months ago, but they've welcomed me in with open arms, giving me some much-needed relaxation amid the chaos in my life.

After wringing the water from my hair, I settle into a spot beside Cass. Cecily passes me a red plastic cup filled to the brim with sangria—so full, in fact, that the liquid sloshes down my arm when I move it.

"So, I'm sorry the invite is super late, but Aus and I would love it if you'd come to our wedding in three weeks."

Lowering the cup from my lips, I swallow the sweet liquid and nod excitedly. "Of course I'll be there. I'm honored you'd invite me."

"I was worried you'd be offended because I waited this long!" She smiles sweetly, stretching her legs out in front of her. "I just didn't want anything to be awkward for you and Denny."

Kate turns to look at us from where she's stacking rocks with Rhett. "But now it won't be, since word on the street is that you two are"—she creates a circle with her finger and thumb and glides her other index finger in and out of it. The other two women begin howling with laughter, creating such a scene that even Odessa stops what she's doing to stare at us in confusion.

"Good God, the town gossips never rest, do they?" I groan, tossing my head back to feel the sun bake my face. When we were teens, I purposely skipped sunblock on my cheeks because Denver loved my summer freckles. "For the record, we're not doing that."

"Well then, if it's weird for you to be around him, know there's no hard feelings if you decide not to come," Cecily says.

"I wouldn't miss it for the world." I shoot her a smile. "Anyway, Denver and I are fine. We agreed to be friends—no awkwardness."

Friends. We've nearly kissed a few times when we've hung

out alone as "friends," but that's likely because it's muscle memory. For years we couldn't handle a single moment of privacy without jumping each other's bones. Friends is easier, because I have no interest in being part of his fuckboy games, despite my admission in a moment of weakness.

Do you ever think about me the way I think about you?

All the time.

"Kudos to you. I don't think I could be friends with any of my exes," Kate remarks. Wide-eyed, Cecily nods aggressively in Kate's direction.

"We were best friends for a long time before we started dating, though, so maybe that's why it doesn't feel weird to me? Plus, that was years ago. Seems silly to hold a grudge over mistakes we made as kids."

Cass reaches over and silently squeezes my thigh.

"We've actually hung out a few times now, too. *As friends.* He came over to visit my mom, and gave me a ride home from the rodeo, and brought lunch to my office."

Kate raises a brow. "And you haven't . . ."

I hold up three fingers. "Scout's honor. Haven't even kissed."

Admittedly, we were close, though. If Brickham hadn't barged into my office, I'm not even sure we would've stopped at kissing.

"*Incredible.* You have some serious self-control," Kate says. "Well, I'm glad we can all hang out without anybody feeling weird."

"Definitely. No weirdness."

None at all. Except he and I still haven't discussed our conversation from a few days ago.

Everyone slowly becomes preoccupied with books or babies, so I grab the AirPods from my beach bag and lean back on my elbows. When I pick up my phone to choose a playlist, I find a text message instead.

Denver: If you could be any
inanimate object for the day,
what would you be?
Blair: Depends who's asking and
how they got my number.

Somehow, he seems to have kept the same number since
his very first cell phone. But I ask anyway, because I don't
want him knowing I've had it saved in every phone I've ever
owned.

Denver: You left in the middle of a
conversation. I had no choice
but to grab a business card from
your desk.
Blair: Refrigerator, because
they're full of food all the time.
Why?
Denver: I told you I want to know
all about you.
Blair: And that's what you chose
as your first question?
Denver: It popped up in my head
first.
Denver: Are we going to talk
about the other day?
Blair: That was the second
question to pop up, or what?
Denver: It hasn't left my brain
since the moment it happened,
actually.
Blair: Give me a ride home after
we finish our drinks by the river.
We'll talk then.

Denver: Only if you promise not
to puke in my truck
Blair: I make no such promises,
but I bet it's a risk you're still
willing to take

Part of me is aching to chug the rest of my drink and go find Denver. Another part of me is terrified about what will happen when I'm alone with him again. The moment he looks at me, I'm a goner.

A little over two hours later, Cass stares at me from her front porch with a look that speaks volumes. "Be careful, okay?"

"I will be." My lips crook into a smile I'm hoping is reassuring.

"I don't have a problem with Denny, or even with you two together. I love both of you. But I know you had a bit of a hard time after you broke up, and I also know what he's like now."

A bit of a hard time is the understatement of the century. Never wanting to worry the people around me, I put on a brave face back then rather than confiding in my best friend about the extent of the situation. Queen of *fake it 'til you make it.*

"Babe, I'm fine—swear."

"You love really hard, and I don't want you to get hurt if the feelings aren't reciprocated."

"It's just a ride home because, between the heat and Cecily's potent sangria, I probably shouldn't drive. Nobody's falling in love."

She points her head toward where Denver's leaning against the hood of his pickup. "Have fun."

I turn and smile at him, waving a quick goodbye to Cass over my shoulder and trying to disguise the extra spring in my step while I walk across the crunchy gravel to his truck. Obviously, it's not the same truck he had back when we were seventeen, but sliding onto the dark leather passenger seat, breathing in the faint smell of his cologne, and rolling the window down to feel the sunshine on my bare arm still feels a lot like it used to. Like home.

Denver hops into the driver's seat, and the diesel engine rumbles to life, filling my nostrils with yet another nostalgic scent. I swallow hard, watching his tanned forearms flex as he shifts the manual transmission. Thick veins branch under his skin, begging to have my fingertips tracing them. I keep an eye on his strong jaw, with light brown stubble catching sunlight, in my periphery as we pull away. It's no wonder all the girls in town have been chasing after him in the years since I left, and a dull ache takes up residence in my chest when I consider how many of them have sat in this seat.

"Do you need to go straight home?" he asks when the truck rattles over the cattle guard at the end of the driveway.

"Why? Have somewhere else in mind?"

I'm openly flirting now, I'll admit. If the rumors are true, he's incapable of any commitment beyond a single night. Cassidy says I love too hard, but I had plenty of one-night stands and short-term relationships in Vancouver. They were a welcomed distraction. Something to quiet the storm in my brain. Maybe I can do the same thing here. Get it out of my system, then move on to the things I *should* be prioritizing.

"There's a place I want to show you," he says.

"I have nowhere else to be." Nor anywhere I'd rather be than here with him.

Rather than heading left, toward town, his large hands glide over the steering wheel, spinning it to the right. When we reach cruising speed, I twist my hair around until it creates a makeshift bun at the nape of my neck, and sink into the seat. Warm summer air whips around in the cab, carrying the aroma of freshly cut hay and the crackling sound of tires on a dirt road.

Aside from Koe Wetzel's hushed voice coming from the radio, it's comfortably silent between us. We've never needed to fill the space with unnecessary chitchat, and there's something magical about being with a person who feels so much like an extension of yourself you don't need to do anything except coexist. Despite the years, the trauma, the heartbreak, Denver Wells is always going to be that person for me.

"I missed this," he says after a few minutes of silence, which he clearly spent lost in thought with me.

"Me too," I admit. "It's been really nice to be home, actually."

"So much so that you're referring to Wells Canyon as home again?"

They say home is where your heart is. Fourteen years away, and I didn't give my heart to anyone else. Because how could I? It was back here in Wells Canyon . . . with him.

So—

"Yeah, it's always been home." I shift in my seat. "I loved my life in Vancouver, and didn't expect to be back here, but . . ."

"I get it." His hands aggressively twist around the leather-wrapped steering wheel. Then he turns off the road onto a trail that's barely wide enough to fit the truck. And he stops.

"Okay, it's safest if we walk from here." He leans an elbow on the center console to get a better look at my footwear. Strappy sandals with a slight heel—hardly appropriate for walking on pavement, never mind on an uneven dirt trail. "But that's not an option, since you're a city girl now, apparently."

"I take offense to that statement. Just because I dress nicer than I used to doesn't mean I can't hold my own in the country."

"Then unbuckle your seat belt, and be ready to bail out of the truck if I tell you to."

My face twists in horror. "What the hell are we about to do?"

"I'm taking you somewhere special."

"To my early grave?"

"Not if we're lucky."

With a groan and a lurch, the truck starts up a steep hillside, along a path that the majority of civilization wouldn't deem worthy of being called a road. Twisting and winding along the mountainside, up steep embankments, past terrifying cliffs. Denver grips the steering wheel, never letting his eyes leave the path, giving the truck just enough *oomph* to get over each knoll and pothole. The views are stunning—not that I can look out the window long enough to appreciate them, because I'm staring at the door handle, and having a mild panic attack about the idea of leaping from a truck as it careens off the edge of the road.

Reaching the top, both he and the truck shudder an exhale when we come to a stop in front of the best view of the Wells Canyon valley I've ever seen. And finally I'm able to quit nervously picking at my cuticles.

I throw open the passenger door, taking a deep breath, and step onto compact earth. The view extends far beyond Wells Canyon, likely allowing a sightline all the way to Sheridan, if you squint hard enough. The ranch, the distant ski hill, and a sea of treed hilltops.

"Wow, it's gorgeous up here. How did you come across this place?"

He walks around the truck and drops the tailgate, motioning at me to come over. "I did a lot of driving around by myself after you were gone. Eventually, even the never-ending backroads come to an end, so I started driving wherever I thought was wide enough for my truck."

He gives me a hand onto the tailgate, then reaches into a

strategically placed cooler and pulls out two bottles of beer—hesitating for a moment before offering me one. "All I have is beer-flavored water, or whatever your hoity-toity ass called it."

"The dirty ice water sloshing around in the bottom of the cooler probably tastes better," I tease, elbowing him in the side but accepting the beer with a smile. "But the beer's more sanitary, so thank you."

The cool liquid goes down better than expected, with the sun on our backs and a picturesque view, legs dangling from his tailgate. I press the amber bottle to my neck, sighing at the refreshing cold against my flushed skin, and beads of condensation run down my chest.

"How often do you come out here?" I ask.

How often do you bring other girls here?

"Not as often lately." The bottle rim hovers in front of his parted lips for a moment as he thinks. "We split up Mom's ashes because the three of us couldn't agree about what to do for her. I actually tossed my portion into the wind up here the spring after she died. So for a while, I was here all the time."

My heart sinks, and I spin to sit cross-legged facing him, resting my elbows on my knees. "I'm so sorry I wasn't there."

"It would've been weird for you to be there . . . considering everything. But I thought you'd like to come see it now."

I nod silently, internally battling with the urge to reach out and touch him. His right hand is resting on the truck bed, ripe for the taking. His callused palm, warm and strong, would fit in mine perfectly.

"How are you doing? Your mom, moving back here, Brickham's dumbassery. You have a lot going on."

I laugh under my breath to keep from crying. "Not to mention babysitting Hazel, helping wrangle my nephew, making sure my dad's okay, being around you all the time. But honestly, I'm fine. It's nothing I can't handle."

So maybe I'm actually flailing, fighting to keep my head

above water. But I'm not drowning—*not yet*—so that's basically the same as being fine.

He stares at me, breaking down every wall with the hollowing of a dimple in his right cheek. As he takes a swig of beer, his eyes don't leave mine, and right when it feels like every atom of oxygen has left the air between us, he opens his mouth.

"You're fine." His look of disbelief has me feeling the need to double down.

"Yep, sure am." I give him a weak smile. "Other people have worse things going on, so it feels silly to complain about my life."

"You don't have to do that."

"Don't have to do what?" I pick at the corner of the beer bottle label.

"Diminish everything you're going through. Pretend like you're managing totally fine. Cut the crap—give me five seconds of honesty."

If looks could kill, I'd be telekinetically tossing him off the cliff. "I'm not *pretending*."

"Bullshit." His voice echoes in the beer bottle, and in my skull.

"Sorry, do you want to talk about who among us isn't managing life well?" The label would've peeled in one clean strip, if I wasn't suddenly shaking. I cram the small piece of ripped paper into my pocket and glare at him. "I have responsibilities, Denver. Yeah, it fucking *sucks* sometimes, but there's no sense crying about it. Crying isn't going to change the fact that my mom's slowly forgetting her whole life. It's not going to change the fact that I left my job, apartment, and friends to move back here. It's *definitely* not going to take any work off my plate. I think my method of keeping my head down and quietly handling shit is a lot more mature than partying and sleeping with every girl in town."

I pray he didn't notice the way my voice cracked at the end of that last sentence.

I shut my eyes, taking a long, calming yoga breath. And when I finally work up the nerve to look at him, expecting to see him ready to throw down, Denver's just smiling at me.

"See? Was a little bit of honesty so hard?" His bottle clinks against mine. "All I was getting at is you don't need to pretend like you have it all together. Not around me. I know you well enough to know when you're faking it."

I shake my head. "You don't know me—"

"That's also how I know you weren't lying in your office the other day."

Did the sun crank the heat right up? I tug at the hem of my shirt, desperate for a light breeze, anything to help with the sudden hot flash I'm experiencing. His predatory gaze nearly has me tripping over myself to get to him, to sit on his lap like I did in Colt's truck. That night it took everything in me not to invite him into my bed, and yet he was still there—not literally, but figuratively, Denver was there. He was the throbbing pulse between my legs when I lay in my bed alone. And the memory of his hand grabbing my belt buckle on the dance floor, and of him toying with the inseam of my jeans, was the reason I came so hard I screamed into a pillow.

But I can deal with the hallucination version, because he won't break my heart. The real deal is far messier.

"Denver, I can't . . ." When his face falls, I add, "I didn't mean to give you the wrong impression by asking for a ride. I really missed having you as a friend, but I'm not the kind of girl who has casual flings."

Five seconds of *dishonesty*.

Casual is all I've been for the past decade. But staring at him here, with the setting sun illuminating the gold streaks in his eyes, I know I can't do that with him, as much as I'd like to. The lovelorn piece of me can't handle it.

Then his downtrodden expression turns into a dimpled smile. "You think that's what I want?"

"I mean . . . yeah. It's what you do, right?" I throw my hands up. "It's a small town, and for some ungodly reason, people thought I should hear about every girl you slept with while I was away. It was a lot."

Both a lot, in terms of numbers, and a lot, in terms of the effects every story had on my mental health.

"So when you mentioned me doing things *to women,* you weren't talking about the murders? Good, *good.*"

"Denver, please." I roll my eyes.

"They usually beg for their lives more convincingly than that."

Typical. Change the subject by turning this whole thing into a joke the exact moment I try to get serious.

"Okay, I'm not having this conversation with you then. Forget I said it, and take me home."

"Sorry, I'll quit fucking around." He drags a slow hand down his face with a groan. "I really hate this place sometimes, ya know?"

"Same."

"I didn't know things would get back to you. . . . I also didn't think you'd care, if I'm being honest. You actively avoided me when you came to visit—people told me things too, Blair. I know you did everything you could to avoid seeing me. Then you didn't move back after graduation like you said you would."

"Why would I move back? For what? You were the only reason I ever planned to, and you'd moved on." A tremor racks my body, and I chew my bottom lip to keep from crying while I frantically turn away from him. My calf smacks into the tailgate when I swing my legs down and a curse slips out under my breath. My eyes flit from treetop to treetop, intentionally avoiding looking anywhere in his direction.

The fucker notices, too, because the truck rocks with the

movement of his weight, and he jumps off. Then he's standing in front of me, caramel and chocolate eyes studying every movement in my face.

"There's no moving on from you. Not then, now, ever."

I scoff. "Now I'm calling bullshit. All the other girls—"

"Weren't anything serious. You were my first love, and you'll be my last. I'm done. I found the girl when I was thirteen, and I haven't been serious about anyone since. I'm not looking for a quick fuck with you, Blair. The younger me messed up, but I would never do something to intentionally hurt you."

"The *fucking* audacity," I mutter under my breath. Wouldn't do anything to hurt me, except he has time and time again, whether he knows it or not.

"What?"

"Oh, just wondering to myself how you can sit here and say that, when you know people have told me things. Things that make your last sentence complete and utter *bullshit*. Because you've already done shit to intentionally hurt me."

"I genuinely don't know what you're—"

"Shelby!" I yell. My friend's name rattles down the valley to town, repeating in a cacophony of echoes to haunt me. The pain of hearing it repeatedly is almost worth it, because Denver looks like he's ready to throw himself off the cliff. And, even though I know I would jump immediately after him, a part of me wants the satisfaction of his cries reverberating in the canyon.

"What the fuck about Shelby? You thought that wouldn't hurt me?" I'm breathing fire, and still he doesn't back away. "You thought I wouldn't care about that? Guess what, Denver. I *fucking* cared."

"I can explain."

I tilt my head, waiting to hear what garbage he spews before I fully unleash every emotion I've bottled up over the years. Ready to drop the act, lose the smile I've worn while listening to people talk about my ex like his behavior should be a funny joke to me.

"Well, the explanation is shit. But, honestly, I didn't think you were ever coming back. You were gone *fourteen years*. A full fucking decade of sleepless nights, of drunk phone calls from any number but mine so I could hear your sleepy voice, of driving up here on the hard days so I could scream at the top of my lungs." He rubs quickly at his eyes, and when his hands fall on top of mine, I don't pull away. I remember the calls in the middle of the night with nobody on the other end of the phone—in fact, I eventually changed my number, paranoid I had a stalker. The calls stopped after that, of course. Now knowing it was him, the knot in my stomach cinches tighter.

His thumb rubs across the back of my hand. "Shelby and I never had sex, for the record. Just drinking, dancing, kissing. And I know that's still not right. I shouldn't have slept with anyone, or even fucking *looked* at anyone. If there was a single shred of hope left in me that you'd come back, I would've held out for as long as I needed to."

"I didn't expect you to take a vow of celibacy. But, come on. . . . She's one of my friends. I don't get why you thought it was a good idea, if you've really cared about me all this time."

There's a slow bob of his throat and he gnaws at the inside of his cheek. "I wish I could say I made better choices over the last decade. You might not have asked for celibacy but, damn, would I love to tell you there's been no one since you. And I knew Shelby was a bad idea, which is why I didn't let it go any farther . . . *fuck*, I should've stayed away altogether."

I shake one of his hands away so I'm free to dab at the corner of my eye to stop the stupid, dramatic, unnecessary tear from falling. Lord knows, I've cried enough over him.

"I'm sorry. For Shelby. For every other girl. The last thing I wanted was to do anything that would hurt you again. I fucked up, and I understand if you don't trust me, but I can swear on my dead mom's grave—which is *literally* right where we are now—it's only ever been you for me."

"Why?" I squint to make out his face through blurred vision and stinging eyes. "Why me, when I wasn't willing to give you the life you wanted?"

"I only wanted a life with you, Bear." The nickname rolls off his tongue and sends my stomach somersaulting with it. "I'm painfully uninterested in any future that doesn't involve you."

"How many girls have you brought up here?" I ask, praying for the answer I need.

"Nobody knows about this place. This is where I come when I need to scream or swear or throw things off the cliff. When joking and laughing through the pain isn't cutting it."

A tear falls from my jaw, ricocheting off my bare thigh. "I shouldn't have left."

"If you hadn't gone away to school, this town would be forever stuck with Brickham as the only medical care. And I'm definitely biased, but you're better than he could ever hope to be." His smile matches mine, small yet genuine, only he has deep dimples in both cheeks. "So I lost you, but it was for the greater good."

"You're such a martyr." I drop his hand. "You said you come out here to scream?"

"Sometimes."

Placing my palm against his firm chest, I give him a push back and hop off the tailgate. The ground's made up of reddish rock, which crumbles underfoot, and I gingerly walk toward the cliff's edge. The closer I get, the more hair every wind gust is able to grab and twist.

Smoothing a hand over my wild locks, I take a deep breath and scream. As loud as I can, until my lungs are aching and my throat is on fire. I scream even when tears stream down my face, and I scream even when Denver grabs my hand and joins me. Our voices fill the valley, and soon it feels like the air in my lungs has been replaced with helium. The weight I've been quietly shouldering for months has disappeared, and if it weren't for the man holding tight to my hand, I might float away.

He turns to me when I've stopped to catch my breath, reaching with his free hand to wipe the wetness from my cheeks. "Feels good, doesn't it?"

The warmth of his touch makes my heart thunder in my chest like a zoo animal rattling the bars of its enclosure.

Fuck my fears—my heart is screwed anyway.

I grab a fistful of his shirt in my free hand and yank him toward me. Wasting no time, my mouth finds its way to his, and Denver wraps his arms snug around my waist. His tongue drifts along my lips, parting them, allowing a soft moan to escape me. He steals my breath and my thoughts and my bones with an explorative kiss. When he pulls back for air, there's a wisp of space between us. Our foreheads touch and, for the first time in years, my entire body relaxes with a deep exhale.

Blair

"**C**an I be honest for five seconds?" I ask breathlessly.

"Always."

"I'm scared." I shutter my eyes, and he presses soft kisses over my dampened eyelashes. "Of what's happening with my mom, of the way I had to toss my life plans aside to come back here, of you . . ."

"Of me?" He grabs either side of my face and tilts my head up, silently pleading for me to look at him. Then he holds my gaze with a worried expression etched into the space between his brows. A single tear—tiny while also big enough to drown us both—sits tucked against the corner of his eye.

"We were kids, and now we're different. You're . . ." I raise my hands like I'm weighing things out, seeking the right word.

A fuckboy, a playboy, a douchebag . . .

A grown man, a sweet guy, more handsome than ever before . . .

"Not the same boy I loved. I don't know you."

"Deep down, I'm the same boy. I still ride broncs, and love my family, and my favorite color is blue. And Blair, I'm still totally fucking crazy about you."

"I'm not the same person I used to be."

"Well, I personally think you're an even better version, based on what I know so far. And I'd *love* to know more."

"What do you want to know?" My wrists link behind his neck, pulling his chest into mine.

"Literally everything. The good, the bad, the random thoughts consuming your brain. I want it all. I want anything you're willing to tell me."

I can't help it. My lips capture his again.

"That's a lot," I mumble against his mouth.

"I have nothing but time." One more kiss, laced with relief, before he continues. "Are you in the mood for ice cream? I heard Lickety Split opened up shop for the summer at the start of the month."

"I should head home to be with Mom."

"Okay, sure, yeah." No hiding the defeat in his eyes, and I realize my words came out wrong.

"Not because I don't want to spend time with you. I just . . ."

"Have responsibilities that you're *totally* fine managing on your own—I know. Let's get you home."

I tug him into me for one last languid kiss, walking him backward to the truck. And when we climb inside, I take the middle seat, letting the heat of our touching thighs warm my bones. For the entire hour's drive to Wells Canyon, he clutches my hand with a grip tightened by fear.

Fear of losing each other. Fear that this moment is for today only.

It started with confusion when I walked in the door; Mom couldn't understand why I was home from school. Doctors had told us to go along with whatever she believed to be true, so we told her summer break had just started, and she relaxed. Then she got annoyed with my dad for insisting she sit down and let him barbecue. But the straw that broke the camel's back was my sister, Whit, showing up and loudly exclaiming that she had Mom's new medic-alert bracelet.

I intercepted my nephew, Jonas, by the front door and told him I needed help with my computer, forcing him to follow me to my bedroom. To my fake surprise, my laptop was working perfectly fine. Jonas side-eyed me, opening his mouth to call me out for lying, when something smashed in the kitchen. Then Mom screamed at Whit for being a bitch, and Dad raised his voice in a way that made the entire house fall still.

Despite the commotion ending a few moments ago, Jonas's hand is still hovering over the doorknob. "Are they okay out there?"

"I don't know," I admit. "Stay here for a second, okay, bud?"

He nods, stepping back from the door to let me brush past. And when I shut it softly behind me, leaving the ten-year-old as far away as possible from the adult bullshit he doesn't deserve to be part of, I take a deep breath.

"Are you guys okay?" I fake a cheery voice, finding Whit sitting on a kitchen stool with her knees to her chest, wiping silent tears. I step up next to her and rub my hand over her back. "I told Jonas to stay in my room for a minute."

Dad looks up from where he's knelt on the floor, picking up large chunks of glass. "Mom went to bed. She just . . ."

"Got confused and scared." I kneel across from him and pick up pieces of what seems to have been a salad bowl. "We know, Dad. If you want to go talk to her, I got this."

He stands with a groan and shuffles down the hall, stopping by my room to say hi to Jonas. In silence, I pick up the remainder of the glass, then wipe up the microscopic pieces with a damp paper towel. Before long, I'm settling in next to Whit with a glass of malbec from Mom's extensive collection. My sister slowly sips hers, furiously wiping the dampness from around her eyes, when we hear Jonas come strolling down the hallway. He flings his lanky body onto the couch, and even though he's wearing headphones, it's loud enough that we can hear the soundtrack to whatever game he's playing on his handheld device.

"This is fucked up," Whit says.

"So fucked up." I take a long drink of the dry wine, letting it linger on my tongue.

"Thank you for coming home, even though I know you hate it here. Dad couldn't manage on his own."

Sucking my teeth, I nod. "I actually don't mind being back. It's been . . . healing, in a way."

She raises an eyebrow.

"I had a change of heart."

"Is that so?"

She's not subscribing to my bullshit.

"Also, I kissed Denver today." I whisper the secret into my stemless glass—a largely hollow space that echoes my words back to me.

"*That* explains it. That's also the least surprising thing I've heard since I got here." She swirls her glass around in her hand thoughtfully. "Be careful, though."

"Cass warned me, too."

"Because we don't want to see you end up hurt again. You deserve the world, sis. If he's willing to give you that, I support it. But make sure he's all in before you fall headfirst."

"I am. I'm taking things slow. It was just a kiss . . . that doesn't mean anything."

She looks at me dubiously, not believing the words coming out of my mouth any more than I am. There's no such thing as *just a kiss* when it comes to me and him. Cass and Whit are the only people in the world who know I used to sneak him into my room at night. My sister's the only person who saw me have a breakdown after losing him, and was subjected to hearing all the details. She knows how deep my feelings for him run to this day.

"Okay, girls and boy." Dad enters the room, clapping his

hands together and smiling broadly. "Who's hungry? I made homemade hamburgers."

We eat in a weird state of limbo, unsure whether we should be quiet and mindful of Mom—who's apparently going to bed at seven p.m.—or be our typical boisterous selves in an effort to maintain some normalcy for Jonas. Opting to prevent another issue with Mom, we talk about nothing exciting, using slightly quieter voices than normal, and Whit leaves with Jonas the moment they finish their last bite of food.

Then Dad and I clean the kitchen in silence, the weight of the evening hanging over us, but neither feeling comfortable broaching hard topics with each other. He and I are the same that way; no sense panicking about the shitstorm when we can board up the windows and weather it alone. It's not that we aren't close, per se. My family's simply never been the type to circle up for a group hug, or talk about hard things, or ask anyone for help.

Retreating to my bedroom, I'm overcome by the need to have the same comforting feeling Denver gave me on the mountaintop.

> **Blair:** Hey, are you busy?
> **Denver:** Not too busy for you, why?
> **Blair:** It was a shitty night with Mom. . . .
> **Blair:** Do you want to come over?

From the moment my finger taps the Send button, I begin to panic. And pacing around my room for the half hour it'll take for Denver to drive to my house isn't feasible. I'll wear out the damn carpet. So I opt for an everything shower, letting water and tears run freely while I soap and scrub and shave nearly every inch of my body. By the time the water's too cold to stand, I'm cried out and wishing I'd held off on inviting Denver over.

That's solidified by a quick glance in the foggy mirror. I swipe my hand across the glass, clearing enough space to discover that my eyes are bloodshot, cheeks puffy, and chest blotchy.

Great, he's going to take one look at me and run the other way.

Clasping the towel wrapped around my body, I trudge back to my bedroom, hoping I can grab my phone in time to tell Denver to stand down. Because all I really want to do is curl up in bed, watch a silly little rom-com, and fall asleep.

"About time. I was starting to think you were pranking me." Denver's leaning back on his elbows on top of my bed, and I momentarily freeze at the sight of him.

I shut the door and hold the towel tighter to my body, moving quickly to the closet.

"You're here already? How?" I glance at the clock to find it's been a full forty-five minutes since I sent the text. "Oh, shit. Sorry, I must've lost track of time. Can you, um, turn around so I can put clothes on?"

"Nothing I haven't seen before, but fine." Lifting his feet onto the bed, he spins to face the headboard. "Are you okay?"

Aside from cursing myself for not owning cuter pajamas?

"Yeah, I'm okay now." I reach for the best available option—a shorts and tank set. Except you can see my nipples clear as day through the thin pink fabric, so I tug the closest available hoodie on over top.

"You don't have to be okay," he says. "Remember?"

I sink onto the soft mattress next to him, tucking my feet under my butt. Our knees briefly collide when he turns to face me, and the most simple of touches reignites the fire in my core that burned for the entire drive home earlier.

And I'm not lying when I say, "I *am* okay now. Truth."

"Did you keep my hoodie for the last decade?"

I gulp, embarrassment creeping from my belly up to my chest and neck. *Yes*, I kept his hoodie—*hoodies*, technically, because I have a number of sweatshirts and T-shirts tucked away—but I wasn't anticipating him noticing.

Denver flicks the wet ends of my hair over my shoulder to check the small logo printed on the front for confirmation, and the dimples in his cheeks pull me in. "Should I tear apart your closet and see how much of it technically belongs to me?"

He moves like he's going to stand, and my fingers wrap around his thick bicep. "Stop. It's a good hoodie. That's the only reason I kept it."

"God, you are the *worst* liar I've ever met. I remember lending you this sweatshirt, and you said it was a complete waste of pocket space because you couldn't fit your hands in the pocket with your mittens on. You complained about it all winter, yet kept wearing the damn hoodie anyway." He toys with the pocket's edge, and the way I feel his hardened hands through the tattered cotton makes me wish I hadn't worn it—*or anything*—to bed at all. I'm tempted to stretch my arms above my head, test him to see if he'd touch my bare skin.

"You got me. It truly is a terrible hoodie. The hood is abnormally small, too." I reach up, blissfully aware of his eyes cutting to the sliver of exposed skin on my lower stomach, and pull the hood over my damp hair.

"Maybe you have a big head." He tugs the hoodie strings, staring into my eyes with a crooked smile as the hood bunches around my face. "Confirmed. Big head. You look like you're starring in *The Shining*."

I playfully slap him on the leg. "You can have it back then, if you're so sure it's a problem with my head."

Hands on the bottom of the hoodie, I pull it over my head in one swift motion.

"I doubt it'll still fit—" His sentence is cut short when his eyes fall to my chest, Adam's apple bobbing with a swallow.

Oh right, I was wearing the sweater for a reason.

"Blair, are tho—did—uh," he stammers, tripping over himself while practically drooling like a dog. It would be a lie to say I'm not flattered. A throaty *fuck* is the only word he eventually manages to get out before I step in to save him from himself.

"Yes, they're pierced. And it's generally bad form to stare."

"I feel like they're staring at me. It's a dominance thing—I can't look away now."

"Told you that you don't know everything about me anymore," I quip.

"And I told you I want to know everything. Never been more true than right fucking now." For a brief second, his eyes cut to mine, and I can see how hungry he is. How close this man is to becoming fully feral. How badly he wants me is painted all over his face, and it makes my thighs clench together.

"Oh, yeah?" Tuning out the warning bells and the percussion of my terrified heartbeat, I place a finger under the thin strap on my left shoulder and slip it down.

There's a dull throb behind my pelvic bone, and I barely breathe while his eyes follow my every move. When I pluck the other strap in my fingers, his hand covers mine, helping slide the strap down my arm.

His tongue skates across his bottom lip, leaving it glistening and kissable. Shaking slightly, he rests a palm on my arm. No more than an inch from where my right breast is ready to be set free. And if my chest was anything more than an A-cup, I'm sure the pajama tank wouldn't be enough to keep them contained without straps.

Denver's thumb stretches to test the waters with a graze of side-boob. Getting no pushback from me, he exhales a strained, rough "fuck it."

Within a heartbeat, my shirt's bunched around my waist, his mouth is ravaging mine, and he's massaging my breasts—

the budded nipples pressed into his firm palms. With a needy moan I tumble backward on the bed. And he hovers over me, pulling the oxygen from my lungs through a mind-altering kiss.

I gasp for air when his lips leave mine to drag down my neck. Then his tongue glides over my skin, along my collarbone and down my chest, spreading gasoline over the fire in my core. I didn't invite him over here intending to have sex. At least, not consciously. But all I want is for him to fill the aching emptiness I'm suddenly overwhelmed by.

He draws back for only half a second—enough to get a good look at my new-to-him jewelry and let me pull my shirt completely off—before diving back in and forcing a hoarse moan from the back of my throat. His tongue encircles each nipple like a halo, flicking over the dainty barbells and sending a jolt of pleasure through me. Feeling my body buck under him, he huffs, and the hot forced air only drives me more wild.

I grip his muscular shoulders, letting my nails sink into his flesh. *I am not seriously going to come already.* I shake the thought away as he flicks across my pebbled nipple again.

Oh, fucking hell.

My toes curl as Denver moves to the opposite breast and licks at one while gently teasing the other between his fingers.

"Den—" I whisper-shout, pulling at his hair to get his attention.

"Mmmm." He hums as he licks a trail down my stomach, stopping at the waistband of my shorts, waiting until I lift my hips slightly and allow him to pull them down. My knees fall away from each other slightly, and he takes me in with a low growl. "*Fucking look at you.* You're the most gorgeous thing I've ever seen. Spread yourself, baby, show me what I've been missing."

I let my hand trail down between my breasts, over my

stomach, and down to my pussy. A dark gleam in his eye, he motions with his head for me to continue. So I press my fingers to my labia, splitting them for him to see.

I'm completely naked and spread wide for him, but I don't feel exposed at all. Even after all this time, his gaze is full of wanton lust when he looks at me. He wants me as badly as I still want him.

"You're already so wet, baby girl. You like when I tease your nipples?" He folds his tongue around one and my eyes roll back in my head for a second. "I can't believe you got them pierced. God, I thought I loved your tits before—but now?"

Insatiable.

Denver grips my hips, leaning to kiss my body, worshipping me from head to toe with the attentive drag of his tongue. Until I'm close to begging, needy for his hands or mouth to be relieving the pressure built at the apex of my thighs. His finger smooths over my clit, and he sucks on my breast, flicking his tongue over my nipple at the same time he slips a finger through my wetness.

There's a rumble in his chest when he slips one, then two fingers deep inside me. And I hold a palm over my mouth, struggling not to cry out as he fills me with a new need. I won't be satisfied until I have all of him. I know it.

He pulls his hand away and brings it to his mouth, then sucks his fingers clean of me with a hum of desire deep in his chest. It's as if he's just tasted the most exquisite dessert on Earth.

With a sated smile, he quietly says, "You keep insisting I don't know you anymore—I've *never* forgotten the way you taste. That sweet pussy of yours hasn't changed, baby. But you know what I really want to know about the new Blair?"

"What?"

"I need to know if you still sound the same when you're

coming for me," he mumbles against the crook of my neck, nipping at my delicate skin.

His fingers slip deep inside, pulling me closer to orgasm, while his mouth focuses back on my nipples. The fire engulfs me, and my back arches to be even closer to his touch. Within seconds of slow, methodical licks and his beckoning fingers, I'm moaning—*loudly*.

"Shhh, baby. You need to be good and quiet." He lays his free hand across my mouth, smiling with pride when I bite down on his flesh at the same moment an orgasm rips through me. And still, he doesn't stop sucking and flicking and fucking while I come back down from the high.

Denver rips his shirt overhead, all abs and tanned skin. Then I'm tugging at his waistband, desperate for him. His cock springs to life from under his sweatpants, and I take a moment to appreciate the man he's become.

Holy fucking shit—praise our lord and savior, or whatever.

He's always been made up of lean muscle, but as a man, there's a smattering of brown hair on his chest. And a thin, lickable trail from his belly button down to the promised land. A cock I've never gotten over. Maybe it's because it was the first I ever had, maybe it's because it was larger than most I've seen since, maybe it's because I've always loved the man packing it. And the tattoo that I . . .

"Wait. Is that a tattoo?" I shift closer to him, squinting to make out the black ink on his thigh—a splotch no bigger than a toonie about halfway between his knee and hip.

Seemingly taken aback, like he'd forgotten it was there, he looks down at his own skin. "Oh . . . yeah."

And when I figure out what the tiny design is, my heart does a weird bobbing action, unsure whether to sink or float. "Den . . . is that a bear?"

"Sheesh, I know Red's tattoo guy was a bit shady, but I didn't think he did *that* bad of a job. Of course it's a bear."

I really don't want to assume. *But how can I not?* Swallowing hard, I run my finger over it and look up at him.

"W-why?"

He brushes fallen locks of hair behind my ears. "Because Mom told me I could get a tattoo over her dead body. So . . . I did. Red hooked me up. I fucking *hate* needles, so it's never happening again."

Naturally, he's fine with the cattle brand embedded into his chest, but a tiny tattoo is too much. He's always been such a wimp when it comes to needles of any kind.

"I mean, why the bear?"

"That's a pretty silly question, *Bear.*" His soft smile matches my own, and his hand finds its way to mine. "You were the only thing I could think of at the time. It was the only tattoo that made sense to me. Right here, where your hand used to rest when we drove around in my truck all summer long."

I fight the burning in my lungs by kissing him, consuming him, and holding tight to his thigh. Overcome with both the need to have him and the need to never let him go again.

My sister and Cass were right about my tendency to fall hard, fast. I'm already in too deep. If he isn't all in, my heart will forever be a shattered mess on my bedroom floor. But if I'm a dead girl walking, I may as well savor every damn moment.

Finally breaking free of the kiss, I let myself get a good look at the intricate browns and golds in his eyes. "I want you to fuck me."

"Anything you want, baby."

"I have condoms in the top drawer." I point in the direction of my dresser and watch as Denver strolls across the room to retrieve one. Every muscle in his unfairly perfect body ripples and flexes with each step.

"I don't want to know why you have condoms." Denver's voice carries a tinge of jealousy and possessiveness.

I take the packet from his hand, and slowly tear open the wrapper. "We've *both* had sex with other people in the last decade, and I stole free condoms from the hospital I worked at."

A grumble starts in his chest, but is promptly stopped by me rolling the condom over the tip of his cock. Replaced by a resounding *fuck*. When it's rolled to the base of his shaft, I give him two slow pumps.

"But Den, you're the only one I've ever truly wanted. It's you, only ever you." I kiss him, stroking him slowly.

"Come here, baby." A hand cradling my skull, he slowly lowers me onto my back, then does a sweep of his palm under my head, making my hair splay out in every direction on the pillow. "I need you to know something, though."

I blink up at him, pressing my heels into his hamstrings. I need his thick cock inside me, instead of the position we're in, with the head inadvertently teasing me. Slipping up through the wetness, lightly grazing my clit, and sliding back down until it's positioned at my entrance. Over and over like a metronome clock counting down to my collapse.

"If we do this, everything else is over." He kisses my jaw. "If you're talking to some prissy bitch boy back in the city, it's done. I'm not sharing. I'm not risking losing you to somebody else. I'm going to keep you for life this time."

"There's nobody else." I tangle my hands in his hair, forcing his brown eyes to meet mine. "There never was."

"There never will be, either." His cock slides into me in one smooth motion, and for a few seconds neither of us moves, allowing me to adjust to him with focused breaths. Despite the slight sting before my muscles relax around his cock, having our bodies intertwined, and his lips pressed to mine, feels like coming home.

All the years feeling like I was missing something, I was homesick. But not for Wells Canyon. I was homesick for him.

For this.

My happy place.

I spent forever trying to forget Denver Wells. And having him claim me again makes me realize it was all for nothing, because I've always belonged to him. Arguing that fact was pointless.

With unhurried passion, we kiss and muffle each other's moans, like he suspected we would. There's comfort and love in his languid movement when he pulls back out before slowly filling me again. I explore every inch of his skin with my hands, skirting down his torso and cradling his firm ass, while he licks and sucks on my breasts, giving them the attention they so often don't get because of their smaller size. And pumps into me, slow and steady, like a calm heartbeat.

When our eyes meet between kisses, I regret every single decision I made in the past. I hate that I haven't had him like this every day. I hate that I broke us—*broke him*—and I can't help but feel like my life would've been better if I had stayed here.

"Baby," he says, stilling while fully seated inside me. "Why are you crying, Bear? Do you need me to stop?"

Oh God, am I seriously crying?

I swipe under my eyes, frustrated when my fingers turn up wet. "No, I'm just . . . I'm fine, honest."

Seeing right through my weak attempt at hiding my feelings, he gives me a look—refusing to move a muscle, even as my heels press to the backs of his thighs.

"Okay, *fine*. I'm overwhelmed. . . . Can you hold me? But don't stop. Just hold me."

If he thinks the request is bizarre, he doesn't say anything. One hand weaves into my hair, while the other wipes my eyes. And he doesn't let go, even as tears dampen my hair and the pillow. With our foreheads pressed together, he kisses me slowly, his tongue pushing past my lips to fill my mouth the same way his cock is filling my core.

Slipping a hand between us, Denver locates my clit and

tenderly massages in time with his thrusts, until my nails are creating small crescent moons in his back, and he's kissing me out of necessity to dampen my needy cries.

"Shhh. I know, baby," he whispers, lips brushing the shell of my ear. His fingers pick up the pace on my clit, and each deep thrust has me ready to come undone. With every sound I make—and every tear rolling past my temple—he simply whispers, "I know, baby. I know."

And I run my hands through his hair, desperate for all of him. Sinking the back of my head into the pillow and biting my lip, rolling my hips to feel him as deep as possible.

"*That's it.* That's my girl. As beautiful under me as I remember," he says softly. "Come for me, baby. Let go."

I whimper, eyes squeezed shut, doing my best to keep quiet as the tension builds between my legs. My skin's crawling with the need for release, and I shove a corner of the comforter in my mouth, racked with so much pleasure I need to scream. And in one crashing wave of gratification and emotion, I relax from head to toe.

Even with my legs shaking, tears pooled on my pillow, he doesn't stop kissing me, holding me, loving me.

"You're so *fucking* beautiful," he groans with his final shuddering pumps punctuating each word. When contentment washes over his face, I pull him to me for another kiss.

Every daydream I allowed myself to envision in my darkest moments comes flooding back, flashing like an old-school film behind my eyelids—dancing in the living room of our first home, walking down the aisle, racing on horseback across the ranch to make love under a tree in the mountains, holding our baby for the first time. A movie I played in my mind whenever I wanted to cause myself irreparable pain. Only now, I see it through a different lens, because maybe there's still time for our love story to happen.

Denver

She cried through most of our first time back together and, while that typically would be a sign to run for the hills, I knew it wasn't because she was regretting having sex with me. Hell, I was holding back watery eyes myself. Blinking back the sting of tears and the burn in my nostrils, I held on to her and fought to keep myself composed enough to be there for her. If I had fallen apart at that moment, Blair would've picked herself back up so she could be my support—and all I've been wanting is the chance to prove I can be that for her.

Being back in her childhood bedroom, holding her and kissing her, is something I've had thousands of dreams about over the years. Finally having her again was ineffable. So I kiss her to make sure she's not a figment of my imagination, wipe the tears from her reddened cheeks, and reluctantly pull out of her warmth.

"I'm sorry for crying." She sniffles, propping herself up on her elbows and watching as I peel the condom from my dick.

"Bear, you don't need to apologize." Tossing the rubber into a trash can next to her old desk, I turn and crawl up the bed to lie beside her.

"I'm sure the women you normally sleep with don't cry during it."

The way she's so hung up on the women I've slept with since her makes my stomach twist.

"Because there's no emotion in that sex. This is different . . . it's us." My fingers run up and down her bare thighs, and I watch her melt under my touch. "You have nothing to be jealous of, okay? None of them are you."

"Yeah?"

"Yes, baby." I give her hip a gentle squeeze on my fingers' slow exploration of her body. "I would rather have been right here with you for the last fourteen years."

"Me too. Maybe not right here, though. I'd hope we wouldn't still be sneaking around in my parents' house."

"Nah, we'd have a big house of our own, with a gorgeous view of the mountains from our king-size bed—not that I'd be looking at anything but you. And we'd be sneaking around so we didn't wake up the kids."

Okay, so I've put some thought into it.

Sniffling, she wipes at her eyes again. "You think?"

"If that's what you wanted. I'd give you anything you want."

Then. Now. Forever.

She sits upright with a groan. "I'm going to go to the bathroom—need anything? A drink? Snack?"

"All I need is for you to hurry back."

Her lips curl into a smile as she leans in for a quick peck, then she's wrapping herself in a fluffy gray robe and slipping out the door. And I'm alone in her room. For the most part, it looks the same as it did when we were kids—beige walls, white furniture, floral bedding. The glow-in-the-dark stars are gone, but after decades of light exposure, the shapes are still visible on the paint. I peel myself from the bed and peruse her room. Barrel racing buckles are arranged in neat rows on top of her dresser, surrounded by photos of Blair and Chief. Then pictures of Blair with her friends, including some that are more recent, with people I don't recognize. I'm thumbing a university graduation photo frame when her door clicks shut behind me.

"Are you going through my stuff?" She hops onto her bed, watching me. I have no shame in my snooping game, so I continue examining her decor.

"Next is your underwear drawer." I throw her a smirk over my shoulder.

"As if you didn't start there, perv." Blair ditches the robe and slides under the covers naked. "I have better drawers, though."

"*Better* than your underwear drawer?" No clue what that could mean, but now I *have* to know. I hover my hand over each knob, waiting to see if there's a reaction from her. She's failing miserably at hiding her discomfort as I move laterally to the far right of her dresser. "Baby, your poker face needs some help."

Bottom right.

Giving it a firm tug, I slide the drawer open to reveal dozens of notes, photos, every single memory Blair's ever had of me. With a breathy laugh, I carefully unfold a wrinkled piece of paper to find a drawing I'd made for Blair in eleventh-grade history class. It's fucking awful—Odessa could draw a better stick figure family—but Blair kept it despite everything.

"I think this was supposed to be a dog." I hold up the paper, pointing to a mess of brown circles.

"A Labrador, specifically. You were pretty proud of it back then."

"We make a very cute stick family. Look at the legs on you—total babe." I wink.

"You're a dork." She pats the bed next to her, and I meticulously fold the paper without creating new creases. Naked, I slip under the soft, cool sheets to hold her.

"You're one to talk. You're the one keeping fifteen-year-old notes, my cute little dork." I kiss the top of her head. "Can't believe you kept my shitty drawings and love notes."

"Of course I kept them."

"Are you okay after whatever was going on with your mom tonight? You know you can talk to me, Bear."

"I'm perfect, now that you're here," she drowsily mutters.

Her body curls around me, a leg slung over mine, soft fingers trailing along my chest. I wish she would lean on me. Let me carry some of her weight. But I understand why she doesn't. She's always been the type to handle hard things without making a fuss, without asking for help. I used to be the exception—she was safe to let down those walls and be honest with me. But I fumbled my responsibility, and now I'm stuck outside her inner circle.

Chest rising and falling against my side, her breathing slows with each exhale, until she's softly snoring in my arms. I stretch my arm to maximum capacity, doing my best not to jostle her, and flip the switch on the bedside lamp.

4,982 nights. That's how many nights I've spent missing her. Hating myself. Begging for sunrise. But the nightmare is finally over—I have her in my arms, and this time I'm prepared to do whatever it takes to keep her there.

Blair

The same as so many nights in our past, Denver slips back out my window before sunrise. I clutch the pillow he slept on to my chest, spooning it and taking slow, conscientious sniffs of his lingering scent, as if inhaling too quickly will make it dissipate faster.

My sister's worried voice rings in my ears. *Make sure he's all in before you fall headfirst.*

He said he was all in. He said I was the only one he's ever loved. He said a lot of sweet things—the same whispered promises he's broken in the past. I'm sure he'll find a way to let me down, and my entire world will fall apart like it did before.

Ignoring the churning in my stomach, I rip the pillow from its case, strip the sheets, and pad down the hallway to the laundry room at five a.m. to remove any traces of him from my bed. Then I spend hours doing anything to shut my brain off. I attempt yoga on the crisp grass, clean the kitchen, make breakfast for my parents, and spend twenty minutes convincing Mom to go for a walk with me.

Standing in the middle of the driveway, I squint up at the midmorning sun while I wait for Mom to find her shoes. In the skintight pocket of my biker shorts, my phone vibrates.

Denver: Hot or iced coffee?

I blink at the screen, debating how to answer. The question in itself seems innocent enough, but the inevitable follow-up scares me. If he asks me to have coffee with him . . . that's a date. And a date leads to *dating,* which lends itself pretty well to me being a wreck when the dating part comes to an end. Except these days I have people relying on me— and being incapable of taking care of my family isn't an option.

"Ready!" Mom calls out from the front door, zipping up her light hoodie. "Took me ages to find these darn shoes."

They were in the front closet, like always, but I know better than to say that.

"Probably because it's been forever since we got out for a walk." I smile at her, pulling my sunglasses from the top of my head and putting them on. "Whit's gonna meet us at the end of the street, too."

"Oh, good. I miss her."

My heart sinks, and I let out a meditative exhale. "Come on, let's go then. She's probably waiting."

Rather than chatting, Mom takes to quiet humming of old Broadway tunes while we walk, which isn't helpful for the chaos happening in my mind. Doesn't matter that the sun is shining, birds are chirping, and my mom's happier than I've seen in weeks; I can't shake the melancholia from my bones.

And when we stop outside of a blue cottage with a yellow door so Mom can tie her shoes, I decide to tell Denver that things need to end.

Denver: That wasn't a question
that typically requires somebody
to think about it for ten minutes.

Denver: Guess I'll bring both
kinds to your office this
afternoon.

Tell him it ends here. Clean break. No pain. I've never been
one for building walls, for setting boundaries, for knowing
how to keep my heart safe. But I need to try.

Blair: I'm not going to the
office today

My fingers and brain don't work in coordination, apparently. I stare at the bubble indicating that he's typing, watching it appear and disappear on repeat. Unable to catch a full
breath, my lungs ache with anticipation.

Denver: I'll deliver it to your front
door, then.
Blair: Denver, that's not a good
idea.
Denver: Another bad day?

I look over at Mom, who finally got her shoelaces tied on
the seventh try. It's not a bad day—*not at all*—and that's exactly why I can't jeopardize my own mental health. I need to
remain strong and put together, so I can relish her good days
and be her support for the bad.

Blair: No, I just need some time
alone with my mom.

Whit's waiting for us at the stop sign, and Mom gives her
a hug that makes up for the disaster from last night. And we
turn toward the Wells Ranch Road, aiming for a walking trail

that skirts town, running beside the Timothy River and through thick forest.

"Night and day difference from yesterday," Whit says quietly, hooking a thumb toward where Mom's a full twenty feet ahead like she's practicing for an Olympic speed-walking event.

"Thankfully. Poor Dad would probably quit the family if both of us were in a weird mood today."

She turns her head slightly, skirting around a tree branch fallen halfway across the trail. "Why are you in a weird mood? Last night you seemed cute and love drunk after kissing Denny."

"I snuck him into my room last night."

Besides Cassidy, Whit's the only person who knows how often Denver used to sneak into my room. Mostly because, at only two years younger than me, she was frequently still awake when he snuck in. I did a *lot* of her homework to stop her from telling our parents.

She slaps me on the arm. "You're close to thirty-two and still sneaking boys into your room?"

"Apparently." I kick a pebble down the trail like I'm dribbling a soccer ball. "I think it was a big mistake though. . . . I was feeling like total shit after everything with Mom. And asking him to come over seemed like a good idea, so I wouldn't be alone with my thoughts."

"Then you hooked up."

I scoff. "How dare you assume? *Okay*, yeah, we did. And now I'm messed up over it."

If we were still teenagers, I'd smack the smirk right off my sister's face.

"Sis, take it from somebody who's had some on-again-off-again with my ex. Follow your gut. If you're not feeling good about this, walk away before you're in too deep."

"You're right." I gnaw at a piece of chapped skin on my

lower lip. "I just . . . what if there's no such thing as getting over your first love?"

"Then I'm doomed to a life where Alex gets to hold power over me forever. I refute that idea." She grabs my hand, squeezing. "Do you think you're simply feeling nostalgic for the way things used to be, or do you actually love him still?"

I think about the way he held me last night, wiping my tears and kissing away every thought in my head. *I needed him, and he came.*

"What if—*hear me out*—part of me wants to take a risk and find out the hard way?"

"Then you should follow your gut, just like I said."

"But I'm terrified, Whit. He might hurt me all over again."

She nods. "He might. And if he does, it's gonna suck."

For a moment I stay quiet, listening to the crunch of compact dirt under my sneakers, waiting for her to add a *but.*

She doesn't.

So I do. "But . . . he also might not."

"Absolutely. He might not." Her lips roll into a flat smile. "Guess you need to decide which 'might' you want to bet on."

We turn a corner on the trail, coming to a fork I don't remember existing. Immediately Whit looks at me with wide eyes, then calls out for Mom.

Holding my palms to either side of my mouth, I scream, "Mom!"

Hearing nothing, I say, "Okay, it's fine. There's only two ways she could've gone. So we'll each take a trail and . . . jog, so we can catch up to her, since she was walking pretty fast."

Without another word, Whit takes off down the left trail, and I take the right. Running until my lungs burn and every breath brings me one second closer to collapse. When the trails converge again, Whit's waiting with her hands on her knees, keeled over, catching her breath.

"*Shit.* We gotta keep going. How long is this stupid trail again?"

Whit snaps her neck to look up at me. "It goes for another ten-ish kilometers. But we're closer to downtown now, so there's a bunch of spots where she could've exited the trail just up ahead."

My fingers comb through my sweaty hairline, and I tug at the roots, trying desperately to figure out a game plan that doesn't involve Whit and me running all over town.

"Maybe we should call Dad?" Whit asks.

"No! He's at work and he doesn't need the added stress right now. It's my morning to keep an eye on her." Squeezing my eyes shut to filter out the vibration of a text message— likely from Denver—I say, "Okay, I think one of us should keep walking the trail, and the other start zigzagging the streets in town."

Thankfully, Wells Canyon isn't a big city, so it shouldn't take long to jog every street. But there's always the possibility she wandered off the trail into the woods, or a wild animal came along, or she started walking down the highway . . . the possibilities are virtually endless. *Especially* if she had a brain fog moment and forgot where she was entirely.

Whit pulls the hem of her shirt up, exposing her stomach and sports bra, to wipe her sweat-slicked face. "Okay, I'll take the trail."

"Okay. I'll call you if—"

My phone rings aggressively in my pocket, and I pull it out to see if it's somebody who might be calling about Mom.

Balling my free hand into a fist, I answer with a harsh tone. "Denver, I don't have time to talk to you about my god-damn coffee order."

"Really? Because it sounds like maybe you haven't had a cup yet this morning."

"Mom's missing."

There's a rustling for a second, then he says, "Well, she's eating a cinnamon roll with me right now . . . so it seems *you're* the one who's missing."

"She's *what?*" Turning to Whit, I let out a sigh of relief, wiping beaded sweat from my brow. "She's at Anette's Bakery having a cinnamon roll."

Denver snorts. "Are *you* lost?"

"No. I'll be there right away. Just tell her to stay put, okay?"

"I'll stay here with her. Take your time, baby."

The way he says *baby* smooths across me like a healing balm. I hate asking him to stay when I've spent the entire morning convincing myself to push him away, but my mom's safety is more important than my discomfort.

"You don't mind staying with her?"

"Of course I don't mind. I figured something was up when I saw her here alone, and I couldn't ignore that."

"Well . . . thank you." I gesture for Whit to keep walking with me down the trail. "We'll be there soon."

Hanging up, I turn to my sister. "I think Anette puts drugs in her cinnamon rolls. If you're looking for anybody in town, that seems to be the place to check first."

She laughs. "They *are* really good. At least she's safe."

"Thank God Denver knew to stay with her when he saw her alone."

When we're finally breathing at a normal rate and able to relax into our casual walk once again, Whit asks, "So, what are you going to do about him?"

"I don't know. He's just . . . he's being very flirtatious, and sweet, and fun to hang out with, and he keeps offering to talk to me about the stuff I have going on. But I also don't know if he's doing all this with a dozen other girls."

"That would be a pretty gutsy move. This town is small. You found out about his dating life when you lived five hours away. Plus, his best friend is dating your best friend." She shakes her head. "I've always thought Denny's a nice guy, but there's *no way* he's smart enough to pull off something like dating a dozen girls at once."

"Okay . . . but what about when he realizes I'm not worth the effort? I kind of come with some baggage now that I didn't have at sixteen."

"What did dating in the city *do* to you?" She stops walking, spinning to stare at me with pure disgust. "You were the older sister who didn't let me say a single negative thing about myself growing up. And now you're telling me you have no idea how freaking cool you are? Any guy would be lucky to have you. If he doesn't see that, he's blind."

I rock back on my heels, cringing at my own irrational thoughts. *Oh God, she's right.* Sure, sometimes I'm on sale, but I know my worth.

"Anyway, half of your baggage came from *him*," Whit says, gesturing angrily toward the imaginary Denver standing in front of us. "If he has something to say about it, I'll give him a piece of my mind."

"No, no. This is just my own insecurities . . . I *cried* when we had sex last night, and he didn't run off. He was actually really sweet and tried to get me to talk to him after. He implied that he still loves me, and he said I was it for him."

"I think I'm going to gamble on 'might not,'" she muses, looking up at the tree canopy.

"What?"

Whit clears her throat. "I think he might *not* hurt you, for what it's worth. Obviously, I'm not a relationship expert by any stretch, but I'd give him a chance."

"I want to . . ." I admit, to both her and myself.

I want more than anything for the love story we told each other as kids to come true. It's something I brushed aside for years when I was away from here—telling myself I was a bad-ass feminist with no desire to settle down with a man. It was true that I didn't have the desire to be with *a man*, because it's only ever been about him.

"Okay, worst-case scenario, what happens?"

I wince, eyebrows scrunched together. "Whit, I don't

think we want to talk about what the worst-case scenario might look like . . . given what happened before."

"Blair, I know you don't think you do . . . but you have support here. You didn't then, and I'm so sorry for that." Her arm links up with mine, our sweaty inner-elbow ditches pressed together, and we take a steep shortcut down a small hill, staggering onto the concrete sidewalk of Main Street.

The smell of Anette's cinnamon rolls penetrates the air, and I smile at my sister.

"Thanks for the talk, sis," I say.

"Figured out what you'll do about him?"

"I think I want to bet on 'might not' . . . but you better have my phone number set to come through even when you're on 'do not disturb,' just in case."

"I'd be a pretty horrible sister if it wasn't already set up that way." She lets our arms fall away from each other as she reaches for the bakery door.

The smell of cinnamon and coffee floods my nostrils as I step inside, and Whit spots where Mom and Denver are seated toward the back of the small café. They're chatting like old friends while Mom cradles her massive mug to her chest, a smile glowing on her normally pallid face.

"Hey." I sidle up next to Denver's chair, while Whit immediately crouches down next to Mom. "Thanks for staying here with her, seriously. You probably could've just told Anette not to let her leave."

"But then if she wanted to leave, she might get scared when they tried to stop her. Figured it was easier to play it off like we're just catching up."

"Thank you." My eyes flit over to Mom. He's right—she would've gotten confused and maybe even combative, if people forced her to stay in the building against her will.

"Don't need to thank me, Bear. It's the least I could do. Besides, I was here getting coffee for her daughter, so ditching her wouldn't have been a good look."

He points to the two coffees on the table—one hot, one iced.

"Unfortunately, you're choosing between *previously hot* and *previously iced*. They're both disgustingly room temperature now." He leans forward to look at the cups with a sour expression.

"I think I'm gonna pass and take Mom home."

"Okay . . . Hey, before you go." His tone drops to barely more than a hushed whisper. So quiet I need to lean in and train my ears. "Are we good after last night?"

"We're good." I force a small smile, still so *fucking* scared, even though minutes ago I was placing bets on our relationship. "It's going to take a bit of time to fully trust I won't get hurt, though."

It's not the answer he wants, or even deserves, given he's done nothing but be honest and kind to me. All I'm able to give him right now is an opportunity to get back to where we were.

And Denver Wells takes his shot without hesitation.

"Good thing I'm ready to prove I can be trusted with your heart."

Denver

Thankfully, Vegas has no issues following the other horses on his own. My mind is so far gone, I'd be walking us in circles if it were entirely up to me. All I can think about is Blair—how fucking badly I miss her after a few days apart. Talking to her over text isn't the same as smelling her perfume and hearing her laugh.

"Should probably get back before that makes its way here," Jackson says, riding up next to me and pointing at a dense black cloud the next mountain range over.

"Won't hear me arguing about heading home early." Red spits his chewing tobacco on the dry soil between our horses.

I tug my cowboy hat down to block the sun from my eyes, getting a clearer view of the rolling clouds. "Yeah, the storms like to race up the valley. But there's enough time that I think we can do the fences until the ravine first."

Both men agree, so we carry on up the fence line, checking for holes, and stopping to tighten loose barbed wire. Despite the impending storm, the sun's beating down, and I pluck at my shirt to get some fresh air across my sweat-dampened back. The water in my metal bottle's so damn close to reaching boiling point, it doesn't even quench my thirst.

I spit the liquid out, wiping the back of my hand across parched lips. "Somebody tell me why the weather here jumps from freeze-your-dick-off cold to sweat-your-balls-off hot with hardly any time in between."

"Think about how Vegas feels having to lug your ass around while you sit there and look pretty," Red shouts over his shoulder from where he's doing a quick farmer fix on a broken chunk of barbed wire.

"You think I look pretty?" I bat my eyelashes at him, and he halfheartedly tosses a clump of dirt at me in response. "Cass is going to be *so* jealous when I tell her you've been checking me out all day."

"Has the heat gone to your head?" He mounts his horse and sprays me in the face with water from his bottle before taking a swig. Despite how warm the water is, it's surprisingly refreshing.

"Wish we could blame the heat for the shit that comes out of his mouth," Jackson quips. "We probably should head back, eh? Storm's getting awfully close."

I nod. "Yeah, good call. I need to head to town, anyway."

Jackson gives me a questioning look, but doesn't say anything.

"Doctor's appointment?" Red smirks.

"Something like that."

Denver: Is Fancy by Reba still your go-to drunk karaoke song?
Blair: Oh God. I'm going to crawl into a hole now.
Blair: I regret telling you to ask questions
Denver: That tells me all I need to know. Thank you.
Denver: Also, will you be busy in about an hour?
Blair: Depends whether your plans involve singing

Denver: Just you singing
my praises

Freshly showered, I run a hand through wet hair and slap a ball cap on. Then head out of my room, passing a bunch of ranch hands in the bunkhouse kitchen on my way out the door. They're drinking beer and playing poker, and all of them stop to stare at me in my clean clothes and going-to-town boots.

"Where ya off to?" Colt cracks a beer, leaning against the closed fridge.

"Appointment." I roll my shoulder, wincing as if it's bothering me.

"Again? Damn. Guess you're an old man now—body's falling apart." He takes a swig. "Grab a two-four of beer on your way home."

I give him a thumbs up before stepping out into the midday sun and crunching down the gravel to my pickup. She fires right up, and I roll the windows down for a breeze on the drive to Wells Canyon. Pulling up in front of Blair's clinic exactly an hour after my initial text message, I grab the bags of stuff I paid way too much for at the home goods store down the street.

"Afternoon." I smile at the receptionist, who eyes me up and down as I stroll across the empty waiting room. I wrestle the bags in my arms, trying to determine how I'll be able to open the door into Blair's office. "Do you, uh . . . mind getting this door for me? Hands are a little full here."

She leisurely rolls her desk chair backward and stands, not caring at all that I'm struggling with an armful of shit, then takes her sweet time getting to the door. Here I thought I'd be a nice guy and do it all in one trip, save her from hearing the front door chime repeatedly. Not doing that again.

"*Thank you,*" I say through gritted teeth as I bump the

door with my hip so it opens all the way. Then I swing my heel to close it in her face.

"Hey." I toss the bags onto an old armchair in the corner and tear into them. "Keep working, I'll be quiet. Just have some things I need to set up here."

I pull a small lamp from a bag and step lightly across the floor to place it on the empty part of her bookshelf. Then another for the back of the room. A larger lamp for the corner of her desk.

Blair sits back in her chair, clicking a pen repeatedly and watching me move around the room. "What are you doing?"

"You hate the overhead light, but there's no way straining to do work with this one shitty lamp on your desk is good for your eyes. And *obviously* I want you to be able to see how handsome I am for many more years." I flick the switch on the new desk light, filling the space with bright, warm light. "Better. Now keep working. You're taking a lunch break as soon as I'm done."

She narrows her eyes at me, and I give the sour look right back until she gives up and returns to work. And I continue on, plugging lamps in and putting together the fancy coffee machine I was finagled into buying at the store.

"Is that an espresso machine?" Blair wheels her chair over to where I'm unwrapping a package of coffee pods.

"Apparently so. I told the lady at the store that you needed a coffeemaker, so you don't have to go out to buy coffee when you're in the zone with work. And she insisted this was the only acceptable thing to buy." I step back to look at it. "Although now I think she earns commission and saw an opportunity."

"You do have the face of a sucker with a lot of money to spend." Blair laughs, and I swear to God, I should record it to play on repeat forever. Sure would've made the morning of fixing fences a lot nicer.

"For sure. She looked at me and said, 'This looks like a millionaire who works as a cowboy for the thrill of it.'"

Getting up from her seat, Blair slowly fingers the various controls on the machine. And I step in behind her, wrapping my arms around her waist and breathing in the subtle scent of her hair. Resting my chin on her shoulder, the silky, light pink blouse catches on my short facial hair, and I press a kiss to her ear.

Blair relaxes into my arms, head falling back to rest against my collarbone. "She played you like a fiddle. What else did she convince you to buy, big spender?"

"A mini-fridge that'll be here next week, so you can have snacks on hand to go with your coffee. Can't have you jittery with an empty stomach." I press my lips to her temple. "Otherwise, who knows? I could've bought a house with a Labrador retriever, for all I know. I think I blacked out."

If only she knew what I'd do for her. *Am doing.*

"Damn, you must be rich if you bought a whole house without realizing." Her eyes shine bright when she looks at me, a reflection of our combined emotions mixed with the warm glow of her five new lamps. "Thank you. This is too much, Denver. But thank you."

"It's not too much. It's a little bit of my time, and a disgusting amount of money."

"I owe you."

"Bear, you don't owe me shit. Taking care of you is my number one priority."

"I can take care of myself."

"Of course you can. But when my mom was sick, you were there. You might not have realized it, but I wouldn't have made it through that without you," I say before planting a discreet kiss on her hair. "I couldn't be who you needed before, and I regret not being there. But I can be here now. I want to be here."

"Why now?"

"Because I know nobody else is looking after you. Not

even you." I squeeze her until she groans, then guide her toward her desk. "Get back to work, baby. Let me take care of you."

I move to turn on the espresso machine, and she practically becomes feral. She might throw elbows over the chance to make her own coffee, so I step back, putting my hands up in surrender.

"This has nothing to do with your last statement, and everything to do with me wanting to try out my new toy, for the record."

"Did I create a monster unknowingly?"

She gives me an evil grin, hitting the power button.

I laugh. "Okay, you make the first one. But then I get to play sexy barista while you work."

"*Fine.*" She flips pages in the manual and taps buttons on the machine, and in a matter of seconds, she's making coffee.

The little moan when the first sip hits her lips makes the money spent more than worthwhile. And she heads over to her desk, cradling the steaming cup with both hands.

Flipping through the manual, trying to figure out what the hell she just made—*and how*—I glance up to see Blair leaning over her work, rather than sitting.

Goddamn.

Maybe I like her fancy work wardrobe more than I was first willing to admit. Because her wide-legged tan trousers are tight across her toned ass, and I can't help but wonder how fucking hot it would be to have her in nothing but the high heels she's wearing.

"Blair, you need to sit down, because I'm looking at you right now the same way you were looking at that coffee machine."

She glances over her shoulder, not bothering to move like I requested. "Like you want to try out your new toy?"

My cock strains instantly against my pants. "Fucking *exactly*, baby."

She doesn't say anything, returning to reading something on her laptop. But she pops a hip, rounding out her ass in invitation. And I can't turn that down.

"Don't stop working. Let me take care of you." I grope her backside, sliding to hold her hips and pull her ass against the bulge in my pants. Trying to free itself from the confinement of my jeans, my dick's practically screaming with the need to feel her, but her pleasure takes precedence right now.

I slip a finger inside her waistband to feel the soft skin underneath, gliding toward the front of her pants to undo them. Blindly feeling for each button, I grind my dick into her ass, searching for any sort of relief in the form of friction.

"I have a patient coming in a few minutes. We shouldn't," she whispers, shimmying out of her pants. When they hit the floor, she gives a swift kick and they slide somewhere under her desk.

"Tell me to stop then." I crouch slightly to trail my fingertips up the backs of her thighs, then they dig into her hips until she gasps. "You're the most stunning woman in the world, I swear."

My girl doesn't make a single peep or move to stop me.

"This ass." I give it a light slap, and heat swells in my balls at the way her butt jiggles slightly. I can't help myself from bending down and biting.

"Den—"

I make a gentle shushing noise. "Get your work done."

My touch wanders down the crease of her ass, lingering for a second when the side of my hand brushes against her wet thigh.

"Blair, *fuck*. You're practically dripping." I collect her arousal on my fingers, gliding easily between her wet pussy lips. "What are we going to do about this? I can't let my girl go about her day with a pussy begging to be fucked like this, can I?"

"No," she whimpers. "You can't."

"But I don't have any condoms, so I guess I'll have to make you come all over my hand instead. Maybe my mouth, too?"

"*Please*." She nods eagerly. "But wait—pause—I've been meaning to ask you to get tested. We can do it right here. I'm on birth control, and I want to be able to have you, even when we don't have a condom on hand."

"I need you to know that's the hottest thing you've ever said."

She laughs softly, and I kiss her tight hamstring while running my hands down her legs. I was right—nothing but high heels is *so fucking sexy*.

"You're a fucking badass who knows how to collect a damn blood sample, *and* you want to do it so I can fuck you bare? Are you kidding me?" Her ass fits perfectly in my outstretched hands as I slowly stand to kiss the crook of her neck. "What're we gonna do right now, though? I always wear condoms . . . I'm sure I'm all clear."

"I want you to fuck me with your bare cock more than anything," she says, sinking her hips back to rub against my lap. "But . . . *I can't, Denver*."

Because she doesn't trust me. I get it. I'll take a fucking weekly STI test if that's what she needs.

"Is there a way we can expedite the process? Like a one-hour photo lab?"

She laughs, craning her neck to kiss me over her shoulder. "I wish."

"Then get back to work, beautiful."

My finger slips inside her soaking pussy, and her eyes shutter. Adding a second finger has her biting her lip. All I can think about is how incredible it'll feel to have every ridge and crevice of her wet heat stroking my cock.

My fingers slowly pump in and out of her tight cunt,

dragging against the grooved walls. She's fucking gorgeous bent over this desk, leaning on her elbows and pretending to be reading something on the computer. Long, muscular legs taut, the extra height from the heels puts her ass up in the air.

I kiss her shoulder, then bite it. And my cock twitches against the inside of my zipper. A sharp inhale whistles between her gritted teeth, and the arms supporting her upper body waver for a moment. Then I pull my drenched fingers from her warmth and rub her swollen clit, and her forehead drops to the desk.

"Oh my fucking God," Blair whines between panting breaths. "Don't fucking stop."

"Oh baby, I'm not stopping until I feel this pretty little cunt shatter on my fingers."

Every little hushed moan and desperate whimper has me closer to coming in my fucking pants. And I can't take it anymore. The throbbing desire is painful.

With my free hand, I undo my belt in a frenzy, suddenly feeling like I might die if I don't get to come when she does. The instant my cock springs free, I'm gripping it firmly, stroking from end to end with an unrelenting fist. Rubbing over her wet clit and staring at her tight ass until my vision blurs.

She blows long huffs of air from her nostrils like a feral animal, biting hard on her lip to keep from screaming. And a wave of muscle contraction works its way from her legs to her neck.

"Atta girl," I say, as my balls tingle and tighten in warning. "*Fuck,* I can't wait to fuck you bent over this desk someday."

Her thighs tremble, clenching either side of my forearm, and her hands scatter papers as they rove the desk, seeking something to grip. Watching her come completely undone is all I need, and with a few tight, fast pumps of my cock, I'm coming all over her lower back and ass.

I'm so fucking tempted to tell her I love her when I see her on display with my cum marking her milky skin. But before she's even fully caught her breath, Brickham's voice booms from the other side of the door. I scramble to pull my pants up in the nick of time, and Blair sinks her bare ass onto her desk chair just as the door swings open.

"Blair, *seriously*. This damn system is— *Oh*, hi, Denny— this stupid computer system is a waste of time. I'm not doing it. Either you come fix this and make it work better right now, or I'm going back to the system that's been working for me for damn near forty years."

Blair swallows, slicking a hand over the wild hair crowning her head, and shuffles the chair closer to the desk to ensure she's fully covered. Thank God for the strong smell of espresso lingering in the air to mask our arousal, because Brickham doesn't even bat an eye. Though he is impatiently tapping his foot, waiting on an answer from Blair.

"Well, I can't help you right this second. I'm . . . uh, kind of in the middle of something."

"This is *your* stupid system. I knew hiring some young girl—"

"Hey, I'm gonna stop you right there." I place a hand on the back of her chair and stare him down. "You couldn't dream up a more dedicated, hardworking employee to have than Blair. And she deserves a hell of a lot more respect than you're giving her for the amount of work she's done to make this place run better."

"Den—" Blair turns to look at me.

"He needs to hear this. She's a grown adult and a damn good nurse practitioner, and you need to speak to her as such. Not to mention, this is a clinic. She could've been in here with a patient. You have no right barging into her office uninvited." I point at him. "*You're* being an asshole."

Brickham stares at me from the doorway with pursed lips. "Miss Hart, would you please assist me with the computer when you have a free moment in your *busy* schedule?"

Blair nods slowly, wide-eyed. "Absolutely, I can."

When the door shuts softly behind him, she practically jumps into my arms, kissing me senseless. "Thank you."

"Told you I want to be here for you. That includes everything from coffee machines to telling off miserable old men."

Blair
(seventeen years old)

The local hockey arena was jam-packed, with cliché songs about growing up blasting through the stands. And it was hot—*so hot*—despite the open garage doors and ceiling vents at full blast. I looked around at my classmates: sweaty, happy, hungover, and sad. A swirling thunderstorm of feelings culminated in this moment.

Graduation.

To be truthful, I blacked out most of the ceremony. As somebody who never wore dresses, my primary goal was to not trip over the gown as I walked across the stage with all eyes on me. Then a second time, when I shuffled onto the stage for my valedictorian speech—yet another part of the day that was nothing but a long-winded blur. Months of reciting the speech to anyone who would listen, namely Denver and Chief, it came pouring out without a second thought. Though, based on the lack of reaction, I was drowning in the words.

But my eyes locked on Denver, and he pulled a funny face to get me out of my funk. His fingers pressed to his lips before forming a ball, which he lobbed to me. I stopped mid-sentence to catch his kiss, smiling out at the crowd and taking a deep breath before continuing with soaring confidence and charisma.

Regardless of how the speech, day, or rest of the school

year went, I had my person. I was one of the lucky few in this world who found the love of their life at a young age. In a couple months, we'd move to the city together so I could get my nursing degree, and he could study agricultural science. After four years, we'd come back to Wells Canyon, or maybe a different small town. Get married, have careers, buy our own chunk of land, have babies. He and I had spent dozens of nights daydreaming out loud as we lay in my bed.

I stepped off the stage to the sound of applause, with Denver's raucous cheers the loudest and most distinguishable. I found his face before taking my seat and mouthed "I love you" to him over the row of students.

God, I loved him.

Naturally, Megan Barlow took it upon herself to host the graduation party. Which was fine—she had a pool, after all. After a lengthy lecture from my parents about the dangers of drinking and driving, and approximately four thousand promises from Denver that he would be remaining sober, we pulled up to Megan's house fashionably late.

"Let's not stay long," I said, leaning across the truck bench to kiss him. "There are better ways I want to spend my graduation night with you."

Sex. By that, I meant sex.

"Just a quick 'hope we never see ya again' to these people, yeah?" Denver laughed, hopping out of the truck and walking around to open my door.

I skimmed my palms across my thighs, which were clad in denim despite my mother's insistence that I should wear a dress to the party. My saving grace was her dresses were too frumpy, and my younger sister's dresses were too small. Anyway, the only person I was ever trying to impress was Denver, and he told me constantly how much he loved my ass in this particular pair of vintage Levi's.

Hands clasped, we entered the party house. It was immediately evident that, unlike parties in our younger years, Megan's parents weren't around. A group of boys were playing beer pong on the dining table, there was already a questionable substance splattered across one of the living room walls, and empty cans littered every available surface. Wells Canyon had forty-six graduates, and there had to be over a hundred teenagers here.

Spotting Cassidy and Shelby in the far corner, I squeezed Denver's hand. "I'm going to go see the girls. Come find me in a little while."

"Okay, baby." He bent to kiss me, then slowly untangled his fingers from mine and headed for the kitchen.

I wove through drunken bodies in the spacious, open-concept living room until nearly collapsing at my friends' feet.

"Who needs a house this big? I almost had to stop for a snack and nap halfway to get to you guys." I grabbed Cassidy's cup and took a sip of the sugary concoction before handing it back.

"Considering Megan's parents don't even speak to each other, having a house so big you never bump into each other is probably useful." Shelby shrugged.

"I think my entire house could fit into this living room." Cass held her cup to her lips without drinking, surveying the space. The three of us stood silently for a second, considering whether Cass was right.

"My girls!" Megan barreled toward the three of us. Personally, I hadn't been invited to any of the parties she'd thrown in years. *But okay, apparently we were her girls.* "Can you believe we graduated?"

"About time." Cassidy clinked her plastic cup against Megan's.

"*Blair,*" Megan said with a bone-chilling shrillness. "Your speech today was so good."

"Thanks. It was pretty nerve-wracking, so I'm glad it's finally over."

"You deserve a celebratory drink." Megan grabbed my hand, pulling me away from my friends and toward a group of people I'd never seen before. Shoving our way between two unnaturally tall boys standing at the kitchen island, she instructed one of them to pour us shots.

"Oh, I don't—" I started to protest, but Megan shoved the shot glass into my hand and clinked it against hers.

Liquor and Blair Hart had never gotten along. A glass of wine, a beer, a cooler—manageable. Hard liquor? One shot and I'd be singing Reba McEntire without music or a karaoke machine. Two shots and I'd start spewing the most embarrassing stories to anyone who would listen. I'd never done three shots before, but I assumed that much alcohol would likely kill me.

But Megan kept chanting "graduation" at the top of her lungs, so I did the second shot of tequila. Then a third in less than five minutes. Megan and the boys, who I found out were graduating from Sheridan High, were awfully convincing with their little chants, drumrolls, and cheering.

Damn peer pressure will get you every time.

The taller of the two, who Megan referred to as Jer-Bear, smelled like bananas. And he had the hots for Megan. That much I could tell despite how glassy my vision had become.

"My boyfriend calls me Blair Bear." I beamed at him as he poured another round. "Also, we should be besties because you're very good at making drinks."

He laughed, sliding a glass over to me, and half the liquid sloshed over the side. I frowned dramatically at him. "Okay . . . maybe not so great, after all."

When the effects of the last shot of tequila hit me, I was astonished that I felt relatively okay. Stumbling? Definitely. A little incoherent? For sure. But I needed to find Denver and proudly show him how well his girlfriend could handle her alcohol. Three and a half shots of tequila, and living to tell the tale.

I found him sitting outside in an Adirondack chair, talking to a couple guys we graduated with. Mid-conversation, I interrupted by sliding into his lap and open-mouth kissing him.

"You okay?" He wiped his mouth with the back of his hand. "You taste like you've been drinking tequila."

"*Ta-kill-ya*, actually. That's what Jer-Bear called it."

He raised an eyebrow, clearly amused rather than threatened by the mention of a strange guy. "Who the hell is Jer-Bear?"

"Some guy from Sheridan. That's what Megan called him. I never did ask if the Jer is short for Jeremy or Jared. . . . Oh, maybe he's a Jerome. Gerry with a G?" I started to stand up. "You know, I should go ask him. This is going to bug me if I don't know."

"Actually"—Denver grabbed hold of my wrist—"we should probably get you home."

I groaned like a petulant child, but followed behind him out of the party, dragging my feet as we walked down the road to his truck.

"Remind me to text Megan tomorrow and ask about Jer-Bear's name." I pointed a finger at Denver as he opened the passenger door and boosted me into the seat.

"Of course, baby."

"I won't rest until I know." My head was sloshy, and I leaned it against his shoulder the moment he got into the truck, my eyes suddenly incredibly hard to keep open.

"I know you won't."

"I bet it's Jeremy. He seemed like a Jeremy. Jeremy Bearemy."

I woke up to Denver trying his best to lift me out of the truck. I flailed on instinct, nearly causing him to drop me, which was enough to convince him I was better off walking. Still though, he slung an arm around my waist for the short walk to my front door.

My dad was sitting in his recliner watching TV, and he looked up at us, then double-checked the time. "You're home earlier than I expected."

"Yeah . . ." Denny hooked his thumb toward me. "This one needs to go to bed."

"All right, well, guess this means I get to go to bed early, too." Dad clapped his hands together, practically jumping for joy to not be obligated to stay up late waiting for us.

We stumbled—*rather, I stumbled,* and Denver kept me upright—down the hall and into my dark bedroom. The instant I heard the door click shut behind us, I threw my arms around Denver and kissed him, walking him backward until he fell onto the bed. Climbing to straddle him, I slid my hands up his shirt until he grabbed my wrists and stopped me with a heaving breath.

"Blair, baby, not now."

"But this was the plan for tonight, right? Quick stop at the party, then we'd have time alone."

"*Right.* That was before you decided to shoot tequila." He sat up, removing me from his lap. "Come on, baby. Let's get you to bed."

I stuck my bottom lip out, letting him pull my shirt off, then lying back so he could wiggle the tight jeans off me. The room spun wildly, and I swallowed down the indigestion rising in my throat.

"I love you," I murmured as he unclasped my bra. My head shoved through the neck hole of a baggy T-shirt, and my heavy arms struggled with the sleeves. "I can't wait to move away from this place in a few months and have our own apartment. Just the two of us all the time."

"Yeah . . ." he said quietly. Even in my drunken state, I could tell he was lacking any sort of excitement in his voice.

"Aren't you stoked to have privacy? No more long drives in your truck so we can hook up. No more sneaking you into my room at night."

"Bear, let's talk about this in the morning." He slipped his own shirt over his head and unbuckled his jeans while I stared in disbelief.

"Why?"

"I love you. Get some sleep, and we'll talk tomorrow." Helping me into my bed, he tucked the covers around me, but I refused—shoving them away and sitting upright to look at him. When he turned the overhead light off, I found the switch for my bedside lamp, turning it on.

"What is there to talk about? Just agree that it's going to be amazing to live together in the city."

"Blair."

"Denver. Give me five seconds of fucking honesty."

"I'm not moving with you. I can't . . ." He reached for my hand, as if it was going to fucking help the way my chest was imploding. "I can't leave Mom."

Looking up at the yellow-green glowing stars on my bedroom ceiling, the world was spinning even faster than it was a few seconds ago. Heart racing out of control, I looked at him, tears welling in my eyes, and vomited straight tequila in his lap.

Denver
(seventeen years old)

On a Sunday morning in late June, we should've been running slack—the overflow and preliminary runs for the main rodeo performance. Or we should've been doing chores around the ranch. Hell, I would've even preferred if we were heading off to church for the first time in history.

Instead, I leaned against the kitchen counter, buttoning the sleeves of my shirt and watching Blair delicately brush out my mom's hair. Her own was pulled back in a twist, held secure with approximately one hundred pins. But Mom's hair was barely chin-length and thin, and Blair used a single clip with a blue flower on it to keep the wispy strands out of her face.

Although I couldn't recall seeing either of them ever wear makeup before, Blair swiped pink stain across Mom's cheeks. And I hated to admit that it gave her more life—color she'd lacked since she wasn't out in the garden every day. Then she carefully added a coat of mascara and a light shade of lipstick, waiting for Mom to roll her lips together so she could touch it up.

"Beautiful." Blair smiled, standing back to admire her work.

"Thanks, honey. I don't know what I would do without you." Mom sighed, looking over at me. "Ready, kiddo?"

"Ready as I'll ever be, I guess." I shrugged as my dad and two brothers sauntered into the room. "*Damn,* this is the best looking all of us have ever been at the same time. I didn't even know Dad owned a button-up that wasn't plaid."

I laughed to cut the tension.

Mom beamed at Dad. "Button-up *and* a fresh shave? Bennett Wells, you haven't looked this sexy since our wedding day."

"And you only get more beautiful every single day." His towering frame moved around the island to lean in and kiss her. She held his face in her hands and whispered something that had him pulling away with a smile—something rarely seen from my father, *except* when it came to Mom.

Mom clapped her hands together. "Okay, we need to go, or we'll be late."

"Well, if there was ever a time we should be forgiven for lateness, it's our grandpa's funeral," I said.

Jackson nodded in agreement. "Not like they're giving away our seats."

"Front row, reserved, *baby.* They won't even start the show until we're there. We may as well roll up fashionably late." I grabbed hold of Blair's hand, following Dad and Austin as they helped Mom out to the pickup.

She was still fighting hard, despite deciding earlier in the year that she was done with experimental drugs and clinical trials. Most of them only made her feel worse, while also forcing her and Dad to be away from the ranch more often. One night, the house was practically vibrating from the yelling match between my parents—Mom insisting she would be happiest spending whatever time she had left here with us, and Dad insisting she needed to put up more of a fight to beat her cancer. In the end, as with every fight I ever overheard my parents have, Mom won.

Blair slid into the middle seat of my worn-out 1986 Ford.

Her hand found its home on my thigh, and I laid mine over-top, squeezing as we passed under the WELLS RANCH sign at the end of the driveway.

"How are you doing?" She tilted her head slightly to look at me.

"I can't believe we're doing this." I briefly steered with my knee so I could manually roll down the window. The warm, hay-scented air felt a lot like a balm over the anguish in my bones. "He was healthy and then, *boom*, dead."

A heart attack while we were driving the herd out to graze for the summer. The one blessing is knowing he died doing what he loved, with the people he loved, in the place he loved.

And now we were en route to honor his life at his second favorite spot on Earth: the Wells Canyon rodeo grounds.

"I'm sorry, baby." Blair lightly kissed my cheek. "I'm so sorry."

"It's . . . okay, I guess. I mean, it really solidifies my deci-sion to stay home."

"Your family needs you. I get it." Her thin-lipped smile said she understood, but didn't agree. That she had so much more to say about my choice to defer enrollment in univer-sity, but the drive to my grandfather's funeral wasn't the time.

"Just for the year, then I'll be coming to you. *Promise.*"

"I know." Her head found my shoulder for a long, quiet drive to town.

Thankfully, we also had reserved parking at the rodeo grounds, or we likely would've turned around and gone back home. Vehicles covered every square inch of ground near the arena and lined the roadways for at least half a kilometer.

Walking into the arena, Blair's grip on my hand felt like a heartbeat with the way she squeezed tighter, then relaxed a little when she realized how close she was to breaking my hand, then squeezed instinctively all over again. Whether she knew it or not, she kept my heart pumping. Her hand in mine being the sole thing holding me together. She was the reason I took a seat next to Jackson and managed not to crumble to the floor.

Somehow, even with all the vehicles outside, I didn't expect the stands to be packed with more bodies than I'd ever seen at a rodeo. I wiggled my nose to cut through the burn as I looked around, pulling Blair's hand onto my lap. And I blacked out until my name was said over the speaker. With a reassuring pat on the thigh from Blair, I stood and walked through the thick dirt to where George Shaw, Wells Canyon's official rodeo announcer, was holding a microphone out for me. It was all slow motion, and filled with an anxious gut feeling similar to the way I felt climbing on a wild bronc or bull. Except lacking any sort of exhilaration.

It fucking sucked.

I cleared my throat, making the mistake of looking at the hundreds of beady eyes staring back at me, then found my girl. Her eyes met mine, and she pressed a kiss to her hand, tossing it discreetly my way like I'd done so many times to her over the years.

"My name's Denver, and uh, Charles is—was my grandpa. As you may know, my grandpa wasn't a big talker, and that's a trait he passed down to basically everyone in the family . . . which is why they made the reckless decision to let me talk today." I shrugged at the gentle laughter from the crowd. "Grandpa might not have been a talker, but he still managed to impart some pretty meaningful wisdom. 'If you're gonna be dumb, you better be tough,' 'You can tell a lot about a man by the way he treats his horse,' and 'Shut up, Denny.' Sorry, Grandpa—last one didn't stick too well."

Blair smiled. Dad gave me a subtle head bob. Mom winked. So I pushed on: "Grandpa's idea of a compliment was 'you didn't screw that up too badly,' but he always made it clear how much he loved us. And by us, I don't just mean his immediate family. He loved the ranch, the town, the people, and the animals. He'd give the shirt off his back, drive a tractor twenty minutes down the road to pull somebody out of the ditch, and give anybody a job if they needed back on their feet. We'll miss the old cowboy—may his pastures be forever green, his horses fast, and his coffee always hot."

Licking my chapped lips, I handed off the microphone and practically sprinted back to my seat—heart suddenly racing faster than it had been throughout the eulogy. Blair was waiting, ready to grab my shaking hands and hold tight. Jackson gripped my shoulder when I sat down, giving silent approval. And Mom leaned forward to give me a small smile, whispering that I'd done a great job.

When the final words were said, the crowd trickled down through the gates to where we'd been sitting. Despite clearly feeling exhausted from the trip out of the house, Mom put on a smile for about ten minutes before Dad insisted they leave. And, with the only other outgoing family member gone, it fell on me to accept condolences. Austin tried—shaking hands and nodding along as people felt obliged to share stories about our grandpa. Jackson, too. Although he was too much of an awkward motherfucker to even engage in conversation, for the most part.

But Blair stood with her arm around my waist, keeping me grounded. She talked when I couldn't. She laughed at my illtimed, and often dark, jokes.

"I'm never doing this again," I said as we walked back to the truck. "It doesn't matter how lighthearted you try to make it. It's sad and it fucking sucks."

There was no sense saying that, because we both knew I *would* be doing it again. Likely in the very near future. And it would be *so* much worse.

Denver

Denver: I found your old saddle
while I was cleaning shit out of
the shed. Should test it out
sometime.
Blair: Found it? Or went looking
for it so you had a reason to text
me?
Denver: As if I couldn't think of a
million other reasons to text you.
Blair: Name one.
Denver: I saw a lab puppy in
town, there was a grumpy cat
meme that looked like you, I
wanted to tell you how beautiful
you looked when I saw you at
the big house earlier
Blair: Did you just compliment
and insult my appearance in the
same text?
Denver: It was a cute cat, and you
looked really good

The past couple weeks have been a frenzied mixture of
our typical summer work on the ranch—getting the hay cut

and stored, checking on the grazing herds, fixing fences—combined with a lot of wedding prep for an event the women keep insisting is "low-key." Plus, Blair is in a state of constant motion, always moving between a million tasks. So I'm left pining.

The way we're texting every day while pretending like there's nothing else going on is awfully reminiscent of when we first started dating as teens and were too nervous to tell our families. But back then, we could steal kisses in the barn or hold hands on the bus to get us by. Now it's glimpses from afar when she's on the ranch, our daily text conversations, and a couple of midnight phone calls to keep me on the hook.

And God, does Blair Hart know how to keep me hooked. Last week, she wore a miniskirt that the fashion gods obviously designed for quickies bent over her fucking desk. Today, a low-cut tank top and something spread across her freckled chest to make it shimmer in the sunlight as she helps Cecily decide how to lay out the reception tables. It doesn't help knowing our tests both came back negative, and the next time I fuck her will be with nothing between us.

They say absence makes the heart grow fonder, but the only thing happening for me is that I'm becoming accustomed to my dick being in a permanent semihard state, because I can't stop thinking about how badly I want her.

Staring intently while I pretend to check the oil in a ranch pickup, I don't notice a group of guys come up behind me until a hand slaps me square between the shoulder blades. Colt grins, sidling up next to me. With a rough throat clearing, I adjust my hat and give him a curt hello.

"Staring at the hot nurse?" One of the ranch hands, Rob, chuckles, and a few join in.

"Nurse practitioner. And shut the fuck up." I glare over my shoulder at him.

He snorts. "*Fucking hell.* Nobody drink the water 'round here, there's gotta be something in it. First Red, now Denny."

Colt glances in my direction out of the corner of his eye, giving me a look that says he's considering punching Rob on my behalf.

"Sounds like you could use some, Rob." I jab my finger into his side. "When's the last time anybody touched your ugly ass?"

Colt howls, punching Rob in the upper arm. "No magical water is going to get this guy laid, that's for sure."

I shake my head and drop to the ground, sliding back under the truck. At some point, the sound of a dozen or so cowboy boots crunch across the rocky driveway, slowly fading into nothing. Dolly Parton's playing softly somewhere in the distance—likely back at the house—and I hum along while I daydream about Blair, preparing to drain the oil pan at a painstakingly slow pace.

Something taps my boot, and I shake it away. *Probably Colt's dog dropping a stick on my foot to play fetch.* Then an unmistakable kick to the heel.

"Jesus, all right, *all right.*" I finish up and shimmy along the piece of cardboard laid on the ground. Ducking under the bumper, I nearly smoke my skull on the metal when I realize it's Blair crouched at the front of the pickup.

"Hey," I croak, reaching for a rag to wipe my filthy hands. "What's up?"

"You can't be over here with a fucking backwards hat on, doing all this manly shit, and expect me not to notice."

I raise an eyebrow and smirk at her. "*Really?* This is what does it for ya, eh?"

Her soft, clean hands brush against the stubble on my cheeks and she kisses me. Slow, deep, and like she's not worried at all about somebody coming across us. Which, given how many people live and work on this ranch, is pretty damn likely.

"I needed to do that before I go," she says against my lips. "It's been a *long* couple weeks."

"You know I'll sneak in your bedroom window anytime." I kiss her again, my arms aching from the restraint it's taking to not touch her.

"We're in our thirties. That's fucked up."

"What's fucked up is that we're alone for the first time in weeks, and you're fully dressed still."

Despite her expensive-looking trousers and shoes that don't belong on a ranch, she sits down on the grass and squints in the sun. "Well, get back to work, and maybe watching you pull wrenches will be sexy enough I won't be able to stay dressed for long."

"You're a weirdo."

"So I've been told. Anyway, how is this different from you watching me in my office? Go back to work now." Her hand flaps to shoo me away. "Turn the wrench, or change the thing, or whatever it is you're doing."

"Yes, boss." I duck under the bumper, skidding across the cardboard laid over rocky ground. "Let me just turn the wrench and change the thing."

"Good boy," she coos.

"If I get a hard-on while changing the oil, I'll never be able to live it down."

Her laugh reverberates through the chassis overhead, and I steal glances from under the truck as a steady stream of engine oil flows out into a bucket. *Fuck,* she's gorgeous. Leaned back on her hands in the grass, more freckles than stars in the galaxy, and the tiny natural uptick on the right side of her mouth.

It's always been her for me. I just need to prove I'm still the one for her.

When I climb out from under the truck, I wipe my clean-*ish* forearm against my sweat-soaked forehead. And Blair, my perfect weirdo, eye-fucks the shit out of me.

"As fun as it's been to watch you with that backwards hat, covered in dirt and grease, duty calls. I have to head to the clinic to meet with a patient, then go pick up Jonas because Whit's convinced he's going to cause trouble if he sits around alone all summer. Plus, I need to work out. . . ." Her nose crinkles, and if she didn't look quite so concentrated, I'd offer up that riding me could count as exercise. "Oh, and make dinner because Dad's working late. *Then* I promised Mom I'd do puzzles with her tonight. If I skip it, this will be the one time she remembers that I told her I'd do something."

"And then, and then, and then . . ." I roll my eyes playfully. "And then, when you're ready for bed, you're going to text me so I know it's a safe time to sneak in your window."

She salutes. "Yes, sir. I'll add it to the to-do list for the day—fingers crossed I remember it all."

"You're the only thing on my to-do list, so I'll send you a reminder. Or thirty. Probably in the form of nudes."

"Nudes and cat memes, if our text history is any indication."

Her phone beeps from within her purse, and she grimaces when she looks at the screen, her pretty shoe tapping on the gravel driveway. "*Fuck.* I knew I was forgetting something. *Shit.*"

"What's up?"

"It's Dad—I totally forgot to pick up Mom's prescription before I came out here this morning. *Fuck.* Now I'll have to find the time. . . ." As she stares off toward a tree line beyond the closest hayfield, I swear I can see the gears turning in her brain.

"Does she need it right away?" I ask. "If not, I can grab it when I'm done here. Bring it over tonight."

She shakes her head no. "Well . . . she doesn't need it until tomorrow, but fuck, I can't believe I forgot—yes, I can. I forget everything."

"*Hey.*" I interrupt her runaway train of words. "I'll pick it up."

"You will?" She bends down, letting her pristine, painted fingers dance across my filthy jawline.

"Of course."

"Thank you," she whispers against my lips before planting one last kiss.

Blair turns to walk away and I lean back against the bumper, watching her practically skip across the grass, with dark hair bouncing over her shoulders. Opening the car door, she turns to look in my direction, and her fingers leave the metal door edge in a half wave before she slips inside and drives off.

The dust hasn't settled from her leaving, and I'm picking up the phone to call her dad. I might not be able to lessen the pain of giving up her life to move here, or the devastation that comes with knowing your mom is dying, but I can pick up prescriptions and help with her nephew. I can check a box on her to-do list. It's not enough, but it's what I have to give. So I make polite small talk with Frank Hart, wrap up the phone call by asking for his younger daughter's phone number, then clear my plan with Blair's sister, Whit.

> **Denny:** Need you to go pick
> something up for me
> **Colt:** Right now? What is it?
> **Denny:** A 10-year-old up in Wells
> Canyon. Bring him to the ranch
> and give him some chores to do.
> **Colt:** That sounds like a crime.
> **Denver:** Don't make it creepy, and
> you'll be fine. It's Blair's
> nephew.

Then I finish the oil change and strip out of the filthy coveralls before heading over to the big house. Heat waves radiate off the gravel, and there's a slight hint of smoke in the air from a forest fire raging a few valleys over. Between the heat and unseasonably dry conditions, we're in for a doozy of a summer. Possibly even worse than the drought and crappy haying season we had last year.

Brushing dirt from my pants at the bottom of the porch stairs, I stick my tongue out at Odessa, who's currently fucking with some flowers she's *definitely* not supposed to be fucking with.

And she knows it.

"Uncle Denny," she yells, jumping up with a startled expression, pretending she wasn't doing anything wrong.

"Oh, Kaaaate," I sing—not loud enough for Kate to actually hear, given how loud the music is blasting inside the house. I just want to scare the kid straight.

"No!" Odessa charges toward me. "Don't call her. I wasn't doing nothin'."

"Quit fuckin' with the flowers, or your mom and aunties are going to kill you."

She puts her hands on her hips and stares me down. "Swear jar."

"Yeah, yeah." I tousle her hair. "Serious, though. I won't have your back if you wreck the flowers right before the wedding."

Heading inside, it's no surprise to find the women, along with Cecily's mom, frantically prepping food. Once again, I'm questioning if they understand the meaning of "low-key," but this doesn't seem like a good time to call them out. Instead, I make eye contact with Austin, raising my brows at the commotion.

Openly singing along to Dolly Parton, I scooch past Beryl and Cecily to get to the coffee machine, then back again to sit across from my brother. Dropping the loose change from my pocket into Odessa's swear jar on the way by.

"How full of regret are you about asking her to marry you?" I ask Aus, tilting my head in the direction of the gaggle of women huddled around the kitchen island.

"No regrets."

"Not even about choosing to have coffee here even though your house has perfectly good coffee and a quieter kitchen?"

"Nope." He shakes his head, bringing the white mug, full to the brim, to his lips. Then he mumbles, "I'll put up with the loud to make her happy."

If that isn't the most raw thing I've ever heard my brother say. But I get it, because I would put up with my worst nightmares for Blair with zero hesitation.

> **Denver:** Reminder: I'm coming over tonight
>
> **Denver:** No nude, because I think my family would frown on that at the kitchen table
>
> **Denver:** And remove Jonas from your list, I got it covered and cleared it with Whit.
>
> **Denver:** Yes, I know you could've handled it yourself, but now you don't have to.
>
> **Blair:** You didn't have to do that
>
> **Denver:** You can thank me tonight
>
> **Blair:** I have some ideas

I'm staring at my phone like a love-drunk fool when Cassidy sits next to me to nurse Hazel. Except I'm pretty sure she didn't come here *just* for that purpose—not when there are a hundred other places to sit.

"What are your intentions with my best friend?" Never one to beat around the bush or worry about being polite, she stares me down, and Austin snickers under his breath. "Because I'm prepared to hurt you, if I need to."

"Very threatening, Cass." Hazel's tiny socked foot kicks

my arm and I grab it, gently encompassing her entire foot in my hand. "You even have the baby doing your dirty work for you."

"I'm serious, Denny. You can't treat her like all the other girls around here."

"Good thing she's from Vancouver, so I guess I'll treat her like an out-of-towner then." I reach across the table, stealing a cookie from Austin's plate. He reaches to smack me, but misses and gives up. Eyes jumping between Cassidy and me, he probably assumes she's going to give it to me worse than he could anyway.

"Denny, cut the shit," Cass says, only taking her death glare off me for long enough to adjust Hazel. Then she's right back to calling me out. "I'm doing my best-friend duty. I've watched you fuck around with God knows how many women over the years, until you get bored and move on. You can't do that to her."

"I'd never do that to her."

"Just everybody else?"

My heart sinks, and I look to my brother for backup. What a time for him to be silently reading, ignoring us entirely.

"They're not Blair, and you're not stupid. You know this is different."

Like it or not, there's never been any denying Blair's incomparable to any other woman from my past. Whether she would've come back a week after we broke up or twenty years from now, no amount of time would change how I feel. Sure, way back then I was more than a little pissed that she didn't seem to care about my feelings or opinions—disregarding the fact that I loved her and wanted to make it work. But now I understand why she did what she thought she had to do, and I'm not too proud to admit I fucked up by letting my selfishness come between us.

"*Please* don't fuck it up, okay? I don't think Chase would appreciate me murdering his best friend."

Austin's mug clunks against the tabletop. "And don't fuck it up before this weekend, because a murder would put a real damper on the wedding."

"What would put a damper on the wedding?" Cecily slides onto Austin's lap, clutching a mug in her hands.

"We're just reminding Denny to keep it in his pants for a few days so I don't have to kill him," Cass says.

Cecily turns to look at Austin over her shoulder. "Should we go down to the courthouse right now? Because I think we're doomed if we're relying on your brother to keep things to himself."

"*Jesus*, have a little faith in me, Filly." I laugh to disguise how much I fucking *hate* this.

I hate knowing this is the way everyone thinks of me—despite understanding that their perception is entirely my own fault. After losing so much, I kept women at arm's distance. No room for hurt if you don't fall in love. So I insisted on keeping things casual. Refused to see the same person for more than a few weeks.

And now I know there was never a risk I'd fall for any of them, anyway. Because they weren't her.

"Starting to think Austin's hired you all to keep his guys working nonstop, because nobody wants to hang around here for long. No such thing as a relaxing coffee break with you ladies here." I hold up my mug, still three-quarters full of steaming coffee, and shake my head. "Besides, I'd be a lot more worried about all the other ways I can accidentally fuck up the wedding. If Blair and I decide to be together again, none of you need to worry about me ruining shit. I learned my lesson."

Before anyone can argue further, I stand and head for the door, bringing my entire coffee—which is distinctly *not* in a travel mug, but fuck it—along with me. With everyone doubting my ability to not fuck this up, I'm feeling inspired. Blair's worried about other women, her friends are sure I'll get bored and dump her right away, and my brother thinks I'll manage to fuck it up within the next forty-eight hours.

Nine. Ten. Eleven. Eleven-thirty. I'm sitting in my truck at the end of Blair's street, head resting against the steering wheel. My phone illuminates the dark truck cab when I tap the screen for the hundredth time to check if she's texted me.

Nothing.

Shortly after eight o'clock, I was too antsy to sit in the bunkhouse for another second. So I drove here and parked in my usual hiding spot, just out of sight of her house. Too bad she's not answering my texts or calls now.

After a long day of doing mechanic work on tractors and pickups, there's no way I can stay awake for the drive back to the ranch. I either fall asleep on my truck's bench seat, or I go confront Blair.

I steal across the field next to her house. My feet crunch along the rock pathway to her back garden gate, and the hinges squeak when I let myself in. I freeze in place for a moment, staring at her parents' window, waiting for signs of life. After no lights have turned on in the few heartbeats I stand waiting, I take my chances and head for her windowsill.

Blair's bedroom window slides open with ease. A good sign for me that she left it unlocked, but also something I don't want her to do anymore, for her own safety.

The first-floor window's low enough I can pull myself up and in with relative ease. Although I'm sure I looked much cooler doing it as a teen.

Stepping foot into the room, I whisper her name, then fall silent to wait for a reply. Within a few seconds, my eyes adjust to the lack of light.

She's asleep.

My palm slaps my forehead, and I sit on the window ledge, questioning my next move. Either I make do with an uncomfortable-as-fuck truck bench seat, or I curl up behind Blair and have the best sleep of my life.

The choice is obvious, and the payoff worth it, even if she gets mad in the morning.

My shoes fall to the floor with a thud, and I strip down to boxer briefs, then slide under the covers next to Blair. Fully asleep, she responds to the dip in the mattress by feeling around until she finds me. Shimmying until her ass is pressed against me, she grabs my arm and wraps it around her. Small whimpers of contentment fill the room. She's in a tight tank top and shorts, and I hold a gentle caress of her breast, the sexy barbell pressing into my palm. My lips smooth over her bare, freckled shoulder, then I nuzzle my face into her thick hair and fall asleep faster and deeper than I've ever experienced.

A loud knock on the door jolts me upright in bed, and I'm only more alarmed when a gruff voice comes from the other side.

"I made breakfast—come get it while it's hot." Blair's dad clears his throat loudly in the way dads tend to do. "And, uh, there's enough for Denny, so . . ."

Blair and I stare at each other in silence, listening to Frank's footsteps carry down the hallway toward the kitchen. Then she starts silently laughing, holding a palm over her mouth.

We didn't even have sex last night, and my truck is parked down the road . . . how did he?

"I forgot about the cameras." Blair laughs under her breath, eyes squeezed tight in embarrassment. "We put up cameras outside the house, in case Mom wanders off. I didn't think about that."

"Thank God those didn't exist when we were younger." I mindlessly stroke her forearm.

"What are you doing here, anyway?"

"You were going to text me when I was clear to sneak in, and I waited outside for an embarrassingly long amount of time. I'm shocked nobody called the cops."

"*Crap.* I'm sorry." She winces. "Mom was in a mood, which put Dad in a mood. And I came in here to get some space, but I must've fallen asleep. I can't believe I forgot to text you."

"I thought maybe you'd changed your mind." I press a kiss to her lips and haul myself from the warmth of her bed to get dressed. Austin might kill me, considering it's well past daybreak and I should've started work hours ago.

"Yet you snuck in here and slept in my bed anyway?"

"You looked awfully lonely in this big bed all by yourself. Anyway, you left the window open, which is basically an invitation."

"That sounds . . . slut-shamey."

"*Jeeeeesus.* Not what I meant." I buckle my belt, watching her search for an outfit in a closet that looks like a bomb went off. *Organized chaos* is how she used to refer to the way everything in her life is messy, yet she knows exactly where to find the specific item she needs among the disaster.

And when her hands find their way to the hem of her pajama top, I can't help but step in to help. My fingers skimming down her arms to mingle with hers, she doesn't stop me from grabbing the shirt and tugging it off in one swift movement. Her breasts bounce slightly when her arms fall back to her sides, and my cock's pressing against the inside of my jeans already.

"*Fuck.* I can't get over your goddamn tits."

"Mmm." She contemplates aloud as she cups them in her hands, staring down at her own chest. There's no way she doesn't know that holding her tits together like this has me envisioning cumming all over her chest. "I'm sure you're used to way bigger. But I mean, at least when they're this small, there's less opportunity for sagging. So that's a nice thing as I get older, I guess. Like, these aren't even a good handful."

She stretches her hand wide and palms her left breast. I don't even know why I bothered putting my pants on this morning. There's no way I'm not sucking on those nipples while I'm fucking her thirty seconds from now.

"They're a *great* mouthful, though." I lean in and kiss her bare chest, pulling a nipple into my mouth and flicking my tongue across it.

She moans softly, letting go of herself to run her fingers through my hair while I kiss and suck and lick her skin. I gently pinch the barbell between my teeth, and she clamps a hand over her mouth. Then I make my way across her chest, sucking at her, leaving small red marks over every freckle. After a few seconds of making sure her other nipple doesn't feel unloved, I smile up at her.

"Baby, they're perfect." I kiss her, inching our bodies toward the bed. "Everything about you is."

I slip my hand into her pajama shorts, and her hips buck when I press my middle finger against her clit. Falling onto the bed with me, she bites at my bottom lip.

"Denver." Our lips smack together. "We. Really. Need. To. Start. The. Day." Every word punctuated by a kiss, a moan, or a combination of the two. My fingers circle her clit, my cock begs to be inside her, and then her dad pounds on the door again.

"Breakfast is getting cold," Frank shouts through the door.

"Goddamn it, Frank," I whisper against Blair's mouth, eliciting a small snort of laughter from her. I pull my hand from her shorts, capturing her lips with mine one last time.

She slips into a fitted pair of navy trousers, and I reluctantly help clasp her bra—taking one last opportunity to kiss each breast goodbye. Then she stands in front of her vanity mirror, slowly buttoning a striped blouse.

"I can't believe you gave me hickeys." She scrubs a finger

over a prominent purple-red mark, slightly above the cup of her bra. Based on the look in her eyes, she likes that I marked her skin up.

"Needed to make it clear exactly how much I love your tits. Something to show they belong to me, just in case."

"In case of what?" She laughs, stealing a glance at me in the mirror between swipes of mascara. "With the exception of you, nobody is seeing me topless. If anything, I should do something to you, *just in case*."

"There's nobody else." I gently hold her face in my hands, staring into her expansive eyes, begging her to believe me when I say it's always been her for me. Even if I did a shitty job of showing it for the last decade. "*Nobody. Else.* I know I can shout that until my lungs turn blue, and you likely won't believe me. But the second you came back into town, I couldn't so much as look in the direction of any girls without thinking of you."

"I want to believe you," she mutters.

"Will it help if I get on my knees and beg for forgiveness?" I drop to my knees in front of her, and stare with the best puppy-dog eyes I can muster up.

"I'm not asking for a grown man to beg for forgiveness." She shakes her head. "I just think we should keep working on getting to know each other again."

"Oh, so I shouldn't propose while I'm already down here?" I jokingly clear my throat. "Blair Hart, would you do me the honor of—"

"*Denver.*" She grabs me by the upper arms, tugging me to a standing position. No hiding that cute smile on her lips, though. "You're being ridiculous. Let's enjoy the summer, then see where we stand."

"No, you're right. We shouldn't steal Aus and Filly's thunder by getting engaged the day before their wedding." I wink at her. "Speaking of which, are you bringing a date?"

"Why? *Are you?*" Her voice goes up an octave.

"Well, that would be pretty fucked up, considering I just slept in your bed and vaguely proposed marriage." I step into Blair, feeling her relax into me when I cradle her head against my chest. "Be my date for the wedding, and we'll take it day by day from there, if that's what you want. *Please.* I'm very clearly not above begging."

"Day by day, I can do."

Blair

"Day by day, I can do."

Taking it slow . . . I can try. Even if I'm already in so much deeper than a person should be for an "enjoy the summer, then take it from there" type of relationship.

I exhale, letting him wrap his arms around my shoulders in an embrace that eases years of pent-up tension in my muscles. He said he wants to be here, so I'm doing my best to let him.

Dad's booming voice cuts through the air like a lightning bolt, sizzling with electricity in the morning air. I instinctively tense, letting Denver grip tighter.

"I need to go see what that was about. Wait here," I say, attempting to pull away.

Naturally, Denver holds me back with a smile. "I'll come with you."

"No, Den—"

"I'm here with you, for everything."

"It's probably Mom. She . . . it hasn't been great, truthfully." I fiddle with the front of his shirt, scrunching the soft fabric between my fingers and refusing to meet his eye. "Sometimes she's really depressed and doesn't want to be around us. Other times, she's straight-up mean—to Dad, mostly. But then we get days where the fog seems to have lifted and she's her normal self. You got lucky with a normal day when we had dinner . . . but it's not all cute little memory slipups like when she thought we were still dating, unfortunately."

"Unfortunate about the moments not always being cute, or unfortunate that she was wrong about us dating?" He runs his thumb over my bottom lip. "Because I know a way to solve the second one."

I acknowledge his comment with a tighter hug. "I don't want you to walk out there unprepared. I'm guessing it's a mean day."

He kisses my forehead softly. "We can sneak out your window and grab a cinnamon roll at Anette's for breakfast."

Seriously tempting. Except I'll need to be a mediator if Mom's in the mood to fight with Dad. My shoulders sag, and I glance over at the window.

"Or—and hear me out before you say no—I'll suss out the situation in the kitchen while you pack a bag of clothes." He puts a hand up to stop me from saying anything. "Assuming things are good, we leave and go to Anette's. I can wait around while you see your patients. Colt's grabbing Jonas again, so you don't have to—speaking of which, I lined up some work for him on the ranch this summer, so he's out of Whit's hair *and* one less thing for you to worry about all the time."

"You did?"

"You can't be babysitting a ten-year-old on top of everything else. Plus, we can always use free labor to muck stalls and shovel shit. Win, win."

Yeah, I'm a total goner for this man.

I kiss him, running my hands down his torso and looping them behind his waist.

His lips press softly to the end of my nose. "Once you're done with work, we'll head out to the ranch and spend all weekend together. I already claimed one of the cabins for us."

"Of course you were cocky enough to assume I'd want to spend the night with you after the wedding." I give his chest a light shove, letting my hand linger over the spot where the Wells Ranch cattle brand is scarred. "I thought we just agreed to take this slow. Day by day, remember?"

"Baby, this *is* slow for me. If I wasn't taking it slow, I'd be proposing for real right now. It's a weekend—I'm not asking for forever."

"We can suss out the kitchen together. I'm not sending you to the wolves alone."

Without a word, he heads for the door and gestures for me to follow. He's waiting with a perfectly sweet smile on his face, and if he swears he's going to be here, I guess there's no reason to hold on to secrets. If it makes him run for the hills, I'd rather it happen now than later.

I hold a finger up to stop him. "There's . . . uh, something I need to do first."

With my back to him, I shut my eyes and tug on the underwear drawer he was close to snooping in last time—until I drew his attention away by mentioning other secrets I kept hidden. And I clutch a small bottle, shakily opening it and tossing a small white pill to the back of my throat.

"Okay. Now I'm good." I turn to him, praying secretly that he didn't notice me take it. Even though, in theory, I *wanted* to have that conversation, I'm not sure I actually want to have the conversation.

"What was that?" He tilts his head.

Fuck.

"Live, laugh, Lexapro." I scrunch my nose, cringing at my attempted humor. "Uh . . . depression meds."

"Okay." He holds his hand out to grab mine, entirely unfazed. "Are you ready to go face your parents?"

I don't say a fucking word. Because all I can think about is shoving him against the wall and kissing him, so I do. I press my chest into his, backing him against the bedroom wall, and his arm accidentally triggers the light switch. Leaving us in the dark—save for light trickling down the hallway from the kitchen—and I kiss him like my life depends on it. Maybe it does, a little bit.

"Mornin'," I say with a false cheeriness in my voice when Denver and I enter the kitchen, as if we didn't hear the commotion a few minutes ago.

"Hey, sweetie," Dad says, not bothering to look up from the pan he's scrubbing a little more aggressively than usual.

The atmosphere's charged like somebody dumped gunpowder over every surface, and one comment might be the match to kill us all. But Denver plops down into the seat across from my mom, and leans on his elbows to see the crossword puzzle set out in front of her—likely the thing that put her in a bad mood in the first place. Crosswords are said to help with memory retention as you age, but the daily puzzles my mom's completed with ease for my entire life have quickly become the part of her memory that's slipping away fastest. Some days she'll spend hours obsessing over a single puzzle.

"Shit, Mrs. Hart, this one looks hard," he says with a smile.

I wince when she looks up. Prepared for him to face her wrath, but that damn boy with his disarming smile. She never stood a chance.

Mom gives him a warm look, nodding keenly. "I think a lot of people underestimate the Sheridan newspaper's weekly crossword, but I've always said it's one of the harder ones out there."

"Oh, I have no doubt about it." He taps a word she has filled out. "I wouldn't have figured that one out in a million years."

"Ire? Oh, you're being silly. It's one of the most common

crossword answers out there. A three-letter word for wrath? Simple."

"Simple for you, maybe." Denver laughs. "I clearly need to learn more vocabulary, because I've never heard that word in my life."

Mom gently smacks his forearm. "Oh shush, give yourself more credit. You've always been a smart boy—I'm sure you know plenty."

I fill two mugs of coffee slowly, exchanging a look with Dad while he dishes up a plate of food for Mom.

"Here's one that shouldn't be *too* hard for you." She spins the newspaper so it's facing him, and her thin finger finds the clue.

"Oh, come on now. You're giving me the easy ones." He smiles up at me when I set a mug of coffee down in front of him with a look. I'm sure Dad provoked her ire with a simple word suggestion, but Denver put her back in the teacher mindset and she's essentially a new person.

Mom takes a slow sip of her coffee, waiting for his answer. With a shake of his head, Denver grabs her pen and jots the letters into their respective squares, then spins it back around to Mom.

Mom shrugs. "I think anybody outside of the agriculture industry would say that 'freemartin' is not one of the easy ones here."

"Free what?" Dad timidly asks, leading Mom to raise her hands with an expression that says, *See!*

Denver plows into a lengthy speech about the negative effects that arise from a female calf being born alongside a male twin—a condition referred to as freemartinism. Dad listens intently, and I can't help but stare in awe at this man who would've been top of the agricultural science program in university, if he hadn't deferred. He gave up his own dreams for the sake of his family, because he isn't just funny, smart, and handsome. Denver's unwavering ability to love is unlike anything I've ever known. When he finishes his spiel, Mom gives him an encouraging wink, and I squeeze his knee under the table.

Crisis averted, Denver makes no mention of sneaking away for cinnamon rolls, and neither do I. Instead, we talk casually with my parents over breakfast, and it's like no time has passed at all. He keeps a hand on my thigh, drawing hearts with his fingertips, and we share quick glances in our periphery.

"So, we should probably address the elephant in the room," Dad says as Mom heads outside to finish her crossword after breakfast. He waits for her to shut the sliding glass door before clearing his throat and pointing at Denver. "I don't want you sneaking in through her bedroom window."

The muscles in Denver's jaw tick. "Right. I'm sorry, sir."

"If you two are dating, then that's fine. I'm happy for you. Obviously Blair's living under my roof, and that changes things a bit as far as . . . uh, adult sleepovers." My burly, hardware-store-owning dad *blushes.*

"Yep, got it, Dad." Desperate for this conversation to end, I start to slide my chair back, frantically collecting dirty dishes.

"*But* you're also both adults. So . . . I think we need some rules." He runs a hand through thinning gray hair. "The main one is that Denny uses the front door like a civilized person. Clean up after yourselves. Don't be too loud." The blush deepens on his face. "I mean . . . keep the TV at a reasonable volume. Uh . . . I don't know. Just . . . be responsible when you . . . you know what I mean."

What the fuck. I could curl up and die. Here I thought Mom would be the embarrassing parent this morning, and now I'm wishing she would've had a moment where she called us names or made an inappropriate comment. Would've been immensely preferable to this bizarre sex talk from my father—

a man who refused to even utter the word "period" when I was growing up.

"Okay, well . . . *with that* we're going to head out." I slam the dishes into the dishwasher as fast as humanly possible.

"One question," Denver pipes up.

The hell kind of question could he possibly have as a follow-up?

"I want to steal Blair for the weekend. Austin's wedding is tomorrow, so I figured it might be fun for her to come stay at the ranch. And I know she has a lot going on here. Before I kidnap her, I thought I'd check if you'll be okay without her for two nights."

With unadulterated relief, I sigh and lean a hip against the kitchen counter.

Dad smiles, looking between the two of us. "You kids go have fun."

Denver
(eighteen years old)

Denver: It's officially been too
long since I kissed you
Blair: It's been two days
Denver: Two days too long :(
Blair: I miss you too
Blair: I'll make it up to you when
you visit next weekend

Blair had never lived with us, but that didn't change how empty and quiet the place had been since her move to Vancouver a couple days earlier. I'd driven down with her family to drop her off in a small dorm room—the apartment plan didn't make sense anymore, since I was staying in Wells Canyon. It was a long five-hour drive back with her parents, and an even longer forty-ish hours since.

Coffee percolated in the corner, and I took a long inhale, staring down at the unending text message chain between us. *Nine months.* That's how much time I had to survive before she would be back home for summer, and it didn't matter what state my family was in come September, I'd be moving with her.

Mom's new care aide, a young girl—couldn't be much older than I was—walked into the kitchen. Kate had moved into Grandpa's old bedroom two weeks after he died to help care for Mom, since it was all hands on deck with the ranch. Turns out, Grandpa had taught us how to be cowboys, but not much else about how to operate a cattle ranch. We were fumbling things left and right without him, so Dad made the executive decision to hire help.

"Hey," Kate said, sliding a cup of tea across the table. "Do you mind taking this to your mom for me?"

"Uh, sure." I stood up, sliding my phone into my pocket and picking up the tea, careful not to slosh it as I trudged down the hallway to my parents' room.

The old door squeaked a little when I pushed it open, and I gave my mom a weak smile. She was in bed—where she was more often than not, since quitting cancer treatment—and watching *Happy Days* on the small television sitting on top of her dresser. Dad was famously anti-TV, but when Mom started chemotherapy, and had plenty of days where she couldn't leave bed, he cracked pretty easily.

"Baby boy, what are you doing hanging around the house on a Tuesday morning?" She shuffled in the bed to sit upright and patted the blanket. Kicking off my boots, I set the tea down on the bedside table and crawled in next to her.

"Wasn't feeling great when I woke up," I admitted, leaning back on the pillows and half-watching the show.

"I know it feels like she'll be gone forever, but she won't be, honey." Mom took my hand in hers. So much softer, without hours spent in the garden or saddle, and everything about her seemed tired. Her movements slow and wary, like a chameleon unsure of the next branch.

"Yeah, she'll be back in the spring. And I'm going to go visit her as often as I can. I mean . . . not much different than driving five hours to a rodeo for the weekend."

"You two are lucky to have each other." Her fingers cinched around mine. "Reminds me a lot of your dad and me. I decided I was going to marry him when I was twelve years old. When I got my driver's license, the only signature I'd ever practiced was one with Wells as my last name, so I just signed my first name."

"Damn, you're like Cher." I nudged her gently, and her laugh crinkled the skin around her fatigued eyes.

"I bet Blair only knows what her signature looks like with your last name, honey. She's loved you for longer than you realize, and she'll be back. She's gotta set herself—and your future family—up for success first."

"No way Blair's taking my last name. Knowing her, our kids are going to be hyphenated. *Although*, there are worse names out there than Hart-Wells, I guess."

Her exhale rattled, so I turned to make sure she was okay. Quickly wiping the wetness on her washed-out cheeks, she licked away a tear clung to her lip.

"What's up?" I asked.

She coughed quietly into her elbow, then dried the last of the tears dampening her eyelashes. "I hope you two have the perfect wedding one day. All the Hart-Wells babies you dream of. And . . ." Her voice cracked. "I hope you have all the happiness your dad and I have had, and *more*."

"Mom . . ." The words caught in my throat. Torn between wanting to argue that she'd be around for my future wedding and kids, and knowing all too well that she wouldn't be.

"You have no idea how happy it makes me to know you found your person, and I got to live long enough to see it."

She slung an arm around me, and I leaned into it, resting my head in the hollow of her shoulder. Her gentle heartbeat and the *Happy Days* theme song creating a core memory deep in my soul.

"Honey, I have something I want you to give Blair. Can you grab my jewelry box from my dresser?"

I peeled myself from her embrace, sniffling back the stinging in my nostrils. Her jewelry box was small, and didn't have a lot in it. Mom was never the type to wear necklaces, and she didn't even have her ears pierced. But she had a few pieces passed down from her own mother and grandmother, so Dad hand-carved her a wooden box to keep them safe. My fingers ran over the delicate tooling when I passed it to her.

"I love having you boys, but I hate that I don't have a daughter to give any of these things to." She opened the box and pulled out a necklace. "This one came all the way from England when my grandmother immigrated to Canada after the First World War. It would be a shame for it to end up in a pawn shop or something."

"I'll give it to Blair. She'll take good care of it."

"No, no." Mom shook her head, dropping the gold chain back into the box. "If she wants it, make sure she gets it. But that's not what I need you to give her."

Her finger slowly dug around in the small puddle of silver and gold, and she pulled out a simple gold band with a small diamond on it. *Mom's engagement ring.* A smile spread across her face when she slipped it onto her ring finger.

"I haven't worn it in ages"—she wiggled it up and down, showing it was clearly much too big for her slender fingers—"and, as much as I'm sure your brothers might be a little pissed off with you for getting to have it, it makes perfect sense. Blair's the closest I've ever had to a daughter. If she wants something different, you can melt down the gold and maybe add more diamonds to fancy it up?"

"Mom, I can't take your engagement ring. Besides, we won't be getting married for *years* still. She needs to finish school first." I pushed her hand back when she tried to offer me the ring, refusing to accept it because that felt like she had given up entirely. She was handing her eighteen-year-old son a diamond ring, expecting she wouldn't be able to give it to me when I was older. I'd never be older than eighteen in her lifetime. "If you really want her to have it, I'll get it closer to when I'm ready to propose."

"*Honey.* I'm giving the ring to you now out of necessity. I don't know how much longer I have, or whether we'll get another moment like this—just the two of us. You're my baby boy, and I'm so proud of the man you're becoming. I *need* you to take this. And I need you to give it to her one day, when you're ready."

"Mom, I—" My voice broke, tears falling in steady streams down my cheeks while I choked on pooling saliva. "I wish you could be there."

She tucked the ring into my palm, folding my trembling fingers around the gold circle. "I will be, baby."

Denver

An extended exhale flows out of Austin when he sits down on the sun-soaked porch steps next to me. A shaky hand reaches for the beer I offer up, and I grab my big brother by the shoulder.

"Love you." I pinch his trap muscle with love. "Glad you found your person. You deserve this."

Nodding, he swallows a mouthful of beer. And we sit in the heat, overlooking the massive white tent the girls spent all day yesterday decorating for the reception. The lawn's pristine, flower beds bursting with blooms, and the morning sun blankets the Earth. I swear even the distant barn looks like somebody took a pressure washer to the exterior. This place is arguably the best it's ever looked; you'd hardly even guess it's a working cattle ranch.

"Wish Mom could see it looking like this," he says.

I smile at him, watching his throat bob with a hard swallow. "She sees it, buddy."

The air is still and quiet, save for a distant tractor engine. Nobody's around, and his shoulders fall as he chugs the last of the beer. So I slide across the stair to sit closer, and I hug him—something I don't think I've done since the day of Mom's funeral. But it feels right in the moment and, shockingly, he doesn't shove me away like I would've expected from my prickly oldest brother. His arm slings around my shoulder, and he pats my back.

"Let's go get you married before Filly realizes she picked the wrong brother." I smack him on the back, encouraging him to get a move on. "Besides, you'll be pleased to know I *didn't* fuck things up before the wedding—in fact, I convinced her to be my date."

"Lots of confidence considering there's four more hours to go. Plenty of time for you to screw shit up."

Standing under the late afternoon sun, in brand-new jeans and button-downs, with a view overlooking the ranch, I reach over and give my brother a love tap on the shoulder right before his bride starts down the aisle.

Everyone stands to stare at her, but I can't take my eyes off the brunette in a floral dress. Lower cut, but so long it sweeps the earth, with flowers the same light shade of blue as my shirt. She picked the dress to match my button-down long before I officially asked her to be my wedding date. I know, because she made me send her a photo of the exact shade of "dusty blue" Cecily had the groomsmen buy.

Her eyes meet mine as she elegantly sweeps the fabric around her hips to sit, and a small smile spreads across her painted lips. When the pastor starts speaking, Blair flits away only for a moment before returning to me. That's where we stay, trapped in a staring contest, throughout the vows.

I spend the entire time thinking about what our wedding might've been like when we were younger. Maybe it would've been a big event like this, filled with family and friends. Though I don't imagine Blair would've wanted anything extravagant. It could've been just us, under the tree out beyond the top hayfields.

Hearing the words "kiss your bride" forces me out of the

daze and back to Blair, who reaches up to dab at the corner of her eye. Feeling the heat of my gaze, she tilts her head to squint at me through the sun's glare. Only it looks like she's winking at me, so I wink back.

Everyone cheers for Austin and Cecily, and my fingers press to my lips so I can toss my girl a kiss. The gesture I did before every single bronc ride when we were kids, and again at the rodeo a few weeks ago. Blair's smile breaks free, and she catches it like an old pro.

While the wedding guests rode to the ceremony site on horse-drawn wagons, the groomsmen—Jackson, Red, and I—naturally showed up on horseback. Untying Vegas from the tree, I spot Blair watching me and beckon her over.

"Ride down with us." I pat the saddle.

"We can't both ride this horse—his poor back."

"Lucky for you, I have a spare." I point to Austin's horse. "Aus is gone with his bride. Looks like we need another rider."

The specks of gold burn up in her eyes, fiery and more full of life than I've seen in years. She licks her lips and takes a step toward Vegas, running her hands down his neck.

"You probably want to ride sidesaddle because of your dress, eh?"

Her nose scrunches. "And be uncomfortable while walking at a snail's pace? I don't think so. I'll take the dress off, if I have to."

When she showed up in town with her fancy clothes and perfectly placed makeup, I was under the impression she had drastically changed over the years. Knowing how wrong I was makes my heart float, and I rush to her side to boost her into the saddle before she hurts herself trying.

Wedged sandals in the stirrups, bare legs, and a long dress bunched around her waist, she's a beauty. She pets Vegas every chance she gets, and he soaks up the extra attention from her. Side by side, we cross the grassy field and start down the hill toward the barn, like we have hundreds of times before.

"Fuck, I missed this so much. It's been too long, and it kills me." She smooths a hand over her wild hair and closes her eyes for a second to revel in the sun on her face. "This is better than therapy."

"You can come out here and grab a horse anytime you want."

"Don't tempt me with a good time," she says, stopping outside the stables.

"Serious, Blair. Take any of my horses. Maybe we can even get you one of your own."

"I don't have the time for my own horse . . . but I'll gladly come riding sometime."

Jumping down, I reach to help her dismount. Then we slowly walk the alley, until I point to the stall we need to put Vegas in.

A few seconds later, she comes out and nearly mows me over on her way to the tack room.

"Where ya going?" I grab her bicep to stop her. "Filly will commit murder if we show up at the reception with a speck of dirt on us. The ranch hands can clean up after us today."

With a sigh, she runs a hand through her hair, letting it fall loosely around her shoulders.

"You're beautiful, Bear." My fingers find their own way to the top of her dress, and suddenly I'm slipping the fabric edge between my fingers like a plucky guitar string. "So fucking beautiful."

She blinks up to stare at me just beyond the tips of her thick, dark lashes. A loose lock of hair falls between us, and I push it behind her ear. The wedding emcee's voice floods the ranch, and Blair gives me one slow kiss before insisting we go partake in the wedding festivities.

We can say we're taking it slow. Day by day, even. Tell

sweet little lies about how we feel, if that's easiest. But I fell in love with Blair once before, and I had that bliss for years. Now? I'm not falling. That sounds too accidental for what I'm doing. I'm jumping in headfirst, praying she loves my level of crazy and jumps with me.

Denver
(eighteen years old)

I stared down at my socked feet, pressing firmly into the hardwood to send the rocking chair backward. I couldn't bring myself to look anywhere else. Not at Austin, who was sitting in a chair next to mine, slumped over with his head between his knees, white-knuckling his skull. Not at Jackson, who was staring into fucking space, not bothering to stop the tears falling down his cheeks. Not at Mom, who didn't look anything like my mom anymore, but a sickly stranger in her bed.

And the last place I could ever look was at Dad. A man who had never shown emotion. A man who routinely told us to "toughen up" as kids, insisting there was nothing in this world worth crying over. A man who didn't so much as well up when his own father had died just a few months earlier. Because now he was clutching his wife's hand to his cheek, tears streaming as he whispered I love you's to her over and over.

If I looked at that, I'd never recover. Hearing it was too much, which was why I kept incessantly rocking. Thankful for the repetitive thumping of the rocker ends hitting the floor, because it meant a couple seconds without hearing his pain.

And *fuck*, it was stuffy in the small bedroom with five bodies breathing the same air. Not that any of us were truly breathing—at least, *I wasn't*.

"Stop," Dad croaked in a voice wet with emotion.

That one word was my final straw.

"What the fuck else am I supposed to do? Sit here in fucking silence and wait patiently for my mom to . . . *die?*" I shook my head, voice cracking. "She wouldn't want that. She *doesn't* want that. For us to just sit in our separate fucking corners and wait in goddamn silence? We should—*I don't fucking know*—play some music she loves and talk to each other and maybe just make it feel like she isn't already dead. Because she *fucking isn't.*"

"Son, enough." Dad shot me a look, and I ran the back of my hand under my snotty nose, seething. "You're going to make this stressful for her."

I bit back everything else I wanted to say, rocking the stupid fucking chair *harder*.

Finally, Austin lifted his head. Placing his hand over mine on the armrest, he said, "No, I think Denny's right. Some music might be good. Mom loves music."

Without instruction, Jackson stood and turned on the small stereo on the dresser, hitting play on the classic country CD already inserted. A twangy Hank Williams song filled the room, and Austin cleared his throat.

"Mom hates this song," he said under his breath.

Jackson skipped to the next one, and within the first few notes, Dad sighed. "She *really* hates this song, too."

The third track on the CD started up, and I immediately began laughing uncontrollably. Like a man possessed, I couldn't help the snorting laughter from bursting out of me. And that sent Jackson into a fit of giggles so hard he couldn't bring himself to change the song. Austin placed a hand over his mouth, shoulders heaving with silent laughter.

And Dad looked right at Mom, shaking his head and throwing his hands up in the air like he was genuinely pissed off with her. "Why on Earth do you possess a goddamn CD with so many songs you absolutely fucking hate?"

For a solid minute, we were a deranged pack of hyenas, laughing partially because of the situation. Mostly because it felt so much better than crying.

Kate poked her head into the room as the last bit of giggles were leaving our lungs in slow spurts. "Are you guys okay in here?"

"Yeah, yeah," Jackson said in a flustered tone, hitting buttons on the stereo until a slower, melodic classic country song started up. "All good here."

"Just thought we'd see if we could find a song Mom hated enough to make her wake up and scold us." I shrugged, glancing over at Mom's peacefully sleeping face.

Kate cocked her eyebrow. "Okay then. Well, if you need anything . . . I have lunch made for whenever you're feeling up to eating."

She shut the door without another word, and the four of us settled back into our slump. For a while, there were significantly fewer tears. Still no talking, but at least we had music to ease the pain. At least Mom had music to ease the pain.

Then there was Garth Brooks singing "If Tomorrow Never Comes," and the tears came back with a vengeance when my dad moved to lie next to my mom, moments before she took her final breath.

"Sh-she's—" He didn't have to say the words.

My eyes squeezed shut, and hot tears snuck through to fall to my lap with a rattling breath. Nobody moved. Nobody said a word. For so long it felt like maybe time had stopped altogether.

Then Austin stood silently, and I watched him give Mom one last kiss on the cheek before slipping out of the room.

When I sat down next to her, her hand was still warm, and I squeezed it so tight I thought for a second I might break her bones. And when I realized it wouldn't matter if I did, a choked sob escaped me.

I leaned in close to her, letting my tears soak her cheek, whispering, "I love you, Mom. I love you. So much. I-I can't do this without you."

Overcome with a need to get the fuck out of there, I stumbled into the hallway in a daze, feeling like my chest was about to implode, unable to take a full breath. Vision blurred, my fingers skimmed the walls as I waded through waist-deep sand to get to the front door. Stepping onto the front porch, I let the screen door slam behind me, rattling through my bones, and a cool breeze left me gasping for air and clutching my chest. I grabbed the front porch railing in a panic, spilling the contents of my stomach over the flowers below.

Suddenly, Kate was rubbing slow circles between my shoulder blades with gentle, motherly shushes. "What do you need?"

"Blair."

"I already called her. She's on her way." She hooked an arm around my waist and sat my spiritless body in an Adirondack chair. "I'll grab you a blanket and water. Do you need anything else?"

"Just Blair."

Blair
(eighteen years old)

My car rattled over the cattle guard to the place that had always felt the most like home. And I found Denver sitting on the front porch steps alone, looking small and weak despite his six-foot-something, muscular stature. I popped the seat belt buckle with my thumb before I'd come to a stop, and the car was hardly in park by the time I was bailing out.

"Baby." I ran to the stairs, throwing myself at him. My arms held tight around his neck, tugging his head against my chest. "I'm so sorry I wasn't here sooner."

My nails scraped across his scalp and he groaned, leaning into my touch and wrapping his arms around my waist. I sat in his lap, playing with his hair. Holding him as he held me.

"Bear, I don't know what I'm supposed to do."

"You're not supposed to do anything. Just let me take care of you." I kissed his forehead. "I'm here for you. Let me take care of everything."

Together, we walked into the silent house, and the stairs to the second floor groaned under our combined weight. But I kept my arm around him, scared he could collapse, and we fell to his bed together. Within minutes of my fingers sifting through his hair, and his head nestled between my collarbone and jaw, Denver fell asleep. Slow, gentle snores—his brain finally able to take a break, and his heartbeat slowing to normal, quite possibly for the first time in days.

We knew it was close to her time. We'd known all week. But with midterm season and looming project deadlines, I selfishly insisted I stay in Vancouver until the weekend.

Lucy was supposed to make it to the weekend.

But she couldn't. On Thursday, she fell asleep and didn't wake. By the time Kate called me, it didn't matter that I dropped everything to drive five hours to Wells Canyon. It was too late. I was too late, and I didn't get to say goodbye.

When Denver woke up an hour later, I suggested we get some food, and his only reply was a groan. Then I suggested a shower, and he groaned again. So for another hour, we just lay there holding on to each other without a word.

"Come on, let's go have a shower and some food. You'll feel better." I sat up, tugging on his arm to take him with me.

"Can we stay here a little while longer?"

"Just humor me with a shower and dinner before my stomach consumes itself. Then we'll come right back." I pulled on his hand, digging my heels into the floor until he reluctantly sat up and followed like a dejected puppy.

Shutting the bathroom door with my foot, I gripped the hem of his T-shirt and pulled it over his head, slowly stripping him. The Wells Ranch brand he'd burned into his skin to match his brothers and dad was finally nicely healed, but still pink and raised, and I ran my fingers over it, pulling him toward me for a kiss.

His hand flew up before my lips met his. "Oh, God. I threw up earlier. Just . . . hold on."

He brushed his teeth while I undressed, our eyes constantly meeting in the mirror over the sink. Then I let the water run until it was warm, and we squeezed our bodies into the small shower together. Letting it wash away the pain and dried tears and warm our weary bones. I held him tight, kissing his chest and shoulders.

Fearing we might run out of hot water any minute, eventually I took a step back and reached for the soap to spread over his tanned skin. I raked shampoo-coated fingers through thick hair, and kissed his jaw when he tilted his head back to rinse.

"Thank you," he muttered against my lips before kissing me. "I don't know what I'd do without you. You're everything—all I have."

"I'm here, baby. I'm always here for you."

That was something I wore like a badge of honor: being his person. We had each other, and that was the only thing that mattered.

Even though it had been two months since I'd been to the house, and Lucy hadn't been filling the space with her joy for months before that—it suddenly felt empty without her. The one-hundred-year-old farmhouse was in mourning, cloaked in stormy skies that let sadness seep into the cracks in the floorboards. A heaviness hung in the air, and no one but Denver and me seemed to be around.

After a quiet meal of toast with jam in a kitchen lit only by the glow of a stove light, I handwashed the dishes and led Denver back upstairs. Since we'd changed into pajamas after our shower, we climbed into bed and I wrapped my arms around him. Praying he'd fall asleep, so all the pain could stop for a little while.

But he kissed me. A soft, closed-mouth peck good night. Then his hands slid to either side of my face, pulling me into him with a deeper kiss, his tongue forcing its way between my lips. The moment a small whimper left my lungs, he was feral. Kissing me and pulling my legs to straddle his waist. I couldn't breathe, giving him every bit of oxygen I had in my lungs with an all-consuming kiss. It seemed like he needed the air more than I did, anyway.

His touch trailed down my body, snapping the waistband of my pajama pants, and his fingers slipped underneath. I broke free of his kiss, giving him a confused look. "Denver, I don't think you want to do this."

"Please, baby. *Please.* I need to feel you. I need things to feel normal—like this is a regular sleepover—just for a little while."

I'd give him anything he asked for. So I nodded, shimmying my shirt off and letting him kiss my breasts while I grinded my hips against him.

"God, you're so fucking wet," he murmured into my neck, slipping his hand between my legs. "I missed touching you like this."

"I missed it, too." I rolled my hips, forcing the heel of his hand to graze my clit, needing friction. "Denver, I love you."

I hovered above him while both of us slid our pants down, and when I felt his hard cock graze my inner thigh, I nearly came undone. It had been too long, and no amount of sneaky phone sex when my roommate wasn't around was enough. Nothing like the real deal.

So lost in the feel of his lips on mine, and the way his eyes were welling, and the need to make him happy for a single moment of this godawful day, I didn't think twice before sliding down the length of him.

"*Fuuuuck,*" he groaned, lifting his hips to push his cock deeper. "Holy fuck, this feels so fucking good."

"*So good,*" I moaned in agreement.

There was something special about having him bare inside me. Nothing, not even air, between us. And I leaned down to kiss him, tugging his lip between my teeth while I rocked my hips.

"This—so incredible." His chest heaved against mine.

"We're never using condoms again," I said. "I'll get on the pill before I come back for Christmas."

"God, yes." He drove upward, and I nearly buckled at the sensation flooding through my hips.

With each thrust, I watched the sadness leave his eyes,

replaced with lust and need. And when I started touching my clit, rubbing with my middle finger while getting lost in his expansive eyes, he threw me off of him with a low rumble in his chest.

"I'm going to come, and if you're on top, I'll end up coming inside you." He gulped, shifting to lay me down and spread my thighs wide. Then he shoved back inside me with an attempt at a quiet moan that came out strangled and hoarse. "Holy fuck, Blair. You feel so fucking good."

Circling a fingertip over my clit, I arched my back, relinquishing power to the tidal wave rushing over me from head to toe. Moaning—*loudly*—and not giving a single fuck because Denver and I were adults now. We were adults, he'd lost his mother mere hours ago, and fuck it if we wanted an orgasm to get us through the pain.

His breathing stuttered and he pulled out of me, pumping his dick in his hand until spurts of cum fell on my stomach.

"Thank you." He collapsed on top of the sheets, tears and sweat dampening his face.

"I love you, baby." I kissed his forehead, swiping my thumbs under his red-rimmed eyes. "I'll be right back."

Wrapping one of his oversized hoodies around me, I cracked open the door and, seeing no one in the hall, slipped out. Mid-dash toward the bathroom, I nearly crashed into Kate as she stepped out of Jackson's room.

"Oops, sorry." I grabbed her bare shoulder. Then it dawned on me. Kate sneaking out of Jackson's room, wearing a blanket. "Oh. Um . . . go ahead and use the bathroom. I'll, uh, use it later."

Not even thirty seconds had passed, and Denver was already asleep when I shut the bedroom door behind me and crossed the dark room to his bed. Telling myself I'd get up again the moment I heard the bathroom door, I snuggled under the covers next to him, tucking his heavy arm across my chest. And fell into the best sleep I'd had in ages.

Blair

Sitting in a chair off to the side of the dance floor, my body sways naturally to the melody of a slow country song—"I Cross My Heart" by George Strait. With Hazel tucked in my arms, a heavy warmth on my chest, I swallow down the emotions bubbling within me. Couples move around the wooden dance floor in the center of the tent, lost in the music and each other.

I guess I'm lost, too, because I don't notice Denver until he's settling in next to me. "I don't think any of you understand what low-key means. There is nothing casual about a fucking make-your-own-sundae bar."

"The flower girl is very demanding, and her Uncle Austin has a hard time saying no."

He holds a white bowl in front of my face, backdropped by the cutest dimpled grin I've ever seen, and I start questioning if it's too much to tell him I love him because of some ice cream.

"*But* the upside is you can have your senior citizen ice cream. Now"—he digs around in the bowl with the spoon, getting the perfect scoop—"for some ungodly reason, they don't have Neapolitan. Something to fix for our wedding, clearly. Um, but I got all three flavors separately, and topped it with walnuts."

Our wedding. He breezed past it as if we're already engaged and actively planning a wedding. I half-expect to look down and see a ring magically appear on my finger.

He stares at me expectantly, holding the spoon in front of my face so I can do the taste test. I swallow, unable to stop a small moan in the back of my throat. "You're the best. That is seriously good."

Gesturing with his head to the sleeping baby in my arms, he says, "That looks good on you."

The words might as well have been a semi truck crashing into me. I choke on my own spit, frantically reaching for a glass of water left over from dinner.

"Now you sound like my grandma anytime I'm around small children. Talk about a demanding woman."

"She just wants a grandchild before she dies."

"Jonas doesn't count?" I rock Hazel gently, tucking her thin receiving blanket over her feet. While the day was *hot*, it cooled off quickly post-sunset.

"Nope. Nothing like that ever counts until the oldest sibling does it." He shrugs impishly. "Sorry about your luck— looks like you're having a baby because I know you can't say no to Grandma Dorothy."

"Considering I haven't had a long-term relationship in over a decade, it's insane she still has hope."

"Not a single one?" He looks at me like I just informed him that I've recently grown a tail.

"Never. Not since you."

"Me neither."

I snort. "Yeah, I'm well aware, thanks. People love telling me about the parade of women in your life."

"Bear, I can't take back the fact that I was with other people, and I'm sorry you heard all about it. But before my bronc ride, I thought I saw you near the chutes. And everything— *everyone*—else stopped mattering at that moment." He shuffles his chair closer so our thighs are touching. "That's all I can offer you. The promise that I was completely yours from the second you stepped back into my life. Can that be enough for you?"

I think for a second, looking down at Hazel, then out at the dance floor. It's not fair to judge Denver for whatever he did while we were apart, especially when I wasn't exactly running a nunnery. But jealousy is a *fucking bitch*. With a hard swallow, I kick the green-tinged emotion from the back of my brain to the curb.

"It's enough." I reach out and pat the top of his thigh, over the spot where his tattoo is. "It's enough, Den. Do you ever think about how things could've turned out if I hadn't left?"

"Every day of my life," he admits quietly. "The house we'd have, how good it would feel to come home to you every day, our kids."

With a slow musing nod, I smooth a hand over Hazel's soft red hair. "We could have a *thirteen-year-old* right now. That's wild to think about."

I haven't let myself dwell on that piece of history in a long time. It brings a rush of pain, and longing, and self-loathing— *saudade*. And my eyes burn when I stare down at the sweet baby in my arms, then over at the man who would've made an amazing father, had I given him the chance.

He runs the thumb of his free hand across Hazel's cheek. "I think about that the most."

Cassidy comes traipsing toward us, fanning herself with her hands, and Red's hot on her heels. She bends to pick up her peaceful baby from my arms and stops short, clearly noticing the glassiness in my eyes.

"You okay?" she says under her breath, quiet enough the guys can't hear, while sliding a hand under Hazel's head.

"Yeah, we were just reminiscing, and I've had too much wine." I half-smile, blinking back the tears and plucking dress fabric away from where it's clung to my stomach. "Denver? Do you want to dance with me?"

Wasting no time, he jumps to his feet and takes hold of my hand, leading me to the center of the dance floor. My arms loop lazily around his neck, and he holds tight to my waist, a hand splayed over my lower back. He motions something to the DJ, and mid-chorus, the song's cut short, replaced by a beat I don't recognize at first.

But when it hits me, I give Denver a look. "You didn't ask for my favorite karaoke song because you wanted to get to know me, did you?"

He laughs. "*Maybe* Cecily and Austin were talking about a wedding playlist in the kitchen, and I offered up a sugges-tion. Come on, Fancy. Sing it. *Don't let me down.*"

Shaking my head, I start singing quietly, only to him. And he beams at me.

"If I close my eyes, it's like Reba is right here in front of me."

"I hate you. You know that, right?" I tease.

"You don't hate me. In fact, I bet you think I'm the best catch here, and you're trying to think up a way to ask if you can have my babies, because they'd be top-tier children."

With a laugh, I twirl around in his arms. "That *would* make Grandma Dorothy happy."

"You're in luck, because I hate disappointing grandmoth-ers," he says, fitting my body against his again. "But you know what's great about us not having those kids yet?"

My mind gets entirely hung up on the way he talks about a wedding and kids with so much confidence, like they're simply an inevitability. And after years of thinking I'd forever be Auntie Blair, stuck in an "always the bridesmaid, never the bride" situation, there's comfort in how sure he is about us. Lost in the way his words calm fears I've never had the cour-age to say aloud, I'm not even the slightest bit tempted to remind him we're supposed to be taking things slow. We both know we never really were, anyway.

I twist my fingers around the hair on the back of his head. "The ability to sleep in? Not spending all our money on diapers and extra food? No fear about raising humans in this fucked-up world?"

"Tonight we're staying in a cabin here, and we don't have to worry about being quiet or sneaking around." His fingers clench around the dress fabric just above my tailbone, and suddenly this thin slip of a dress is too much between us. His lips brush my ear, hot breath blowing against the goosebumps scattering up my neck. "I'm going to rip this fucking dress off and make you come again and again. You'll be begging me to ease up, and I still won't stop. I've had fourteen years to think about what I'd do to you if I had another chance. And tonight you're mine, baby. All mine."

"Is that a threat or a promise?"

"Whichever turns you on more."

I press my pelvis into his, tempted to tell him we should ditch this party early. Finding myself so lost in the depths of his eyes, I can't hear the music anymore. I don't care that everyone is around, or that I told him we needed to take things day by day. We might not be the same kids we used to be, with a few smile lines around our eyes, and even a gray hair or two, but he's still my Denver Wells.

And I kiss him with the intent of never letting him go again. His tongue brushes mine, our bodies still in the middle of the floor while everyone flows in slow motion around us. When my lips break away from his, the backs of his fingertips brush a wispy strand of hair off my cheek.

He looks like he's about to say something, searching for the words as his eyes search mine. But something tugs him away from me, and a tiny voice brings us crashing back to reality.

"Uncle Denny, it's our song," Odessa yells over the opening notes to "I Gotta Feeling." She's practically vibrating—

likely from overindulging in ice cream—and her white and pink flower girl dress swishes around her legs. With hair a frizzy mess and sweat beaded on her hairline from dancing, she holds out a hand for him to grab with a wild look in her eye.

"Sorry, baby, there's a super cute girl asking me to dance. I can't turn her down—you know how it is." He winks, running his hand from my back to my waist, struggling to tear his touch from my body.

"I knew it was only a matter of time before a prettier girl grabbed your attention. Hopefully it doesn't come to this, but I'm prepared to fight a literal child, if I have to."

"I never pegged you for the jealous type when we were younger, but I like it." He kisses my cheek. "One—*maybe two*—dances, and you'll get me all to yourself again."

"I'll be waiting with drinks." I feel the loss of his touch everywhere the second I pull back, and I nearly trip over myself walking backward off the dance floor. Because watching Denver twirl his niece around, laughing and goofing off, is simultaneously the hottest and most gut-wrenching thing I've ever experienced.

I don't take my eyes off them for the entire trip to the bar and order our drinks while keeping tabs in my periphery. My time back in Wells Canyon has been a continual reminder of all the things I could've had. From trips to the ice cream shop to the time spent with Mom. Weddings and babies and building a life with him.

"I was looking for you." Cassidy leans an elbow on the bar—Hazel, now wide awake, is nestled in the other, chewing on her tiny hands. "They're about to wind things down here, and some of us are going to have drinks and a fire, if you're in. Chase and Colt went to set it up."

"Is it bad if we don't come because I kind of want to jump his bones right now instead?" I motion toward where Denver has Odessa on his hip, and they're spinning in fast, stumbling circles while she throws her head back laughing.

"Honestly, that's fair. Careful, though. Baby fever is a hell of a drug. I've come close to trashing my birth control a few times because Chase looks so hot holding Hazel." She cracks open her water bottle and takes a sip while watching them with me. "So you two *aren't* taking it slow, I assume?"

"We're kind of . . . picking back up where we left off. Like time stood still for the last decade."

"But it didn't."

"That's okay. Time stopped in the ways that matter. Don't get me wrong, I'll probably have some jealousy flare-ups when girls he's slept with flirt with him. But I'd be an idiot if I pushed him away—or into the arms of somebody else—because I couldn't admit to myself that I still love him."

"Wow, what's it like to have all your feelings so well sorted out?" Cassidy laughs.

"I wouldn't say well sorted, but at least I'm not going to say 'thank you' if he decides to drop the L-bomb on me."

"*Ouch.* That's a cheap shot. I retract my invite to the fire, asshole."

"*As if.*" I blow her a kiss. "Your reverse psychology worked. We'll be there shortly."

Spinning on her heel, Cass turns to leave. "I promise not to judge when you two sneak away after fifteen minutes."

I grab our drinks and find a seat with a good view of Denver and Odessa. Spinning, laughing, and busting out their silliest moves in a freestyle dance-off. Sipping the chardonnay does nothing to ease the burning in my core. Instead, my head's floating, warm and fizzing like I'm submerged in a hot tub. Sinking deeper into the chair, I cross my legs to fight the need for him.

As the last song of the night draws to a close, Denver indulges Odessa in one final twirl before scooting her toward her dad's waiting arms. Then he saunters over to me, dimples catching the twinkling ceiling lights, wiping sweat from his forehead.

"Quite the moves you've got there." I hand him his beer bottle, watching the muscles in his neck as he takes a pull.

"It was all those hours practicing when we were younger. I'm basically the best dancer in town now." His fingers find their way to my thigh, absentmindedly toying with the silky fabric of my dress. It's the way touching me seems to be his natural instinct anytime we're together. A constant need that I pray never fades—his hands belong on my body every moment of every day.

"There's a fire set up outside. I told Cass we'd go." Finishing off my glass, I stand up, nearly changing my mind about the fire when his palm slides across my ass, stopping for a quick pat on the cheek before finding a home on my hip.

And that's how we walk across the tent, weaving through the last remaining party guests. Denver stops off at the bar, grabbing two bottles of beer and an open bottle of wine.

Our hips bump into each other at random while walking down the gravel road to where a propane firepit is flickering. Thanks to the dry summer weather, we're not allowed real fires, but this works as a good substitute for the ambience. Denver plops into an oversized cushioned lawn chair and tugs me by the waist so I fall into his lap with a startled gasp. Within seconds, I'm conformed to the memory foam of his body like I never left. Cuddled in his arms, my legs slung over his, and the thumb of his free hand lightly stroking my upper arm. Giving up on the wineglass, I sip straight from the dark bottle and stare at the amber fire glow.

By the time Kate and Jackson join us about five minutes later, we're a group of twelve—including a few ranch hands and a handful of Wells cousins. Kate sits down with a mischievous smile, holding up a bottle of Fireball in triumph.

"I have liquor, no children to be responsible for tonight,

and my bed is within walking distance. I'm ready." She cracks the bottle, still held up in the air, and chugs the most Fireball I've ever witnessed a single person consume in one go.

Jackson finally snatches it from her hand, shaking his head with a laugh, and Denny releases his hold on my arm for just long enough to whistle enthusiastically at her. Then Jackson takes a much more acceptable drink from the bottle before passing it along to Colt. Slowly, it works through Denver's cousins, skips Cass and Red, and ends up in my hands.

"Oh God. I don't think you guys want me drinking this. Things will get weird in a hurry."

"Oh, just do it!" Kate shouts, then quickly mouths "sorry" when Red points out the sleeping baby in the stroller next to him.

I lock eyes with Denver, who raises a daring brow. "Maybe don't drink quite as much as Kate."

"I would be lying facedown in the dirt if I did." I press the rim to my mouth, and it clinks against my teeth accidentally when I take the smallest sip possible.

The cinnamon-flavored liquid burns down my throat, and I wince while handing it off to Denver.

"We should play a game." Kate claps her hands together, waiting anxiously for the Fireball to be passed back to her.

"Oh, Cassidy loves Seven Minutes in Heaven," Red quips.

She smacks him on the chest, mouth agape, and he coughs dramatically like she knocked the wind out of him.

"Way to throw me under the bus at your first opportunity," she says.

Denver tosses his hands up in the air. "Every girl here is taken, so how exactly would that work, anyway? I didn't think this was that kind of party."

Every girl here is taken. With a relaxed exhale, I melt into him.

"Never have I ever," Kate suggests. "I'll go first. Never

have I ever . . . had sex in that barn." Her finger sloppily points in the direction of the large white barn . . . a place Denver and I spent *many* hours in as teens.

He and I both drink without question until I lower my bottle and find everybody staring. Kate gives us a slow clap, elbowing Jackson.

Clearing my throat, I clarify, "Not *recently,* for the record. At least . . . not for me."

"Not for me either," Denver whispers into my hair. "Although . . . for old times' sake."

Jackson thinks for a second, staring at Denver with the look of somebody prepared to spill every secret about his brother. "Okay . . . never have I ever had sex in a stock trailer."

I turn to Denver and gasp. *"You told him that?"*

He stares at me like a deer in the headlights, slowly raising his beer to his lips. His free hand nudges the bottom of my wine, telling me to drink.

Red's howling laugh carries around the fire. "Where *haven't* you two done it?"

Licking a droplet of wine from my top lip, I turn to him. "We were teenagers trying to get it on whenever we had the opportunity. It led to some creative choices."

"Okay, okay, okay. If you two have done this, I have some serious questions." Colt leans forward in his seat, ready to drop a doozy. "Never have I ever had a threesome."

A reminder of fourteen years apart crashes into my chest when Denver sheepishly takes a drink. For a second, I quit breathing; staring at him, I'm willing myself not to cry. Because that's stupid. This is a game. We only *just* got back together—*if we're even technically together?* Everyone else is laughing, but his eyes meet mine with a shameful glance, and I find his hand to give it a squeeze.

It's fine.

Thankfully, the moment is saved by Cassidy's shriek when Red tries to discreetly turn to the side and take a drink.

"Oh. My. God." She cackles, then points between Denver and Red. "Wait . . . *together?*"

"Okay, I'm starting to really feel targeted by this game," Denver says with a groan.

Next to me, Cassidy pokes Red in the stomach. "Oh, you're so telling me all the details about this later. I can't wait."

He responds by choking on his drink. "Can we play a different game? *Please.*"

"Was there sword crossing?" Colt asks casually, touching the tips of his index fingers together. The entire group busts out laughing, and both guys nearly jump out of their seats with a synchronized, resounding *no*. Colt puts his hands up in surrender. "Okay, okay. Just thought maybe things got a little extra freaky."

We're all quiet, trying to work out the last of the giggles, when Colt raises a hand—presumably because he has another question—then steeples his fingers in front of his mouth. He's way too deep in thought for one a.m. and a dozen beers in. "Eiffel Tower, then?"

"*Jesus Christ, Colt,*" Denver yells, massaging his temple.

"Okay, you're all getting weird. I'm heading to bed." Jackson's face is scrunched in disgust as he stands. Kate—who seems rather intrigued by the entire conversation—reluctantly takes his hand and follows.

"Yeah, same." I fake a yawn. I'm not actually all that tired, and I'm only half done with my wine. But the thought of trying to stomach any new information about Denver's sex life is making the Fireball slosh around a bit more than I'd like.

Denver's quick to follow, linking our hands silently as we start up the moonlit path. The bonfire party becomes quieter with each footstep until our friends' voices are overshadowed by cricket chatter. The night air is still and Denver's grip on me is steady.

"I'm not mad at you. It's hard to hear or think about

sometimes, but that's on me." I glance over at the twitching muscle in his jaw. "Won't lie—part of me wants to know how the hell you ended up in bed with Red."

"I'd rather be dead than in bed with Red." A goofy grin cracks his tired expression when he catches the way his sentence rhymed. "That's the start of Dr. Seuss's new explicit sequel to *Hop on Pop*, in case you were wondering."

My cheeks burn with the need to laugh, and a squeaky noise resembling an unoiled door hinge slips between my lips. Denver pokes me, and a full-on guffaw escapes as I double over.

Gasping for breath, I look up at him. "You're the biggest dork I've ever met. *God,* I love you."

Not leaving room for me to clarify or backtrack, his mouth crashes into mine with unbridled lust. His hands slide to my lower back, pulling me close enough the pulsing between my thighs presses against the bulge in his jeans. And I frantically kiss him back, taking everything I've needed all night. Everything I've needed for fourteen years.

His tongue tangles around mine, hands raking through my hair to mess up the loose curls, and my hips meet his in desperation. I want him to fuck me right here in the middle of the driveway.

"*Fuck,*" he mumbles into my mouth, his voice drowned out by my moan as I feel him cup my pussy through the thin dress fabric.

"I need you inside me. Right fucking now."

Denver

Thank God for a lack of locks—the cabin door swings open and we stumble through, attached at the lips. Kissing her with primal need, I kick the door shut and cage her against the grooves of the log wall. Her moans echo through the small space, and my tongue meanders down her neck, across her dainty collarbone, to the freckles speckling her shoulder. Kissing each freckle individually, I slip the dress strap down her arm, doing my best to ignore the way my cock's already pressed painfully into the zipper of my jeans.

"I thought you promised to rip the dress off me." She hooks her fingers in my belt loops, forcing the bulge of my erection against her stomach. Grinding into me, her eyes meet mine with a fiery stare.

"Rip the dress, then make you come until you can't take another second."

"And then you still won't stop, right?" The corner of her mouth crooks upward, taunting me.

"That's right, baby. You're in for a long night." Reaching behind her slender body, I grab either side of the zipper and tug. She bites her lip at the metallic sound of zipper teeth tearing apart and nods slowly for me to keep going.

"Rip the *fucking* dress for me," she commands, spinning so I get a lovely view of her back and ass.

Without hesitation, I pull on the slippery fabric, letting

her enjoy the sound of every thread being ripped to shreds. Goosebumps trail down her spine in the wake of the torn fabric. One more harsh tear exposes her ass, which I grab, digging my fingers into her flesh.

"No underwear," I observe, exploring the softness of her bare skin.

"I was waiting for you to notice all night."

Blair's chest is heaving, and when I let the torn garment fall to the floor, she turns to grab either side of my face, kissing me feverishly.

"Good boy." *Fuck,* her praise makes my cock twitch. Her hands slide up my jaw, plunging into my hairline. "Now about the second part of your promise."

Tightening my grip on her ass, I walk us backward toward the bed. Her pierced nipples are pebbled and needing attention, and I take full advantage of the opportunity to mark her skin. Kissing and sucking her perfect tits, knowing how close she can get to coming from a little nipple play. Her head lolls back, the tips of her long hair tickling my forearms, and I toss her onto the bed.

She innocently pats the blanket, slipping a nipple between her fingers and giving the slightest pinch. I doubt there will be any gentle lovemaking filled with tears tonight. Not with the way she's looking at me like a predator hungry for a long-overdue meal. "Lose the pants and come here."

No belt in history has ever been removed so quickly. With a single snap, the belt and buckle fly across the room, landing on the hardwood floor with a twang as my pants fall to pool around my ankles. Blair sits up, grabbing my shirt in both hands, and tears. The row of pearl snaps fly open, and she kisses my stomach, working her lips over me until she's reached the waistband of my boxer briefs.

My dick's so fucking hard, it only takes a simple flick of the elastic for it to spring out, bobbing in front of her kiss-swollen lips. Her killer brown eyes look up at me through long lashes, and Blair slowly licks from the crease of my balls to the twitching tip of my hard cock.

I whimper, my hips bucking forward when she laps up the pearl of pre-cum. "Fuuuuck."

Hands on my hips, she pushes me back from the edge of the bed and drops to her knees on the hardwood.

"Baby, no. Hold on." I reach over her to grab a pillow for her knees. Then give her a few seconds to get comfortable, shifting side to side on the pillow, before I run the backs of my knuckles across her cheek.

Dainty fingers around my cock, she gives a firm tug to force even more pre-cum, and her thumb spreads it across the head. All the while, her eyes never leave mine. Teasing, with slow licks swirling the crown and dragging down the shaft, and fingers caressing my balls. Until I can't take another second of the torture.

"Suck my fucking cock, Blair." I grab hold of the base with one hand, her hair with the other. "I know you're dying to. Open your pretty mouth for me. It's been a while . . . I want to see how well you can take me now."

She hungrily drops her jaw, eager to let me slide my cock between her pouty lips, tongue instinctively rolling to cradle my shaft the deeper I go. I push forward until she's forced to breathe through her nose, spit pooling to lubricate my way into her throat. Her lips close around me, and I pull part of the way out before thrusting deeper into her wet mouth.

"That's it, baby. You're so fucking good at that. So goddamn greedy for my cock, aren't you?"

She digs her nails into my ass, forcing me even deeper, until she makes a small, sputtering, choking sound. With watery doe eyes looking up at me, eager for praise, and saliva spilling from the corners of her full mouth, she's the hottest thing I've ever seen. I can't help the grunting, whimpering mess I'm becoming with every thrust into her beautiful face.

Mouth stuffed with my cock, a drop of spit barely clinging

to her lip, she reaches between her legs, and the relieved moan reverberating in her throat encourages me to plunge forward.

I groan. "I can't wait to feel how wet your perfect cunt is from this."

She's fucking intoxicating. Sucking me, wet and sloppy, and with the occasional popping sound when she breaks suction on the tip of my cock. Every greedy sound that buzzes under my skin sends me closer to the edge of oblivion.

"Fuck, you look beautiful with your mouth full of me." I struggle to remain upright, shoving myself to the back of her throat and practically ripping the hair from her head while I fight to maintain some composure. Moaning her name like a goddamn prayer.

This moment. *Blair.* It's everything. My undoing and my saving.

And holy shit, she's working me over like it's her fucking job. The perfect combination of tongue, suction, firm hands, and a way of looking up at me that has me wanting to see her from this angle every day for the rest of my life.

"I'm going to come, baby," I say between groans of pure bliss. "Where do you want it?"

She pops off my cock and smirks. Blair's cutesy, mischievous smile turns into her eagerly waiting for me to come, with glimmering eyes and a wide-open mouth. Her fingers wrapped around me, jerking until it feels like a heavy weight is pressing on my lower spine. An electrifying jolt of pleasure forces its way out in a staggering moan, and hot spurts of cum shower Blair's face and tongue—the last few pumps falling short and trickling down her bare chest.

With most of the white substance collected on her tongue, my girl takes my pulsing cock back into her mouth and swallows around me. Muscles working to draw out every last drop as my knees threaten to buckle and my body convulses. She pulls away with a devastating *pop* sound, then rocks back on her heels, licking her lips and wiping a hand across the mess on her cheek. It takes more than a few seconds, and multiple deep breaths, before I can think or see straight.

"That was a big mistake, Blair." I pant.

Her face quivers, running through a gamut of emotions in half a second.

"Now that you made me come, I'm going to take all the time in the world with you. Pick your safe word, because that's the only way to stop me from forcing you to come over and over, until I decide you're done. And, *I fucking promise,* you'll be wanting to use the word long before I've had my fill of you."

She gulps. "Neapolitan."

I snort. *That's my fucking girl.*

"Spread your legs, baby. I have some promises I need to keep."

"Get over here then." She scoots up onto the bed, propping herself up with a plethora of pillows against the headboard, letting her knees fall apart. Gorgeous cunt on full display. After the way she just sucked me dry, she deserves to be a pillow princess while I worship her pussy for the rest of the night.

I start toward her, and her thighs slam shut. "Not like that. Show me you deserve a taste. *Crawl.*"

Fuck. She wasn't kidding when she said I don't know everything about her. But I'm the luckiest goddamn man alive to be here getting firsthand knowledge.

I drop to my hands and knees at the foot of the king-sized bed, and I fucking crawl. Because I'd do anything this girl asked me to do. Because I'm a fucking goner for Blair Hart. Because crawling across the bed to lick her sweet pussy is the absolute bare minimum when it comes to the things I would do for her. This comforter could be covered in broken glass, and I wouldn't hesitate for a single second.

When I finally reach her, my palms press to her open

thighs, steadying my orgasm-drunk body. And she inhales sharply with the smoothing of my fingers over her entrance. I can barely catch my breath, smelling her arousal, seeing it glisten on her pussy. It's too much.

"So pretty when you're soaking wet like this. I can't wait to see how perfect you look around my bare cock."

"First I need you to be a good boy and make me come." She wiggles her hips so my finger moves closer to her clit.

"Oh, baby. Pretty soon you'll be begging me to let you stop coming." I trace the delicate skin at the apex of her thighs, loving the way her chest rises and falls in rapid commotion, until I get close to her clit. Then she quits moving altogether, waiting with bated breath for pleasure.

I slip a finger halfway inside her. "Sucking my cock turned you on, didn't it?"

She nods, then shuts her eyes for a second to quietly say, "But . . . not as much as you coming on me did."

My heart stutters, and I think my brain's malfunctioning. *Goddamn*, that's a kink I will enthusiastically participate in. "You like that? What do you like about it, baby?"

"Being yours," she whispers.

I kiss her, tasting traces of my salty cum on her tongue. "You're mine, Hart. This sweet cunt of yours has always belonged to me. I was the first one to make you wet"—my middle finger sinks into her—"the first fingers and tongue across your clit, the first cock deep inside you. You've always been mine, but I'm happy to mark you as a reminder."

"*Yes, please.*" She whimpers as my finger swipes through a drop of misplaced cum on her chest, and I rub it over a nipple. My touch rolling over the hardened bud has her instantly writhing, frantically trying to slip a hand between us to flick a finger over her clit. And I fully seat a second finger deep inside her.

"More," she moans loudly. So I slip a third finger into her, and her eyes shut tight. "*Oh God.*"

"You need something more?"

She moans, thrusting against my hand, and a frail *yes* escapes her lips.

Her legs are already shaking when I bend down to taste her. Nudging her hand out of the way, I drag my tongue up her pussy and devour her.

She's sweet and all mine.

I circle her clit—smiling inwardly as she begins to fall apart—then suck it into my mouth. And she flings an arm down onto the mattress, grasping at the bedding. Her pussy walls clench around my fingers, holding on to me as she shatters. In a drawn-out, raspy moan, Blair comes undone with a final flick of my tongue across her swollen clit.

"You taste so fucking good." I lap up her wetness, feeling aftershocks vibrate through her thighs. "So goddamn beautiful when you come, too. *Do it again.*"

I dive back in, reveling in the way she squirms with the slightest touch. Working her with my fingers and tongue, it's not long before she's back to the brink of ecstasy again. Digging her nails into my shoulders, dragging her heels across the bedding underneath us.

And by the fourth time, she's begging me to stop, but she's not mentioning ice cream. So I don't.

Blair

"*Jesus Christ. Oh my God. Lord have fucking mercy.*"

Denver looks up from between my legs, where it's officially taking very little effort to draw out another orgasm. My clit's so sensitive, I'm convinced I can come from him staring at it with intent. I wiggle on the bed, the sheets sticking to my sweat-soaked back, and temporarily release the hold I have on his hair. It's a miracle I haven't ripped it all out, although I don't think he'd mind. He hums against my skin anytime I yank his hair or press crescent moon shapes into his flesh with my fingernails.

"Baby, this is definitely not the time or place to be praying." *Jerk.*

"I think I need to," I say breathlessly—a small part of me thankful for the conversation, because it means there's a break between the most intense orgasms of my life. "It might be the only way I survive this."

"All you have to do is say the magic word and I'll ease up." He homes in on my protruding nipple, flicking his tongue gently over it while he waits for my answer. Becoming impatient, he turns to biting and sucking at my tits. No doubt leaving the same type of hickeys he marked me with last time.

My problem, it turns out, is I'm too stubborn to admit

defeat. Instead, I need to win at his game. Make him come so hard he can't go on. "*Fuck me.*"

His tongue darts out to lick his lips, and he slowly fists his cock between my legs. "Yeah?"

"I need to feel you, and I want to watch you come all over my pussy."

This time, it's him who has to catch his breath. "Blair . . . *fuck.*"

I sit up, pulling him to meet me, and kiss him. His lips taste like my arousal, and I relax into the way he's loving me with a tenderness I've only ever had with him. Sure, he might be pleasure domming the fuck out of me, leaving me squirming and crying out for him to stop. But he also checks in to see if I'm ready to use the safe word, gently massages my lower belly while I come down from an orgasm, and presses featherlight kisses to my thighs despite the way they tremble out of control. It's the difference between random hookups and sex with the love of your life.

"One more first." He winks, and I groan as I fall back onto the pillows, but my hips instinctively lift when he brushes my torso with his lips.

"You know something?" he muses, drawing small patterns on my pink, tender skin with the pad of a finger, touching everywhere *except* my clit. In theory, I should be touched out, but I find myself silently pleading for release again. Needing him to never stop touching me.

"Mmm?" I drowsily grumble.

"I could spend the rest of my life right here. It's warm and comfy, I can have the tastiest meal on Earth anytime I want, and the view is stunning."

Then his tongue makes unexpected sharp contact with my clit, and I cry out. "Denver, *fuck.* Fuck me, please. I can't take it anymore."

"Are you feeling ready for some ice cream, baby?" He

rocks forward to trail the flat of his tongue from my clit to my belly button, like he's licking soft serve.

"I'm not tapping out—I need something more than your fingers. I need you."

He stops to think for a moment, looking around the room with mussed-up hair and a wild look in his eye. "I'm sure I can find something around here to fill you."

"No!" I sit straight up in a flash. "I've done rotations in emergency. You are *not* putting a random object inside me."

"Well, you need something, because I'm not giving you my cock yet." He chews on the inside of his cheek, eyes still scanning the small cabin.

"I-I have something . . . in my duffel bag."

"You've been holding out on me?" He scoffs, practically tripping over himself to get to my bag on the floor. The unmistakable zipper noise echoes through the room, and he laughs softly under his breath. "*Blair Hart*. You love making things easy for me, don't you?"

"I just love giving myself a challenge."

His chest rises and falls in a wild commotion as he's crawling back up the bed and filling the air with a heavenly hum. "I bet you're going to come so fucking hard with a bit of help from our little friend here."

I packed my vibrator because my mom often tears the house apart looking for items she's misplaced, and the last thing I need is her finding my hot pink dildo. I didn't expect I'd need to use it during my first weekend alone with Denver, but this is a nice bonus.

The rabbit vibrator slips between my thighs, filling me almost as good as his cock would. The small ears press square on my clit, rocking my body with an intense wave of pleasure.

Denver cups my chin and gives me a soft peck. "You want me to fuck you?"

"More than anything," I whimper, trying and failing splendidly to hold the impending orgasm at bay.

"Mmm. I think I'll let our friend have a turn first. See exactly how many times you can come in a single night. I want you fucking feral for me." He grips the base of the vibrator, shifting it slightly so my cries fill the room. "Come on it. Show me what you're going to do with my cock."

His tongue flickers over my nipple, and I'm a goner. Muscles quivering and jaw clenched, I unravel in under a minute. Crying his name as my feet drag across the sheets, making a corner pop off the mattress. When I finally come back down from whatever part of heaven he just sent me to, I find him holding up the saturated vibrator like a trophy.

"Fuck, I can't wait to see my cock dripping with your cum like this." He smirks before giving the silicone a languid stroke of his tongue to clean my mess. "Get on your knees and turn around."

Denver sits back on his heels, stroking himself from end to end while I switch positioning. His palm falls to my right thigh, demanding my legs farther apart.

"Get comfortable, but keep that ass up for me."

I lower my upper body, leaving my ass up and practically right in his face. My forehead resting on the cool pillow, I let out a deep exhale, waiting to feel him stretch me. His cock rubs down the seam of my ass, then he taunts me with the tip pressed to my pussy. My hips roll involuntarily, enough to feel the head of his cock slip inside, and he inhales sharply through his teeth. Doing my best to make him come undone, I push back against the bruising grip he has on my hips. Hopefully, I'll get him sunk deep enough that he loses control and fucks me senseless.

Clearly able to read my mind, he pulls out, leaving me even more needy and desperate. "Tough luck, baby girl. I warned you I was relentless."

Denver plunges three fingers deep inside, and I slam my fists down on the bed. A small, amused puff of air escapes his mouth at my temper tantrum, and his thumb briefly touches the sensitive skin of my inner thigh, encouraging me to spread wider. To give him everything.

"*Denver,*" I whine, nearly collapsing to the bed.

He laughs. *Fucking laughs.* "Should I give you what you want?"

There's no sense in even saying yes, because he's going to ignore it until I say the damn word. So rather than wasting my breath, I groan into the pillow. My legs are shaking uncontrollably, and I'm incredibly tempted to quit the game so he'll finally give me what I want. He has me ready to climb a wall.

But my competitive streak kicks in, and I reach between my legs, joining his hand—touching my clit in time with his undulating fingers.

"Fuck, Blair. Your pussy's squeezing my knuckles together." His teeth sink into my backside with desperation. He kisses, nips, sucks at my skin.

Then with a tenderness that takes my breath away, creating momentary panic, his tongue makes barely-there contact with my asshole. The sensation's unlike any I've experienced, and when I finally allow myself a new breath, I relax into the swirling of his tongue over the intimate area.

Feeling the shift in my body language, he breathlessly asks, "Does that feel good?"

"Don't stop," I whisper back, nodding like a broken bobblehead, body trembling with a mixture of nerves and anticipation.

Blush creeps from my chest to my cheeks when I think about what he's doing. But the way his tongue is bringing me bliss in skilled, rhythmic motion makes it too hard to tell him to stop. I clench the sheets under my head, pushing my hips back to force his fingers into perfect position, while he continues his assault on my senses. In one smooth motion, he replaces his fingers with the cool silicone of my toy, hitting my G-spot and rocketing a vibration through my entire body.

"Fuck, I'm going to—" I can't finish the sentence, because I'm suddenly on the brink of ecstasy. Overwhelmed with pleasure in so many places at once, the most intense orgasm of my life builds at the base of my spine, and I moan his name into the musky cabin air.

"Mmmm," he hums an agreement against my asshole, and I fall apart. Toppling to the bed with a convulsion that has me breathless and clutching at the sheets for dear life, I rip the toy from between my legs with a relieved gasp for air. My nerve endings are shot, and I might be dying, but what a fucking incredible way to go out.

And this *fucking man*. Slips a hand under my body, still drunk on the post-orgasm glow, and touches me with the insistence of back-to-back orgasms. But it's too much. My clit's sore and uncomfortably sensitive, the veins in his thick cock are dark purple and bulging, and I need him inside me before I wither away.

"You win." I rip his arm away from me. "*Fuck me.* I want the fucking ice cream. Neapolitan."

"Okay." He smiles, instantly moving away from my ragged body. Then pads over to the tiny kitchenette.

"But—" I start as he pops open the freezer door and pulls out a literal tub of ice cream. Standing completely naked in the dim light, he holds it up triumphantly, a devilish grin spread across his face.

In my wildest dreams, I wouldn't have expected my face to fall when looking at ice cream. But even after so many orgasms I've lost count—despite my legs being too tired to hold my own body up, and my muscles spasming at random—I'm still fucking desperate for this man.

I frown. "I thought . . ."

His nose scrunches up with a broad smile, and he tosses the ice cream back in the freezer before taking a running leap at the bed. "I'm just fucking with you. *That* is your reward for afterward. But I couldn't resist the opportunity—you played yourself by choosing Neapolitan as your word."

"*Denver Wells*, I swear to God." I side-eye him. "Fuck me."

Propping my ankles up on his shoulders, he slips his thick cock between my thighs, settling against my damp skin. Then he slaps it on my pussy, forcing a throaty whimper from me.

"I can't fucking take it when you make that noise." He notches the head at my entrance, and he bites my calf while pushing into me in a slow, smooth motion. "*Fuuuuck.*"

Despite my weary body, I prop myself up on my elbows and stare as his cock slides perfectly in and out of me. Filling me to the hilt, then slipping out covered in my arousal.

"You like watching the way you stretch around me?" He thrusts forward with more power, forcing my head to loll back.

"The perfect fit." I reach down to feel where our bodies meet. Where his shaft is pumping in and out with ease.

"I told you this pussy is mine. It's been mine since the first time we made love, and I don't plan on going another day of my life without feeling you strangle my cock until you shatter."

His words make heat rise from my core to my chest. I watch him watching us, a sated look in his eye. This feels like coming home to him, too.

He picks up the pace, punishing my cunt with forceful thrusts. Beads of sweat caught in his hairline and his fingertips bruising my shins.

I arch my back and he grabs frantically at my hips, pushing as deep as he can go. "Fuck, Blair. *Fuck.*"

I might not have the muscle strength to ride him—or do much of anything, based on the way my legs are quivering. But I want him feral, losing all control. So I slip my hands over my breasts, letting my nipples poke out between my fingers to grab his attention.

"Play with your fucking tits." He's losing control, with an ardent groan and sloppy thrusts. I pinch my nipples lightly, and he slaps the side of my thigh. "Harder, baby. Those pretty pink nipples need some attention."

I do as he says, toying with my nipples while he watches. "Like this, baby?" I ask innocently. "You want to come all over my tits, don't you?"

He nods silently, biting and sucking at my ankle. Finally, I have him like he had me. Out of control, reckless, and willing to do anything.

"Or maybe my face again?" I lick my lips, quirking an eyebrow. "Mmm. But I want you to come all over my sore pussy. I want you to be a good boy and make a fucking mess of me."

He whines against my bare leg, moving at a neck-breaking speed, getting so fucking close to coming apart, I can feel the hum under his skin.

"Blair, *shit*. I'm gonna—"

Leaving the sentence behind, he pulls out just enough to pump his cock and coat my aching, reddened skin in cum. Letting my legs fall with a thud to the bed, he collapses beside me.

"That's my good boy," I mutter between heaving breaths, wiping the sweat from his brow with my fingertips and giving him a long, slow kiss.

His arms wrap tight around me, pulling my head to rest on his chest. The steady percussion against my ear has me drifting in and out of consciousness, spent from the long day and perfectly sated by him. He presses his lips to my hair, mumbling something about ice cream that I'm too exhausted to catch.

"Bear," he nudges my shoulder. "Let's go get you cleaned up and ready for bed."

"Can't move," I grumble.

He slips out from under me, then scoops my body into his arms and starts to lift me from the bed—clearly struggling, but trying to pass it off like he's fine.

I shriek, flinging my arms around his neck. "Stop, you're going to throw out your back or something."

"Just . . . let me . . . carry you." He heaves me upward, and my life flashes before my eyes for a second when I'm momentarily suspended in the air. Then I'm clinging to him, and he's grinning. "See. It's fine. I lift heavier things than you all the time."

"*Bullshit.* I probably weigh as much as you do. Let me try to Bambi my way to the bathroom on these shaky legs."

He takes a couple shuffling steps across the small room, teetering with each one. "Just sit back and be impressed by how strong your man is."

My lips roll together, reining in a laugh. "Very strong. So impressive. Please stop before you hurt yourself."

"Baby, let me take care of you." He stops outside of the bathroom, considering how he'll fit both of our bodies through the narrow doorway.

"Unless your plan is to take care of me while I'm bedridden with broken bones, let me down." I scrub a hand across his jaw and kiss the short stubble. "You're already doing enough to care for me."

With a sigh, he slowly lowers my legs until the soles of my feet are firmly on the cold bathroom tile. Then I sit on the edge of the tub—at his insistence—and let him meticulously clean my skin with a warm washcloth.

We share sleepy, loving glances in the bathroom mirror as we go through our bedtime routines. And I can't help but picture how perfect life would be if every night was spent getting ready for bed encased in the comfort that comes from a gentle pat on the butt, or a raking of fingers through hair, or a wink in the mirror. Having the love of my life stand next to me at the bathroom sink, with a drowsy smile while we brush our teeth, is a fairy tale.

Both too tired for ice cream, we groggily crawl into bed and fall asleep tangled in each other's arms.

. . .

The next morning, I wake up to find Denver sitting in wait with a pint of ice cream and two spoons. His smile's brighter than the sun pouring in through an easterly-facing window.

"Little early for ice cream, isn't it?" I yawn, squinting at him with hazy vision.

"Ice cream for breakfast is one of the only perks to being an adult. Live a little, Hart." He hands me a spoon, and cracks the lid off the tub while I sit up.

Honestly, I feel so drained and parched and the most relaxed I've ever been, ice cream for breakfast makes sense. I hold a spoon heaping with strawberry ice cream in my mouth, letting it slowly melt all over my tongue, and my head falls to rest on his shoulder.

"You good after last night?"

I'm deliciously sore, and overwhelmingly content. "Perfect."

"Blair, you're everything to me," he whispers, his lips brushing my hairline.

I lick my lips, pulling the spoon slowly from my mouth, considering biting the bullet and telling this man, with no uncertainty, how in love with him I am. Lay it all out in front of us like a picnic. Admit to myself that it was silly to think for a single second we could take things slow.

But an obnoxious sound blares from his phone, making us both jump out of our delicious stupor.

"Oh, see. *This* is why I set the alarm." He hands me the tub of ice cream and slips out from under the thin sheets. Once the alarm's shut off, the room falls silent, and he looks at me. "Where are your meds? In the end pocket here?"

Immediately he starts rummaging, turning up with my antidepressants in hand before I even have the chance to tell him where they are.

"What . . ." I start to ask a question, but I don't even know what to ask, honestly. "Do you have an alarm for my pill?"

"Just one more thing I figured I can take off your plate.

Obviously, I can't take them myself. But I can make sure you do." He thoughtfully reads the label, then cautiously pours a single white tablet into his hand. "I didn't see any other pill bottles there, but if you have something else you need to take, I'll grab it."

"N-no. Just this one." The way he's so nonchalant makes my heart skip a beat. I lick my lips, slowly reaching for the pill. "Is it, um, weird to you that I take these?"

"Would it be weird to me if you had to take prescription medication for literally any other reason? No." He jumps back onto the bed, pressing a super fast kiss to my forehead. "Just . . . I know I'm repeating myself by saying I'm here if you need to talk. And I also know you'll ignore my offer, because you don't like needing help from anybody. But I want to be the one you tell everything to. Your good news, bad news, anything, everything. I want to listen to whatever you're willing to tell me."

Releasing a deep breath, I close my eyes and whisper, "Okay, well, I've been taking these since I was eighteen. . . . I had my first major depressive episode right after the abortion."

Denver
(eighteen years old)

When Mom died, we didn't anticipate Dad disappearing in the middle of the night less than a week later. But he did.

With fucking impeccable timing, too. He ducked out right before we had to bring the herd home from grazing land, leaving my brothers and me to call in favors at damn near every ranch within an hour of ours. You don't expect losing one man to have such a huge impact, but Grandpa died and Dad took over all the ranch operations, not bothering to teach any of us. So when he left, it meant my brothers and I were essentially handed a cattle ranch we had to learn how to operate from scratch. Austin didn't sleep for at least a week straight—trying to wrap his mind around the ranch's finances all night, then helping with chores all day. Jackson, Red, and I were working a minimum of fifteen hours daily.

Not to mention, Dad wasn't around for the funeral. Thank God for Kate, who took care of pretty well everything. By the time the date came three weeks after Mom had died, I was so spent, I did nothing but hold tight to Blair's arm and wait for the day to end. My mind erased every detail of that day, wiping the slate clean so I could jump back into cattle sorting the following morning.

I didn't complain about all of this—*not really*—because

it's hard to think about the fact that your entire world has fallen apart in the past few months when you're too tired to think at all. The work was a welcome distraction.

Blair and I hadn't talked a lot, simply because of our busy schedules. While I was busting my ass at the ranch, she was trying to play catch-up from the week she spent with me after Mom died. She drove to Wells Canyon the night before the funeral, and back to Vancouver the morning after, so I didn't even get time with her. Otherwise, we were surviving on the occasional text message, and a phone call once a week.

Despite all that, I assumed we were in a good place, until I got back to cell service just before dusk on a random weeknight and found a cell phone crammed full of missed calls from Blair.

I hung back, letting the rest of the guys get ahead on their horses, and called her.

"Hey, baby. I miss you," she said softly, with a waver in her voice that told me she'd been crying.

"What's going on?"

"I . . . well, um, I don't really—" Her breathing was short and snappy. Gasping.

"Take a breath, Bear. Are you okay?"

"Please promise me you aren't going to freak out or be mad or anything. Okay?"

My stomach twisted, preparing for the worst possible scenario. And to be honest, I was so exhausted, I couldn't even begin to picture what that scenario might be.

"*Please*," she pleaded against my silence.

"Okay, I promise."

"Denver . . . I—*fuck*—I'm . . ." Her words trailed off as the tears made it too hard for her to talk between heaving sobs.

"Are you—" I took a second to clear the lump in my throat before letting the words fly out at high speed, hardly taking a breath while I spoke. "Are you breaking up with me? I'm sorry

I've been so busy, and I haven't been able to come visit you, or even call very often. But I love you more than—"

"Oh my God, no. That's not what's happening here. I'm pregnant."

It's a small miracle I didn't fall off my horse, but—*fuck me*—I gripped the saddle horn for dear life. My eyes instantly glazed over, covering the hills around me in a disorienting fog.

"Blair, *shit*. Okay . . . when are you coming home?"

"I can't. I just took time off school for your mom, so I can't." The air was silent for a long while, then she quietly added, "I had an appointment at the school clinic today to confirm it. I didn't want to stress you out when I took the test yesterday, in case it was wrong."

"Baby, you should've called. Okay, so . . . you'll be home for Christmas in two weeks, right? The day after your last exam?" My brain spun in circles in an attempt to figure out a way to see her sooner.

"Um . . . I already scheduled my appointment at the hospital for right after I finish exams. So I might be coming home a couple days later than I thought."

My stomach flopped around like a dying fish. "Wait, why?"

"Denver . . ." Her voice dropped, thick with emotion. "I can't keep this baby."

I could've thrown up. Don't know how I didn't, honestly. Instead, I let my horse slowly bring us home—couldn't even find the wherewithal to hold the reins. "Well, don't you think we should discuss this?"

"I don't really know what there is to discuss. We can't have a baby . . . we're *eighteen*. I'm in school, you're killing yourself on the ranch."

"So you quit school and stay here—"

She cut me off with a new sharpness in her voice. "I quit school? One semester in and you think I should quit to be your housewife?"

"I can take care of you and the baby. You can live here, and I'll take care of us."

"We're eighteen." She sniffled. "I don't want that."

"What about me? What about what I want?"

"I don't think you want it either."

Wrong.

"Besides, I'm the one who has to give up everything in this scenario," she said.

Except she wasn't. Because this seemed so much like fate—after so many shitty things happening all at once, there could be a tiny glimmer of hope. If she didn't keep the baby, I would give up the chance to have a family again.

"Blair . . ."

"I didn't call you to have this fight. You promised you wouldn't freak out or get mad."

How was I supposed to not freak out?

"That was before I knew you were pregnant, and not letting me be involved in any decisions."

"Please, don't make this harder on me. *Please.*" She sighed into the phone, and I hated that I could perfectly picture the heartbreak on her face. "I'm trying to do what's best here."

"Baby . . ."

"I need to go. I have a class soon."

"Blair, can we talk more about this before you make any decisions? Let me have a say."

My words fell on deaf ears. I could tell by the exasperated exhale she responded with. "I have to go. I'll talk to you later."

"Please? I love you."

"I love you so much," she said quietly before hanging up.

The instant the line went dead, I rode back to the barn relying solely on muscle memory while my mind went a hundred miles per hour. I needed to talk to her in person, then she'd see how serious I was about making the best of this situation.

A baby at eighteen wasn't ideal, obviously, but we could make it work. My parents had kids when they were young, and it worked out. If Mom had waited for another five or ten years, she would've died long before we reached adulthood. So maybe having kids young was some sort of divine plan.

Fuck, what I would've given to get her input on things. If anybody had the power to change Blair's mind about something, it was my mom.

I went through the motions as though I'd been sedated, my limbs moved by marionette strings. By the time I was done getting my horse put away and fed, I was the last man around, the other ranch hands likely halfway through dinner already. Not that I was in a position to eat with my queasy stomach, nor did I have the time.

Without allowing myself a second to overthink, I beelined for the big house, stormed up the stairs, and packed a bag.

Sure, Blair's appointment was weeks away, but that didn't stop the urgency from coursing through my veins. I *needed* to be with her. The only way I was having another discussion about the situation was in person, and we desperately needed to have another discussion.

When I barreled back down the stairs, I collided with Austin rounding the corner. His massive hands gripped my shoulders to keep me from toppling backward—center of balance shot, thanks to the overstuffed backpack slung over my shoulder.

"Where are you going?"

I white-knuckled the banister. "I need to get to Blair."

"Denver." He fisted my shirt to prevent me blowing past him. His tone stern and fatherly. "You can't drive five hours to Vancouver right now."

"I need to see her. Talk to her."

"So pick up the goddamn phone."

"If that was an option right now, I would, Aus. But I need to see her. You don't . . . you don't understand." I peeled his fingers from my shirt one at a time. "I'm sorry, and I'll be back as soon as I get things sorted. Love you."

"*Denver!*" he yelled, following me outside. "You're not leaving here, too. You need to stay."

Realizing he probably thought I was taking off for good, like our father, I decided he deserved more. "Aus, I'm coming back. Don't say a word to anyone—Blair's pregnant. I need to go get her. I need to bring her home."

His entire demeanor shifted, along with the shifting of his weight as he stood on the front porch. His hand dragged down his face. "*Shit*. Okay. Okay, go get your girl."

The five-hour drive to Vancouver took just over four, but I spent an extra two trying to navigate the city streets. And forty whole minutes wandering through the campus looking for her building.

Standing in front of her door at two a.m., I briefly considered going somewhere to catch some sleep and coming back in the morning with a level head. But I also desperately needed to see her. And the selfish desire to look into her eyes outweighed everything else, so I knocked. Softly, at first, mindful of her roommates. Then a bit harder.

When a random guy opened the door, blood rushed past my eardrums and I gripped the doorframe to keep from passing out. I'd never been the jealous type—never needed to be. Blair was my girl. Everyone in town knew it, and she'd never given me reason to doubt her.

Until this motherfucker.

"Can I help you, man?" the tall, football-player type said. Sure, he had a solid fifty pounds on me, but I was pretty fast. I could potentially dodge punches for long enough to do some damage to this guy.

Clearing my throat, I tried to deepen my voice. "I'm here for Blair."

You know. My girlfriend.

"Denver?" Blair's voice came from somewhere deeper in the dorm. Then she popped up beside him in a tank top and pajama pants, hair falling over her bare shoulders.

"Brennan, it's fine. I got it." She grabbed his arm, shuffling him to the side. My eyes briefly flitted between them and, clearly noticing, Blair added, "Brennan's my roommate's boyfriend."

With a small huff, Brennan disappeared into the dorm, leaving Blair staring at me with a worried look in her eyes.

"What are you doing here? Did you drive straight here after our phone call?"

"Of course I did. I couldn't leave things like that."

"Den—you being here isn't going to make me change my mind."

"Can we talk about it? Please?"

She backed away from the door, and I walked into the small dorm space; it looked completely different from when I'd tagged along with her family to move her in back in August. The walls were decorated with posters, dirty dishes littered the counter, and a set of bikes leaned against the only spare wall.

"So, your roommate's boyfriend . . . Does he live here?" I looked around for traces of his belongings.

Blair rolled her eyes at me, locking the front door. "No. He stays here with Ashley sometimes. Come on, we can go talk in my room."

I followed her through the tiny, dark living space to her tiny, dark bedroom. Plopping down on top of her bed, I waited for her to sit next to me before breathing. And her hand fell to my thigh—a surefire sign she still loved me.

"Okay, what do you want to talk about?" she asked.

"Well, for one . . . how are you feeling? Are you sick?"

She shrugged. "I've been better, but it's honestly not too bad. Apparently I have an iron stomach when it comes to—"

Her hand quickly draws a circle around her stomach. "But I throw up anytime I drink. It makes zero sense."

"Well, better than being sick constantly." I connected the freckles on her forearm with my index finger. "Bear . . . I think we need to discuss all the options here. Maybe it's not ideal, but this could be something really good. You can always go back to school later, or get a job, or neither. I meant what I said about taking care of you."

She pinched the bridge of her nose between her shaky fingers. "I don't want you to feel obligated, and I don't want—I *can't* give up on school."

"But . . ."

"Denver. I can't have this baby."

"I thought we both wanted to get married and have kids one day." My voice wavered, and I had to talk around the mass quickly growing in my throat. Frantic about the way I was stroking her arm, because it suddenly seemed like this might be my last chance to touch her. She was pulling away. That much was clear in the way her palm slipped off my leg, and she didn't bother to replace it.

"*One day*. Not right now. We're barely adults. . . ."

"My parents got married at nineteen, and look at how happy they were. We can be like that. We can make the best of this. Be a family *now*." I had half a mind to be embarrassed over how weak and pleading my voice was, yet I couldn't bring myself to stop. "All I want is you, and this baby, and us. The house, the ranch, the kids. I want that with you. I want to give that to you, Bear. *Please*."

She wiped away the tears from under her eyes, sniffling. "Den . . . I love you, and I know that's the plan for one day. But I wasn't expecting this to happen right now."

I shoved my hand into my front pocket, eyes brimmed with tears as I dropped to my knee in front of her. My hands were so clammy I fumbled with opening the small jewelry box, pulling out my mother's ring. "You're my entire world. I would give up anything to have you—to have a family with you. If there's even a tiny part of you that wants the things we talked about, a tiny part that loves me, *please* marry me."

A sob racked her body. "That's not fair."

"Just like it's not fair for you to make a life-changing decision without caring about my input."

"I'm trying to do the right thing for myself . . . for both of us. I love you." The words barely left her mouth before she was clasping a hand over it to stop a gut-wrenching cry.

"Then marry me." I leaned forward, still on my knee, and grabbed her face so she was forced to look me in the eye. "Marry me, and I promise to make you so fucking happy. Please, Blair. *Marry me.*"

She was so quiet for a minute, I couldn't help but get my hopes up. Until I reached to wipe the tears from her jawline, and she ducked her head away from me—cutting me off and wiping her own tears.

I choked out her name with the last breath left in my lungs. And when she didn't respond, I sank back to sit on my heels and cried the hardest I had since the day my mom died.

Finally, after what very well could've been a century, she spoke back up. "I love you, but—"

"The word 'but' instantly means the first part of your sentence is bullshit."

She flashed a derisive sneer in my direction. "Now you're being a jerk."

I threw my hands up. "A jerk for wanting to give you the life we've dreamt about together? For wanting to have a family?"

"A jerk for not realizing that maybe your dream isn't the same as mine."

"Since *fucking* when? That's not true."

It couldn't be true. I knew Blair better than anyone else on Earth. She wouldn't have said all those things just to make me happy. She wanted it. I was sure.

I rubbed my watering eyes with the back of my hand. "We've talked about this so many times, and not once did you make it sound like that wasn't what you wanted."

"I want to finish the program I busted my butt to get accepted into. I want to enjoy being young, figuring out who I am. What if I decide I love being in the city? Or I get a job offer somewhere else?"

"What if you decide you love living on the ranch and being a mom? You can go horseback riding every day. We can be together every night."

She shut her eyes, squeezing tears from the slivered crack in her eyelids. "Denver, I *can't*. A few years from now, maybe I'd feel differently. But I can't right now. You're asking for a life I'm not ready for. If this is what you want—a sweet little housewife and a bunch of kids—maybe you need to find a girl who's ready to give that to you. It's not going to be me, though."

Bullshit. Every word spewing from her lips had to be complete bullshit. I refused to believe she actually felt this way because it felt a lot like . . .

"Blair, are you breaking up with me?"

She shook her head no, but the rest of her body language screamed yes—arms crossed, scowl painted across her tear-stained cheeks. Then she finally whispered, "I don't know."

I bit my lip *hard* to keep from screaming. "You can't. Blair, I came here because I can't live without you. I needed to talk to you. I needed—"

"You came here because you thought you could talk me out of a decision that affects *my* body, and has way more of an impact on *my* life than it does yours."

"I guess because I thought this was impacting *our* life. The one we've been planning *together*." I stared up at her as I sank further into the personal hell that was her bedroom floor, when all I wanted to do was crawl into her bed and hold her.

"I love you, but I can't be who you want me to be, or do

what you want me to do. I'm sorry. *So sorry.* I love you . . . and I hope one day you see this is for the best." She gulped, wiping away the tears that clung to the twitching muscle in her jaw. "My appointment is on December third, if you want to come be supportive."

"So that's that? Fuck me, right?"

"I'm not doing this to hurt you. I would never. I just . . . *can't.*"

On shaky legs—like a newborn horse—I stood and rubbed the pads of my fingers over my eyes. I leaned in and, to my surprise, she let me kiss her softly on the forehead.

The ring box fell from my hand to her bedspread, and I said, "You can keep this or sell it or have it melted and made into a necklace. Whatever you want. Mom wanted me to give it to you."

She didn't fight me leaving her room, or her dorm, or her building. She didn't text or call. And despite how exhausted I was in every sense of the word, I drove the entire way home and then continued right past the ranch. Until I found a road I'd never been on before, and when the road turned into something resembling a trail for ATVs—with a cliff on one side—I didn't even hesitate to continue.

Maybe it was dramatic and morbid and insane, but I didn't care a whole lot in that moment if my truck went off the road and rolled two hundred feet to the bottom. Instead of dying, I found a place where I could scream and nobody would ever hear me.

So I did. Until my lungs nearly collapsed the same way my knees did. Bloodied legs from falling on the rocks underfoot, I bent down so my forehead hit the dirt, and I unloaded every ounce of emotion left in me.

Then I sat there for hours before returning mid-afternoon to find Austin waiting in my room for me.

"No Blair?" he asked.

"No Blair." I stripped off the clothes I'd been wearing for

two straight days and slid into a pair of sweatpants. "I proposed, and then I think she broke up with me, actually."

"I thought you were going there to bring her home. . . ."

"She called me yesterday and said she made an appointment for an abortion. Thought maybe I could change her mind." My eyes were instantly heavy when my head hit the pillow. "Thought wrong."

"That's a piss-poor reason to break up."

"Suddenly everything we've talked about over the years has apparently been a lie, according to her. Seems like a damn good reason to me." I rolled to my side, facing the wall. "Can I get some sleep, please?"

"You two will work it out, buddy." Austin slapped his palm against my leg, and didn't say a single word when I spent the rest of the week in bed.

Blair
(eighteen years old)

"He's going to come," I muttered under my breath to Cassidy, while staring at the glass front door.

"You're probably right. I'm sure he got lost." She gripped my hand tight in hers. "Vancouver's pretty overwhelming for those of us who never leave Wells Canyon."

"I got so lost trying to find my classes at first." I used my free hand to keep my knee from anxiously bouncing into another dimension. "We haven't talked since he showed up at my place. I just . . . Cass, I don't know what to do."

"Well, that seems like a question you maybe should've asked *before* we came to your abortion appointment, but . . ."

"No, I know I need to do this. I'm in no place to have a baby. *Especially* since Denver and I aren't in a good place right now." I glanced over at the door again. "I don't know how to handle us. I don't know if we can ever come back from this."

"You will. I may have *zero* dating experience, but I know you two are the real deal. Everyone in town knows it."

Suddenly a nurse called my name from the swinging double doors.

"Oh, um. Can we wait another minute? I'm waiting for somebody."

The middle-aged woman gave me an earnest smile. "Honey, your appointment was supposed to be twenty minutes ago . . . we can't keep waiting, unfortunately. I'm sure whoever you're waiting for will be right here when you get back."

Cassidy let go of my hand with a nod. "I'll stay right here in this chair, so he won't panic when he gets here and you're gone."

Blinking back tears, I turned to follow the nurse, leaving my best friend and the baby-poop-yellow waiting room behind.

When the procedure was over, so was any chance of fixing Denver and me. Without explanation, the one person I'd always felt safe relying on—*trusting*—didn't show up when I needed him more than ever before.

Blair

Letting his ice cream spoon drop into the tub, Denver tugs me into his side, smushing my cheek against his warm, bare chest.

"I carried—*carry*—so much regret about everything that happened. I know having an abortion was the right choice, but I also know I could've handled things differently." I breathe the musky scent of his skin, holding as tight to him as I can. "I'm sorry I didn't talk to you about it first."

"You were right—we were in no position to have a baby. I was in no condition to actually make good on the promises I was making. Hell, I was acting like a baby myself."

"I wish we would've been in a situation where we could've kept the baby, because then I could've kept you. It sucks knowing I'm the one who broke us," I admit with a tear-filled sigh.

"You didn't. It wasn't your fault." His lips press to my head. "Good to know we've both been blaming ourselves, though."

I settle into the grounding thump of his heartbeat and say, "Can I ask you something?"

"Of course."

I take a deep breath and center my palm over the small bear tattooed on his leg. "Why didn't you come to the appointment back then? Or come to check on me after? You didn't—" I pause to compose myself, fighting the burning in my lungs. "I needed you to be there. I needed you to be with me."

"I hate myself for not being there. There's no excuse that's worth the air it would take to speak it. I was being a selfish kid, and you deserved better from me."

"Okay, so no excuses. Give me five seconds of honesty and tell me what you were doing that day, even if it hurts me to hear it."

I've always told myself I don't need to hear whatever excuse he had for not being there, thinking it would only cause more devastation. Now here I am, practically begging him to destroy me with his words. If there's any hope for a future, we can't sit with a live bomb in the room anymore.

"It's fucking stupid, though, Blair. I don't want you to hate me all over again."

"I *never* hated you," I admit. "I was heartbroken."

"To-may-to, to-mah-to."

I give his side a little pinch. "You're breaking the rules. You're supposed to be giving me your truth right now."

"I drove to Vancouver the night before and knew you were with Cass, so I stayed away. In the morning, I went to Stanley Park and walked along the seawall trying to clear my head—ended up scaring some old ladies because I was crying so hard. I had no reason not to be at your appointment. Hell, I sat in my truck in the hospital parking lot the entire time. And I knew I was being a complete piece of shit by skipping it, but I just *couldn't*."

My eyebrows pull together, and I tear myself from his arms to look at him. "I waited in the lobby for an embarrassing amount of time, hoping you'd show up. And you . . . were sitting in the parking lot?"

"See, I told you it was a shit excuse. I was so fucking lost that day." In a rapid succession of blinks, tears pool in his eyes, then dissipate. "After I left, I convinced somebody to bootleg alcohol for me, then I sat in the back of my truck bed drinking for the rest of the day. Cassidy sent me some threatening text messages, and I didn't bother responding because there was no explaining myself."

"What about after? Why not come after? Or call me. *Something.*"

"Figured I'd already lost everything I cared about, and there was no way you'd forgive me after that, so I gave up. Losing you was my punishment."

"You're my person. I would've forgiven you in a heartbeat."

"I-I wish I could change the way things went down. I shouldn't have proposed to you in the middle of the night in your dorm room in a last-ditch effort to keep you. I shouldn't have tried to make you give up your dreams because I saw a way to have a family while mine was crumbling. And I really shouldn't have made you go through it alone." His fingers press so hard to the inner corners of his eyes, I begin to worry he'll blind himself. "*That* is the biggest regret of my life. Followed closely by every action that made you think I'd moved on over the last fourteen years."

"I forgive you. A thousand times over, I forgive you." I pull away from his chest to look into the rich browns of his sad eyes, then I kiss the worry away from his face. Letting my tongue swipe across his lower lip and trailing my fingertips over the muscular ridges of his shoulders. "I hurt you, too. You needed me there for you just as badly as I needed you there for me. Can you ever forgive me?"

"I forgave you so long ago, Blair."

We didn't break—not completely. Years ago we splintered, but every whispered truth and healing kiss is bonding us back together. Stronger than before, with any luck.

Licking my lips between kisses, I test the way telling him I'm in love with him would feel. Last night it was said in a way that made it seem like a throwaway statement, rather than the emotional confession it should be. And he deserves more. He deserves the world.

My phone rings on the bedside table, and I groan at the intrusion, reluctantly peeling my skin from his to reach for it. If it were anyone but my dad, I'd ignore it without a second thought, never wanting to leave this moment with Denver.

"Hey, Dad. What's up?"

"I know you're having your weekend away, so I hate to bug you." His voice is quiet, like he's trying not to let anybody overhear. "But Mom grabbed a hot pan and burned herself pretty good here, so uh, if you could come take a look at it."

"*Shit.*" I watch Denver take a slow bite of melty ice cream in my periphery. "Yeah, I'll be there as soon as I can."

He's already out of bed and slipping into a pair of blue jeans when I hang up. And for a second, I do nothing except watch him with adoration.

"You gonna get dressed, or continue to eye-fuck me?" he quips. "Maybe do both at the same time, so we can get to your parents faster."

"You're coming with me?" I throw back the sheets, and stand to find my legs still wobbly from last night.

Covering the last traces of bare abdomen, he pulls the hem of his navy T-shirt down. "Of course I am, silly. One day you'll understand how serious I am about being here for you."

The antibiotic burn cream smooths across Mom's blistered palm, and the muscles in her forearm contract under my touch in an attempt to pull away.

"Almost done, Mom. Those painkillers kicking in at all?"

"Maybe a bit," she says through gritted teeth, clarifying that *no, they're not kicking in.*

Despite the pain of a second-degree burn—one which hopefully we'll be able to keep from getting infected, so long as Dad and I can stay on top of her to ensure she doesn't mess with the bandaging—she's smiling and cheerful. The entire drive to town was tense as I prepared myself to deal with an indignant Alzheimer's patient. Instead, I found my lovely mom sitting with a cool washcloth over her hand, watching *Wheel of Fortune* while eating a chocolate chip cookie, seemingly without the dementia fog clouding her memory and judgment.

She's herself today.

Thank God.

"Thanks for taking care of your clumsy old mom, honey." Her free hand brushes across my cheek, and I continue the methodical wrapping of her hand. Hopefully if it's wrapped in the perfect way, it won't annoy her, and she'll be less tempted to rip it off. "I can't believe I grabbed a cast-iron frying pan—I *knew* your dad had just used it to make breakfast, too, because I watched him cook it."

"It's our klutzy nature."

"Thank God there's a nurse practitioner in the family."

"You just like that you didn't have to waste a whole day going to the Sheridan hospital for this."

"Thank you for taking care of me instead. I know it's hard on you sometimes."

With a gulp, I dare to look at her red-rimmed eyes. A crease is wedged between her eyebrows, and the corner of her smile falters for a mere second before coming on even stronger than before. It's not genuine—I know the expression because I've worn it well many times. It's a smile despite it all. A smile to spite it all.

"It's fine, Mom. It's totally fine—I went to school for medicine for a reason, right?"

"I don't just mean the burn, although this part of it sucks a lot, too." Her injured hand squeezes mine despite the bandages, and she blinks away the flash of pain in her eyes. "I hate knowing you're here when you should be out enjoying your life."

"There's nowhere else I'd rather be." My voice cracks—an unstable attempt at reassuring her again.

"Oh, bologna, Blair." She laughs quietly, stealing my gaze as her eyes cut to the patio door. We're both staring out at my dad and Denver relaxing under the summer sun, chatting over a beer in a pair of lawn chairs. "I know you'd rather be with him right now."

"Honestly, I want to be with you." The bandage tucks around her hand, and I release a pent-up exhale. "Good as new."

"Thank you. Go have fun, and don't skip out on another second with him. I know that's where you'd rather be, although the lie was fairly convincing."

Wanting to spend time with him on a day when Mom's mind isn't muddied, and the fog's cleared, feels selfish. I should be taking advantage of the opportunity to be with her.

The one thing Denver and I regained when I moved home is time.

Time to learn each other again. Time to fall in love. Time to be together.

Time is the thing my mom fights every day, because there's a constant countdown ticking in the back of our minds. A foreboding reminder that we don't know how much she has left, but it's insufficient.

"I know what you're thinking, hon. But it's okay to want to get back to your weekend plans with your boyfriend." She winks, clearly grasping the full reality of my situation with Denver today—a nice change of pace from her typical confusion. "By some miracle, you're one of the lucky ones who found their soulmate. Spend every second you can with him."

"But I . . . I feel bad ditching you, with your hand and you—"

"Who said I wanted to hang out with you today?" She pulls a face that fosters shared laughter between us for a moment, and I smack her lightly on the arm with a scoff. Our giggling's loud enough the men outside turn to check on us with raised eyebrows. "I found my soulmate, too. And I'm so thankful for the years we've had together . . . you never know when it might end, so take advantage while you can."

"Thanks, Mom. I love you."

"I love you, honey." Her frail arms wrap around my shoulders, and my forehead knocks into hers. I swim in the comfort of the embrace, and the floral scent of her perfume, and the feel of her thin hair tickling my cheek, and all the things I pray I'll never forget. I lick away the tears sliding onto my lip and squeeze tighter.

"I love you," I whisper once more, with thick emotion clung to each word.

Letting up as Denver and Dad step into the living room, Mom hooks her thumb toward the front entryway. "Okay, kids. Go have fun, and I promise to do my best *not* to hurt myself again this weekend."

"You can't even make those kinds of promises. You've always been a klutz," Dad says with a chuckle.

Mom nods. "Put me in a bubble, and I'll break an ankle walking on the uneven surface."

"If there's any issues at all, I'll come straight back. We don't want this burn to get infected, so keep it clean." I wiggle a finger between both of my parents, because Mom's lucid enough to comprehend at the moment, but eventually it'll be up to Dad to keep an eye on her.

Clutching Denver's forearm with the grip of somebody about to be torn out to sea, I follow him to the truck. The tremble in my lip unnoticeable. The stinging in my eyes minor. The fickle beating of my heart insignificant.

Until it's not.

He slips into the driver's seat, asking where we're heading next, and my carefully constructed walls implode in one fell swoop.

"W-what happens . . ." I heave a panicked breath, not able to fill my lungs. "What happens if . . . if . . ."

"Bear. Take a breath." He demonstrates as if I don't understand the concept of breathing. Like it isn't something I've done without issue for thirty-two years—save for the time I caught a virus in ninth grade and it damn near took me out.

Television static pulses under my skin, and he's hauling me into his lap, cradling my skull so our faces are close enough his exhalations become my inhalations. Our souls intertwined on his truck's bench seat, Denver's palm is warm on my chest, and it tugs at my heart and lungs like a marionette until the panic dissolves.

"Talk to me," he mumbles against my cheek, sifting fingers through the hair at the nape of my neck.

And my biggest fear crashes down on us. "What if I end up like Mom?"

"Then we'll take it in stride, like every other possible thing that might happen in our lifetime. Dying is inevitable, living isn't. I want to live as much as I can with you, Bear." His lips press delicate kisses to every freckle on my face. "No matter what happens in the future, I'll be there."

He'll be there.

And so will I.

Blair

The air's still and quiet for the first time all morning, thanks to the seven children under the age of ten who turned the clinic into a playground while I gave their sweet, tired mother a Pap test—and twenty minutes relaxing alone in my office with a coffee from the machine Denver bought.

Now my brain's fried, and it's not even ten o'clock. I wheel my desk chair over to the new mini-fridge again, grabbing an individually wrapped chocolate and pushing myself back to my desk. Popping the treat into my mouth, I stare at the X-ray results in front of me for a middle-aged patient who's been complaining about hip pain. I'm trying to do my work, *truly,* but my eyes refuse to focus and my brain rejects any words I manage to read. So I glide back over to the fridge and try again.

Rolling my neck, I crack my knuckles and reach for my phone. Clearly work isn't happening today, and I desperately need out of my head.

> **Blair:** Hey, does that offer still
> stand for me to borrow a horse?

I toss the phone down on the desk and shuffle through papers, trying to look busy even though nobody's here to notice. I could be sleeping at my desk and it wouldn't matter. I glance at my phone, huffing over the fact that Denver hasn't texted me back within two seconds of receiving my message. After our long conversation the morning after the wedding, he's been even more adamant that I do some self-care, so I was expecting him to jump at this opportunity.

I'm swiping an obscene amount of chocolate wrappers into the trash can, silently cursing Denver for buying them, when my phone buzzes.

> **Denver:** Always. Grab the buckskin in paddock six. I'm pretty far out, so I can't join you, though.
> **Denver:** Think you remember how to tack up?
> **Blair:** Bet I can saddle a horse faster than you can
> **Denver:** Loser gives a BJ
> **Blair:** Sounds like a win for both of us either way

Shutting my laptop, I grab the light hoodie from the back of my chair and head out. It's finally a slightly cooler day, but the sun's shining. The perfect weather to clear my head somewhere on the back of a horse. Get a little taste of Blair Hart circa mid-2000s, before adult life stamped out my spirit. Now I'm back home, eager to pick up the fragments of my old self scattered around Wells Canyon like puzzle pieces. And I might finally be ready to let Denver help put me back together.

After a quick stop at home for a pair of jeans and my old boots, I'm flying up the mountain with the windows down and the playlist Denver made for me when we were kids blasting into the midsummer air.

·   ·   ·

"Buckskin in paddock six," I mutter to myself, standing out-side the barn and staring at pen after pen of horses. "Why do they need so many damn horses?"

I squint, counting away from the barn. *Okay. No.* There's nothing but a sea of bay horses in the pen six away. *Okay. Closest to the barn?*

That really feels like the most ass-backward way they could possibly do it, but truthfully, I wouldn't put it past them to number the paddocks in the dumbest way possible. I mean, clearly they didn't do it the way any normal person would, or my first guess would've been correct.

There *is* a buckskin gelding in the pen closest to me, so I walk to the gate, halter swinging at my side. Given the way he saunters over immediately, this must be the horse Denver was talking about taking.

"Hey, bud," I say softly, letting him greet me before open-ing the gate and walking in. "Wanna go for an adventure? It's been a while, so go easy on me."

I lead him over to the barn, get him ready, then take an embarrassing amount of time to find the right-sized saddle and get it on him. Thank God Denver isn't here, because he'd never let me live this down. Odessa could probably beat me in a race.

"I forgot to ask Denver what your name is, but I can't just call you 'hey you' all day. . . . I mean, I guess I *could*, but that feels ridiculous. So I'll call you Sandy for today, okay?" I settle into the saddle, getting acquainted with the feeling and mak-ing sure Sandy feels good about it.

I might've been a bit spoiled with Chief. I could do any-thing I wanted with that horse—there was mutual trust and love. And I was double-spoiled, because I had Lucy Wells to show me the ropes *and* help train my horse. But Sandy is one of many horses in the remuda, and he's likely only used to Denver.

So we start slowly, walking across the ranch to a trail I

know well. One that switchbacks up the mountainside, leading to the upper hayfields. From there, it branches to the lake, the upper part of Timothy River, unending pasture, and beyond for infinity. If you head in the right direction, you can ride for days into the middle of nowhere. No roads, no signs of civilization.

Sandy hikes the steep terrain in a series of grunts and huffs, shrinking the ranch buildings with every step closer to heaven. The scent of cattle slowly dissipates, replaced with cut hay and summer air. I'm breathing the deepest I have in ages by the time we reach the top, and I lean forward to give Sandy a loving stroke on the neck.

Shutting my eyes while we cross the open field, I let my mind think of absolutely nothing. Nothing but the way the sun feels on my face, and the summer breeze lifting up the ends of my hair, and the steady movement of the horse under me. Everything about this little slice of heaven is astonishingly poetic—something I forgot to miss while I was so busy missing everything else about this place. And I don't bother stopping the tears or wiping them before they fall.

I also don't check the time or touch my phone in my saddlebag. I simply ride and talk to Sandy, treating the saddle like a therapist's couch. "The thing is, I don't know what it's like to rely on someone, because I don't ask for it. My sister always needed help from my parents growing up, so I didn't ask. I didn't know how to ask for help, and when the time came when I desperately needed it, Denver didn't know. Because how could he? And yet I blamed him. . . ."

We stop at the river so Sandy and I can both have a drink in the shade. I need something to soothe my sore throat from talking so much. And I scoop glacier-fed water into my cupped hands to splash away the tear streaks down my cheeks before climbing back into the saddle. My legs ache from going so long without riding, but the warmth in my chest keeps me pushing on.

"I love my career choice, and I loved most of my life in Vancouver. It was just missing something. And I shrugged that off for years, going back to school for a master's degree, dating people casually, signing up for team sports. Searching for something to make me feel like myself."

We cross at a shallow section of the river and continue along a trail weaving among thick trees. The air has a sudden coolness to it that I assume is from being so deep in a thicket and close to the river. "All of the people and things and prescription medications couldn't fill the depressing-as-fuck emptiness. Between you and I . . . getting dicked down in a small town hasn't magically cured all my problems, but I feel more like the person I want to be than I have in a long time."

We carry on past the spot where we spread Grandpa Wells's ashes years ago—a cliffside overlooking the entire valley. On a clear day, you can see into town and well beyond, but dense, dark clouds seem to have settled in the valley during our ride. I smile at the indication of rain cloaking the mountain range beyond the ranch. Farmers pray for rain during a normal year, but a particularly dry summer like the one we've had elevates that to a new level. It's not simply about losing crops or struggling to water your animals. It's about losing *everything* with a single spark turned deadly forest fire.

"Let's get home, Sandy." I nudge his sides and start back down the mountain.

Within minutes, thunder's rolling down the valley, and Sandy's ears perk at the crashing roar. I gnaw the inside of my cheek, trying to remember if there's a faster route home rather than going back the way we came, which would mean two hours on the trail. Two hours and a *guarantee* we'll be riding through a thunderstorm.

We stop in the middle of an expansive field. Grass brushes across Sandy's knees with a whistling, damp gust. His body tenses under my legs, ears pricking at the swirling sounds of wind and rain and thunder that seem to be all around us. I run a palm over his neck, other hand anxiously rubbing the saddle horn until it creates hot friction against my skin.

I've been caught in storms before. I've driven cattle in intense rain and howling wind. But that was then—when I was young and reckless and trusted my horse with my life—now my head's getting the better of me.

I was an idiot to think I could still do this after fourteen years.

A crash of thunder has Sandy sidestepping, and my blanched knuckles curl around the reins. With a series of desperate soothing sounds, I manage to steer him toward a thicket of poplars as the first few droplets of rain fall.

We both just need a minute to get our bearings, and we'll continue on to the ranch.

It's fine. I got this.

I can't get out of the saddle fast enough by the time we reach the trees. The claps of thunder come from directly above, rattling my bones and sending shivers up my spine. Sandy throws his head back, backing up in a threat to run.

"Hey, whoa. Let's *not* ditch me here, okay?"

Though whale-eyed and blowing hot huffs of air on my face, he's no longer testing my grip on his hackamore bridle—freezing in place as another bout of thunder rolls through the dark clouds.

Rain litters the canopy overhead, trickling down through the fluttering leaves, until only a few drops crash to the earth. And in the field we just crossed, it comes down in sheets, sideways and hitting the earth with such force it bounces back up. I've ridden around this hillside enough to know the trail back to the ranch is treacherous in bad weather—a combination of slick mud and smooth, slippery rockface can spook even the most bombproof horse.

With a hard swallow, I look over at Sandy, catching my reflection in his deep brown eyes. Seems the fear in his dilated pupils is a damn good mirror of my own.

"Fuck," I mutter, rubbing a clammy hand down the damp

denim stretched over my thighs. "We need to get home some-how. . . . Maybe if we take it slow, it'll be fine."

Standing next to him, I stare at the saddle, racked with a sudden, irrational fear.

It's not irrational. You don't know this horse, he could spook and throw you off.

Swallowing my fear, I reach for the saddle horn and step a boot into the stirrup.

You used to spend every free moment in the saddle. You know how to ride. You'll be fine. Like Lucy used to say: do it afraid.

My right foot anxiously bounces on the ground before I swing it up and over. And I'm in the saddle. Sure, I can't breathe, and my sternum might be collapsing in on my heart. Black speckles distort my vision, and I can barely get my right boot into the stirrup because my entire leg's trembling out of control. But I'm here.

Lifting the reins, I encourage Sandy ahead. And for a mo-ment, he obliges without question, until lightning strikes so close I hear the sizzle of electricity and he's sidestepping through thick forest. I duck to narrowly avoid an oncoming branch, frantically shushing him with hoarse noises that only seem to make the situation worse.

I yank a foot from the stirrup just before his side smacks into a thick pine tree, and I'm out of the saddle faster than a relay horse racer. I nearly lose hold of the reins when he threatens to rear, tossing his head around like he's headbang-ing to the drumming thunder.

"Okay, okay . . ." There's no convincing him I'm calm, but I cautiously reach to rub his neck anyway. "Let's walk home."

I don't want to think about how many hours it'll take to get back if we walk, but it's a better plan than sitting in a clump of trees waiting for somebody to find us. In my experi-ence, nobody ever magically appears when you need them to. I lost myself in that purgatory before—waiting for the help I was too afraid to ask for but assumed people would know I needed. So I learned to help myself. I'm the only one I can count on.

It's a slow start, moving through thick underbrush on foot, tugging a flighty horse behind me with an aching grip on the reins. After about fifteen minutes, and barely any ground covered, I head for the tree line. I'd rather become sopping wet in the storm than trip over a fallen log and break my ankle.

Sandy and I step out into a wet blanket of fog socked in all around us, so dense it cuts the sun, and I genuinely can't tell whether we spent fifteen minutes in the forest or five hours. No valley or mountain views to indicate how much farther we need to walk. No recognizable boulders or trailheads.

And I don't know where I am, but it feels like I should know where I am. Everything's familiar and completely foreign simultaneously.

Reaching a spot where the fog doesn't lie so heavy on the earth, I'm finally able to get a good look around. And I'm hit by a slug to the chest over the view of a tree just beyond this forested strip. I'd know it anywhere, even though the world around it has grown and changed. New growth, a million tiny blue flowers freckling the soil, and one unmistakable carving etched deep into the bark.

The deep carvings are weathered and smooth, yet everlasting despite the tree's best efforts to heal itself with a thin sheen of hardened sap. I trace the lines with my fingertip, heart skipping with the reminiscence of Denver's love-drunk smile as he marked up this tree.

I slowly wet my lips, tasting tears I hadn't noticed were slipping down my dewy skin. What I would give to be just as sure about our love and our future as I was that day. As sure as Denver is now.

Never loosening my hold on Sandy, I rest my back against the bark and run my free hand through my hair before sinking to the cold grass, inhaling the petrichor and waiting for my heart rate to slow to normal. I'm not sure how long I sit there since every second feels an awful lot like an hour. But eventually the sky's brighter, the clouds sit a little higher, and the percussion of rain slows to a light tip-tap.

"Think we can go now?" I hesitantly ask Sandy, making no move to actually leave.

The thought of walking back to the ranch exhausts me. The thought of riding back to the ranch by myself . . . *fuck*, it terrifies me.

Why does it terrify me?

I study the horse casually grazing on a patch of clover, no longer affected by the storm. He seems okay—surely safe enough to ride. And yet the idea of sliding into the worn leather saddle makes my stomach clench and my lungs collapse.

A leaf twists and twirls through the air, flitting down to land on my shin, and I glance up at the sturdy tree. Standing solo in a field of tiny blue forget-me-nots, the tree stands strong in the worst of storms, cutting the harshest wind. Entirely alone.

My eyes snag on the spot where Denver carved our names.

Denver . . . Maybe . . .

I shake the thought aside, though it pops back up less than a second later.

I can ask him for help.

My knees threaten to buckle when I stand and make my way to the saddlebag to grab my phone. Reflexively, I'm talking myself out of calling before the phone's even in my hand. He said he was busy today, so surely he won't be able to come help me. The preemptive ache in my chest says it's not worth asking in the first place, when *no* is such a likely answer.

But . . . he loves me. Maybe even more today than he did back then. And what if he's serious about wanting to make things right? What if those promises actually mean something now?

I what-if myself for so long, even Sandy is giving me the side-eye. I've suffered in silence countless times because it felt easier than asking for help. And now there's a man who insists at every turn that he *wants* to help, and he's already been doing so without me asking for it. We aren't eighteen and misguided by heightened emotions anymore. He's here. He loves me.

Clutching my fear close to my chest, I shakily hold the phone to my ear.

"Denver?" I let out a pent-up breath. "I need you."

Denver

Stomping through a sprawling puddle, I take a deep breath of humid summer air. The brief torrential downpour was a welcome sight after weeks of drought, and it left the earth so drenched, the soil needs time to drink it all in.

I rode damn near halfway across the ranch to help Red fix one of the many tractors we have working the hayfields this time of year. The old thing broke down halfway through baling the field, and we've been at it for hours trying to figure out what the hell's wrong with it.

"I think we need to call it quits and burn the damn thing to the ground," Red says, wiping his brows with his forearm.

"Light the match." I hold my hands up in the air. "I didn't see anything."

With the amount of hours we've spent replacing old parts and repairing shit in the field over the past few months, having the practically vintage piece-of-shit disappear would be welcomed by me. Austin might have other thoughts, since he'll have to come up with the money in the ranch finances for a new one. But I don't see him out here fixing tractors in the pouring rain.

I stand back, staring at the torn-apart engine and scratching my head, wishing I was out riding with Blair instead. Hopefully she managed to find a dry spot during the storm.

Standing next to me, Red packs his tin of chew with a quick snap of his wrist. "If only I had a lighter."

"Fuck. Guess we have to fix 'er then." With a resolute sigh, I pull a crescent wrench from the back pocket of my jeans like a soldier pulling out his weapon for battle. "At this rate, every damn part on this thing will be brand-new before the end of haying season. Get in and try to fire her up again."

Waiting for Red to climb into the cab, I stroke my knuckles across the sharp stubble on my jaw. I'm usually pretty good at diagnosing issues with machines. I'm not a mechanic, by any means, but we all fell into various roles around the ranch after Grandpa passed, and this is where I landed. Now I handle most maintenance and repairs so we can save an expensive service call-out whenever possible. But this one might need the help of somebody who knows what the hell they're doing.

To neither of our surprise, the tractor doesn't start, and Red sits in the cab shaking his head in annoyance. Austin's not going to be happy, but there's no way we have the ability to fix whatever's wrong with the engine.

"Fuck," I mutter angrily, chucking a wrench at the ground at the same moment a loud ringing chimes from my pocket.

Blair.

That's all it takes to still the tense air around me. After years of wishing every phone call was from her, seeing her name flash on my screen is something I'll never get over—the reminder that she's mine again soothing my erratic, irritated pulse.

"Hey, baby." My voice instinctively softens when I pull the phone to my ear. A rush of summer air blows the back of my shirt up, and I reach behind with my free hand to tuck the fabric into my jeans.

"Denver." It comes out in a half-sob. "I need you."

"What's wrong? Are you okay?" I toss my arm up in the air

to get Red's attention, signaling for him to wrap it up. We're going home. "Where are you, Bear?"

"I'm okay. I just . . . sorry, I didn't mean to bug you. I know you're busy."

"Where are you?" I repeat.

"By our tree."

Our tree. I've actively avoided that section of the ranch for years. When forced to take the trail past the thicket of trees that keep our little clearing hidden from the world, I ride as fast as my horse can go. And even still, I feel the emptiness and regret tucked deep into my chest for days after each pass.

"I'll be right there," I say, already mounting my horse.

Red slams the cab door and yells at me to ask where I'm going. I shout something incoherent over my shoulder about Blair, and cleaning up our mess, and telling Austin I'll talk to him later.

"It's not a rush," she says. "You can finish helping Red first. I'm okay, promise."

Fat chance I'd leave her sitting alone somewhere when she needs me. I might not have known better at eighteen, but I do now. I also know exactly how much it must've taken for Blair to ask for my help.

"I'm already on my way. Wanna tell me what's going on?"

In the time it takes for her to waver between telling me and not, my mind reels with possibilities. And unless she's lying about being okay, none of them seem plausible.

Thrown from the horse? Nah.

Fell off? Nah.

"I'm . . . scared," she finally answers.

"Scared? Of what?" I chuckle under my breath, heart pounding as my horse flies through the open air.

She tries to laugh it off with me, but it comes out awkward and laced with sadness. "Riding."

Shit. That was definitely not the answer I anticipated from her, of all people. Blair Hart scared of riding? The girl who jumped on the back of a horse at thirteen without a single trace of fear in her eyes? Who was running barrels only weeks later, letting the wind stream through her long hair, smiling like she'd never felt more alive?

But I don't say that. I know better.

"That's okay, baby. I'll be right there. And I'll get you home."

I push my mare even harder, and my heart beats in time with the clap of her hooves over well-packed soil. Less than ten minutes later, I'm crossing through the tree line and leaping out of the saddle before I've even gotten to her. She looks up at me from where she's cross-legged on the grass, rolling a blade of grass between her fingers, and smiles meekly.

"Bear." I hustle across soft dirt and drop to my knees next to her. "Are you sure you're okay?"

Despite the red eyes and tear-stained cheeks which indicate otherwise, she nods. "Yeah. I just feel really stupid."

"There's nothing to feel stupid about." I pull her into my lap. My palms hold steady on either side of her face, her hair dances around our faces in the wind, and I kiss her, sweeping my tongue across her bottom lip. She opens her mouth with a relaxed sigh, looping her arms around my neck.

"I do, though. I was doing perfectly fine until we got caught up in the storm, and Sandy was starting to get a little spooked—"

"Sandy?" I interrupt. "Who the hell is Sandy?"

"I didn't know what your horse's name was, so I was calling him Sandy. It felt weird not to have a name for him." She gestures toward a horse . . . not my horse, that's for damn sure.

"Don't know who the hell that is, but he's not my horse." I laugh. "Blair Hart, you're a horse thief."

Her wide eyes bounce between the buckskin and me. "I

assumed paddock six was the sixth one moving away from the barn, but there wasn't a buckskin there. So I grabbed one from the paddock closest to the barn."

"Oh, shit. I'm a moron." My palm slaps to my forehead. "We did some shuffling because Jackson got in some new horses for training. My buckskin's in . . . *actually*, shit, I don't even remember where Austin moved him."

She gawks at me. "You were *trying* to kill me, weren't you?"

"You caught me. I wanted to murder off my future wife." Fuck, does that word feel good rolling off my tongue. "This must be the gelding the McKinney Ranch down in Fox Ridge sent over. I don't think Jackson's even been on him yet, so clearly you've still got some riding skill up your sleeve."

I jokingly reach for her shirtsleeve, pulling it away from her arm so I can peek up it. Anything to earn the slimmest smile from my girl.

"Stop." Her lips lift into a half-smile, and her fingers rap against mine. "I got in my head and . . . well, I wanted you."

My heart's real close to bursting from my chest. Stroking her head and using the weight of my arm to pull her against me, I say, "I'm here, baby. You want to try riding with me? Or I can call Austin and see if he'll drive a truck up here. Tell me what you want me to do."

Blair hesitates for a moment. "Um . . . I think I can ride."

"I don't want to push you."

She shakes her head, interlacing our fingers and holding them tight in her lap. "You'll be right beside me?"

"Nope, gonna take off at a gallop. Make you eat my dust." I kiss the top of her head. "I'll be *right* next to you. Hell, we can even share a horse, if it'll make you feel better."

The attempt at a glare she gives me is more adorable than threatening. "You *would* ditch me, jerk."

"Bear, I'm never leaving you." I brush my free hand over her chin, cupping it to hold her eyes on mine. "*Never.* Thank you for calling me, instead of doing something that scared you all by yourself."

This is the man I want to be for her. Maybe now she's finally ready to let me prove myself.

Her full lips press softly to mine, and she breathes out the words I thought I might never hear again. "I love you."

"I love you, Blair. I don't even know how to express it in a way that'll ever show you exactly how much."

Slowly, without letting my touch leave the small of her back, we move to stand below our tree. I can't help myself from pushing her against the rough bark and crashing my lips to hers with a heart-stopping, breathtaking kiss. She quivers under the skimming of my fingertips beneath the hem of her shirt, and the kisses turn frantic. We're teenagers stealing a moment of privacy, tongues colliding, moans stolen, fingers wandering.

She wraps a hand around the fabric of my shirt, breaking the kiss for a single moment. "Denver, thank you for coming when I called. I didn't . . ." Her voice cracks, and she kisses me again, as if the taste of my lips and the feel of our bodies pressed together is what's giving her the courage to open up. "I wasn't sure you'd come. I almost didn't call because I didn't know how I'd handle it if you didn't."

"You call, I come. Always." My eyes search hers. "I don't care if I'm a million miles away, or if you think the reason is stupid, I want you to call me every single time the urge strikes you."

"I love you," she repeats against my lips. "I love you, Denver Wells."

"Let's get the heck out of here before it starts raining again. I think we need a hot shower together and some ice cream in bed."

She nods, and I grab her hand to lead her toward the horses. As steady and sure as she was while kissing me, she's noticeably shaken now. It's not that I thought she was exaggerating when she said she was scared—Blair wouldn't ask for help unless she felt backed into a corner in some way. Which means she was *fucking* terrified. And it's scrawled across the panic in her rich brown eyes, the slow worrying of her bottom lip, and the anger etched between her brows.

Every horse person has been where she is before. It's easy to say *you fall off and get right back on again,* but a bad moment can plant seeds of doubt, and eventually the deeply rooted fear can become debilitating.

I squeeze her hand to remind her I'm here, and I've got her. "Let's ride double just until we get out of this clearing. On my actual horse this time."

"Well—" She looks over at me tentatively, and I smile back. "Okay."

We both know she doesn't need any help getting on a horse, but that doesn't stop my hands from finding her waist and boosting her into the saddle. Once she's settled, I slip a foot in the stirrup and hop up behind her.

Holding one hand around her and the other leading the buckskin she rode in on, I ask, "You okay?"

Blair's heart is racing, the hand resting over mine clammy. And naturally, she insists she's fine. I'm not buying it for a second. Never have. I don't understand why she still does this, when it's so obvious I know her better than she knows herself.

"Bear, I love you. You can tell me if you're not okay." I kiss her shoulder, hoping she feels the warmth through the fabric. "Five seconds of—"

"I'm a little nervous. Only because it's been fourteen years, and the horse was getting spooked, and he's not even your horse, anyway."

"One spring a couple years back, we were out here driving cattle. The season had been really warm and dry already, and there was a fucking snake on the trail. Well, my mare reared up before I even realized what the hell was happening, and down I went." I hold tighter around her waist, rejoicing in the slow melting of her tense muscles. "Physically, I was fine. But for some reason I was fucking terrified to get back on. It felt stupid, considering I spend my weekends getting bucked off horses for fun, but it was different somehow."

"You weren't prepared for it," she offers up, glancing over her shoulder.

"Maybe." I shrug. "Either way, it took a few days before my confidence returned. And that trail probably spooked me even more than it spooked my damn horse for *months* afterward. It's okay to be scared, baby. We'll get you back running barrels before you know it."

For a minute or so, she's quiet and contemplative. Her back against my chest, head resting on my collar. Her breathing becomes easier with each step, and she reaches back to stroke my cheek. "I can't believe I found you."

My eyes narrow on hers. "Are you sure you didn't get thrown off and you just don't remember because you smacked your head? I think you meant *I* found *you*."

"If that happened, I wouldn't remember because I smacked my head. I meant I can't believe I came back to Wells Canyon and you were still here. That I found you, and you still love me. You didn't meet somebody else you wanted to marry, have babies with, and do all the things you wanted."

"I never wanted those things with anyone but you." It's a slow ride across the golden field, with Blair shivering in my arms.

"D-do you want those things still?" she asks after a long period of silence. "A wife and babies?"

"I want whatever you want."

"No, give me five seconds of honesty." Her hand moves to rest on my thigh. "Tell me what *you* want."

"*You*. I want you, Blair. If you're the bride, I want to get married. If you're the mother, I want kids." I swallow the lump in my throat. "What happened back then was a downpour.

There was this constant, agonizing, crushing weight on my chest that I couldn't shake—believe me, I tried. I woke up every morning feeling that way for fourteen years. But you walked back in bringing all the sunlight with you. You didn't notice how much brighter my life's been since the ambulance ride, because you weren't here during the dark days. So I want you. I want your sunlight and your love—whatever comes with that. Understood?"

I feel her head nod slightly against my shoulder. "I came back here after getting the worst news imaginable, and despite the grief of it all, I'm the happiest I've been in years. I get it. My life's been brighter since the ambulance ride, too."

"I can't wait to spend the rest of our lives together," I say before pressing a kiss to her temple, just as we skirt around some tall brush, and we're home free. I'd love to ride the rest of the way home with her safely tucked against my chest, but I'm afraid it'll only make things *that much* harder when I want to get her on a horse again. "You feel ready to ride by yourself?"

There's immediate rigidity where a second ago she was loose and free.

I add, "I'll give you this horse. I promise she's as bombproof as they come. And I'll be right next to you."

With a hefty exhale, she agrees. And seconds later, I'm mounted on Sandy, or whatever the fuck his name actually is. I look over at Blair, gauging her reaction. Definitely tense, but she's still breathing—albeit each breath seems calculated.

"Okay, I'm good," she says, giving a tiny nudge of her heel to get the horse moving underneath her. "I'm good," she quietly repeats to herself.

When I give my horse a nudge, he stomps his front hoof in defiance. When I give a tiny spur prompt, he goes from zero to one hundred in about two seconds. Little fucker thinks he's a bronc or something.

"Oh, you fucking bastard, whatever your goddamn name

is." I tighten the reins in, bringing him to a halt that he's making it clear he's unhappy about.

"His name's Sandy," Blair offers, suddenly looking a lot further from a panic attack than she was a minute ago. In fact, she has a teasing smile that makes this entire shitshow feel worthwhile.

"His name's about to be glue," I reply.

"Hey, that's not nice. He was a very good boy to me for our entire ride."

My head's on a swivel as I make Sandy-or-whatever walk in a wide circle—clockwise, then counterclockwise. I'm no horse trainer, like Jackson is, but I subscribe to the belief of *fuck around and find out*. And this gelding is about to find out, if he doesn't want to follow my lead.

"Wanna trade?" I ask over my shoulder.

"Come on." Blair gestures toward the trail with a tip of her head. "Or do I need to teach you how to ride a horse? I know you're used to getting bucked off, not staying on."

"*Hilarious.*" I stick out my tongue at her. This time Sandy makes a wise choice by listening to my cues and starting toward the trail without issue.

True to my word, I ride so close I'm able to reach out and give her thigh an empathetic squeeze from time to time. The journey may be slow, but that gives us time to talk. About then, and about now. There's reminiscing and laughter. And slowly but surely, Blair eases into the saddle with the exuberant confidence she had at sixteen.

When we crest the hillside, staring down the final, steep descent to the barn, I'm genuinely sad it's over. "We should do this more often. Like . . . every day."

"Every day?" Her sweet laugh carries over the wildflower-painted mountain. "I don't know how I'll find the time to do that. But maybe weekly. Aside from my little moment of panic, it's nice to be on a horse again . . . and even better with you here."

"I shouldn't have let you go out alone today. Count on me being there for every ride from now on." The warm breeze that's been following me this entire time encircles us again. Call it crazy, but I'm starting to think it's Mom. "I'll always be here, Bear."

Blair

"I think I want to try running barrels," I say as Denver and I ride side by side along the ranch road.

In the two weeks since the day I scared the crap out of myself in the storm, we've ridden together four times. It's brought me more joy than anything has in years, and I'm ready to feel the rush of ecstasy I've only experienced barrel racing—the invincible, weightless air in my lungs and galloping beat in my chest.

"Yeah?" He veers left, toward the riding arena, instead of the barn. "Let's do it, Blair Bear."

My heart rattles against my sternum, begging to be set free, adrenaline coursing through my veins as Denver shuts the arena gate behind me. I'm not anticipating it being a smooth ride, given I'm out of practice and this horse has likely never seen barrels in its life.

We take the barrels easy the first time, curving around the last section of the clover pattern and bringing it on home to Denver, who's leaning on the fence rail. For a moment, I genuinely expect to see Lucy Wells standing next to him, cheering and jumping up and down. My eyes burn harder than my chest. I sniffle back the urge to cry and rake a hand through my windswept hair.

I was right. I needed this.

"Baby, you're a natural," Denver calls out. "And I fucking love you."

Pawing at the strands of hair strewn across my face, I look up at the vibrant blue sky and let the sun soak my bare skin. Once my breathing is mostly normal, I set up to go again.

Faster.

Without a second thought, my heels strike the gelding's sides and we charge toward the barrel, rounding the first without question.

On the next, my focus has already shifted to barrel three, and there's a roller-coaster-like drop in the pit of my stomach when the horse's feet slip. He tries to catch it, and I ease up on the reins, leaning left as if my body weight will be enough to keep us from going over.

In a cloud of dust, I land so hard it knocks the wind from my chest, and I'm left gasping under a horse who's fighting like hell to stand back up.

I'm okay, I tell myself silently, assessing whether there's any pain.

In a pleasant surprise, there's not. Until the gelding finally gets his footing, directly on my boot, sending fireworks radiating under my skin and a scream clawing up my throat.

Within seconds, Denver's hovering over me, face blanched. "Blair, holy shit. Are you okay?"

"Um, I think my ankle might be broken."

Also, I'm most definitely in shock, because I'm way too chill right now.

"Can you move it?"

With gritted teeth, I try to roll my ankle gingerly. "N-no."

"Let's get you to the hospital," he says, already scooping an arm under my armpits to pick me up. "Prepare to be *very* impressed by your man's strength again."

There's no argument from me this time—looping my arms around his neck and letting him hoist me into the air.

"You good?" he asks, adjusting his grip on me before attempting to take a step.

"Been better." I hold up an unconvincing thumbs-up. "But I'll live."

As we awkwardly stumble down the driveway, each jostling movement has me clenching my jaw to keep from crying out in agony. Holding my breath, I press my forehead against the crook of his neck, and a loud sigh of relief escapes my lungs at the sight of his pickup.

Setting me gently in the passenger seat with a kiss on the forehead, he says, "I'm gonna go grab my keys and wallet, and tell somebody to put the horses away. Stay here."

I raise my eyebrow and point at my leg. "I can't exactly run away."

"Knowing you, you'd hop away on one foot to go get in your car and drive yourself to the hospital simply to avoid accepting my help."

I scoff. "Calling me out like that is rude. I *promise* I'll wait here for you."

"Good." He reaches to buckle me in, despite the look of absolute horror I'm giving him. "Let me love you, Blair."

How can I argue with that request?

He jogs over to the bunkhouse, stepping back outside less than a minute later to slide onto the truck bench seat with a natural smile.

"Why do you look like that?"

"Like what?"

"Like you're enjoying yourself way too much for somebody who's taking their girlfriend to the—" I catch myself, but not fast enough.

"*Girlfriend?*" He turns in his seat, tucking his tongue to his cheek while he beams at me. "Do I need to be worried that you might've hit your head?"

"It accidentally slipped out. Shush." I shift awkwardly in

my seat, pretending to be stabilizing my throbbing limb. "Please just drive."

"Well now, hold on a second." His hands leave the steering wheel, and I toss my head back against the seat with a groan. "If it accidentally slipped out, that tells me you've thought about it. So much for taking it day by day, eh?"

"Says the guy who's mentioned marrying me *how many times* since we started hanging out?"

He winks, *finally* deciding to start driving. "The difference is I've been straight up with you about what I want since the ambulance ride months ago. I cut things off with Peyton because you showed up. From day one I was fully committed to winning you over, until you threw me for a real loop when you wore an engagement ring, and I backed off for a bit."

I bite back a laugh knowing the fake-as-hell ring I paid ten dollars for tricked him into thinking I was taken.

"Well, it's a good thing you did. Mark might be a plastic surgeon, but he's not afraid to fuck up his money-making, insured hands to defend my honor."

That's the exact second his brain malfunctions. Face pinched, he blinks rapidly, clearly struggling to process the information.

"Mark is fake," I clarify before he spontaneously combusts from the mental gymnastics going on in his head. "I mean, he's real in my heart. But he's fictional."

"So it *was* a fake ring." A statement rather than a question, putting two and two together. "I'll kick the absolute shit out of Mark, for the record. Those bitch-boy surgeon hands ain't got nothin' on me. I'd love nothing more than to steal you away from him."

I can't help but smile, an increasingly common occurrence whenever he's around. "For some reason, I like you better anyway."

· · ·

"I promise, I'm fine," I insist, getting comfortable on the couch while Denver slides a pillow under my foot.

Turns out, I was right about the broken ankle. Denver drove to the hospital in Sheridan, sat with me for hours, and slept in the waiting room while they performed surgery to align the bones. He kept my parents updated, fed me, and softly stroked my hair when the drugs made me nauseous.

And now he's in my house, propping my ankle up and completely ignoring my requests to let me do anything myself.

"You broke your ankle and had surgery last night." He shakes his head, dragging the coffee table closer so I can reach the million drink and snack options he has laid out for me. "Take full advantage of the royal treatment, princess."

Mom looks up from her recliner with a smile. "Hopefully your ankle is healed up in time for your wedding, Blair."

Her confusion about the relationship between Denver and me is the one thing she's consistent about. To be fair, I'm also unsure about our relationship. Are we officially together? We are, aren't we?

"That's why I gotta take good care of my girl, isn't that right, Mrs. Hart?" He gestures at me to sit up straight so he can plop down on the couch, then I fall back into his lap. "She needs to be able to walk down the aisle."

Mom laughs. "She's a klutz—I bet she trips walking down the aisle, anyway. At least it's harder to fall if she's already in a wheelchair."

"Oh, good point." Denver smiles over at her. "Although, if anyone can have a wheelchair accident during a wedding, it's Blair Bear."

"Um, you two know I can hear you, right?" I toss my hands up in annoyance. But a big part of me is also relieved Mom seems to be having a good day. I don't think I could handle the pain in my ankle while also managing Mom's symptoms, and the emotional pain that comes with it.

"It's said with love." Denver rubs his thumb over my cheek, looking down at me with a softness in his eyes.

Mom flips on her daily *Wheel of Fortune* binge, and Denver sinks deeper into the couch, stroking my hair.

"How old are these reruns?" he quietly asks. "There's no way this was filmed more recently than the nineties."

"Eighties, for sure. Look at that Madonna hair." I pretend like I'm reaching for my drink, and tap the info button on the remote, much to my mother's chagrin. A box pops up in the corner with the original air date, and I smile up at Denver. "April 24, 1986."

With a deviant smile, he pulls his phone from the front pocket of his blue jeans and taps away on the screen during a commercial break.

"I know the answers," he mouths. "All of them."

When the commercial ends, there's a *T* and an *N* on the board. And Denver sits there pondering alongside Mom. She leans in to study the board, and Denver clears his throat before innocently asking, "Could it be demolition derby?"

Mom glances over at him, shaking her head. "No, I don't think so. It's too soon to guess, anyway."

"Hrm." He grins at me. "My vote is demolition derby."

A few minutes, and a *lot* more letters later, his answer is right. Because of course it is. And Mom is in a state of shock, gawking between the television and Denver, asking him how on Earth he knew the answer.

"I don't know. It just seemed right . . . with the *T* and the *N*." He shrugs impishly.

"You're evil," I whisper up to him, shifting my head on his lap to get comfortable. "Tricking her like that."

"Not evil. *Smart*."

And when he gets the second puzzle correct with only a *P* and an *S*, Mom nearly loses her shit entirely.

Smacking the armrest of her recliner, she practically shrieks my name. "Did you know how smart this boy of yours is? *Gosh*, I can't believe it. The two of you—*ugh*—you're going to have perfect children. Smart, beautiful, funny."

"I mean, if our kids are anything like Blair, I'd say I'm pretty damn lucky." He smiles softly at my mom, and suddenly I'm considering asking him to impregnate me right this second. Broken ankle and all—just prop the entire lower half of my body up with pillows, and kill two birds with one stone.

In the middle of a lady with the poofiest hair I've ever seen buying a U, an obnoxious beeping starts playing on Denver's phone. I thought the only alarm he had set was in the morning for my Lexapro, but it's midday.

Silencing his phone in the nick of time—just before my mom snaps at him—he taps my shoulder. "Hey, time to take your meds."

"Oh, okay." Honestly, thank God he's keeping track, because I already forget when I last took anything. "I have to go pee, so I got it. You can stay here."

"*Knock it off.*" He glares at me as I sit up. "You can go pee on your own, but for God's sake, let me help with *something*."

I'm not trying to be difficult. Although I've been slowly letting Denver in, my gut instinct is always to turn down his offers to do anything for me.

"Okay. Thank you."

He hands me the crutches, then follows closely as I hobble my way down the hall, struggling to get accustomed to my new mode of transport. I can sense his hand hovering behind me, ready to catch me the entire time.

"I'll go grab your drugs while you're in the bathroom, and I'll be right back, if you need me." He opens the door to let me in. "Please keep it unlocked, just in case."

"You're naughty. My parents are right down the hall." I waggle my eyebrows at him.

"Under any other circumstance, I wouldn't give a shit

that they're right there. That would even add to the thrill. But right now, you need drugs, a snack, and a nap."

"*Boring*," I tease, even though drugs and a snack sound wonderful. Not a nap, though. During my depressive episodes, I'd pray for sleep because staying forever with my dreams meant forever without pain. With him now, being awake is better.

After the most complicated pee of my life, I swing the bathroom door open to find Denver leaning against the frame. Once again, he hovers over me on the short journey back to the couch. And when I'm settled with my leg propped up, he thrusts a fistful of pills toward me.

"I grabbed your antidepressant, since you didn't have one this morning." He squeezes my thigh. "And your painkillers . . . which you should take with food. So let me grab you a snack."

"Thank you," I whisper, picking up the pills one by one and popping them in my mouth as I lean back on the plush pillow.

My heart billows at the sight of Denver in my parents' kitchen. On the outside, it looks like he's dumping a bag of tortilla chips in a bowl and grabbing guacamole from the fridge. But it's so much more. He's making up for lost time. Picking up where we left off. And he's loving me the way he should've all those years ago.

Blair
(nineteen years old)

Cassidy, Shelby, and I interlocked our arms, shuffling strategically along the icy sidewalk with an unspoken rule that one woman down meant all of us were going down. No way would one person embarrass themselves alone in this crowd.

Finally finding an empty space to squeeze our bodies in among the throng of paradegoers, I rubbed my mitten-covered hands together, shimmying on the spot to stay warm.

"A year down in Vancouver and you can't handle the cold anymore?" Shelby laughed, despite the fact that her own nose and cheeks were fuchsia, and Cassidy was violently shivering. You would have had to be a literal snowman to not be cold.

"We're at a parade when it's twenty below zero. And for what?" I shook my head at her.

Cass pulled a flask from her coat pocket and handed it to me. "Because we're good citizens of Wells Canyon. Doing our part to be engaged with the community."

I took a swig of the Fireball, then wiped my lips with the backside of my mitten, grimacing at the hot cinnamon flavor lingering on my tongue. It didn't help the chill on my skin, but it churned warmth throughout my insides. A second shot did the trick, leaving me fuzzy and flushed all over.

The parade started with a herd of 4-H kids and their animals—a questionable way to start the parade, since they left various types of animal shit scattered across the road for the Wells Canyon High School band to try and dodge while playing instruments.

When a kid stepped directly into a cow patty, Cassidy lost it. Descending into a fit of giggles, she leaned into me, and I gave apologetic smiles to the judgmental old people around us.

"Sorry, sorry," Cass said, taking a deep breath to compose herself. "*God,* Wells Canyon really puts on a shit Christmas parade."

"Hey now, the parade might have literal shit in it. But look! Those kids in elf costumes are adorable," I said. "Plus, I've never heard of another town that shuts down Main Street for a giant game of hockey afterward—have you?"

Shelby looked at me with a threatening stare, cracking her knuckles. "I'm going to fuck some kids *up* in the game today."

My mind drifted to a few parades prior, when Denver and I were about sixteen. Our families came together, and when our team won the street hockey game, he spun me around in the middle of Main Street, kissing me while snow fell around us. Like something out of a Hallmark movie.

That haunting memory was already making me feel queasy, but sometime between a parade float for the local church and a tractor covered in Christmas lights, I saw him.

On the opposite side of the street, Denver Wells was at the parade. With another girl. A pretty petite blonde I'd never seen before. His arm around her waist, her head resting on his shoulder.

My heart stopped, seizing with a stabbing pain. Shutting my eyes, I focused on my breathing, scared I was about to die from a heart attack at nineteen.

When I could finally form a sentence, I turned to Cass. "I need to go home."

"Oh, *shit.* Are you okay?" She looked me up and down worriedly. "You look . . . rough. Come on, I'll take you."

"No, I can go alone. It's fine. I'm fine. I just . . . Fireball isn't sitting well. Fresh air."

Ignoring that we were outside, surrounded by fresh air, Cassidy nodded slowly. "Okay . . . text me when you're home, yeah?"

"Yeah." I nodded aggressively, already spinning to escape this personal hell.

This is why I don't come home.

I lied to my parents the Christmas before and said I didn't feel comfortable driving on the winter roads to come home for only a few days. Mom cried. The truth was I couldn't bring myself to leave my bed. When Cassidy left two days after the abortion, I called Denver.

He didn't answer.

And that was the first time my life fell apart. I lay in bed sobbing, sleeping, and hating myself. For the entirety of Christmas break, I survived off saltine crackers and slept up-wards of sixteen hours a day.

When school started, I tried my best to go to class, but more often than not I simply couldn't. I was failing, at risk of losing my scholarships and my seat in the program. I'd lost twenty pounds. And I only hated myself more with each pass-ing day—both for ruining my own life in every possible way, and for lying to my friends and family. Sending cheerful texts daily while lying in bed with bloodshot eyes and matted hair.

Finally my roommate, Ashley, stepped in. She drove me to the hospital to be admitted, contacted each of my profes-sors individually, and cleaned my dorm room while I was gone. When my grippy sock vacation came to a bittersweet end a couple weeks later, she set up a wall calendar in my room with reminders for medications and therapy appoint-ments.

Ashley was there when it should've been Denver.

And I didn't know if I could ever forgive him.

So seeing him happy and carefree only one year later

killed me. I stormed through the crowd, desperate to get as far away as possible from this parade. This town. Him. All of it.

"Blair," he shouted my name. Convinced it was my imagination, I didn't look back, breaking into a jog as the end of the parade route came into view.

"Blair," he said again, closer this time. And he grabbed my arm as I rounded the corner at the end of Main Street.

Lip already quivering, I turned to look at him.

"You're home." For some reason, it seemed like there was a glimmer of hope in his eye. "I was starting to think you'd never come back."

"Yeah, well . . . life got busy." I faked a half-smile.

"How . . . uh, how are you?"

"I'm fine."

No need to ask him the same question. He's *clearly* doing great.

"Good. Good, I'm glad." He swallowed hard, Adam's apple bobbing along the column of his throat. "Chief misses you. Should come by and see him while you're in town."

Biting my lower lip, I let my eyes meet his for a split second, and that was all it took for me to be sucked in. Deep brown eyes I'd spent so much time lost in. But he was here with somebody else, and she could probably give him all the things I couldn't.

"I'm not staying long, so I won't really have time," I said quietly. "And I should go home now."

He stepped toward me, stealing the air from my lungs and stilling the world around us. Time stopped with him—always had.

"*I miss you,*" Denver whispered.

A fiery need to cry took up residence behind my eyes, and I blinked up to the sky to will it away. "Don't. *Please.*"

"Blair . . ." His knuckles grazed my jaw, igniting the spark that had been dormant all year.

"Please," I begged. But the problem was, neither of us

knew if it was a plea for him to stop—to walk away from me forever—or a plea to be kissed.

Denver, of course, decided it was the latter.

His lips pressed softly to mine, and suddenly the entire previous year hadn't happened. He backed me into the brick exterior wall of a hardware store and kissed me like his life depended on it. And I soaked him in. Everything from his tongue clashing with mine to the feel of his callused hands on either side of my face.

A police car in the parade sounded its siren, breaking our spell, and the memories crashed into me like a tidal wave.

"Denver, we can't." My hand pressed to his chest, pushing him away for good. "I can't do this with you. I can't do this *to* you."

He looked at me with the same devastation he had the night he proposed in my dorm room. Unable to bear the guilt that racked me after everything we'd been through, I turned and ran. Vowing to *never* spend a single second longer than necessary in Wells Canyon.

Denver Wells shattered my heart, and I shattered his. He was finally picking up the pieces of himself and moving on with someone who could give him the life he wanted. Who was I to come back to town, be involved in him *cheating* on his new girlfriend, and hurt us both all over again?

Racing through the front door of my childhood home, I found my younger sister alone on the couch watching a cheesy Christmas movie. Independent, stubborn side be damned, I fell into her lap in a fit of sobs that racked my entire body. And *finally,* I told somebody every painful secret I'd been carrying.

Blair

For three days, he didn't leave my side for anything longer than a bathroom break. On day four, he sat in the waiting room and listened to Wanda talk about her Yorkiepoo for a full hour while I worked. Day five he left me home alone only so he could venture to the grocery store with my mom. Ignoring my insistence that I would be okay if he left for a while, Denver stuck it out through hard moments with Mom, kept track of the little day-to-day things I was constantly dropping the ball on, and held me close at night. And on day six, he finally agreed to go back to work under one condition—I would hang out at the ranch with the girls.

With my nephew, Jonas, tagging along to give my sister a break, we turn off the dirt road to spend the day at Wells Ranch. Drinking, watching the cowboys sort out cattle to ship off, and eating Beryl's fire-cooked feast I've been hearing rumors about for the last two weeks.

"So, I'm not allowed to ride any horses today?" I glance at Denver in my periphery as the truck rattles over the cattle guard, teasing him. "No barrels—*promise*."

"If I say no, you'll do it for sure. So fill your boots. I think Jackson has a new horse in—never been ridden before." Denver winks, testing me. "I'll get tickets to that show any day."

"I think I'll leave the bronc riding to you."

"That's right, leave it to the pros." He dusts some pretend

dirt off his shoulder. "Maybe we can get Jonas on there, though."

"Absolutely not. Whit would kill me."

Jonas clears his throat from the backseat. "I've been bucked off before."

"Wait, what?" I spin to face him, catching the way he and Denver share a mischievous smile. "When your mom agreed to let you come work here for the summer, I don't think she was agreeing to you being involved in ranch-hand shenanigans."

"Your nephew's getting branded next spring. He earned it," Denver says, shutting the truck down and grabbing his hat from the middle of the bench seat.

"He's *ten*!" I smack him on the arm before stepping out into the sun. "It'll be your funeral."

Jonas hands me the crutches from the backseat before sliding out, and I start my hobble across uneven ground toward where the girls are sitting in folding camp chairs. Denver's close behind me, as always—convinced I'm mere seconds away from toppling over any time I'm not on perfectly level ground. I swear he doesn't take a breath until I plunk down in a padded chair, dropping the aluminum crutches beside me.

"You need anything?" he asks.

I know better than to say no, because he'll look like a dejected puppy if I do.

"A drink would be wonderful."

"We got you," Cecily pipes up from a few seats down, quickly pulling something that looks a lot like a homemade Capri-Sun juice pouch from a large blue cooler. "It's sangria! I found these reusable pouches when I was looking for wedding stuff online, and they're perfect."

"It's nine o'clock in the morning," I exclaim.

"Five o'clock somewhere," Kate quips.

CHANGE OF HART 361

Denver laughs, passing me the juice box. "Okay, well, looks like they've got you covered here."

I take a long drink of the sweet nectar, closing my eyes blissfully. "Oh, yeah—*shit, that's good*—I'm fine here. Go do your hot cowboy shit now."

"Hot cowboy shit? Jesus, how strong is that drink?" He leans in for a sip, and I clutch it to my chest, nearly tipping the chair as I play keep-away, giggling like a love-drunk teenager. "*Go away.* You can't drink and ride."

"Mmm. I think the night of their"—he points at Cecily— "wedding proves that wrong."

I blush furiously, and he smirks in response. Dimples highlighted by the summer sun, he gives me a playful wink just as Kate starts getting riled up.

"All right, you're nauseating me." She swats her hand in his general direction from her chair next to mine and he quickly dodges it. "Either go away or go get a room. There are kids around!" She gestures at Hazel, who is literally an infant incapable of understanding what we're talking about, and her own two kids, who are playing in a pile of dirt too far away to hear us.

"Okay, okay. I'll go do hot cowboy shit now. Make sure you're paying attention."

Boy, am I. I don't care that I'm openly gawking. I sink into the chair with a long, continuous chug of sangria and watch his toned, denim-clad ass saunter over to where the rest of the guys are. Tight Wells Ranch branded T-shirt, fitted jeans, and a cowboy hat.

No words.

"I need you to know how bizarre it is to see him like this," Kate says, leaning into me and breaking my focus from the incredible man I'm staring at unashamedly.

I blink over to her. "What do you mean?"

"I mean, he's always going to be a bit of a jokester and a

goofball. But it's nice to see him joking around because he's in love, not because he's hiding behind it."

Out of the corner of my eye, I watch him mount his horse and instantly turn to look at me with a boyish smile that makes my heart skip.

"Yeah?"

"Trust me, I was here dealing with him like he was my own annoying little brother for years. I've never seen him like this. He looks at you like he's trying to commit every little detail to memory . . . and he's *always* looking at you. It's adorable."

Cass places a sleeping Hazel in the bounce chair at her feet and leans in to join the huddle. "And you're *always* looking at him. Just go get married already."

"Weren't you the one telling me to be careful and take things slow at the start of the summer?"

"You two have always been inevitable. Sure, I was worried after how he hurt you before but . . . I don't know. Seems different now." Cass studies him with narrow eyes for a moment, then catches Kate's eye with a look I don't quite understand. "I don't want to say he's matured, because that is *false*. It's pretty damn clear how in love with you he is, though."

"I love him, too."

"This is the closest we can possibly get to becoming sisters, unless Whit and I have a simultaneous bi-awakening one day in the future. I'm not ruling that out but . . . this feels more likely. So I love this for us." Cass does a little dance in her seat, and I shake my head at her with a laugh.

Suddenly Cecily comes along, dragging her chair and the cooler behind her. Settling down in front of me so we become a misshapen circle. "I was feeling left out over there. What are we talking about?"

"How my fear of Denny being the next one to have a Wells baby is going to come true." Kate grips Cecily's knee for emphasis, pressing her lips together. "Nothing against you, Blair. I'd actually be thrilled. This is a slight at Cecily."

Cecily scrunches her nose and shrugs. "I mean . . . maybe he won't be first."

"Wait, are you pregnant?" Kate jabs a finger at the sangria pouch in Cecily's hand.

"No!" She laughs. "No. But I did remove my IUD, so . . ."

Kate sits back, shaking her head with a sigh. "You're all going to make me get pregnant again so we can have little babies together, aren't you?"

Cecily snorts, sangria leaking out of her nose, and we devolve into a fit of giggles that doesn't stop until we accidentally wake up Hazel. And even then, it just becomes slow, silent laughter while we sip our juice boxes like a bunch of small children on the playground. Listening to the steady sound of hooves as the men head out to round up the herd and drive them back to the sorting pen.

A little after noon, Beryl steals Kate and Cecily away to serve a massive amount of various hot and cold dishes to the dozen or more cowboys. In typical fashion, I'm feeling awfully useless and awkward sitting in my chair, despite Cassidy sitting next to me. Although, she's technically busy feeding Hazel. So I zone out and pick at a loose thread on the seat, unblinking until something passes by my field of vision multiple times and breaks my focus—or lack thereof.

I look up to find Denver placing a plate on my lap as he sinks down to sit on the grass. "Did all that cowboy shit do it for you, or what?"

"I think you better do it again, for science."

"It's your lucky day, baby." He grins, sliding his palm up and down my bare calf in a soothing way; something about feeling his skin on mine is grounding. "So, what evil schemes did you get roped into over here this morning? It looked like there was a lot of sinister plotting happening."

"A pregnancy pact." I shrug nonchalantly, and Cassidy spits out her drink, narrowly missing Hazel.

"Sheesh, Cass." Denver stares at her wide-eyed. "Are you in on this?"

"God, no." Cassidy pulls a face.

Denver returns his focus to me. "But you are?"

"What if I was?"

"*Okay*. That's my cue to leave." Cass stands up, shaking the water droplets off her legs from her accidental mouth-sprinkler incident. "You kids make good choices."

I snort. "Rich, coming from you."

She flips the middle finger over her shoulder, then strolls over to where Red's filling two plates with food.

"So, hey," Denver says. "Want to take a drive with me when we're done here?"

"And leave Jonas—"

"Got it covered. He and Colt have something potentially delinquent planned, so he'll give him a ride."

I open my mouth to protest, and he puts up a hand to stop me. "It's *fine*. Colt's been managing Jonas with his chores all summer, and so far nobody's gotten seriously injured or thrown in jail. They'll be okay."

With an exhale, I nod. No sense in arguing when I know he's right—from what I know about Colt, he's not going to do anything that would put a kid in danger.

"I'd love to go for a drive. Where do you have in mind?"

"You'll see." He adjusts his Stetson in the sun and hops to his feet. "Back to doing more hot cowboy shit for your viewing pleasure."

"You're never going to let it go that I said that, are you?"

"*Never*. Just like I know you love a backwards hat." He flips his cowboy hat around. "Is this working for you?"

I toss my head back with a breathy laugh. "You're a dork.

But please wear it exactly like that, so somebody other than me can make fun of you, for once."

"Just sayin', if this makes you want to ride me, I'll put up with some heckling."

"A cowboy hat the *wrong* way is definitely not doing it for me. You look like a city boy at a rodeo for the first time."

He leans in, putting his hands on my thighs. "Like Mark with his bitch-boy hands?"

"Precisely."

He contemplates his words for a second, then chooses to continue with the Mark discussion, for some ungodly reason. "I mean, you liked him enough to get engaged. Which is more than you can say about me."

His laughter does little to ease the bruising blow of his words.

"Are you jealous of a fictional man? You realize how insane that sounds, right?" I tilt my head, giving him a look.

"Well, I'm pretty sure these rough hands"—he glides his work-worn palms up my thighs—"make you come better than his fancy surgeon fingers could."

"*Correct.* Because *again*, he's fictional." I grab his face, middle fingers falling into the divots of his dimples. "Please turn the cowboy hat back around and go do some good work, because you know what *really* turns me on? A competent, hardworking man."

"You've single-handedly convinced me to work the hardest I ever have. Bet the ranch can pay you, if you want a side-gig watching me work." He winks. "I'm gonna be such a good boy for you."

"You already are *such* a good boy."

With a glimmer in his eyes, Denver kisses me softly, then turns to head back to his horse.

Picking up a massive slice of watermelon from my plate, I watch him sort the cattle and try not to drool at the way his shoulder muscles flex under his shirt. His body's perfectly relaxed yet sturdy, moving with his cutting horse like they share a soul, completely trusting the animal to do its job. The cows fight separation from the herd, always looking for a way to get back. And it seems entirely chaotic, with Austin yelling at his guys from the top fence rail, horses moving through the cattle, guys working the cow squeeze to check ear tags and confirm every animal is safe to travel before they're loaded onto a massive livestock trailer—destination: Alberta.

And Jonas, my short, skinny preteen nephew, is right in there. When Denver mentioned lining up some work for Jonas over the summer to keep him out of trouble, I didn't expect *this*. He's using every ounce of energy in his tiny body to open and close the backstop on the cattle chute—the sliding door that keeps cows from backing out of the chute once they've been loaded in.

I pull out my phone and zoom in to discreetly take photos for my sister. Then I turn the camera toward Denver, and when he looks at me with a smile, I snap my new favorite photo of him.

Denver said I brought the light back into his life, but I don't think he'll ever understand how badly I needed him to anchor me here. Before I came home, I had a career and a fancy apartment, but I was anxiously flitting about. Working as much overtime at the hospital as I could manage and spending a concerning amount of my free time at the gym— being busy kept my mind from wandering, and I confused that with my brain being calm.

But this? This is calm. Sitting in the sunshine with my best friends, catching smiles from the love of my life, and eating the most flavorful watermelon I've ever had.

Mildly sunburned, exhausted, and feeling the tiniest bit tipsy, I let Denver boost me into his truck and buckle my seat belt. Hopping into his seat, his right hand instantly finds mine in the center of the bench, and we pull away from the sun-soaked ranch. He insisted on showering at the bunk house before we left, and now heading down the long driveway, he rolls the windows down to get a breeze through his damp hair.

When he turns left—as if heading back to Wells Canyon—I look at him confused. For us, going for a drive has always meant heading farther into the middle of nowhere, not closer to civilization.

"Where are we going?"

"Just sit back and enjoy the drive. You'll see it when we get there."

Rolling my eyes, I do what he says, leaning my head against the back of the seat. Denver drives along the tree-lined dirt road, with classic country softly playing. Stretching my fingers, I stick a hand out the open passenger window and let it swim through the wind current. The other takes its natural place on his thigh.

The sun chases us down the mountain, threatening dusk. Then he turns onto my street, and I cackle. "The *drive* was a ride home?"

"Something like that."

Denver

The sun's barely hovering above the skyline when I pull into the driveway of a modest blue cottage. *The* blue cottage Blair didn't shut up about any time I drove her home back in high school. Just down the street from where her parents live, it's set back from the road in a heavily treed lot. But there's no missing the blue siding, white front porch, and sunshine-yellow door.

And the confusion on Blair's face kills me.

"Why are we at Mrs. Weaver's house?"

"Figured you haven't had a piano lesson with her in close to twenty-five years, and since your leg is busted up, you need *something* to do—other than eye-fuck me at work every day."

"Funny guy."

"C'mon, I'll show you." I pop open the glovebox and rummage around to find a key. "She gave me a key. In case you're worried there's some funny business going on. Nobody's coming to arrest us for this."

Her face remains scrunched, with confused wrinkles on the bridge of her nose, the entire time I help her out of the truck and up the porch steps. The key slips into the lock with ease and I swing open the door, careful to catch it before it hits the interior wall.

"Key or not, I'm still not convinced we aren't breaking and entering." She hesitantly steps inside, and I flip the light switches, walking ahead of her into the living room and lighting it up.

But the space is empty, and the harsh, cool ceiling light reverberates off the white walls and recently polished hardwood floor. Blair squints when she steps through the archway.

"Wait—is Mrs. Weaver moving?"

"Moved already, actually. Last week. Down to Florida because apparently she's sick of the cold winters here, and they have some pretty bomb seniors' communities. I was tempted to dye my hair gray and tag along. Maybe find me some cougars down there."

"I bet you could find some really wonderful women in need of a pool boy." She leans on a crutch and runs her hand through her hair. "So she gave you the keys to her empty house? Like an Airbnb situation . . . sans the furniture?"

God, she's really not understanding where I'm going with this. She's supposed to be the smart one here.

"Blair. *I fucking love you*, but sometimes . . ." I massage my temples. "She gave me the keys because I bought the house from her."

"Um, no you didn't." She laughs under her breath.

I swing the key around on the end of my index finger, smiling at the adorable look she has painted across her face. "Well, it's weird that they took a mortgage payment from my bank account last week, in that case."

"Why did you buy a house in Wells Canyon when you already have a place to live at the ranch? Plus, like . . . endless space to build a house there, if you wanted."

I drag my hand along the live-edge wood mantel. "I bought it because it's close to your parents—so you can still help out with your mom whenever you need—and you didn't shut up about how cute it was when we were younger, and I was also kind of hoping that *eventually* we might want to live together."

"So you bought it . . ." Her voice trails off, her eyes flitting around the room, taking it in with a new appreciation.

"For you. Yeah, I did. I actually stopped in here to talk to Mrs. Weaver the same day I came over for dinner with your mom. Completely unsolicited, too. She's an old softie, and ate up our entire love story like I was giving her a live reading of *The Notebook*. Turns out, she was already debating putting it on the market before winter, so it was meant to be."

"Do you know how ridiculous it is that you bought a house for us to live in before we even went on a date?"

Ridiculous? *Maybe.* But the way she's admiring the room with a hopeful glimmer makes me think it was the smartest thing I've ever done.

"I figured it would either turn out to be the most romantic thing I could possibly do, *or* it would be a great business decision. Even if we didn't work out, eventually you'd get tired of living with your parents and discover that your dream home is available for rent. Either way, I figured my mom would approve of me using my inheritance from her as a down payment."

Looking around the empty room, she nods softly, traversing the hardwood floor until she's in my arms. Her warm lips find mine immediately, and her hands wander over my torso. We sway to the music of our combined heartbeats until she tosses her crutches aside, relying solely on me for support. The simplest gesture means so much. And I hold her close, reassuring her I'll never drop her—not again. I'll be the man she can count on through thick or thin.

"So, is this place available for rent?" she asks with a teasing lilt. Hands clasped behind my neck, her mind's clearly running a million miles a minute as she thinks about what this all means, until she blurts out, "We might need some furniture in here."

"The thing is, I used my meager inheritance and basically every penny of my savings for the down payment. *But,* I got the next best thing. Hold on."

I run to the master bedroom closet on the opposite side of the main floor, returning a minute or so later armed with all of the makings of a top-tier floor bed. Her laughter fills the room, making this place feel more like home by the second.

We kneel together on the hard floor, setting up layer upon layer of thick blankets and pillows until it's a bed fit for a princess. And Blair flings herself backward in the middle of it, a radiant smile stretched across her freckled face.

"You're the cutest thing I've ever seen," I admit. My cheeks are aching from how much I've been smiling since we walked into the house, but I can't fucking stop.

When my mom died, the house I grew up in didn't feel like a home to me anymore. And when Blair and I broke up, that became even more evident. It was cold, and lonely, and I suddenly couldn't stand being in a place with so many memories that had since been tainted by my own melancholy.

But this is a place to make new memories with her. And that's all I've ever wanted.

Staring up at the ceiling, she asks, "How the hell did you keep this a secret in such a tiny town? Even when I lived in Vancouver, I knew everything that happened around here."

"Oh, everybody knows. I will say, Mrs. Weaver has a damn good poker face. She kept telling people it was an out-of-towner who bought it, but word got out eventually. They all just know not to tell you."

"This might be your best trick yet, Wells." She pats the blankets with a small smile. "Come snuggle."

"Let me do one more quick thing for you."

After setting up a dozen or more candles, I shut off the bright overhead light and practically collapse next to her.

She nuzzles against me like she's seeking warmth, and yawns into the crook of my neck. Candlelight flickers across us, and I kiss her temple.

"You're sure you want to leave the ranch?"

I chuckle. "Be pretty silly for me to buy a house in town without considering that, wouldn't it? It's more important to me that your mom's nearby."

That's never been more true than in the last week since Blair's horseback riding accident. Spending so much time around the Hart family's home has shown me what she goes through with her mom—from the extravagant safety measures to the general caretaking Blair does for her. Living in close proximity doesn't just mean Blair's close by in case of an emergency; this house allows her to pop over and style her mom's hair, or help her find things she's misplaced, or any number of little tasks to help out.

"It'll be so nice to have some distance from my parents but also be close by when they need me. Mom's only going to need more and more help as time goes on. And eventually we'll put her into a care facility, but I know both of my parents want her to be home for as long as possible. That really only works with all of us helping."

"Count me in. I want to help," I say.

"I love you." Her fingers tug lightly on my hair, pulling me into a kiss. "I don't know what I did to deserve somebody as incredible as you. I hate that I lost you all those years ago because I wouldn't hear you out."

"Bear, I told you I forgive you. We're here now, and that's all I care about."

She tilts her head to look up at me. "If we were in that situation now, I'd make a different choice, so you know."

"No, I'd want you to make whatever choice you needed. I meant it when I said I only want you. The plan to have the house, wife, kids was taken off the table years ago. I want you, and whatever you want." I scrub my hand over my stubbled jaw, staring into her eyes, which are ignited with the dancing flames of candles lit around us. "But I'd love it if you decide to live in this house with me . . . since I already bought it and all."

"I'll miss you sneaking in my bedroom window, but I can't wait to make this place our home."

"It's already feeling more like home than anywhere has in a long time."

With slow, sleepy kisses, I soak in the comforting warmth of being wrapped around the most incredible girl in the world.

"Denver?" She breathes out my name like a question.

"Yeah, Bear?"

"I never stopped loving you. It's never stopped being you for me."

"Even when I thought you might not be mine in the end, I was always going to be yours."

"Morning, baby," she mumbles into the skin covering my collarbone. Her fingertips feather across my chest, and when I open my eyes, she smiles up at me.

"Hey, you." I lick my lips slowly, letting my eyes adjust to the sunlight streaming in through the living room bay window.

The woman I love is wrapped in my arms, on a makeshift blanket bed, after spending our first night in *our* house. One day she'll decorate this space with furniture and anything else she wants. One day I'll carry her through the front door on our wedding night. One day, I'll stand in this spot rocking our baby to sleep.

She squirms against me, covered only by a thin sheet, grinding my leg. When I scoop her chin in my hand, tilting her face so I can kiss her, she rolls her hips. Catching friction on my thigh, she lets out the sweetest moan, and the sound goes straight to my cock. Each movement of her hips has the leg of my boxer briefs riding up, until I realize she's already ditched her underwear, and there's a soaking wet pussy riding my bare thigh.

"Baby, *fuck*. Are you this wet for me?" I reach down and

swipe my fingers up her slit, collecting her wetness. When I pull my hand away, it's glistening in the sun, and I suck my fingers clean. That's all it takes to turn my semihard morning wood into a fully erect blanket tent.

"You promised we wouldn't have a single day where I'm not on your cock. It's been a full week."

"I think I said *strangling* my cock, specifically." I kiss her, tangling her tongue around mine. "It's not enough to just have you on it. I need you falling apart with my cock deep inside you. I need your pussy milking every drop of cum from me."

"What else do you need?" She's found the perfect pace now, rubbing herself against my leg with a symphony of lip-biting whimpers.

"I need to suck on your perfect tits." I gently roll her nipple between my fingers, the metal barbell hot against my callused skin. I bend slightly, trying to keep my leg still between her thighs, and kiss her chest. "I need to see my cum all over you."

She moans, with a breathy, "Yeah?"

"Fuck, Blair. I need *you*."

"You have me. All of me is yours for the taking." A whimper slips free from her lips, pussy hot and wet on my thigh. And I bite down on her nipple piercing.

I want nothing more than to be inside her, but I also promised I'd take care of her. And that means putting aside the things I want, if she's not feeling up to it.

"How does your ankle feel? Any pain?"

The instant her head starts to rock side to side on the pillow, I'm tearing her from my thigh and aggressively pulling my underwear down. My cock snaps to attention without the restrictive fabric, and the slow lick of her lips has me ready to burn the world down for a taste of her pussy.

So I kneel between her legs and drag my tongue up her

slick cunt, savoring the sweetness. Then I sit back and admire my girl—her breasts jiggle slightly with every panting breath, and a few barely-there hickeys fill the empty spaces between the smattering of freckles painting her skin. "Look at how perfect you are."

I slip a finger inside her, pulling my bottom lip between my teeth when her back arches, hair splaying across her pillow. I suck and bite at the delicate skin around her pussy, creating a watercolor smattering of light purple bruises on her creamy skin, encouraged by the slap of her hand down on the blankets and the accompanying moan.

"Holy fuck, why does that hurt so good?" She squirms under me.

"Because you love being mine."

Blair shifts to force my lips close to where I know she's desperate to be touched, with a panting, exhaled "Yes."

I dive back in for meaningful licks, flicking the tip of my tongue across her clit until she's grinding against my face, tugging my hair at the root. Thighs constricting around my head.

Suffocate me, baby.

She comes with a stuttering contraction of every muscle in her body, her good leg wrapping around my skull to make sure I don't let up until the hurricane tearing through her is over. And all at once, her muscles fully relax.

I look up at my girl, licking the taste of her from my lips, and she stares back with a needy glint in her eye. Rocking her hips and grabbing at my shoulders, nails dug into my flesh to force my cock toward her pussy. The head of my cock slips inside her tight entrance, and it steals my breath like a blow to the chest. Nothing has ever felt as good as being with her.

"*Fuck.* Don't think I'll ever get used to how good it feels when you stretch me with your cock," she pants.

"It's so fucking good, baby. So fucking tight."

Sliding my hand under her ass, I lift up and her muscles get even tighter around my dick. It takes a deep breath to adjust to the sensation, so I don't come before I've even moved inside her. Then I slip a pillow between her and the floor bed and fill my girl to the hilt. The moan that escapes her only makes me more wild with need, turning each thrust into a rough, hungry attempt at getting another sound to slip from her kissable lips.

She claws at my thighs, eyes rolling into the back of her head, and when I ease up on her mouth, she replaces it with a pillow. Her muffled voice cries out my name, and a string of expletives, into the down. And I punish her hips with my fingertips, pulling her to meet me with every push, bearing down on her.

My cock's swollen, begging for release with the feel of her ridged inner walls squeezing it. "Lose the fucking pillow and look at me. I want my name to echo off the fucking walls when you come."

Her eyes snap to meet mine, and she eases up on the pillow clenched between her teeth just enough to whimper, "*Fuck*, you're so deep."

"This pussy's perfectly made for my cock, isn't it?"

"Your cock's perfect for me."

"That's right it is, baby. Made for you. Now come on it. Show me how perfect we are for each other, and come with me."

I brush the wild hair from her face and lean in to suck on her pretty pink nipple. Swirling my tongue to push her over the edge as she grips my skull like she's trying to crush it between her palms, and her body convulses under mine.

"Don't," she pants. "Stop."

She pulls me into a kiss, my fingers traversing her clavicle and dropping down to play with her nipple. Toying with the barbell, and coming closer to falling apart inside her with every perfect moan from my satiated girl's throat.

"Come in me," Blair whispers. "Put a fucking baby in me. *Please*. Let me give you everything you want."

"Blair." I choke on her name. Vision blurring, heart racing at the vision I've denied myself for years—Blair pregnant and happy here with me. *Fucking hell,* I want to fill her with cum, pregnancy or not. I want to come on and in her, I want her covered so she knows exactly who she belongs to. Watch it leak out of her pussy and run down her perfect ass.

"I need you to remind me who my pussy belongs to."

"Baby, that's the hottest thing I have *ever* fucking heard. Your beautiful cunt is mine, and your ass"—I slap her butt hard enough to leave the outline of my hand in red—"and your perfect tits. And I have no problem marking up every part of your body so you never forget it."

Leaning forward to suck on her skin, my lips leave behind dark welts on her breasts. Just in time, too, since last week's bite marks are almost fully faded. She glances down and sucks an exhilarated breath through her teeth, grinding her pussy on my cock. And I hit a tempo I've never found before, fucking her until I'm dripping sweat and my fingers working her clit are getting a muscle cramp.

Blair grabs my ass, forcing me to stay fully seated inside her while I pant and struggle not to come. "*Come. In. Me.* I want you to fill me so I can't move for the rest of the day without it leaking out of me."

How the fuck do I say no to that?

I pump into her repeatedly, succumbing to the electric heat coiled at the base of my spine, letting her pussy grip my cock and pull out every last drop of cum, until I'm throwing my head back with a hoarse moan.

"Holy fuck. *Holy fuck.*" My brain's broken, unable to do anything but revel in the aftershocks of her pussy hugging my cock, sending shivers up and down my spine.

"I love you." She kisses my forehead. "I love you so fucking much."

My lungs strain with every aching breath.

"Bear . . ." I talk through the exertion. "About the baby thing—"

She shushes me, pressing a finger to my mouth. "I wasn't lying about birth control. I just . . . it was the heat of the moment."

"*Fuck,* you have such a filthy mouth on you." I trace her lips with my thumb. "I love it."

"For the record, I *do* want to have your baby one day. I'm ready for the future we planned, whenever you are."

"Given up on your bullshit about taking it day by day?" I slowly pull out of her and, if I were physically capable of it, I'd be immediately trying to fuck her again after watching a small stream of my cum run down her ass.

Her elbow's crooked over her eyes in a post-orgasm glow—the most gorgeous she's ever looked to me. Face awash with perfect contentment, she shifts her arm to look at me. "We spent fourteen years without each other. And, in the absolute worst-case scenario, we could have our time together cut short like our parents have. I mean, you could've killed yourself when you fell off that bronc, and I never would've been able to forgive myself for not telling you how badly I missed you for all those years. And I could've suffered worse things than a broken ankle, considering a horse fell on top of me. Luck's been on our side. But it might run out, eventually."

Her eyes track mine as I settle in next to her on the blankets. And she continues in a hushed tone while my kisses roam her goosebump-covered arm.

"When one of us dies or loses our memory one day, I want to know we had as much time together as possible," she says. "I don't need more time to figure out whether I still love you. I do, and I always have."

"And you're finally ready to let me love you?" I smile.

"Actually, can you grab me my purse?"

Weird segue to avoid my question, but at least she's asking me for help. A couple days ago, even with the cast on her leg, she would've insisted on dragging her ass across the floor to get it herself.

"Of course, baby." I hop up and grab her small black bag from beside the front door.

"Okay, ask me that question again." A smile dances across her face, and she looks like she's ready to explode with giddiness.

I side-eye her and hesitantly ask, "Are you ready to let me love you?"

She digs in the bag for a few seconds, and I'm fully anticipating that she's going to dump her clutter all over our laps to find whatever it is she's looking for. But instead she produces a box.

A black velvet box I haven't seen since that night in her dorm room.

"You kept it. . . ." I stroke her milky-white upper thigh, waiting with bated breath for her to explain herself.

"Of course I did. Not just because it was your mom's, either. Part of me hoped I'd have the chance to give it back to you one day."

My fingers stop, and I stare at her with my heart pounding in my ears. Maybe this was all in my head, and I was chasing the same dream I had as a kid. Back when I tried to coerce her into marrying me and having my baby, all in a futile attempt at piecing together a family to replace what I'd lost. Without realizing it, that's what I just did again with this fucking house. I put her in a place where she felt pressured to tell me what I wanted to hear.

Noticing my spiraling, she slides a hand along my jaw, bringing me back to her.

"Hey, I don't mean it that way. I mean . . . will you take this ring so you can give it back to me?" She slips the box into my open palm. "Denver, I want to know if you'll marry me."

Everything in my body turns to Jell-O—brain included. My unsteady fingers fumble frantically with the box, desperate to pry it open and give her back the ring before she changes her mind. I lift myself up so I'm on one knee, determined to do it right and make my proposal stick this time.

But she laughs, pulling me back down to sit in front of her. "It's weird for you to be hovering above me."

"Baby, I'm trying to give you the proposal you deserve."

"So quit leaving me hanging—tell me you'll marry me."

"Bear, I've wanted to marry you since I was sixteen." I pull the delicate gold band out, and the small diamond sparkles light beams across the empty wall. It slips onto her finger with ease, and she smiles up at me with tears dotting her lower lashes.

"And I promised you I would one day."

Blair kisses me, melting her body into the cradle of my arms. The years of feeling broken and lost disappear with the soft touch of her lips. It's always been us. In any lifetime, any universe. We were meant to end up here.

Blair
{two months later}

Denver walks around the side of the barn leading two horses, with the autumn sun on his back and a breeze toying with the hem of his shirt.

"Are you sure it's safe to do this with your ankle?"

I roll my eyes with a smile. I have to admit, it's nice having someone who worries about me. "Who's the medical professional between us? Yes. I ditched the walking boot a full week ago. I'm fine."

Stopping to tighten a cinch, he takes a quick glance at me over the top of the saddle. "Next question—are you sure you don't want to drive? I don't know if I trust you on horseback."

"I'm *great* at riding, for your information."

"Oh, I know that." He winks at me as he hands me the reins. "You're excellent at riding . . . if we're talking about something other than horses."

"I'm great at both. Some might even say a *natural*, thank you very much."

He watches intently as I mount the horse—as if he expects he'll need to launch in my direction to catch me at any moment. And since my ankle doesn't immediately shatter when I put weight on it to swing my other foot over, he exhales and sinks down into his own saddle.

Adjusting the dress bunched up around my hips and thighs, I smile at him. "Ready?"

"Whenever you are, Bear."

Our horses side by side, Denver and I link fingers as often as we can. Brief touches when our horses converge and diverge repeatedly, hooves sinking into the dry dirt and rattling over rocks. And each time, we share a look. Locked eyes reflecting all the emotion and heartache that's led to where we are now. None of it matters anymore, because I have him and he has me. Neither of us are going anywhere.

The trees lining the top hayfields are quickly losing their amber and goldenrod leaves with every passing gust. Like a rolling fire tumbling along the yellowed field, they blow ahead of us. It's absolutely stunning—the perfect day in every possible way.

We stop to take in the scenery, when Denver sidles up next to me and leans in. I think he's going for a kiss, but instead he removes the shiny floral clip I had keeping my hair in the pretty updo Cass spent twenty minutes on this morning.

"Hey!" I swat at him.

"Thought you'd want to feel the wind in your hair while we race across this field. You ride best with your hair down."

"So I've been told." I smirk at Denver, giving the gelding under me a little kick. "Last one there has to assemble the dresser I just ordered."

"You've always been a cheater," he shouts after me.

I give it all I've got, and so does the horse, tearing across the open field. A cool breeze flows down my back, and my dress billows around my legs.

"You think I'd give you a horse with a lot of giddy-up in him?" Denver cackles, quickly catching up. "You're not winning this one, Hart."

"That's Wells to you now, mister." I turn to smirk at him, my hair whipping around my face. He's right—I needed to feel the wind in my hair again.

I win by the skin of my teeth, and Denver refuses to admit

it. Grumbling his disagreement, he dismounts and ties our horses to a tree, then helps me down.

"You also got a head start. Had it been a fair race, I would've won." He smooths my hair down with his palms and lightly kisses my forehead.

My jaw drops at the accusation. "Nuh-uh. You gave me a horse you knew was slow, then asked me to race. It was rigged from the start."

"Okay, okay. We can trade horses for the way back and see who wins."

"Either way, you're building the dresser." A quick close-lipped kiss. "With the backwards hat. No shirt on."

It's a picture I've been blessed to see multiple times since we started the process of moving into the house he bought. At first, he was doing all the work because I was in a cast. Then it basically became foreplay—a game to see how long we could tease each other before christening yet another room or piece of furniture in our new home.

"Ready when you two are," George Shaw—rodeo announcer and, in true small-town fashion, the only licensed officiant in the area—calls out from under the tree where our initials are carved.

There beside him are our siblings, best friends, parents. . . . I nearly choke on my own spit when I see Bennett Wells standing toward the back of the group in a dark green button-up. How our people managed to pull this together in two weeks is beyond me. At first, we were talking about a lovely summer wedding next year, but it didn't feel right for either of us. With Mom's illness, and the constant niggling reminder that tomorrow may never come for any of us, we chucked the wedding planning in the garbage and went all in on an intimate gathering at our tree. Austin even allowed vehicles to drive along the outskirts of the hayfields—slowly, to help protect the sensitive grazing land—so my mom could safely get here.

"Oh, wait. Isn't it bad luck to see you?" Denver jokingly covers his eyes.

"You're a dork. Bad luck would be you tripping in a hole. Just because I'm fully healed doesn't mean it's your turn to injure yourself." I grab his hand, smoothing out my white midi dress with the other, and making our way across the soft grass.

In front of our closest friends and family, Denver and I hold hands. Each shaking, with glassy eyes and relentless smiles. Years later than either of us initially thought this would happen, but also so much sooner than I ever expected. Maybe it's quick—too quick, some might say. But it's always been him for me. I've wanted to marry this man since we were two goofy kids in love, and I've waited long enough to finally do it.

"Short but sweet, because we all know if I get too serious for too long, I combust." Surrounded by the low chuckle of his brothers, he lets out a big exhale, squeezing my hands. "Blair, the first time we hung out, you tricked me into spending hours sitting next to the least-used railroad tracks in the province with the promise of a 'really cool' flattened penny"— he releases his grip on one hand to dig in his pocket, pulling out the same penny we squished a million years ago—"and I hate to admit it to you now, but the penny wasn't *that* cool. That's not why I stayed there with you, or why I insisted we go back the next weekend to flatten toonies."

He smiles, turning the coin over in his hand, then placing it in my palm. "I fell in love with making you smile that day. From that moment on, the only thing I ever wanted was for you to be happy. And I know I lost sight of that for a while, but the second you came back home, I knew I needed to be the reason for your smile again. That's all I want, Blair Bear. Let me love you, and I'll spend the rest of my life making you happy."

I could kiss him—but I can't, because . . . *wedding.*

"I can't believe you kept this." I tighten my grip around

the coin, and before I can reach to wipe the tear rolling down my face, he catches it with the pad of his thumb.

"Of course I did."

When George, our officiant, gives me the go-ahead, every muscle begins to quiver. Denver holds my hands, tightening and loosening like a heartbeat until my pulse regulates. Taking care of me without needing to be prompted. *This* is why I'm marrying this man.

"Even when you weren't in my life, you were. You were in the country song on the radio, the sound of a diesel truck, and the creak in my apartment floorboards. Finding our way back to each other has felt like coming home after a long trip, and I can finally drop the heavy bags that have been weighing on me all these years. I didn't know if we'd get back here, or if we'd be able to make up for lost time, but time's never mattered when I'm with you. You're my person, Denver, and I'm so happy we're picking back up where we left off. I love you."

The tanned skin around his eyes crinkles with his smile, and he mouths an "I love you." George has us repeat the marriage vows after him, while slipping rings onto each other's trembling fingers, and two small pools of tears form in Denver's dimples.

Then we kiss, with his hands sliding into my hair and my arms looping around his neck. Kissing him comes as naturally to me as breathing. Making our love for each other known in the same place we have time and time again, wrapped in a warm wind that feels a lot like his mom's reassuring hug. He and I are as inevitable as the passing of time, and as ineffable as a Wells Ranch sunset.

Denver

M y *wife.*

Even in a crowd, I find her in a heartbeat—that invisible string between us tighter than ever. She and I have always shared a soul, but now we share a last name.

Blair Wells. My wife. *Finally.*

"Fuck, she's gorgeous," I mutter, mostly to myself.

Cecily nods enthusiastically. "She's absolutely stunning. And you look so happy."

"Never been this happy before, Filly."

She leans into Austin's chest. "And who would've guessed you could be so sentimental. You kept a penny from when you were thirteen?"

"Sure did." I shift on my feet to get a better view of Blair standing with her parents. "Thirteen-year-old Denver Wells was a pretty damn romantic guy."

"What happened to that guy?" Austin raises an eyebrow.

"Turns out, there was only one girl out there I wanted to do romantic things for."

"Ooooh," Cecily coos. "That's pretty dang romantic, Denny."

"Yup, that's me," I practically crow, nonchalantly brushing off my shoulder and stealing yet another glance at my beautiful wife.

Austin stares me down, seeing clear through the charade. "Proud of you, bro."

At the same moment he says that, I'm startled by a deep voice paired with a massive hand clamping down on my shoulder.

"Proud of you, too, son." My dad steps in next to me and peers around at Austin. "You too, Austin. And Jackson."

My spine stiffens, hands slowly pulling out of my pants pockets in preparation for breaking up a fight. As far as I know, Austin and our dad haven't said a word to each other since the day Dad left the ranch. The fact that Austin didn't immediately leave the moment Dad showed up today is a small miracle. No chance he doesn't bolt now.

Austin clears his throat, nodding but refusing eye contact. "Thanks."

Holy fucking shit.

I speak up to take the heat off Austin. "Thanks for coming, old man. I know it was pretty last-minute—wasn't sure you'd come."

"Wouldn't have missed it for the world," Dad says. But fuck, he's still staring down his eldest son. "Speaking of which, I hear congratulations are in order."

Now it's Cecily and I both trying to keep the peace. She beams at her new father-in-law, and gives him a firm handshake. "Cecily. So nice to finally meet you. I've heard plenty of stories from when the boys were kids."

"Ah, yeah. They were a handful." He squeezes my shoulder.

"Especially Blair and I," I chime in.

"Whoever said having a daughter was less chaotic than sons never met Blair Hart."

"I knew my ears were ringing for a reason," Blair says, popping up between Austin and me, and sliding perfectly into the space under my arm. We're a pair of puzzle pieces, and I'm only whole when she's tucked against my side like this.

I press a kiss to her hair, pulling her tighter. The dress fabric slips between my fingers, and we share a quick glance that says I'm not the only one thinking about tearing it off her shortly.

"We were never *bad*," Blair clarifies. "Denver and I just enjoyed a good prank."

"I'm still not convinced you agreeing to marry me wasn't the ultimate prank," I say to her.

She throws her hands up with a laugh. "*I asked you.*"

"Ultimate prank. Like I said."

With a head shake, she slowly rubs my back. "I've always been a Wells—figured it was about time I made it official."

"Damn right," Dad says. And for the first time since she died, my dad utters a name that sounds awkward and foreign coming from his lips. "If she were here, Lucy would be so happy to see you two together."

"Just like I told Aus before his wedding, I know she's here. She's always here," I say.

Blair pulls me in like a life raft, securing her hold on my waist, and we don't separate again until the last guest dwindles off the mountainside.

Blair

After the wedding guests trickle off, heading back to the ranch to set out food the girls have spent days preparing, Denver tosses a cooler bag down below our tree and lays out a simple plaid blanket. And before long, I'm sinking into his embrace under the warm autumn sun. Golds and yellows and reds stretch as far as the eye can see, and the occasional fluttering leaf from our tree floats down to us.

"I love our spot," I say with a contented sigh.

"Maybe one day we should build a house right here." He tugs the cooler bag toward us and starts unloading the picnic he insisted on packing by himself.

I raise an eyebrow. "Not sure how it would work for a house—what with being so far from the ranch or any roads."

"Sounds perfect. We can be nudists because nobody will bug us all the way out here."

"And during the winter we'll get cabin fever and kill each other. *Perfect.*"

"Hey," he scolds, uncorking a bottle of sparkling white wine and handing it to me. "No talk of murdering me on our wedding day. Save that for your next girls' night, at the very least."

I smile behind the bottle of wine, letting the bubbles pop and fizz on my tongue. It's a lot like the way every smile of Denver's makes me feel.

He pulls out a pint of ice cream and a spoon, and laughs when I eagerly set down the wine in response.

"Told you we'd have your perfect ice cream at our wedding." He carefully feeds me a heaping spoonful of the perfect blend of all three flavors. Then takes a bite himself.

"Mmm. You got a little . . ." I lean in and kiss away the small dab of chocolate ice cream on his upper lip.

With a smirk, he smears the spoon across his lips, leaving a trail of melting ice cream for the taking. His playful eyes meet mine with a daring stare. This time, I laugh softly before dragging my tongue to lap up the sweet treat.

"You're a shit," I say. Before he realizes what's happening, I dip my finger into the ice cream and tap it against his right dimple.

The perfect fucking snack.

And he palms the back of my skull, consuming me with an ice-cream-flavored kiss. We savor it, reveling in the feel of our tongues exploring one another like they're licking the most decadent cone. I melt into him, dropping my hands to his button-up shirt and slowly undoing the tiny metal buttons until my fingers can weave into the fine hair across his chest.

I kiss his bare skin, trailing my tongue to trace the branded scar on his pec, and grabbing at the buckle of his pants. All I can think about is recreating our first time—making love on a picnic blanket under our tree. And maybe this time, Denver can carve our wedding date into the tree below our names to memorialize this place once again.

I pull back and look at his perfect fucking face. *This man.* This handsome, smart, hardworking man with boyish charm and so much love to give.

My husband.

He holds up his spoon to offer me a bite, and I take it without hesitation. Until halfway to my mouth, when I have a new idea.

Slowly, the metal handle spins between my fingertips, and when the cold ice cream hits his bare chest, Denver inhales sharply through gritted teeth.

"*Shit.*" He moves to wipe it with his hands when I aggressively stop him with the swat of my hand.

And I lick my man like a goddamn ice cream cone. Weaving up his abs, cleaning every groove in his muscle until I swirl around a nipple and smile up at him.

The column of his neck quivers with a hard swallow. "*Holy fuck,* Blair. You're so goddamn hot."

"Yeah? Come here, baby. Let me have my dessert and eat it, too." I jerk at the waist of his pants, and he lifts his ass up enough to let me pull them off, until he's wearing nothing but an unbuttoned shirt and a thick erection.

My palm wraps around his girth, and I give a couple slow tugs to elicit a moan from him. With my free hand, I push hard on his chest, forcing him back so he's propped up on his elbows. And without breaking eye contact, I suck the head of his cock into my mouth for a moment. Just enough to have him grumbling when I pop off.

"That's my good boy." I bite my bottom lip, watching the steady rise and fall of his chest, and the way his cock flicks when my nails run along the soft skin of his inner thigh. "My husband needs his cock sucked, doesn't he?"

"Fucking hell. Call me your husband again."

"Does my *husband* need his wife to take care of him?"

He nods, then groans when I take his pulsating cock back into my mouth. He's needy in the best way, grabbing at my hair and moaning under his breath while he fills every bit of space left in my mouth. Thrusting forward with a spontaneous convulsion that makes my eyes water. Whimpered curse words slip from his lips with every dip of my head; he's practically feral, and that only makes me want to please him so much more.

"Such a good wife. Always so fucking greedy for a mouthful of my cock." He wipes a dribble of spit from my chin, thrusting his hips upward to fuck my face.

His dick slips from between my lips, taking a strand of saliva with it, and I stare up at him while I lick it away. He quivers, and I reach for the ice cream with a devilish smirk. Denver eyes me as I take a heaping scoop, tilting his head with a blend of confusion and excitement.

Strawberry pink droplets fall from the spoon's edge, splattering in an uneven row along his shaft, and he jolts with a hiss after every freezing sensation. My lips slide around his cock, taking him as deep into my throat as I can manage with the way his hips buck under me. Letting the warmth of my mouth finish melting the ice cream, and he thrusts deeper when I swallow around his shaft.

"*Fucking . . . damn it, Blair.*" He gasps. "Holy shit, that feels so weird, but *good.*"

So I repeat it, drizzling half-melted ice cream over him. He moans at the cold, tangling his hands in my hair in an effort to get me to suck it off. Only this time, I refuse to rush— slow, attentive licks ensure every last sticky, sweet taste of ice cream has been cleaned from his hard cock. Getting the perfect mixture of salty and sweet when he leaks pre-cum from his tip.

"Tastes even better eating it this way." I dive back in and lick his cock from base to tip in one slow, steady stroke.

Then I take him fully into my mouth, clenching my thighs together at his sounds of pleasure. My hair wrapped around his hand, Denver guides me to bob in his lap.

"Yes," he hisses. "That's it. That's my girl. Take all of it."

Reaching between my legs, I press two fingers over my soaking wet underwear and apply steady pressure to my clit. Desperate for relief, overcome with a knotted warmth that's aching to unravel below my belly button.

All at once, he forces my mouth from him with a raspy

moan. "Ride me, baby. I don't want to come before my cock's been inside your sweet, wet pussy."

Me neither.

For safety purposes, I pool saliva on my tongue and go down on him with a final, attentive bob. My cheeks hollow to suck any remaining ice cream from his cock. The back of my hand swipes across my mouth to clean up the excessive amount of spit, and I consider whether the sloppy mess I've made of his lap is enough to clean him well enough.

Fuck it.

Helping shimmy my underwear down my thighs, he stares up at me with a look of bliss. "Jesus Christ, I have the sexiest wife in the world."

The title makes my heart flip. Somehow—by some stroke of fate or luck . . . maybe both—I've been given the opportunity to love this man twice in a single lifetime.

I lean in to kiss him, positioning myself so his cock bobs against my entrance. And I grip it, stroking while dragging the head between my pussy lips, eagerly watching every telling expression on his face.

"Fuck, you're so wet." His fingers dig into my thighs. "Be a good wife and sit on my cock. I want your cum dripping down me like ice cream."

The tip slips in with ease, and I slowly settle onto his lap with a moan. The stretch of my muscles around his cock makes me throw my head back in ecstasy, with hair cascading down my back and the autumn sun warm on my face. His hands find their way to my hips, bunching my dress up so he can watch himself sink into me, and keeping me steady as I come close to falling apart. Being here with him is heaven on Earth, and when he drives upward to ensure I'm getting every last damn millimeter of his cock, I swear there are angels singing.

Denver adjusts the angle slightly, hitting my G-spot with a whimper. I moan and fall forward until our foreheads touch.

And he thrusts with a new primal need while sweeping my hair away from our faces.

"I know, baby," he replies to the whine escaping my lips in short bursts. "Feels so fucking good for me, too."

Placing a soft kiss on my lips, he holds his palms to my shoulders to sit me upright again. His jaw ticks when he looks up at me, entire body shuddering while my pussy clenches around him. Every muscle in my body is stiffening with an impending orgasm, and he rockets me up and down on his lap, forcing his cock to hit my G-spot until I'm crying out so loudly they can probably hear us back at the ranch.

"I." *Thrust.* "Love." *Thrust.* "You." *Thrust.* Sweat beads on his forehead, and his eyes close.

"I love you so much," I say through an elated exhale, stroking the pad of my middle finger over my clit in rhythm with every bounce. Heat curls in my core and fireworks out when I feel the heat of his cum fill me, a low moan escaping through his gritted teeth.

Denver squints up at me with a satiated smile, eyes brimming with love, and pulls me into him for a slow kiss. If it weren't for his unshaken hold on me, I'd be crumbling to the earth. And if that isn't the perfect metaphor for our lives together, I don't know what is. Time standing still when I'm encompassed by his touch, and the branches of our tree swaying above us, it's like I'm sixteen again—madly in love with Denver Wells.

It's always been Denver Wells.

Epilogue—Denver
(five years later)

Standing next to Blair's dad, I keep a hand firmly on my son's back so he doesn't fall off the fence rails he insists on climbing. Constantly trying to keep up with his older sister and cousins, he's already a bit of a wild child. Though I guess he comes by it honestly.

The rodeo stands are packed, and Oliver wiggles his tiny butt to "Hell on Heels" by the Pistol Annies, when the world's cutest barrel racer comes out of the alley. Frank leans on the rail, recording the run on his phone to show his wife during his daily visit to the care home. And Blair's standing just beyond the timer in the arena, hands anxiously clasped over her mouth as her horse rounds the first barrel at a trot. Circling around to the second barrel, our adorable four-year-old is bouncing in the saddle with the biggest smile I've ever seen on her face. Her light brown hair whips out from underneath the pink helmet—just like her mom's always does—and when Avery rounds the third barrel, I swear the entire rodeo ground hoots and hollers collectively. All the way home, to where my gorgeous wife is jumping up and down, dirt clouding around her dusty jeans as she cheers on our baby girl.

"Come on, Oll. Let's go congratulate your sissy." I scoop up the two-year-old, settling him onto my shoulders, and we walk with Frank over to where our truck and horse trailer are set up.

Blair's in the middle of tying up her horse. A wedding gift from Jackson and Kate that five years later I'm still convinced was meant as a gag—the buckskin Blair accidentally rode through a thunderstorm, thinking it was one of mine. It turns out Sandy makes a decent barrel horse. And he has a pretty undeniable bond with Blair. Something magical happens to her after a few hours spent in the saddle following a hard day. Between running her own clinic, coping with her mom's mental decline, and raising two feral children, she deserves the escape.

"Dad!" Avery shouts, already eating a celebratory Rice Krispies square on the fender of the horse trailer. "Did you see me go super fast 'round those barrels?"

"You bet I did. *Super* fast." I smile at her, lowering her brother to the grass. "You're going to have more winning buckles than your mom pretty soon."

Blair loosens off Sandy's cinch with a breathy laugh. "I think we'll both be adding another one to the collection today. Sandy's on a roll this afternoon."

The two kids—*and their grandpa*—immediately tie into the plastic container filled with homemade marshmallow treats, courtesy of Beryl. The troublesome trio giggle away like absolute fiends. As hard as it is sometimes to be away from the ranch, it's been a blessing to have a loving grandparent a couple doors down, especially since we moved Blair's mom into a permanent care facility three years ago. If we're not at Frank's house, he's at ours. And recently, we've even been able to stand out on the porch and let Avery walk alone down the quiet street to his house.

It's a bittersweet reminder of the relationship I had with my grandfather, and something I didn't know if my future children would get to experience. My own dad's around more often now than ever before, but he has no interest in moving back to the ranch or Wells Canyon, and I don't fault him for that.

Blair scratches Sandy's shoulder, making his entire body

shudder. Then she pulls the hat from my head to plant her warm lips on mine. Five years and two babies later, I can't get enough of kissing my wife. I also haven't gotten over the fact that she's my *wife*.

"Hopefully all three of us will go home winners today," she says.

"Baby, winning bronc ride or not, I'm still going home a winner."

"Right answer." She plops the hat back on my hair.

Adjusting it, I rub my other hand up and down her arm. "I'm gonna go say hi to Mom quickly before my ride, if you got time?"

"Always." She looks over her shoulder, confirming Frank and the kids are all good. Interlacing our fingers, we saunter toward the barn with our hips bumping into each other at random. Her hair flounces over her shoulders, and I let go of her hand to sling my arm around her waist when we step inside.

The barn my family built when I was a kid is dimly lit and quiet, filled with the familiar smell of horses and alfalfa. Blair and I were near-strangers the first time I saw her in this barn at thirteen, not realizing that mere weeks later my mom would coerce me into buying her a pop that would change my life. A simple drink—one I bought reluctantly, no less—gave me the family I've always dreamt of. Maybe that was Mom's plan all along; she always seemed to know exactly what we needed before we did.

I hold on to Blair, silently thanking Mom for bringing her into my life—at thirteen, and again when I was finally ready to be the man she deserved. A man my mom would be proud of. A man I'm proud of.

"Do you know how happy I am that you found your way back to me?" I whisper against her hair.

"I was always coming back to you, Denver. No one else has ever felt like home."

Acknowledgments

What is life?! That's what I've been asking myself repeatedly. The last year has been beyond anything I could've imagined, and I have so many people to thank for that.

To my incredible family for coming on this journey with me and taking the chaos in stride. I wouldn't be able to do any of this without your love and unwavering support. Sometimes I'm too much like Blair for my own good, so thank you for recognizing when I need help, even if I'm too stubborn to ask for it.

Speaking of which, I'm not sure I would've finished editing this book in time if it weren't for the help of our bonus family, the Bremners. Thanks for wrangling the wild four-year-old for an entire long weekend to make sure I had time for edits.

This book wouldn't be what it is if it weren't for my brilliant beta readers: Abby, Albany, Amanda, Ceilidh, Chelsea, Danie, and Maddy. Thank you not only for providing helpful feedback, but for constantly making me laugh with your unhinged comments. I'm forever thankful for your willingness to help, even when I had you reread certain parts of the book on the fly as I made a million changes.

Speaking of making this book shine, a huge thank you to Alicia and Bhavna for loving this book as much as I do.

You've helped me turn this into something I'm incredibly proud of, and somehow I love Blair even more now than I did before. I'd apologize for making you cry, but you know I'm not sorry for that.

A huge thank you to my agent, Carly, for making my dreams come true. Having you by my side throughout this entire process has given me so much confidence and determination. I can't wait to see what we accomplish together next. LFG!

"Queens of Wells Ranch"—I love you. Thank you for giving me a place I can celebrate, cry, vent, or ramble incessantly when I need to work out a tricky plot hole. Abby, Chelsea, and Danie, you've become three of my best friends, and I can't wait for the day when we can be together eating our weight in Nerds Gummy Clusters.

Special shout-out to my one-bed trope girlie, Ceilidh. I would probably be a *lot* more productive if we didn't spend so many nights voice-messaging each other, but I wouldn't be as emotionally fulfilled. Here's to many more nights full of vodka-crans and McFlurries.

I've been blessed to meet, and become friends with, so many authors I look up to. This career can be really isolating, but there's something magical about a group of badass women supporting one another. I'm sure I could name a million names here, because this community has been incredibly welcoming and supportive, but a special shout-out goes to: Kayla Grosse, Sarah A. Bailey, Albany Archer, Karley Brenna, Ruth Stilling, Elliott Rose, and Elsie Silver. You ladies are such an inspiration in so many ways.

I could fill an entire book with the names of readers I love. So if there's ever been a point where we've talked, laughed, or I've spilled secrets to you, just know that it means the world to me.

To my readers, who have waited so much longer for this book than they initially expected: Thank you for sticking by me through all the changes the last year has brought. Thank you for your patience, even though I know how hard it is to wait for a book you're anticipating. Thank you for sharing your love, telling friends to read my books, making gorgeous edits, and flooding my social media with support. I continue to be overwhelmed by the love you all have for this series. Seriously, what is life?!

BAILEY HANNAH is a Canadian romance author with a passion for strong heroines and rugged men who aren't afraid to love their women hard. Born and raised in small-town British Columbia, she always includes a touch of rural Canadian flair (dirt roads, rodeos, and ketchup chips) in her stories. Bailey lives with her husband, daughter, dogs, and chickens. In her spare time, she enjoys reading, spending time in the outdoors, and daydreaming about her characters.

baileyhannahwrites.com
Instagram: @baileyhannahwrites
TikTok: @baileyhannahwrites